P9-AOA-517

anything for you

Also by Kristan Higgins

IF YOU ONLY KNEW

*

The Blue Heron Series

IN YOUR DREAMS
WAITING ON YOU
THE PERFECT MATCH
THE BEST MAN

*

SOMEBODY TO LOVE
UNTIL THERE WAS YOU
MY ONE AND ONLY
ALL I EVER WANTED
THE NEXT BEST THING
TOO GOOD TO BE TRUE
JUST ONE OF THE GUYS
CATCH OF THE DAY
FOOLS RUSH IN

KRISTAN HIGGINS

anything for you

Recycling programs for this product may not exist in your area.

ISBN-13: 978-0-373-78975-7

Anything for You

This edition published by arrangement with Harlequin Books S.A.

For questions and comments about the quality of this book, please contact us at CustomerService@Harlequin.com.

www.Harlequin.com

Printed in U.S.A.

This book is dedicated to Catherine Arendt,
my wonderful friend since our very first week of college,
godmother to my daughter and a true-blue pal all the way.

CHAPTER ONE

"Get up, doofus."

Though the words were said with a smile, they definitely weren't what Connor O'Rourke was hoping to hear. He was, after all, on a bent knee, holding up a diamond ring.

"I just asked you to marry me, Jess," he said.

"And it was adorable." She ruffled his hair. That didn't bode well, either. "The answer is no, obviously. What were you thinking? And boy, I'm starving. Did you call for pizza yet?"

Okay. Granted, Jessica Dunn was...different. They'd been dating for the past eight months—or ten years, depending on how you counted it—and getting her to this moment had taken as much strategizing as, oh, D-Day. Still, he hadn't quite anticipated this.

He tried again. "Jessica. Make me the happiest man on earth and say you'll be my wife."

"I heard you the first time, big guy. And I did wonder about all these candles. Nice touch, if a little on the fire-hazard side of things."

"And your answer is?"

"You already know my answer, and you knew it long before you asked anything. Now come on, Connor. Upsy-daisy."

He didn't move. Jess sighed and folded her arms across her chest, giving him a patient look, eyebrow slightly raised.

Her phone buzzed, and she pulled it out of her pocket, because she always checked her phone, no matter what they were doing. "Iron Man is killing all the bad guys in the cave," she said, deadpan.

This was normal—her brother dictating text updates on whatever movie he and Gerard, his occasional babysitter, were watching. It could be funny. At the moment, not so much.

"Can we be serious here?" he asked.

"I'm really hungry, Con."

"If I feed you, will you say yes?"

"No. So up you go. Let's have a nice night, okay? Weren't we gonna watch *Game of Thrones*?"

Hail Mary, full of grace, she was really turning him down.

He didn't get up. With the hand that was not holding the little black velvet box, he rubbed his hand across his jaw. He'd shaved for this and everything. The diamond winked in the candlelight, taunting him.

"Look, Jess," he said. "I'm tired of feeling like you pay me by the hour. I'm tired of you breaking up with me. Why don't we get married and stay together for the rest of our lives?"

"You ever hear that expression, if it ain't broke, don't fix it?"

"Do you see me here on one knee with an expensive ring in my hand?"

"Yes. You're hard to miss. And it's very pretty. But I get the feeling you think you *should* love me for the simple reason that we've been sleeping together on and off for so many years—"

"No, it's genuine love."

"And secondly, you know how things are. I can't marry you. I have Davey."

"Well, I have Colleen, and she's a lot more trouble than your brother."

"Funny." Jessica's *three feet away* face was erasing any emotion. It was a face he'd seen all too often in the past two decades, as if she was saying, very politely, *keep three feet away from me or you'll lose an arm.*

His knee was getting sore. "I know how things are with your brother, Jess. I don't think you're supposed to martyr yourself because of it."

"Don't go there. I love my brother. He comes first."

"So you basically have a life sentence."

"Yes," she said, as if she was explaining it to a two-year-old. "Davey's life. My life. They're inseparable. You think I should put him in a kennel for you?"

"Did I say the word *kennel*? No, I didn't. But I think you *could* tell him you're getting married and he can come live with us." Or in the group home in Bryer, which seemed like a very nice place. Yes, Connor had checked it out.

Her phone buzzed again. Again, she checked it. "Iron Man can fly."

"Jessica. I'm asking you to marry me." His jaw was getting tight.

"I know. And really, thank you. It's very sweet. Are we going to eat?"

"So you're not saying yes, is that it?"

"Yes. I'm not saying yes." She pushed a strand of silky blond hair behind her ear.

Jaw at one hundred percent lockdown. "Then it's a no."

"Sadly, yes, it's a no. Which I'm sure doesn't come as a huge surprise to you."

She was really turning him down.

Somehow, he'd seen this all going a bit differently.

Connor stood up, his knee creaking a little. Closed the little black velvet box and set it carefully on the table. He'd gone into

Manhattan to buy that ring—a simple and flawless emerald-cut diamond that suited her, because she was simply, flawlessly beautiful, too. Not a drop of makeup on, her long blond hair in a ponytail, wearing jeans and a faded T-shirt that said *Hugo's* on it, she was still the most gorgeous woman he'd ever seen.

"Shall I call for pizza?" she asked.

He sat down across from her. In the fridge were two lobsters, scallops, potatoes au gratin, artichoke and arugula salad, a bottle of Dom Perignon and *pots de crème au chocolat*, since his plan was to slide the ring on her finger, make love to her and then cook her the best meal of her life.

He did not want pizza.

He did not want a rejection.

His pulse was throbbing in his temples, a warning sign that he was mad. Brain-Vein, his irritating twin called it. He took a slow breath, looked around the room, trying not to lose his temper. The dining room…maybe that had been a mistake. It wasn't exactly warm and romantic. No pictures on the walls. His whole house looked like a furniture showroom, now that he thought about it.

Certainly, there were no pictures of him and Jessica.

He leaned back in his chair and folded his arms across his chest. "How do you see us going forward, Jess?"

She was as cool and still as a stone in Keuka Lake. "What do you mean?"

"You and me, our future, our relationship, not that you can really call sneaking around at the age of thirty-two a relationship."

"I see us doing this. Getting together when we can. Enjoying each other's company." She wasn't the type to be goaded into an argument, that was for sure. Pity. A little yelling and some Olympic make-up sex would be more Connor's style. And that ring on her finger.

He made sure his voice was calm. Jess didn't do anger. "Do

you ever think about us living together or marrying or having kids?"

"No. This works for me." She twisted the silver ring she wore on her thumb and gave him a pleasant smile.

"It doesn't work for me. Not anymore, Jess."

A person would need a magnifying glass to see any reaction from Jessica Dunn, but Connor was something of a student of her face. Right now her lips were pressed together the tiniest bit, indicating a disturbance in the Force.

"Well, thanks for letting me know," she said smoothly. "I'm sorry to hear that. You said you understood how things were and how they had to be. Nothing in my life has changed, so I'm not sure why you thought things would be different now."

"Davey can adjust."

"No, he can't, Connor. He has an IQ of fifty-two. And he hates you, or have you forgotten that? He can't even see you in the grocery store without having a meltdown. You remember the head-banging when he saw you with our dog?" Yes, Connor remembered. It had been one of the scariest moments of his life, as a matter of fact. "I don't have room for marriage and kids," Jess continued. "My brother is my responsibility in more ways than you could ever know. I'm surprised you brought marriage up at all. We've had this conversation a million times."

"Actually, we've never had this conversation."

Her cheeks were getting pink. Finally, something more than calm, cool and collected.

Good. It didn't seem fair that he was the only one feeling something here.

"Well, I thought you knew," she said. "I've always been very clear."

Blood thrummed through his temples, too hard, too fast. Another slow breath. "You're using your brother as an excuse. He'll adjust. He's held you hostage for years now."

"Do *not* go there, Connor."

"What I mean is—"

"What you mean is, put him in a home."

She was really digging in now. "No, I don't," he said. "I bought this house with you in mind. There's an apartment upstairs, in case you forgot. It's for him. I love your brother."

"No, you don't. You've never even had a conversation with him, and he *certainly* doesn't love you. And let's not rewrite history. You decided to buy a two-family house without even talking to me."

Fair point. But it *had* seemed like a perfect solution; him and Jess downstairs, Davey upstairs. Instead, his sister had moved in after Jess turned him down.

Jessica sighed, some of the steel leaving her posture. "Connor, look. I think it's sweet that you made this gesture. Maybe it's because your sister's pregnant and you're feeling sentimental, but this just can't work. And I also think you're saying it because you're sure I won't say yes, and you're right. I won't."

"I wouldn't have asked if I didn't want you to say yes, Jessica."

Her phone buzzed again. She looked at the hateful device. "Great. Davey clogged the toilet, and Gerard can't get the valve to shut off. The last time the bathroom flooded, and I had to pay to replace the whole floor."

"Jess, I want you to marry me."

"I have to go. I'll see you Thursday, okay? This was a nice thought, Connor. I appreciate it. I really do." She stood up, kissed him on the head like he was a dog—which he basically was, just some half-brain Labrador retriever you could ignore until you were lonely, and it was always happy to see you and would cheerfully forget the fact that you'd locked it in the cellar for a year or so. She grabbed her denim jacket from the hook by the door.

"Jessica." He didn't look at her, just stared at the candles flickering on the table. "This will be the last time you break up with me."

Well, shit. He hadn't really planned on saying that, but now that the words were out, they sprang up between the two of them like an iron door.

She froze for a second. "What do you mean?"

His head was killing him, every heartbeat stabbing behind his eyes. "I'm talking about all the times you've broken up with me, all the times you said life was too complicated, and you couldn't make any changes. I want a wife and kids and to be able to kiss you in public. If you leave now, make sure you mean it."

"Are you breaking up with me?" She actually sounded indignant.

"I'm *proposing*!"

"Well, I have no idea why!" she snapped back. "You *know* this is the best I can do."

"Okay, then." His jaw clamped shut.

Her mouth opened a little. "Really."

"Yep."

"Fine," she said. "Do what you want."

"Thanks. I will."

"Good."

"Fine."

She gave him a long look. "Have a nice night, Connor."

And with that, she left, and he picked up the stupid little black velvet box and threw it across the room.

CHAPTER TWO

Twenty years before the proposal…

Connor Michael O'Rourke fell in love with Jessica Dunn when he was twelve years old.

The feeling was not mutual.

He couldn't blame her. After all, he killed her dog.

Well, he didn't actually kill him. It just felt that way.

The fateful, terrible day had been a Friday afternoon in April, and he and Colleen had been riding their bikes home from school, a new privilege, and one their parents gave only if they rode together, which took away much of the thrill. It was the curse of being a twin, Connor often thought. It would've been so much cooler if he could've ridden to the village, maybe bought some candy at Mr. Stoakes's store or found a snake by the lake to put into Coll's bed.

Instead, they were together. Colleen talked all the time, usually about things he didn't have much interest in—which of her friends had gotten her period, who flunked the math test, who liked whoever else. But that was the way it was—Coll talking, him half listening, the occasional mild sibling violence that marked a healthy childhood.

But even if she drove him crazy most of the time with her talk of magical twinsy bonds, which yeah, they did have, and the way she followed him around all the time, he couldn't imagine it any other way. And he did have to look out for her; she was his little sister, even if they were only three minutes apart in age.

Connor and Colleen had about as normal a life as could be had. They had a nice house, a two-week vacation most years, and recently, Connor had become aware of the fact that they were pretty well-off, something you didn't really notice when you were little. But his father drove expensive cars, and if Connor wanted the latest Nike running shoe, his mother never suggested he get something a little less expensive. He was his mother's favorite. His father… Well, his father was kind of tricky. Tense and—what was that phrase? Full of himself, that was it. Only happy when he was the center of attention and admiration, and even then, only happy for a few minutes.

If Connor was Mom's favorite, Colleen seemed to get all of Dad's approval. These days especially, it felt like Connor was either at fault or invisible, his only value coming from his role as Colleen's protector. "Watch out for your sister," Dad had said just this morning, giving Colleen a hug. There was no hug for Connor. Which was okay and all. He was a boy. A guy, even. He wasn't supposed to want hugs anymore.

But today was a good day. The apple blossoms had popped, and the breeze was warm, finally. He'd gotten three tests back, A+'s on all of them, much to Colleen's chagrin; Connor never studied. And all day, there was the thrill of the bike ride home. Friday afternoon meant they could take their time, maybe stop at Tompkin's Gorge and climb up the top and listen to the roar of the waterfall and find bits of mica and quartz.

Colleen rammed his back tire. "Whoops, sorry, brainiac," she said, not sorry at all.

"Not a problem, simpleton."

"Did you eat the pizza at lunch today?" she asked, pulling alongside him. "It was nasty. I mean, you could wring out the oil, it was so wet and disgusting. You should show them how to do it, Con. Your pizza is the best."

He suppressed a smile. Whenever their parents went out, Connor cooked for Colleen. Last weekend had been pizza, the dough made from scratch. They ate a pizza each, it was so good.

He heard a car coming behind them and pulled ahead of his sister, his bike wheels hissing on the damp pavement, the wind in his face. He and Colleen had taken the long way home, the better to enjoy their freedom. Once you left the Village section of town, there wasn't much out here, mostly woods and fields. West's Trailer Park was just up ahead, and then nothing for a good mile. Then they'd round up the back side of the Hill, where all the vineyards were, and wind their way home.

After the long winter, it felt so good to be outside. He pushed harder, lengthening the space between him and Coll. He'd had a growth spurt over the winter, and it was easy to outpace his sister. He felt the satisfying burn in his muscles and answered the call for more speed. He'd wait for Coll at the top of the hill. She was lazy, after all.

And then he heard a noise he couldn't place—was Colleen coughing? Was it a motor? No, that wasn't—

Then there was a brown blur streaking at him, and he was falling before he even realized it hit him, his bike on top of him. It wasn't Coll making the noise, it was a *dog.* The brown thing was a dog, and it was *furious.*

There was no time to react, no time even to be scared, just hard pavement under his shoulder and hip and his hands trying to keep the dog's head away from his throat. The world was full of sound—angry, raging snarls and Colleen's screams. Was she okay? Where was she?

All Connor could see was the dog's mouth, huge, gaping

and snapping, its neck thick and strong, and that mouth went way, way back like a snake's, and he knew once those teeth bit into him, he'd be dead. It was trying to kill him, Connor realized distantly. This might be the way he died. *Not in front of Colleen. Please.*

Before the thought was even finished, teeth sank into Connor's arm, and the dog shook its head, and *Jesus*, it was so strong, Connor was just a rag the dog was whipping around, and he couldn't yell or fight; he was nothing compared to the muscular fury of the dog. Colleen was screaming, the dog snarling, Connor silent as he tried to hold on to his arm so it wouldn't be torn off.

Then Colleen was hitting the dog with her backpack and kicking it, and no cars were anywhere. It would've been *so* great if someone stopped and helped; he wanted a grown-up so badly right now. His arm was on fire, and there was blood, and still the dog pulled and shook, as if Colleen wasn't even there.

The dog finally released his arm and turned toward Colleen, who kicked it square in the face. *God*, she was brave, but what if it bit *her*? And then in a flash, it seemed to do just that, and Connor kicked it in the leg, and it turned back toward him—good, good, better than Colleen—and then it was on him again.

His face this time, and this was it, he was going to die. Those huge jaws clamped down, and a searing burn flashed and throbbed, the whole left side of his face. The dog didn't let go. Colleen was hysterical now, kicking and kicking the dog, and Connor could see her eyes, open so wide he could see the whole gray circle of her irises.

Get out of here, Collie. Run.

He was passing out. Colleen's screams were fainter now.

Then there was a yelp, and the dog was gone, and Connor instinctively held his hand up to his cheek, which was hot and throbbing and way too wet.

"Oh my God, oh my God," Colleen sobbed, dropping to her knees to hug him. "Help us!" she screamed to someone.

"Are you okay?" Connor asked, his voice odd and weak. Was his face still on? "Coll?"

She pulled back, shaking. "You're bleeding. It's bad."

They were in front of West's Trailer Park, where the poor kids lived. Tiffy Ames and Levi Cooper and Jessica Dunn.

And there was Jess now, holding the dog by its collar, trying to lift it up. Her brother, who had something wrong with him, had latched on to the dog, sobbing and saying one word over and over. Cheeto or something. "Is she okay?" Connor asked, but his voice was too weak to be heard. "Is her brother okay?"

"Call the ambulance," Colleen yelled, her voice high and wobbly.

"Are you all right, Collie?" he asked. The gray was back.

"I'm fine. But you're…hurt."

"How bad?"

"Bad. But it's okay. You're okay." Tears dripped off her cheeks onto him.

"Am I gonna die?"

"No! Jeez, Connor! No!" But he could tell she didn't know. She wadded up her sweatshirt and pushed it against his jaw, making him see black-and-white flashes of pain. His hand was shiny and slick with dark red blood. "Just take deep breaths," she said, biting her lip.

It helped. The sky became blue again, and Colleen's shirt was pink. And bloodstained. The town siren went off, such a good sound…but so far away, it seemed.

"They're coming. Just hang on. Help is on the way," Colleen said. She sounded way too adult. Tears were streaming down her face, and her lips were trembling.

There was a bang of a door, and Connor looked over. Jessica Dunn's father had come outside. "What did you kids do to my son?" he asked, staggering a little, and Connor couldn't help feeling bad for Jessica. Everyone knew her parents were drunks.

"Get that fucking dog inside!" Colleen shouted.

Yikes. He'd never heard her swear before. It made him think that his face was pretty much gone, and he might in fact be dying.

Jessica pushed her little brother aside, finally, then bent down and picked up the dog. It was heavy, Connor could tell. Connor *knew.*

"Chico!" her brother screamed. "Don't take Chico away!" He ran after Jessica, punching her on the back with his fists, but she went into the trailer—the rattiest, dirtiest one—and closed the door behind her.

Then Levi Cooper's mother came out, a toddler on her hip, and seeing Connor, ran over to him. "Oh, my God, what happened?" she said, and Connor realized he was shaking, but at least there was a nice grown-up here now.

"The Dunns' dog attacked him." Colleen said, her voice breaking. "It came out of nowhere."

"God," Mrs. Cooper said. "I've told them that dog is a menace. You just lie still, honey." She patted Connor's leg.

It was weird, lying there, Mrs. Cooper telling him not to move, Colleen's sweatshirt pressed against his throbbing face, the Dunns standing in their yard. The father was loud and kept saying things like "That dog wouldn't hurt a fly," and "Why were those kids in my yard anyway?" and Colleen was holding his hand too hard.

When the ambulance did come, it was both embarrassing and such a relief he almost cried. There was fuss and questions, gauze and radio. "Minor child, age twelve, attacked by dog," Mr. Stoakes said into the radio. *Minor child.* Cripes. Everyone was shooting dirty looks at the Dunns.

They put a neck brace on Connor and packed him onto a gurney. Mrs. Cooper said she'd called Connor's mom, and she'd meet him at the hospital. Colleen rode in the front of the ambulance, sobbing.

In the ER, he was told he was very lucky, and that it could've been so much worse. He ended up with eleven stitches in his jaw, eight under his eye. "Don't worry about the scar," said the hip young doctor who was doing the job. "Chicks love scars." Another sixteen stitches in his arm, but it was the bite on his face that was the big concern. A bump on his head, road rash on his back where his shirt had ridden up. He was a mess, in other words. Everything stung, throbbed or burned.

Mom was weepy all that night. Connor was woozy from the pain meds. Colleen made him a get-well card without any insults, which made Connor think he must look worse than he realized. "You saved me," he told her, and she burst into tears.

"I didn't," she said. "I tried, but I couldn't."

"It ran away, though."

"Jessica threw a rock at him. Got him right in the head."

Huh. He was too bleary to think about it further. Good aim, though.

His father was icy with fury. "Those fucking white-trash scumbags," he said, peering into Connor's face, then got on the phone in his study and didn't come out until Connor was in bed. "I'm glad you're okay," he said, putting his hand on Connor's shoulder. Suddenly, the dog bite felt worth it. "You were very brave, I heard."

"It was scary."

Crap. Wrong answer. He should've said something about it not being a big deal. Sure enough, the hand was withdrawn. "It could've been worse, though," Connor added quickly. "At least it wasn't Colleen."

Because if something happened to his sister, Connor would've killed the dog himself. The flash of rage and terror was unexpected.

"Tomorrow we're going to see the Dunns," Dad said.

"Oh, Dad, no." The memory of Jess lugging the dog into the house… There was something wrong with that image, but Connor couldn't say what it was.

"You have to man up in situations like this," his father said. "I'll be with you. Don't worry. They owe you an apology."

The next day, sure enough, Dad made him get into the Porsche and go back to West's Trailer Park. His face was swollen and sore under the bandages, and his arm ached. The last place he wanted to be was here.

Dad knocked on the door, hard. Jessica answered, her eyes flickering over Connor's face. She didn't say anything. A TV blared in the background, one of those court shows with a lot of yelling.

"Are your parents home?" Dad asked, not bothering with politeness.

"Hi, Jess," Connor said. Dad cut him a look.

She slipped away. A second later, Mrs. Dunn was at the door. "What do you want?" she said sullenly. Connor was abruptly grateful for his own mother, who always smelled nice and, well, wore a bra and clean shirts.

"Your dog attacked my son," Dad said, his voice hard. "I'm here to inform you that Animal Control will be here this afternoon to have him put down."

"You don't get to say what happens to my dog," she said, and Connor could smell her boozy breath from the steps.

"What's put down?" asked a little voice.

Connor flinched. Davey Dunn was peeking out from behind his mother's legs. He was five or six, and had the longest eyelashes Connor had ever seen. Everyone knew he had something wrong with him, that skinny head and eyes so far apart, but Connor wasn't sure what it was. The kids on the bus had a word for it, but Connor hated thinking it. Davey just wasn't quite… normal. Cute, though. Jessica reappeared next to her brother, her hand on his head, staring at Connor, her face expressionless.

He and Jess were in the same class. He couldn't say she was nice, exactly; they didn't have the same friends, but she hung out with Levi Cooper, and everyone liked Levi.

And Jessica Dunn was beautiful. Connor had always known that.

"What's going on here?" Mr. Dunn appeared in the doorway, rumpled and skinny. And suddenly, the dog was there, its big brown head, and Connor jumped back, he couldn't help it. Dad grabbed the animal by the collar, roughly. "Put down," he said to Davey, "means your dog has to go somewhere and never come back, because he was very bad."

"Chico's not bad," Davey said, putting his thumb in his mouth. "He's good."

"Look at my son's face," Dad snapped. "That's what your dog did. So he's going to doggy heaven now."

Silence fell. Davey pulled his thumb out of his mouth and blinked.

Dad could be *such* a dick sometimes.

"He's gonna die?" Davey asked.

"Yes. And you're lucky he hasn't torn your throat out, son."

"Don't talk to my boy," Mr. Dunn said belatedly.

"No!" Davey wailed. "No! No!"

"Here they are now," Dad said, and sure enough, a van was pulling into the trailer park.

"Chico! Come on! We have to hide!" Davey sobbed, but Dad still had the dog by the collar.

"Dad," Connor said, "maybe the dog could just be… I don't know. Chained up or something?"

"Have you seen your face?" his father snapped. "This dog will be dead by tomorrow. It would be insane to let it live."

"No!" Davey screamed.

There were three animal control people there, and a police car, too, now. "We need to take the dog, ma'am," one of them said, but you could hardly hear anything, because Davey was screaming, and the dog… The dog was licking Davey's face, its tail wagging.

"Dad, please," Connor said. "Don't do this."

"You don't understand," his father said, not looking at Connor.

"Screw you all," Mrs. Dunn said, tears leaking out of her eyes. "God damn you!"

It was Jessica who picked Davey up, even though he flailed and punched. She forced his head against her shoulder and went deeper into the gloomy little trailer.

Mr. Dunn watched, his mouth twisted in rage. "You rich people always get your way, don't you? Nice, killing a retarded boy's pet."

There was the word Connor wouldn't let himself think, from the kid's dad, even.

"Your *pet* almost killed my son," Dad snarled. "You can apologize anytime."

"Fuck you."

"Dad, let's go," Connor said. His eyes were burning. Davey could still be heard, screaming the dog's name.

It was a long walk back to the car. The Porsche, for crying out loud. A car that probably cost more than the Dunns' entire house.

Connor didn't say anything all the way home. His throat was too tight.

"Connor, that dog was a menace. And those parents can't be trusted to chain a dog or fence in their yard. You saw them. They're both drunks. I feel bad for the boy, but his parents should've trained the dog so it didn't attack innocent children."

Connor stared straight ahead.

"Well, I give up," his father said with a sigh. "You want to worry about that dog coming for you? You want to take the chance that it would go for Colleen next time? Huh? Do you?"

Of course not.

But he didn't want to break a little kid's heart, either.

By Monday, most of the swelling had gone down in his face, and his arm was stiff, rather than sore. But he still looked pretty grim. Colleen was over the trauma, already calling him Frankenstein and telling him he was uglier than ever. The doctor had said he'd have a scar on the underside of his jaw, where the dog had taken a chunk, and one on his cheek, near his eye. "It'll make you look tough," Connor's father said, examining the stitches Sunday night. He sounded almost pleased.

Connor's stomach hurt as he went into school.

Everyone had already heard. In a town this small, of course they had. "Oh, my gosh, Connor, were you so scared? Did it hurt? What happened? I heard it went for Colleen first, and you saved her!" Everyone was sympathetic and fascinated. He got a lot of attention, which made him fidget.

Jessica didn't come to school that day. Not the next day, or the day after that. It was Thursday before she made it. Granted, she was absent a lot, and everyone knew why—her parents, her brother. But Connor couldn't help feeling like this time it was because of him. The bandage on his face came off the night before; the swelling had gone down, though there was still a good bit of bruising.

Jessica played it cool. She didn't talk much; she never did, except to Levi and Tiffy Ames, her best friends, and she managed to spend all day without making eye contact with him, despite the fact that their school was so small.

Finally, after school when he was supposed to go to Chess Club, he saw her walking down the school driveway. He bolted down the hall and out the door. Her pants were just a little too short—highwaters, the snotty girls had said at lunch—and the sole of one of her cheap canvas shoes flopped, half-off. "Jess! Hey, Jess."

She stopped. He noticed that her backpack was too small, and grubby, and pink. A little girl's backpack, not like the one

Colleen and her friends had, cheery plaid backpacks with their initials sewn on, extra padding on the shoulder straps.

Then she turned around. "What do you want?" she said. Her eyes were cold.

"I… I just wanted to see how your brother was doing."

She didn't answer. The wind gusted off Keuka, smelling of rain.

"I guess he's still pretty sad," Connor said.

"Uh…yeah," she said, like he was the stupidest person on earth. He did feel that way. "He loved that dog."

"I could tell."

"And Chico never bit anyone before."

Connor had no answer for that.

Jessica stared at a spot past Connor's left ear. "My father said that in most cases, Chico would get another chance, but since Pete *O'Rourke* told the mayor what to do, our dog is dead now." She cut her eyes to his. "Davey hasn't stopped crying. He's too upset to go to school, and he's wet the bed every night this week. So that's how he's doing, *Connor.*"

She made his name sound like a curse word.

"I'm really sorry," he whispered.

"Who cares what you think, O'Rourke?" She turned and trudged away, her footsteps scratching in the gravel, the sole of her shoe flopping.

He should let her go. Instead, he ran up and put his hand on her shoulder. "Jessica. I'm—"

She whirled around, her eyes filled with tears, fist raised to hit him. Jess got into fights all the time, usually with the oafs on the football team, and she could hold her own. But she paused, and in that second, he saw the past week written on her face, the sadness and anger and fear and helplessness. The…the shame. He saw that she was tired. That there was a spot of dirt behind her left ear.

"You can hit me," he said. "It's okay."

"I'll pop your stitches."

"Punch me in the stomach, then," he said.

Her fist dropped. "Leave me alone, Connor. Don't talk to me ever again."

Then she turned and walked off, her head bent, her blond hair fluttering in the breeze, and it felt like someone was ramming a broom handle through the middle of Connor's chest.

She was so beautiful.

A lot of girls were pretty—Faith Holland and her red hair, Theresa DeFilio and her big brown eyes, Miss Cummings in the library, who didn't seem old enough to be a grown-up. Even Colleen was pretty, sort of, when she wasn't annoying him.

But Jessica Dunn was *beautiful.*

Connor felt as though he'd just stepped on a bluebird, crushing its fragile, hollow bones.

CHAPTER THREE

Eleven years before the proposal…

When Jess was very little, before Davey, her parents had taken her camping once. Real camping, in a tent patched with duct tape, blankets making a nest on the ground. She had loved it, the coziness of the tent, the smell of nylon and smoke, her parents drinking beers and cooking over the fire. Had it been Vermont? Michigan, maybe? It didn't matter. There'd been a path down to a lake, and the stars were a heavy swipe of glitter across the inky sky. She got seventeen mosquito bites, but she didn't even care.

That was it for vacations.

When the senior class trip to Philadelphia was announced, everyone had gone wild with excitement. They'd be staying overnight, seeing the sights, then given four precious hours of freedom to wander. Jeremy Lyon, the newest, hottest addition to their class, had an uncle who wanted to take Jer and all of his friends out for dinner. There was talk of going to the Reading Terminal Market, which was filled with places to eat. The Museum of Art, so everyone could run the stairs like Rocky. Everyone wanted to get a cheesesteak sandwich.

The trip cost $229.

Jessica had been to New York City on the sixth-grade class trip, but it was just for the day. She was pretty sure her teacher had paid her fee so Jess could go.

But in Philly, they'd be *staying* in the city, and the thought of it made her heart bounce like a rubber ball. Based on those five hours in Manhattan, she was pretty sure she loved cities.

Her parents didn't have $229 for field trips, though they might have it for booze. Asking them didn't even cross her mind; she had her own money saved, squirreled away in a hole in the wall behind her bed, secured in a little tin box she'd found by the creek that ran behind the trailer park. At eighteen, Jess wasn't naive; she knew her mom was a helpless alcoholic. *Powerless* was the word used at Al-Anon. Her father was less extreme, but he was cunning and sneaky. Either parent would use her money for themselves, no matter how you cut it.

So she hid her savings. She'd wait until the house was empty then sneak her tip money and pay into the red tin. Her parents generally didn't go into her room, and they sure didn't move the bed away from the wall to clean or anything.

She'd go on the trip. She'd room with Tiffy and Angela Mitchum, maybe sneak out with Levi…maybe for a walk, maybe for sex, though she often felt like that was habit more than anything for the both of them.

Growing up in the trailer park with Tiffy and Levi and Asswipe Jones—born Ashwick, and really, did his mother hate children?—it bonded people. They were the have-nots, some having less than others. You recognized each other, knew the strategies of eating a big lunch at school, because school lunches were free if you were poor enough. You knew how to glue the soles of your shoes when they started to come off, how to keep an eye on the Salvation Army thrift shop. You might even know how to shoplift.

Things like ski trips or island vacations, dinners out and hotel stays…that was foreign territory for the Dunns. Bad enough that Jess's father couldn't keep a job, and Mom had four prescriptions for Vicodin from four different doctors. Add to basic poverty Davey's special programs and doctor's appointments and new meds that might help with his outbursts but were never covered by Medicaid…there was always less than nothing.

But Jess had almost a thousand dollars saved. Her job at Hugo's earned her more than her father made, and when Davey needed a helmet so he wouldn't hurt himself during a head-banging rage, she was the one who'd paid for it. The private summer program that gave him something to do—away from their parents—ditto. His clothes, bought new, also funded by her, because while she'd been able to handle the middle school mean kids who'd make fun of her wearing Faith Holland's hand-me-downs, Davey deserved better. He already had a big strike against him; he wasn't going to wear used clothes, too. She bought groceries and special vitamins that one doctor thought might help raise his IQ. She paid the gas bill last March when the cold just wouldn't let go and they had no heat, and she'd paid for the repair on the crappy old Toyota that got her to and from work.

Even so, she'd managed to stash $987.45 in the three years she'd been working at Hugo's and, for once, she was going to spend some of it on herself. She was a senior, and college was out of the question. For one, she couldn't leave Davey, and for two, well, she had neither the money nor the grades for a scholarship. She'd try to take a class at Wickham Community College, but her plans for the future were pretty much her plans for today. Work. Take care of Davey. Keep her parents from getting into too much trouble, and when that failed, bailing them out or paying their fines.

But this trip…something in her rose up at the thought of it, something bright and clean. She could see another part of the country. Picture a future, magical version of herself, working in the city, living in a townhouse, holding down a great job.

No parents, just her and Davey. The Mid-Atlantic. It sounded exotic, so much cooler than western New York.

Whatever the case, she ran all the way home from the bus stop, fueled by excitement and…well, happiness.

"Hey, honey-boy," she said as she came into the kitchen, bending to smooch Davey's head, then frowned. "Did you cut your own hair again?" It was practically shaved in spots, making it look like he had a disease.

"No," he said. "I let Sam do it."

"Honey, don't. I'm the only one who cuts your hair, okay?" That little shit Sam would be getting a talk from her, and if he peed his pants in terror, that'd be *fine*. The boys were eleven, for God's sake. This wasn't innocent "let's play barbershop" stuff. This was bullying, and it wasn't the first time Sam had decided to pretend to be friends with Davey so he could humiliate him.

"What's for supper?" Davey asked.

"I don't know. Where's Mom?"

"I don't know." He bent over his coloring book. Still loved Pokémon.

Jess glanced in the living room, where her father was in the recliner, watching TV. He seemed to be asleep.

Good. She went into the bedroom she shared with Davey and closed the door quietly. Pulled the bed back from the wall, bent down and stuck her fingers in the hole.

No tin.

It must've fallen back, even if that had never happened before. She stuck her whole hand in, groped to the left, then the right.

It wasn't there.

Her heart felt sticky, its ventricles and valves clogged with dread.

On the wobbly plastic table next to his bed, Davey had a keychain with an LED light on it, in case he got scared in the middle of the night. Jess grabbed it and pointed it at the hole.

No tin. Not to the left, not to the right. It wasn't below, and it wasn't above. It was just gone.

She went back into the kitchen. "Davey, honey, did you find a metal box in our room? In a little hole behind the bed?"

"There's a hole? What's in it?" he asked. "Is there mice in it?"

"No. I had a little metal box in there."

"What color?"

"Red and silver. And there was some money inside."

He chose a blue crayon, its paper soft and furred from use. "I don't know where it is." Davey didn't know how to lie. "Will you make me supper tonight?"

"I have to work."

"But Mom's not home!"

Jess took a deep breath. "Okay." She glanced at the sink; the dishes from breakfast and lunch were still there, waiting to be washed. Seven empty beer cans, too.

So she wouldn't be going on the class trip. She'd just say she had to work. Or that Davey had a thing and she couldn't go. No, she couldn't blame Davey, even if he always did have an appointment and a fear of being left alone. She'd just say the trip wasn't her thing.

Except it was.

Well. She probably didn't deserve it, anyway. Selfish, to be thinking about leaving her brother for the weekend.

She put on some water to make spaghetti and opened a can of tomato sauce. Not much nutrition, but that was about all they had. She'd have to go grocery shopping tomorrow. Then, glancing at the clock, she did the dishes as fast as she could. She had to go to work soon.

Dad had probably taken it. Mom was a little more decent that way. Every once in a while, Jess's grandmother would send Jolene some cash, and Mom would take Jess and Davey out for ice cream…then head for the Black Cat and drink the rest away. If she'd known about Jessica's stash…well, it was hard to believe that she would've taken it all, in one fell swoop. It'd be more Mom's style to filch it bit by bit, just enough to buy a few vodka nips and get her through the day.

So it wasn't Mom.

That left Dad, and he wouldn't admit it with a gun to the back of his head. The money might still be around, but he was too smart for Jessica to ever find it. And he'd never give her an honest answer if she asked, just feign ignorance and blink his big blue eyes...and then go out and buy a hundred lottery tickets or go to the casino. If he ever won something, he always managed to find a way to blow that, too.

She'd bet her life he wasn't sleeping, even though he just lay there, eyes closed.

Sometimes, she wished he'd just die. Without him being a bad influence, such a casual drunk, maybe Mom could get sober. Without him, Davey wouldn't have such a shitty role model. Without him, there'd be one less mouth to feed.

A few days later, Jeremy Lyon gave her a ride home in his expensive little convertible. It was raining, so the top was up, and it was so cozy and clean and pretty in that little car that Jess wanted to live there.

With Jeremy. She loved him. Everyone did.

But boys like Jeremy didn't go for Jessica Does—as in Jessica Does Anyone—class slut, poor white trash. Sure enough, Jeremy had fallen hard for Faith Holland, otherwise known as Princess Super-Cute, one of the rich girls—a little dim, it seemed to Jess, and someone who never wanted for anything.

"So I heard you're not going on the trip," Jeremy said.

"Oh, right," Jessica answered, pretending it had slipped her mind. "I have something going on that weekend."

"Well, here's the thing," he said. "You know how I am. Incapable of having fun if my friends aren't all with me. Curse of the only child or something. So I was thinking, if cost was the issue, please let me cover you, Jess. You'd be doing *me* a favor, because it won't be any fun without you, and I'll be miserable and lonely the whole time."

The guy was such a prince, it hurt her heart sometimes. He was also a liar. He was best friends with Levi, in love with Faith in such a sappy way that it was a shock that bluebirds didn't follow them around. Jer was friends with everyone he'd ever met.

As they pulled into West's Trailer Park, Jess let herself imagine that Jeremy was her boyfriend. That he'd dump Faith and fall for her, and love Davey—he was already good to Davey—and take care of them for the rest of their lives.

"What do you say, Jess? Will you do that for me?"

She cleared her throat. "That's really nice, Jeremy, but it's not the money. Philly's really not my thing, you know? Plus, I'm working that weekend. But thanks." She blew him a kiss and ran inside before the casual act slipped.

That Friday night, when her classmates were in the city of brotherly love, a huge party of middle-aged fraternity brothers came into Hugo's, and Hugo gave the table to Jess. They left her a tip of $250.

Too little, too late.

On Sunday she took Davey to the fair in Corning and bought him corn dogs and popcorn and root beer. She screamed on the roller coaster, and he put his arm around her, laughing with glee. He loved when she was the one who was scared and he got to protect her. They both ate candied apples and then scraped the gunk off their teeth with their fingers, Jess more successfully than Davey.

When he wanted to play Shoot the Balloon, she made sure the carny got a good look down her shirt so that Davey won a huge stuffed animal, even though he only managed to pop one balloon.

It was the best day she'd had in a long time.

"I love you," Davey said sleepily on the car ride home.

In that moment, she was so glad to be exactly where she was, with her brother, her best bud, the boy who'd had an uphill battle since the day he was born.

A battle which was largely her fault.

"I love you, too, honey-boy," she said back, her voice husky.

Nothing was ever more true.

But as Davey slept, his head against the window, snoring slightly, Jessica couldn't help wondering about the view she might've seen from that hotel, and the little soaps and shampoos, which she had fully intended on bringing home to her brother.

Which is why, at the age of twenty-one, Jessica Dunn had never stayed in a hotel before.

It was three years past graduation, and Jess and Angela Mitchum were the only ones who hadn't left Manningsport. Angela was a mother now, having gotten knocked up senior year. She lived on the hill with her parents and was going to school part-time to become a nurse. Sometimes, the Mitchums came to Hugo's for dinner, and Jess always admired the baby, who was really cute.

Jess was doing what she'd always been doing—waiting tables at Hugo's, doing a little home health aide work on the side, looking after her brother. She still lived in the trailer park, but that was going to end soon; she now saved her money in a bank, and in four more months, she'd have enough to rent a decent place in town. Two bedrooms, because of course she wasn't leaving Davey at the mercy of her parents' negligence.

Lately, Dad had been offering him drinks, which Davey was only too happy to take. For some completely unfathomable reason, he worshipped their father, who thought it was *funny* to see Davey tipsy. Mom wouldn't like Jess taking Davey, but in the end, she'd give in. Her Vicodin was now supplied by the grungy guy at the laundromat, since the doctors had finally figured out that there was nothing wrong with Mom except addiction.

It was October, always a poignant time of year for Jess. The leaf peepers, those tourists who came up by the busload to see the foliage and drink Finger Lakes wine, were heading home, and aside from the Christmas Stroll, Manningsport would soon be quiet. Hugo closed the restaurant after Veterans Day, so Jess would have to see if she could get more hours as an aide. It didn't pay nearly as well as waiting tables, but she didn't have a lot of other options.

Hugo called her into his office before she started her shift that night. "I want you to take a wine class," he said without preamble. "Felicia kills you in bottle sales, and the markup is incredible. What do you think?"

"Um…sure," Jess said, scratching her wrist. "But I don't really drink."

"I know, honey." He knew about her family. Everyone did, and just in case they didn't, Dad crashed into the restaurant at least once a year, asking where his "baby girl" was and wondering if old Hugo would give him a drink on the house. "But you're twenty-one now. You should know about wine. What goes with different kinds of food, how to talk about it, what to recommend."

"I just recommend the really expensive stuff," she said.

"Which I appreciate. Still, I want you to do this, kid. It classes us up if you can talk knowledgeably about what people are drinking."

"Yeah, okay." It was true. Felicia could sell a bottle of wine to just about anyone, and was full of phrases like "that particular region of France" and "long, lingering finish with notes of fresh snow and blackberry." It sounded pretty ridiculous to Jess, but Felicia's clients spent more, and that meant bigger tabs, which also meant bigger tips.

"Blue Heron Winery is having a class next week," Hugo continued. "You went to school with Faith Holland, didn't you? Want to go there?"

"I'd rather not take that one," she said easily. "If that's okay. Next week is a little packed."

Hugo nodded. He'd hired her to bus tables when she was fifteen, promoted her to waitress and was now teaching her to bartend. He never asked why she didn't go to college like all the other Manningsport kids, or enlist, or leave town to find something other than a waitressing job.

He knew why. He probably knew more than she wanted him to, including why she'd try to dodge a class at Blue Heron.

"Okay, kid," he said with a nod. "I'll see what else is around."

"Thank you." The words didn't come easily to her, but she rubbed the top of his head, said, "Lucky bald spot," and went back to work, stuffing down her feelings.

Manningsport was a moderately wealthy town. Full of vineyards and families that went back generations, like the Hollands, or wealthy transplants, like the Lyons, or families whose parents earned a lot of money, like the O'Rourkes.

And scattered in between, like weeds in a garden, were families who were poor, and had tussles with the law, and had drinking problems or drug problems and always, always had money problems. Families where the mother was milking the system, claiming a lifetime disability from a vague knee injury she got four days after being hired at the high school as a lunch lady. Families where the father couldn't hold a job and had been driven home in a police car more times than a person could count.

Her family, in other words.

But she had Davey. If not for him, she would've left Manningsport the second she could drive, moved somewhere far away from anyone who knew why she was called Jessica Does. Maybe she'd live in Europe. Italy, where she'd fall in love and learn the language and become a clothing designer or something.

But there *was* her brother, and he was her responsibility and hers alone, so none of those thoughts were worth more than a few seconds. Davey made staying worthwhile and then some.

A week later, Hugo handed her some papers and walked away. "Don't say no," he said over his shoulder. "You can figure it out."

The first page confirmed her enrollment in a day-long wine class at the Culinary Institute of America, down in Hyde Park, a good four hours' drive.

The next page was a hotel reservation at the Hudson Riverview Hotel.

He was putting her up overnight.

Hands tingling, Jess went into the office, which was empty, and Googled the place.

It was *beautiful.* A four-star hotel overlooking the Hudson. Full complimentary breakfast and a welcome cocktail. The beds were king-size; Jess still slept in a twin in the room she shared with her brother. A huge tub *and* a fancy, glassed-in shower. A flower arrangement in the lobby the size of a small car.

She turned around and saw Hugo, smiling sheepishly. "I thought you might like to get out of town."

"Hugo," she began, but her words stopped there.

"Just promise you'll go. I can even check in on your brother, okay? And don't you cry! Are those tears in your eyes? Don't you dare, or I'll fire you."

A few days later she kissed her brother, pried his arms from around her neck, told him Chico Two would take good care of him, warned her parents to stay sober, reminded her mother of the heating instructions for the casserole she'd cooked the night before and got in the car.

She was going to a hotel. The class would be fine, sure, but she was going to stay in a *hotel.*

The four-hour drive flew by, and as the miles passed, Jessica felt…light. Yes, she was worried about Davey, but she'd be back tomorrow afternoon. She fully intended to sleep late and eat that breakfast. But she would be staying in a gorgeous hotel near the Vanderbilt Mansion and the Culinary Institute of America. She planned to have dinner in the hotel dining room, and if there was a wedding there this weekend, she might peek in the ballroom—because her hotel had a ballroom! A bath in that tub, definitely. Her house didn't have a tub, just a shower with mold growing on the caulk, no matter how much bleach she sprayed on it.

When she finally got to the hotel, it was even prettier than the internet pictures. Her heart pounded as she walked in. She should've brought a suitcase, rather than her backpack, but hey, it was fine. She looked casual, that was all.

"How are you today?" asked the older man behind the counter.

"I'm just fine," she said. "Jessica Dunn."

He clicked a few keys on his computer. "And I see all expenses are covered by a Hugo's Restaurant?"

"Oh. Um, yes. My employer."

"What do you do for them?"

For a second, she was tempted to say she was a manager, or the sommelier, not that Hugo had one, or the chef. "I'm on the waitstaff."

He gave her a quick once-over, then handed her a key. "I've upgraded you to a junior suite," he said. "Enjoy your stay with us. I'm off at seven. Perhaps I can buy you a drink."

"I'm afraid I have plans," she said, "but thank you. I really appreciate the offer."

"Let me know if you change your mind," he said.

The one thing her parents had given her was good looks. That, and Davey. She knew she was beautiful, and at this moment, she was glad. Sure, the horny old guy was hitting on her. But it had gotten her a junior suite, whatever that was. It sure sounded amazing.

And it was. It was flippin' huge. There was a couch—a sleek gray couch with orange pillows, and the bed was like an ocean of white with an orange throw draped across the end. Flat-screen TV! There was a Gideon's Bible in one night table drawer, and an "intimacy kit" in another—condoms and massage oil. Ahem. There was even a minibar! Not that she drank, but it was pretty anyway, all the top-shelf booze and snacks. Nine dollars for a pack of M&Ms, imagine that.

The towels were pure white, and the bathroom had so many light switches—one for the shower, one for the mirror, one under the counter like a night-light or something. And holy heck, a bathrobe made of cotton so soft it was like a cloud. Slippers! And the shampoo and shower gel and conditioner were all L'Occitane, which Jess assumed was really expensive and sure smelled that way.

She went to the window, which overlooked a small park and the Hudson River. The day was gray and a little cold. It was maybe the prettiest view Jess had ever seen.

She went back into the bathroom and turned on the faucets in the enormous tub.

This was going to be the best weekend of her life.

As the tub filled, she called home. As expected, Davey answered. He was a total phone hog.

"Hey, Davey," she said.

"I miss you. When are you coming home?"

"Tomorrow. You know that. You want to hear about my hotel?"

"Okay."

"It's got a big bed. Really big. Bigger than Mom and Dad's."

"Did you jump on it?"

"Not yet," she said with a grin. "And a tub. I'm going to take a bubble bath."

"That sounds fun."

"We'll have a tub in our new house."

"Okay! What else is there?"

"Room service, where they bring you food on a tray."

"Did you get some? Do they have cheeseburgers? And cake? That's what I would get!"

Someday, Jess thought as she talked to her brother, she'd bring Davey wherever he wanted to go. Disney World, probably, and they'd stay in a nice hotel like this one.

But this weekend was just hers, and to someone who didn't have a lot that fell into that category, it was a very nice thought, indeed.

CHAPTER FOUR

Eleven years before the proposal…

When Jessica Dunn walked into the room where Connor was teaching Wine 101 at the CIA his senior year, he didn't recognize her at first.

Instead, he felt an instant crush of heat and attraction. It took him a full three seconds to realize who it was—three seconds of *Holy Mary, she's beautiful* before he realized who it was. Not that she had changed; just that it was so strange to see her here, at his school.

The other thing that surprised him was the surge of happiness that followed the knee-jerk attraction.

Most of the students for this kind of half-day class were older people, interested in wine now that they had some time on their hands and money to spend. A lot of couples, a lot of girlfriends looking for something fun to do.

He would guess that Jess wasn't here for any of those reasons. She drifted near him, clearly alone in this class of pairs and groups.

"Hey, Jess," he said when she was within three feet of him.

She was equally unprepared to see him, it seemed, because she jumped a little, her cheeks turning pink. "Hi, Connor. I… I forgot you came here."

"It's my last year. How are you?"

Almost without thinking—almost—he hugged her. She didn't pull away but she didn't exactly hug him back, either, just patted his side.

"Sorry," he said with a grin. "It's good to see a face from home."

"Yeah," she said, but something flickered in her eyes.

Right. She never did like him.

Since the day her dog bit him—well, since the week after her dog bit him—Jessica had given him a wide berth, which made him a rarity among the males of their class. She was never rude to him after that one aborted punch, but she never talked to him, either. Not willingly. Even so, it felt as if an invisible copper wire connected them, occasionally flaring with electricity and light. He could sense her sometimes, just on that particular buzz.

If she felt it, too, she was excellent at ignoring it.

During chemistry their junior year, they were lab partners, and she talked to him then. But only about the lab, and after class, she'd always zipped out, always moving fast, always on her way to meet—and possibly sleep with—some other guy.

Yeah, she was the class slut…very well-liked by the guys because of it. The girls, not so much. Connor couldn't figure her out. She was tight with Levi, and they slept together, too, but she was never Levi's actual girlfriend. And even though she slept around, she had that aura around her—Connor thought of it as her *three feet away* face. Her personal space bubble that was only ever entered with blatant invitation. For someone with the nickname Jessica Does, she sure was…aloof. She worked more than most kids in their class. She never seemed bitter, though…just busy. And she never really spoke to Connor if she could avoid it. It wasn't as if she didn't like him; it was as if he were invisible.

Until chemistry. God, Connor loved chemistry. It was a tough class, and when their final exam results were given back, Connor watched her as the teacher passed their reports. "Only two of you managed to understand the assignment," Mrs. Riordan said wearily. "I'm very disappointed in the rest of you." She handed Jessica her paper, and Jess glanced at the grade then covered it with her hand. Peeked at it, covered it again.

Then she looked over at him and smiled, and it felt like all the blood in his body stopped for a minute, then flooded through him in a torrent.

Connor was used to As. He had the feeling Jessica wasn't. She was never on the honor roll, and yes, he always looked. But she was smart, and he'd been careful to let her do her share of the work, not just carry her, make sure she understood the Krebs cycle in all its glory without overtly teaching her.

That smile made him feel like he'd just won the World Series.

Then Big Frankie Pepitone said something—something dirty, probably, because it was about all he said—and Jess turned to him.

And that was pretty much the end of their interactions. She sure as hell never slept with him, something that a couple of the other guys mentioned once in a while. Nope, Jess might raise her chin at him or say hi in a group, but otherwise, nada.

Wine lovers were milling around them, sitting at the rows of counters in the test kitchen.

"So are you the teacher?" she asked.

"Yep. I'm actually filling in for a buddy of mine. It's a pretty basic class, though. Plus, growing up where we did, we all know way too much about wine, anyway. You probably don't need to take the class. It might be boring for you." He could hear Colleen's voice telling him he had no game. In this case, she'd be dead-on.

"Hugo wanted me to come," she said.

"Oh. Right. Well, I guess I should get started." Real smooth.

He went to the front of the class, cleared his throat and smiled. Three women sat up a little straighter. "Thanks for coming to the CIA," he said, and for the next two hours, he talked about grapes and regions and the different characteristics of wine. Poured and schmoozed, praised people for their excellent use of adjectives—though someone used the word *dewdrops* to describe a flavor, and even in wine circles, that was a little extreme.

Jessica took notes and tiny sips, unlike the rowdy group from Connecticut, a book club, they cheerfully told him. He served cheese and bread made at the school, talked about the texture of wine, the legs, the nose, the body, finish and color and mouthfeel, clarity, harmony. If he felt a little bit like a huckster at a carnival, it was okay. Everyone was happy.

He tried not to look at Jessica too much. It wasn't easy; she was so still and gorgeous, focused on the task at hand, occasionally answering the couple next to her with a smile. He'd seen her two summers ago at the Cork & Pork festival, which was a wine and barbecue event in Manningsport. Her brother was with her; the kid was a teenager now, or close to it. When Davey saw Connor, his expression tightened, so Con didn't bother saying hi, just kept going, feeling like dirt.

But he was teaching this class, so he bent over her shoulder and looked at her notes. *Jam, black licorice, kind of smoky,* she'd written for the shiraz.

"Good comments, Jess," he said, and she looked up at him.

Her eyes were green and clear, like sea glass.

"Thanks," she said. "I thought I was just making it up." Then she smiled, just a flash, there and gone.

"Not at all." At least, that's what he thought she said, but she *smiled* at him, and just like in chemistry class, his blood seemed to stall then rush cheerfully south.

"What would you pair this with?" she asked.

He cleared his throat. He could smell her hair, a lemony, clean smell, and see the different shades of blond, from almost white to honey-colored, straight and smooth and, he'd bet, silky to the touch, the kind of hair that would run through his fingers like water.

"Uh...sorry. Leaner red meat, brisket, lamb, bison, just about any kind of beef, really. There's a nice spiciness to the wine, so you need a meat that will stand up to it. Sausage." Great. He sounded like an ass.

"So not with KFC, then."

She was joking. With him. "No, that'd be a white, maybe a rosé."

"Connor?" asked one of the women who'd been eyeing him. "Can you give me some advice on a nice wine to bring to my parents?"

"Duty calls," Jess murmured, writing something else in her notebook.

He tried to think of a clever comeback and came up empty, but he put his hand on her shoulder and gave it a gentle squeeze as he left.

Glanced back.

She was looking at him.

When the class was over, Connor made sure those who seemed tipsy weren't driving, shook hands, accepted compliments and recommended local restaurants. Jess was putting on her coat. He hesitated for a second then said, "Would you like to have dinner?"

She hesitated.

"It's okay if you don't. It was just good to see you. Someone from Manningsport. You know. But if you don't, that's fine." There was the babbling again. And to think he made fun of Colleen for the same thing.

"Are you homesick, Connor O'Rourke? I'd think your sister would be here every other weekend. And your mom, too."

"Not really. I mean, yeah, Colleen's a pain and shows up here from time to time, but my mom... Oh, you were joking."

She gave a small smile, and his stomach tightened.

"Is that a no?" he asked.

She fixed the collar of her jacket and flipped her hair out of the collar. "Well, the thing is, I'm staying at a really nice hotel, and I kind of want to soak it up, you know?"

"The Riverview?"

"Yeah."

"Great place. I interned there last year." Not that she'd asked. But she hadn't rolled her eyes and walked out, either, so what the hell. "Did you drive over?" The Riverview wasn't more than a mile from campus.

"No."

"Maybe I can walk you back, then."

She hesitated. "Sure."

It was nearly dark outside, and they walked side by side, shoulders occasionally bumping. Connor racked his brain to ask an innocuous question, but everything seemed loaded. *How's your family, what have you been up to, how's work, got any plans...* Everything seemed wrong.

"Do you like going to school here?" she asked.

"I do. I love food."

She laughed, and there it was again, that tugging sensation in his gut. "Most people do, I guess." She looked up at him, her hair fluttering in the cold wind. "I would've guessed you'd end up in law school or medicine or something with your grades. Never saw you as a chef."

"Neither did my parents."

"Are they mad?"

"'Extremely disappointed' was the phrase my father used."

She didn't say anything at that.

"I wouldn't think you'd need this class," he said, more to keep the conversation going. "You must know a lot about wine."

"I didn't grow up in that part of Manningsport, Connor. Wine tastings in the trailer park were few and far between."

"I meant working for Hugo's all these years, Princess Defensive."

She gave a half smile of acknowledgement. "I know a little. I don't sell enough wine, though, so he thought this would help."

They'd reached the hotel's long driveway, which meant his time with her was winding down.

"How's your brother?" he heard himself ask. Kind of hard to stay away from the subject, after all.

"He's good." Another pause. "How's Colleen?"

"She's good, too. Jessica…" He stopped walking. "I always felt so bad about your dog."

She looked at the ground. "It wasn't your fault. Actually, it was mine. I tied Chico up that day. I knew the railing was rusted."

"You're the one who got him off me. Probably saved my life."

She looked up, her face unreadable. "Let's not talk about it, okay? What's that up there?" she asked, pointing ahead.

"Oh, that's really cool. It's an overlook. Want to see it? There's a great view of the Hudson."

He heard Colleen's voice in his head. *Trying too hard, idiot.* Yep. And why would Jessica want to hang out with him? She was just being polite, letting him walk her back to her hotel, where some rich George Clooney older guy would ask her to have dinner with him, and he'd order a $500 bottle of wine, and by the end of dinner, he'd want to marry her and Jess would become his trophy wife, and who could blame her, she'd drive around in a little BMW and have a maid and go to Turks & Caicos and—

"Okay," she said.

It was freezing now, and already the late October wind had gone from damp and raw to razor. She was only wearing a denim jacket. He should've noticed that before. He slipped off his peacoat and gave it to her.

"I'm fine."

"Take it, Jess."

She did. "You're not cold?" she asked.

Not as long as he was looking at her. "Not at all." He took her hand, which was cold and small in his, and rubbed it with both of his. Though it was hard to tell in the dim light, she might've blushed.

No one else was out on the hotel grounds, probably because their survival instincts had kicked in and they didn't want to freeze to death.

But Jessica sure looked cute in his coat, which came down to her knees and past her hands. Her hand slipped out of his as she leaned her arms on the railing and gazed out at the mighty river. Lights winked from the opposite shore, and the wind gusted.

Say something, idiot, his brain instructed. He had nothing.

A barge passed beneath them, almost silent, the motor just a low growl.

"You ever wonder where they're going?" Jessica asked. "What it'd be like to crew on one of those, where you'd sleep, the places you could see?"

"All the lives you could live," he said.

She looked at him sharply then returned her gaze to the river. The barge kept going, downriver toward Manhattan, and from there, anyone's guess.

"I'm sorry if I was rude before, when I first saw you," she said, not looking at him. "I didn't expect to see someone I knew."

"You weren't rude," he said.

"It's just... No one in the wine class knew my reputation, or that I'm just a waitress, or that I still live in a trailer park. For a second, I just got to be some good-looking chick from upstate, maybe a restaurant manager or sommelier or something." She pushed some hair behind her ear. "When I saw you, I was Jessica Does again."

There was a whole lot of history in that statement, and Connor was wise enough not to answer right away.

"If it makes you feel any better," he said, "you were always Jessica Doesn't where I was concerned."

She laughed, surprised, and looked at him. He smiled.

She shifted her gaze back to the river. “Do you remember the time you said I could punch you? After Chico bit you?”

He blinked. “Yes.”

“That...” She straightened up and looked at him. “That meant a lot to me.”

Hell’s bells. The wind howled down the river, gusting into the bridge.

She looked away. “I’m freezing.”

“Let me walk you back to the hotel,” he said. *Nice going*, he told himself. *She gave you an opening and you stood there like a tree.*

They didn’t hold hands on the way back, and though the wind was bitter and the smell of creosote from the railroad tracks was sharp, Connor was awfully sorry when they got to the lobby.

“I hope you have a good time tonight,” he said as she took off his coat and handed it to him.

“Thanks,” she said. She just looked at him for a long minute, her clear green eyes as mysterious as the dark side of the moon. For a second, he thought she might just turn and walk away.

But then she said, “Yes, by the way.”

“Yes what?”

“Yes, I’d love to have dinner with you.”

God was smiling on him, that was for sure. He grinned and let her lead the way to the dining room.

“Connor O’Rourke,” said Francine, the restaurant hostess, a fiftysomething-year-old woman who had flirted with him all last summer, “what are you doing back here?”

“Francine, this is my friend Jessica. She’s a guest at the hotel.”

“Very nice to meet you, Jessica. I hope everything is to your liking.”

“Everything is wonderful,” she said.

“Table for two?” she asked.

And here was the thing about being a good-looking, amiable guy who always had time to flirt with the restaurant hostess.

It got you the best table in the house, in front of the fireplace. And being a hard-working sous-chef who'd tolerated the rages and hissy fits of his stereotypical French boss got them a visit from the self-same diva, who came out to their table to greet them and sent over a bottle of wine and a lobster-and-avocado appetizer that wasn't on the menu.

"Mademoiselle, a pleasure to have you dine at my humble establishment," Raoul said, bending over her hand, and Jess smiled at him then raised an eyebrow at Connor.

"You always get treated like this?" she asked him. Raoul still held on to her hand.

"I think you're the one who's getting treated like this. Watch out for Raoul," he said, separating the chef's hand from hers. "He loves beautiful women."

"Ah, it's true, it's true," Raoul said, completely charming. "My wife, she suffers, but what can she do? She throws things and screams, then I cook for her, she is helpless in the face of my great talent, and everything is happy again. Mademoiselle—Jessica, if I may? Jessica, I would love to cook for you, just the two of us—"

"The kitchen needs you, Raoul." Connor smiled at his old boss. "Go. I smell a filet being cooked well-done."

"Mon Dieu," Raoul said. He bowed again to Jess, then winked at Connor, and then they were alone again.

Jess gave him a small smile then took a tiny sip of wine.

"You don't drink much," Connor said.

"I have two alcoholic parents," she answered mildly. "I'd be stupid to start."

He nodded.

"So what kind of classes do you take?" she asked, and he told her about the CIA, and what he was good at and where he wasn't so hot.

"What's your dream job?" she asked as their dinners were served.

He hesitated. "I'd like to own my own place," he said.

"Something fancy, like this?"

"No, no. Something small and humble but with great food. Really thoughtful food, you know? Not just burgers and nachos, but with the best burger you've ever eaten, nachos with three kinds of cheddar and fresh tomatoes and jalapeños. A place with a really good wine list, and specials based on what was in season and what looked good at the market that day. Nothing frozen or premade, nothing that came shipped in a plastic bag and was offloaded from a trailer, you know?"

Shit. Hugo's had food that came off a trailer.

But she didn't take offense. "It sounds good. Where would you do it? Manningsport?"

"Maybe." He hadn't really thought about it too much; if he followed the course of most CIA chefs, he'd sous-chef somewhere terribly impressive and uptight for a couple of years, probably in Manhattan or Europe. He was one of the best students in the class. He could go to Paris or Milan or Sydney, easily.

"What about you, Jess? What's your dream job?"

She took a deep breath. "Oh, I don't know. Not a waitress. Something where I could make enough to take care of Davey."

His Catholic guilt shot up into the red zone. "Will he ever be able to…uh…live on his own?" he asked.

"No," she answered. "He'll always be with me." She didn't seem bothered by that in the least.

Connor never did know what caused Davey's handicap. It seemed too personal to ask.

"He has fetal alcohol syndrome," Jessica said, pronouncing the words carefully, as if she wasn't used to saying them.

"I'm sorry."

"Don't be sorry," she said. "He's the best thing in my entire life."

"Sorry," Connor said again then winced. Jess gave him a wry look and then smiled.

Dessert was brought out without their ordering it, as well as two cappuccinos. “Raoul made this special for the two of you,” said their server, a girl Connor didn’t recognize. “It’s a *tartin des pommes de terre* with caramelized ginger, served with clotted cream, and he said if that doesn’t make you believe in God, he doesn’t know what will.”

“Please thank him for us,” Jessica said.

Happiness was watching her take a bite, close her eyes and lick her lips. “Oh, God, that’s incredible,” she said.

If he could make her look like that—and not because of dessert—

Better cut that thought off right there. Jess had more than enough men lusting after her.

But come on. Jessica eating that dessert was complete and utter food porn. And he was a chef. It’d be wrong not to enjoy the way her eyes fluttered closed, the little smile, the quiet moan of pleasure.

When the bill came, he grabbed it.

“No, no,” Jessica said. “Let me.”

“Not on your life,” he said.

“At least let me pay my half.”

“Nope.”

“But Hugo—”

“I’m buying you dinner, Jessica. Live with it. And thanks for tolerating me.”

“It was very tough.” She smiled. “It was nice to see you, Connor. I didn’t think it would be, but it was.”

Huh. Mixed praise.

He followed her through the restaurant, noticing the looks she got from men and women both, and wondered if she knew how beautiful she was. He didn’t think so. Or if she did, it didn’t make a lot of difference to her.

At the elevators, she turned to him and thanked him once again.

"Maybe I'll see you at home," he said.

"Probably," she said. "Small town and all that."

He looked at her another minute. "Take care of yourself. And Davey." Then he hugged her for the second time in his life, and this time, her arms went around his waist.

Her hair was as silky as he thought.

He turned his head just a little, to breathe in the smell of her lemony shampoo, and then he felt her cheek against his, and he wished he'd shaved today, because her skin was so soft.

Then their lips were touching, just brushing, not really a kiss at all, and that wouldn't do, not when he was so close to finally, finally kissing Jessica Dunn.

He cupped the back of her head and went for it. Her lips were full and soft under his, a perfect fit, and it was so, so good.

And she kissed him back. Her mouth was lush, but the kiss was innocent and gentle and a little shy, and Connor didn't want anything more than that—*such* a lie—but it was enough, it was so much… Jessica Dunn against him, her lips on his.

Then she stepped back.

"Sorry." He cleared his throat.

"I should… I…" She ran a hand through her hair, not looking at him. "Sorry about that. A guy buys me dinner, I guess it's a reflex."

He wasn't sure she was insulting him or herself. Her hand was shaking, he noticed.

"It was good seeing you," he said.

"You, too." She pushed the button for the elevator. "Take care."

He nodded once then turned and walked away.

Shit, shit, shit. Whatever he'd just done had been all wrong. She probably hated him more than ever now. She told him she'd wanted a night alone, but he'd gone ahead and accepted what had probably been an obligatory offer, and then he'd kissed her as if he deserved something, and seriously, he would never get it right where she was.

"Connor?"

He turned so suddenly he almost fell. She was still there, looking at him, not smiling. "Yeah?"

"Do you want to come up?"

She was very still. Frozen, really. Then she bit her lip.

She was nervous.

"Yes," he said, very, very quietly. "If you're sure."

The elevator doors opened behind her. She glanced back, then looked at him again. "I am."

And much to his surprise, she smiled, and it caught him right in the gut, as strong as a punch and almost painful.

Almost not trusting her words, he walked back to her, and she grabbed the pocket of his coat and pulled him into the elevator, pushed 11, and they were kissing again before the doors even closed, and she tasted so good, like apples and lemon and that hint of wine, and he was already drunk with wanting her before they hit the eleventh floor. When the doors opened again, he just picked her up and carried her out into the hall, smiling as she laughed against his mouth.

She fumbled for her room key, inserted it upside down, then got it right, and they were inside. She stopped for a second. "Beautiful, isn't it?" she said then kissed him again, shoving his coat off his shoulders, and Connor had never wanted a woman as much as he wanted her. She was lean and strong and soft in all the right places, and she smelled so good and clean, like lemons and cilantro. He kissed her neck, tasting her skin, and she yanked his shirt out of his jeans.

"Wait," he said, his voice hoarse.

"There are condoms in the drawer," she said. "Full-service hotel."

"Just...wait."

He was already breathing hard, his heart crashing against his ribs. His body was telling him to just tumble her back on the bed and get her naked and into her as fast as possible.

"Change your mind?" she said, and there was an edge in her voice.

"God, no."

"Then what?" The *three feet away* face was already in place.

"I want to look at you," he said.

Something in her eyes flickered.

He stepped forward again. His shirt was open, thanks to her quick fingers, but she was completely dressed. Her sea-glass eyes slid away from his, then back, and he cupped her face in his hands, smoothing his thumbs across her high cheekbones. Her lashes were soft and feathery. He touched her lips with one finger, then bent to kiss her, softly, softly, then the corner of her mouth, her cheeks, her nose, and back to her soft, pink mouth.

When Connor was a kid, he'd seen a coyote take a rabbit from the woods near their house. He ran after it, even knowing the rabbit was already dead, only to find a baby rabbit there in the leaves, its sides heaving with terror. Connor picked it up and felt its heart flying under his fingers, the animal terrified, but safe. He took it home and fed it from an eyedropper. It had taken a week before the animal trusted him.

It was kind of the same feeling now.

Jessica, for all her bravado and impenetrability, seemed to be a little…scared.

He kissed her neck, gently, slowly, and slid his hands under her sweater. Unhooked her bra and skimmed her skin, then slowly pulled the sweater over her head. Looked at her.

She was perfect. The pulse in her throat was visible, and fast.

"You're so beautiful," he said, and then he sat on the bed and tugged her down with him. He held her hands over her head, and kissed her for a long, long time, tasting her, learning her mouth. Then he let her hands go, smiling as they buried into his hair. Bit by bit, he undressed the rest of her, taking his time, tracing every bit of skin he saw, tasting it.

"You're killing me here," she whispered, her breath ragged, and he lifted his head and smiled, and after a second, she smiled back. It wrapped around his heart, that smile, hot and tugging. "Hurry up, Connor O'Rourke."

This was one of those moments of honest-to-God perfection, and he wasn't going to rush through it. No.

He took his time instead.

There were no complaints.

Jess woke up on her stomach, her head under a pillow. The sun was bright behind the curtains, which they'd thought to draw around 2:00 a.m. after the third round of sex—against the wall, good God.

Very slowly, she turned to see if Connor was still there.

He was.

So that was a first.

In fact, it had been a night of firsts. First night in a hotel, for one. But it was hard to think about the hotel with a rather large, beautiful male in her bed.

He was lying on his back, one arm over his head, looking ridiculously perfect, like an ad for Alpha Male Cologne. His lashes were long and curly, and his jaw was dark with razor stubble. Full lips, and a slight dimple in his chin. Just under his jaw was a divot from where Chico had bitten him, with a faint, corresponding scar curving from his eye to the top of his cheekbone. For a guy who spent all his time eating and cooking, he was pretty damn chiseled, with long muscled arms and a broad, lightly furred chest. Beautiful flat stomach thick with muscle. Those magical V-lines above his hip bones that led to Happy Land.

She knew he was gorgeous. She'd known that all her life, in fact.

It was his smile that was his secret weapon.

And his words.

I want to look at you, he'd said last night, and Jessica had gone from feeling rather lusty and a little irritable when he stopped kissing her to something completely different.

Exposed.

Because when Connor O'Rourke looked at her, she felt… different. She wasn't the type to stop and feel the feelings all the time, because that was dangerous. In that moment she'd felt something she wasn't used to feeling.

Scared. Just a little bit.

A lot, really.

And then he'd kissed her as if she'd never been kissed before. As if he'd been waiting his whole life to kiss her, as if she was the most precious thing in the world.

Another first.

There was no *screwing*, as she used to call it back in high school when she was a slut. It wasn't just a guy looking to get laid and making use of her reputation, a guy she'd be using just as much as he'd be using her. It was something else entirely with Connor O'Rourke, giving and hot and sweet and just dirty enough and then sweet again, and he'd smile at her, and that smile slid like a hot knife right through to her unprotected heart.

This was not screwing as Jessica knew it. The feelings were not feelings she'd had before. Oh, sure, she'd…well, she'd done plenty back in the day. But it had always been hard to turn off her brain. Sex was never just sex, of course. She'd always had an agenda before, with the possible exception of Levi Cooper, who had always been a friend with benefits and nothing more—or less.

So this was another first. Inviting Connor up…just because… She'd never done anything like that before.

Even last night, it hadn't been easy. There was no reason to sleep with Connor other than the fact that, as he'd walked away from her last night, she hadn't wanted him to go.

I want to look at you.

Just the memory of those words made her chest feel tight. Because when he looked at her, she didn't feel like Jessica Does at all.

She felt new.

It was scary, and it was exhilarating, and Connor knew what he was doing, and he could *kiss*, and he knew where to touch, and he wouldn't hurry, but when he was finally on top of her, and they were finally together, she came to the edge…and stopped, hanging there, stuck.

And then he used his words again. "Trust me," he'd whispered against her mouth, and she was gone, lifted on a wave of purple and red with flashes of white, a feeling of her body not being her own, and being held safe at the same time.

Another first. The trust part. The safe feeling.

What to do now was a complete and utter mystery. Should she get up? Should she move closer to him? This bed was enormous. Brush her teeth? Call for coffee? Hide?

Connor took a deep breath and opened his eyes. Turned his head to look at her.

"Hey," she said.

He didn't speak. Just gave her a sleepy smile that made her girl parts tighten and thrum. He reached out and took a piece of her hair between his fingers. "Hey, Jessica Does," he said.

Her heart stopped. She felt it crack the second before it was abruptly encased in ice.

"Oh, shit," he said, bolting upright. "I did not mean that."

"Time for you to go," she said, and her voice was calm.

"Jess, I'm sorry. I didn't— I'm just— I really shouldn't be allowed to speak without coffee—"

She got out of bed, consciously not taking the comforter with her. So she was naked. So what. He'd seen everything last night. Walking into the bathroom, she kept her breathing calm.

No big deal. No big deal. She pulled on the hotel bathrobe and cinched it too tightly around her waist.

No big deal.

"Jessica," Connor said, standing in the doorway, boxers on. "Please forgive me for that stupid-ass mistake."

"It's not really a mistake, though, is it?" she said, picking up her toothbrush. "I put out, as you know. Welcome to the club. Go home and tell the gang another one bites the dust. But at this moment, you need to leave." She started brushing her teeth, not looking at him.

He came to stand behind her. She stared at her own reflection, not looking at his. "Look, that just…came out," he said. "I'm not exactly a virgin, either, you know."

"And now you've slept with me, like half our graduating class. You should've just asked. The whole dinner thing was unnecessary."

"Jessica." There was a reprimand in his voice that infuriated her.

"I have other things to do, Connor. Can you get dressed, please?"

"Okay, since you brought it up, why *did* you sleep with all those other guys?"

"None of your business. Excuse me." She pushed him out of the bathroom and closed and locked the door. Checked her reflection again. Normal enough, she thought, though it was sort of like looking at a stranger. Her throat was killing her, clamped tight, impossible to swallow.

Jessica Does.

That fucking name would follow her the rest of her life.

"Jess," Connor said through the door, "I'm really sorry. I didn't mean it. It just kind of… It was just a reflex. But last night was—"

She opened the door. "Save it for the next girl, okay? I have to get going. I'm working tonight."

"I don't want there to be a next girl. I just want to erase the last five minutes."

"Too bad you can't. Take care. Thanks for dinner."

Then she closed the door again, locked it and turned on the shower.

When she got home that day, her brother was sitting on the steps, waiting for her. "Was it fun?" he asked as she stopped to hug him and pet Chico Two. "Did you eat room service?"

"I did," she lied. The truth was, she'd fled right after her shower, as soon as she was sure Connor had left. "I brought you the little shampoos and bath stuff. They smell really good. Wait till you take your shower tonight." Davey hated showers; maybe the new stuff would entice him into cleanliness.

See? She was back to normal, thinking about her brother. She went into her bedroom.

There was a bouquet of flowers on her bed.

"The truck man said these were for you," Davey said. "They smell nice."

Irises and roses and a fat lily and a bunch of other flowers she didn't recognize. They were just about the prettiest things she'd ever seen, a riot of purple and pink and red.

The card said, *Please forgive me.* No signature.

"Why don't you give them to Mom?" she asked her brother, ruffling his soft hair. "I have to run."

At least he couldn't call her. Jess was so, so glad Connor didn't have her phone number. He sent a note, but she tossed it. And for the next couple of months, she did what she did best—she didn't think about something that was too painful to think about. She just worked. At Christmastime, his entire family came into Hugo's, which opened for the holidays. And yes, her stomach flipped when she saw them. But hey. She was a waitress; they were her customers. Nothing else. "Hello, Clan O'Rourke," she said amiably. "How's everyone tonight?"

"Pull up a chair and chat with us, Jess," Colleen said.

"We're really busy, but thanks," Jessica said. It wasn't a lie. She passed out the menus, took drink orders and checked on her other patrons.

About halfway through their dinners, Abby Vanderbeek spilled her root beer for the second time that night, and Jess mopped up the table, had Felicia get the kid another pop, then went to the bathroom to wash her hands. When she came out, Connor was standing there.

"Jess, I'd really like to explain my idiot comment," he said.

"No explanation necessary," she said. Gave him a noncommittal smile, the one that she'd been using since forever, the *don't worry, I've got this, everything's fine, no hard feelings* smile that made her face ache.

"So a one-word mistake has ruined any chance I might've had with you forever."

It wasn't a one-word mistake, she wanted to say. *It was my reputation, it was "Jessica Does Anyone," it was "That white-trash Jessica," it was my entire past when I'd already told you that this was my chance, my one chance, to be someone other than that stupid, slutty Jessica Does.* "Don't be melodramatic, okay? It was a fun night, and it's over."

"I would really like to see you again."

"Sorry." She let that sit a beat, then added, "I have to get back to work now."

His eyes narrowed. "Okay, Jess. It's your call."

"Yes. It is. Happy holidays." It was as bland as she could possibly get, and it worked.

After all, he deserved bland. That smile, those eyes, his kisses...those were just tricks to get her into bed, and boy, did they work. There'd been candles and dessert and a beautiful hotel, and Connor had figured *Why not? Jessica puts out. This is an easy lay just waiting to happen.*

And she played right along, had been Jessica Does again to him and to herself.

It would've been stupid to forget it.

And no one had ever called her Jessica Dumb.

CHAPTER FIVE

Eight and a half years before the proposal…

The second time Connor and Jessica hooked up was almost exactly two years after the ill-fated first time.

In the time that passed, Connor had surprised himself by moving back home. While at the Culinary Institute, he'd traveled quite a bit—internships in France, Miami and then a prestigious stint at the only restaurant in Manhattan ever to earn three Michelin stars. And while he learned immeasurably, the big, glitzy restaurant scene wasn't for him. Food presentation bordered on the ridiculous…filet mignon topped with a circle of half-inch, precisely cut white and green asparagus tips arranged in a yin-yang symbol; symmetrical dollops of red beet paste making a half circle around a brick of polenta with the restaurant logo branded onto it.

The food was amazing, but it wasn't the type Connor wanted to make. He wanted to make ordinary food taste extraordinary. It was all about flavor and the experience. Happiness should be part of the meal, and at Vue des Anges, where dinner for two could easily cost more than $500, there weren't a lot of happy patrons. Snobby patrons, definitely. Patrons trying to impress their companions. Bored patrons, sullen patrons, patrons a little stressed by the high-pressure dining experience.

What he wanted, especially now, was a place for normal people. A place that served perfect meals without the pressure. Lasagna made with veal and pork and cream and four kinds of cheese and homemade pasta—not fussy, not ridiculous…just perfect, thoughtful, fantastic. Yes, they'd serve hamburgers, which would probably enrage Etienne, his former boss, but hamburgers made with Angus beef and shallots and flat-leafed parsley and garlic-infused butter. His sister's weakness, nachos, served with Cotija cheese and wafer-thin slices of radishes and charred tomatillo salsa.

A place that was home in a way that his own home had never really been.

On the surface, the O'Rourkes had always seemed like the classic American family—two kids, two cars, parents who were still married.

Underneath, though, ran a tension that only Connor felt. Well. Connor and his father.

Connor had never felt particularly close to his father, ever. The dog bite had only cemented that feeling. Pete O'Rourke was too busy being Manningsport's answer to Donald Trump. Growing up, Colleen had always been Daddy's little girl, the more outgoing twin, always with some funny, fast remark, always getting attention. She could do no wrong in their father's eyes. Her grades weren't as good as Connor's, but Dad never seemed to notice or mind… Collie was never told to study harder or help their mother more. She was simply adored.

And Connor was largely ignored, except when they were out in public. Then it was Pete and his gorgeous kids, leave it to Pete to have twins, weren't they just great, good-looking kids, both of them, and on and on and on.

Jeanette, their mom, thought Dad walked on water, never

minding his slight, and not-so-slight, condescension toward her, his long workdays and lack of reciprocity in the affection or praise departments. No, the O'Rourkes were a sitcom family, starring Dad as The Hardworking Businessman; Colleen, the Sassy and Beautiful Daughter; Mom with a supporting role as Slightly Dim Housewife; and Connor as…

As not that much. As Colleen's twin. Barely a walk-on role, at least in his father's eyes. No matter what, Connor always seemed to disappoint his father, and somewhere along the line, he'd stopped trying. Mom was so grateful for any affection or attention that Connor made a point of being her ally, complimenting her when she got dressed up, because his father always had some not-quite-nice comment for her, or watching a TV show with her, rather than have her sitting in the living room, alone.

Connor knew his father was something of a slimy businessman not above some questionable business deals. Pete used money and influence and favor-trading to get his way.

And Connor knew his father cheated on his mom…at least, he strongly suspected it. When he was fifteen, he'd been walking past an empty storefront Dad owned, and there was his father, kissing a much younger woman.

Connor wasn't an idiot. He knew grown men didn't kiss a woman without hoping to go all the way. And the woman sure didn't seem to mind. For weeks afterward, Connor gave his father the cold shoulder…not that his father noticed or cared.

Just before Connor and Colleen had graduated college, their father had announced that he was leaving their mother for his girlfriend. The fact that he even *had* a girlfriend had shocked Colleen and Mom.

It hadn't shocked Connor.

However, Dad's piece on the side was pregnant…and that *was* a shock.

Mom fell apart. Colleen, too, was struggling; not only was her image of their father utterly smashed, but she'd dumped her longtime boyfriend and had been walking around like a ghost all summer.

And then Connor got the call from Sherry Wong, who was the commercial loans director at the local bank, and whom Connor had taken to the prom. The Black Cat, a nasty, run-down bar right on the Manningsport green, had gone into bankruptcy. She'd heard that Connor was a chef... Any chance he might want to buy it?

There was. The building was his before it even went on the market, in a move that surprised and displeased his father, who seemed to own every other commercial building in town.

His maternal grandmother had died the year before and had left him and Colleen each a sizeable nest egg. Con asked his twin if she wanted to be half owner, and she was game. All of August and September, they overhauled the place, sanding the old maple-plank floors, spending an entire day driving to a salvage yard in New Hampshire to buy a gorgeous old bar, hammering and sawing and keeping each other company as their mom fell apart and Gail "the Tail" Chianese—who was a whole four years older than they were—gestated their half sibling.

Oddly enough, it was good to be back. While Connor never quite imagined settling down in his hometown, it felt right. Manningsport was as beautiful a town as they came, perched at the base of Keuka Lake, surrounded by hills and farms-turned-vineyards, filled with families who went back generations. Three seasons a year, the tourists flocked in to taste wine and exclaim over the quaintness of the village, filled with shops and a really good bakery and Hugo's French Restaurant.

And now, there'd be O'Rourke's. Colleen came up with the simple name and message—*You're very welcome here.* It would be the only restaurant open year-round, and in that way, it would give the residents of Manningsport a place to gather in the long, cold winter months. Connor would run the kitchen with the help of Rafe, a less-ambitious friend from the Institute who was happy to live in wine country and work as a sous-chef. Colleen would manage the place and bartend. Two of their cousins asked if they could waitress. In fact, forty-nine people applied to work there.

Jessica Dunn was not one of them. Connor had half hoped she'd be interested, but while she continued to treat him politely if they crossed paths, that was it. The *three feet away* face was always in place.

On a Wednesday night in October while Connor was alone at the restaurant, bolting booths to the wall, Colleen called him. "We have a sister," she said, her voice husky. "Savannah Joy, eight pounds, two ounces. I'm going to the hospital. Wanna come?"

He paused. It was nine o'clock, and he was sweaty and grimy. "No. I'll go tomorrow. Uh…everyone's healthy?"

"Yep. That's what Dad said." His sister was silent. He knew what she was thinking. *You won't make the baby grow up lonely, will you? Just because Dad's an asshole?*

Give me some credit. "A sister. That's nice. Hopefully, she's not as ugly as you are, Collie Dog-Face."

"Me? You're the one who's so ugly, you have to put a bag on your head to get the dog to hump your leg."

"Do you still own a mirror, or did that get too sad?"

"You know what, Con? You'll never be the man our mother is."

That one always got him. He laughed. "You win."

"I always do."

He rolled his eyes. "And yet you work for me."

"Ha! Brother mine, *you* work for *me*."

"Keep telling yourself that. I'm hanging up now because you're annoying me."

"How?"

"By breathing." He paused. "You gonna tell Mom about the baby, or am I?"

"I will, coward. I live with her, after all." It was true. In a glorious spasm of Catholic martyrdom, Colleen had moved back in with their mother. Connor, who felt this only proved he was the smarter sibling, lived in the tiny attic apartment above the bar.

He rubbed his eyes. "Tell them I said…" He sighed. "I guess congratulations. Tell Gail, anyway." He almost felt sorry for Gail. Almost.

"Tell them yourself, dumbass. Love you, even when I hate you."

"Ditto."

He hung up the phone.

A baby sister, just shy of twenty-three years younger than Connor and Colleen.

Christ.

He went upstairs and took a shower. The apartment wasn't much; stifling hot in the summer, and soon to be freezing cold, but it was fine for a single guy who worked a lot. A futon couch, a chair, a TV, a bed and several crates of books. When the restaurant was turning a profit, he'd look into buying a house.

He pulled on some clean jeans and a T-shirt and briefly contemplated visiting his mother. She'd be a wreck about this, the poor thing. She still held out hope that Pete would see the error of his ways and come home again.

That wasn't going to happen. Everyone could see it except Mom.

And while Connor had known his father was cheating, he sure hadn't pictured Gail the Tail as his stepmother. Pete had married her nine days ago, the day after his divorce was final.

He grabbed his motorcycle helmet and went out. Yeah, yeah, he owned a motorcycle. The gas mileage couldn't be beat. Colleen called him a cliché, but so what? It was fun. He had a small pickup truck for winter.

Where he was headed, he wasn't quite sure. The area didn't offer too many places for anonymity, and that was exactly what

Connor wanted. A place to sit in the dark, have a beer and not think.

He thought about calling someone to join him—one of his high school pals, maybe. Levi Cooper was on leave from Afghanistan, and Big Frankie Pepitone was always up for a beer. Then he opted against it. Solitude was the order of the night. He was Irish—brooding was the song of his people. Colleen would kick him into a good mood tomorrow, as he'd been kicking her for the past few months.

His Honda purred its way up the Hill and along the lake. Penn Yan wasn't far; maybe something would be open there. The wind was clean and cold, and his thoughts focused on driving.

The dark miles blurred past, the quiet engine of the bike soothing.

Up ahead was a cement building that every male in a fifty-mile radius visited at least once in a lifetime: Skylar's VIP Lounge.

A strip club, in other words.

Perfect. Beer *and* boobs.

Connor went in. He'd been here for a bachelor party last year, and it was exactly what you'd expect. Crappy drinks, worse food, health department violations by the dozen and nearly naked women, a few of them even good-looking.

The place was mostly empty tonight, a few men sitting around the runway. The requisite pole was being humped by a very lithe and extremely overweight woman in a glittery Wonder Woman outfit, who kept flipping off the customers. It was Tuesday; Connor guessed the management saved the under-fifty strippers for the weekend.

Connor took a seat, ordered a Sam Adams (bottled, so as to avoid having to use a glass from the kitchen). The waitress brought it, and he took a pull. Wonder Woman looked familiar.

"I can't believe you're still stripping," one of the guys down in front said. "A little long in the tooth, aren't you?"

"Take a bite, Ernie. If your dentures are in, that is," said the stripper. "And you," she said to another guy. "Give me a tip or I'm kicking over your beer. You think my job is easy?"

Mrs. Adamson. That was it. Her son had been a year ahead of him in school.

Connor took another sip of his drink.

A baby sister. Savannah Joy.

He'd look after her. Poor kid, with those two morally bankrupt assholes as parents. Yeah. He and Colleen would make sure Savannah turned out okay.

A small part of him, though, couldn't help feeling just a little more invisible.

At least he wasn't eleven, hoping for a few crumbs of his father's approval.

And a little sister…that might even be fun. He could teach her to play baseball and cook.

The beer was mellowing him. Colleen always laughed about what a lightweight he was.

"Let's hear it for Athena, Goddess of the Hunt," said the DJ. Connor frowned. She was supposed to be Wonder Woman, after all. Costume aside, he'd have to leave her a tip, and a good one. She'd made the best cookies, back in the day.

"When do the women start?" called one of the runway patrons.

"You people suck," said the stripper, walking off the stage.

"Making her debut tonight, please welcome the beautiful Jezebel," said the DJ. "Take It Off" by Kiss started up—not the most imaginative song. Connor reached for his wallet. Time to head off before his old catechism teacher showed up.

Then, onto the runway, wearing very high heels and a microscopic bikini, came Jessica Dunn.

Connor froze, his wallet halfway out of his back pocket.

She wobbled down the runway, then stopped.

She was shaking.

"Now we're talking," said Ernie. "Go ahead, sweetheart, start dancing."

She tried. She took a few steps, looking like a little kid. A bob. A bend of her knees. Step to the left. Step to the right.

From behind her, Athena, Goddess of The Hunt, called out, "Try a hair toss, hon!"

Jess tried. It wasn't hot. It looked like she wrenched her neck. Another knee bob.

"Grab the pole. It'll help," said Athena.

"Yeah, sweetheart, just wrap yourself around the pole. We don't need a lot," said Ernie.

Connor closed his mouth. He was fairly sure Jess hadn't seen him, because she was looking straight ahead, as if staring down the angel of death. She had on a ton of eye makeup and red, red lipstick, and Connor had the sudden flash that as exposed as she was, she was trying to hide herself.

"Relax!" called Athena. "You got this!"

She really didn't. She held on to the pole with both hands, like she was strangling it, and shuffled her feet, her ankle wobbling in the heels.

All that perfect skin, those long legs, the gorgeous body, her breasts barely covered by the tiny scraps of fabric.

Connor suddenly wished he had a blanket.

One of the men held up a bill. "Bend over, doll. Do you do lap dances, by the way?"

Connor was on his feet before he realized he was moving, but Jess had already turned, bolting down the runway and behind the curtain.

"Nice. You scared her to death, assholes," Mrs. Adamson called with a hearty double-fisted salute.

"Last call," said the bartender.

Connor jumped lightly onto the runway and followed Jess. No one stopped him, so he went behind the curtain.

There was a little hallway that led to the bar on one end, a small room (closet, more like it) on the other. Mrs. Adamson was talking to someone in the bar and barely flicked an eyelid at Connor.

The dressing room door was slightly ajar. Con opened it a little more.

There she was, face in her hands.

"So rhythm isn't really your thing," Connor said, leaning in the doorway, and she jumped out of her chair like he'd tazed her.

"Shit." She grabbed her jeans and flannel shirt. "What are you doing here?" she asked, pulling on her clothes. She dashed her arm across her eyes.

"I'm a scout for *Dancing with the Stars.* Sorry, we've had to rule you out." He smiled.

Her eyes flickered, then she shrugged, her face neutral. "I needed some extra money."

"Really? It's not your dream to be a stripper?"

"Shut up." She might've been thinking about smiling. He was almost sure of it.

"So, Jess," Mrs. Adamson said, thundering down the hall. "You're fired. Sorry, kid. Stripping's not for everyone."

"You were quite good, though, Mrs. Adamson," Connor said. He handed her a twenty.

"Oh, Connor O'Rourke! Look at you, all grown up! Thanks, sweetheart." She pinched his cheek and took the cash. "We're closing. Off you go, kids." She strutted back down the hall, the floor trembling under her weight.

Jessica tied her hair into a ponytail with a smooth, quick movement. "So you go to strip clubs a lot?" she said.

"No. This is my second time."

"Why tonight? You stalking me?"

"Not consciously." He looked at her for a long minute, taking in the fact that she was jamming things into her bag, moving as fast as she could. "That was really brave, Jess."

She looked up sharply.

"And I won't tell anyone."

Her gaze dropped back to her bag. "Thanks."

"You want to get a drink?"

"It's almost eleven. Nowhere's open."

"O'Rourke's might be. I know the owner."

She hesitated, then met his eyes. "I could use a drink. Which is probably why I shouldn't have one."

"How about a Coke, then?"

She nodded.

The fresh air was welcome after the beer-scented fog of the club. Connor waited till Jess got into her car. She turned the key, but there was only a click. "This night seems to be cursed. Can you give me a jump?"

"I only have my bike." He gestured to his motorcycle. "I'll give you a ride home, though. After your Coke."

She got out of the car. He took off his leather jacket and handed it to her.

"I'll be fine," she said.

"Put it on. This, too." He gave her the helmet, and after a second, she did what he asked.

Mentally thanking the gods that had chosen this night for her battery to die, Connor got on the bike. Jess climbed on behind him and put her arms around his waist.

Driving through the dark, Jessica pressed against his back, was about the best thing that had happened to Connor in years. The drive had seemed long on the way out; now, it was way too short.

He parked the bike behind O'Rourke's, then unlocked the door. "It's not quite finished yet," he said needlessly, turning on just the light behind the bar.

Jessica slid out of his coat and put the helmet on the bar.

"It's beautiful," she said. She took a long look around, then ran her hand over the bar. "You're gonna put a dent in Hugo's business, that's for sure."

"Well. It's…it's just a pub."

"Looks like a lot more than that to me."

Connor saw it through her eyes—the U-shaped bar, the booths with the carefully chosen lighting and comfortable leather seats, the tables that he'd paid extra for so they wouldn't wobble, unlike 98% of all restaurant tables everywhere. The wide-planked floor and tin ceiling, the amber lights that hung over the bar.

Hopefully, yes, it would be a lot more than a pub.

Jess went to sit down on one of the stools, then stopped. "You live upstairs, right?"

"Right." His residence wasn't a secret, but he was surprised Jess knew.

"Would it be all right if I took a shower?" Her voice was businesslike, but she didn't meet his eyes.

"Yeah, of course. Right this way." He brought her upstairs, abruptly wishing his place didn't look like a dorm room. He got a clean towel and handed it to her, feeling awkward. "Take your time," he said. "I'll be downstairs."

He went back down, trying not to think about the fact that Jessica Dunn was taking off her clothes in his apartment. Stepping into his shower. Naked. Wet. Soap suds streaming down her long, smooth—

"Snap out of it," he muttered to himself.

He went into the kitchen, since the kitchen was where he did his best thinking.

He didn't know too much about what Jess had been doing these past two years. She was still at Hugo's, he knew that. Lived with her brother in a little house over near the factory, at the very edge of the residential part of town, where the houses were covered in sagging vinyl siding and the sidewalks were cracked.

A neighborhood that was far better than the trailer park.

He broke three eggs into a bowl and started whisking. Chopped some parsley and cilantro, hoping Jess wasn't one of those people who hated cilantro. Got out the nonstick frying pan that had cost a fortune, turned on the gas and put a dollop of butter into the pan. As it melted, he opened the cupboard where he'd already arranged his salt collection, chose some Peruvian sea salt and added a few flakes, waiting till they dissolved. Sliced two hearty pieces of the peasant bread he'd bought from the Mennonite market that morning and put them in the toaster.

Above his head, he heard the shower turn off.

He told himself that he shouldn't be so happy that tonight had been an utter failure for her, that her car was a piece of crap.

He could still feel her arms around his waist from the ride here.

He added a quarter cup of heavy cream to the eggs and whisked gently. Poured it into the pan, added the herbs and ground in some Tellicherry black pepper, waited twenty seconds, then began folding the eggs gently. Buttered the toast, plated the eggs, added a sprig of parsley and brought it out, just as she came into the bar.

The makeup from earlier was gone, and her wet hair looked darker, pulled back into its ponytail.

She looked about fifteen years old, except for the way she filled out her clothes.

"You didn't have to do this," she said.

"I know. Would you like a glass of wine instead of that Coke?"

She hesitated. "Okay. Just a small one."

"What kind?"

"I don't care."

"Now, now. You took my class. I expect better from you."

She sat at the bar and smiled a little. "Fine. A fumé blanc?"

"An excellent choice." He winked at her and poured her a six-ounce glass. One for himself, too, so she wouldn't be drinking alone, then sat down next to her.

"You're not eating?" she asked.

"Not right now. I'm just a voyeur."

"Pervert." She smiled slightly, then took a bite of the eggs.

"Oh, my God, these are incredible," she said, closing her eyes. "Are they really just scrambled eggs?"

Her eyelashes were dark brown and feathery. "Thanks," he managed. "Uh, yeah."

Watching her eat made his chest hurt from happiness. Her hands were efficient and neat, and she savored the food, really tasting it, not like some people, like Colleen, who ate like a starving coyote; not like his mother, who ate with the careful rhythm of a chronic dieter and then binge-ate junk food later.

No. Jessica tasted. She savored. Her tongue slipped out to lick a little crumb of toast from the corner of her pink mouth, and when she swallowed, he had to look away. He took a pull of his wine or beer or orange soda or whatever the hell he was drinking. It was cold. He should probably pour it in his lap.

"So I figured stripping would be easy money," she said, and he looked back. She was talking to her glass, apparently, because she didn't make eye contact. "There's this new medicine they're trying for kids with fetal alcohol syndrome, and it's expensive, and of course Medicaid doesn't cover it."

"What kind of medicine?"

"It's something to help with impulse control and outbursts. This bread is fantastic, too."

"The Mennonite market."

"Right. Anyway, I figured I could strip for a few months and pay for it. It was harder than I thought." She took the last bite of eggs and wiped her mouth with the napkin. "Those were the best scrambled eggs I've ever had. Thank you."

"You're welcome." He paused. "Jess, I could always—"

"No. But I appreciate the offer."

Sure, he'd been about to offer her money. Who wouldn't? "Do you want to pick up some shifts here?"

"No, but again, thank you. I have a job. And another job, too, actually."

"Okay." If she didn't want to work for him, well…he got that. She'd always been proud.

She sipped her wine, then set the glass down, her movements controlled and precise. Now came the moment that she'd thank him and leave.

She didn't. "How are things with you, Connor?"

The ordinary question sounded extraordinarily intimate, given the amber lighting and the late hour. "Well," he said, "I'm a big brother. My father and his new wife had a baby girl tonight."

"Wow. Congratulations."

"Yeah. My dad's been divorced from my mom for ten days. Married to Gail for nine."

"Speedy."

"He didn't want the family honor stained by bastardization."

Jess laughed. "Interesting definition of *family honor.* Not that I'm one to talk."

"I'd say you know quite a bit on the subject."

She swallowed. Took another sip of wine, and put the glass back down exactly in the spot it was in before.

"Are your parents still married?" he asked, more because he was afraid she was going to leave than because it mattered.

"Yep."

"That's good, I guess."

"That's not the word that leaps to mind. At least I got Davey out of there. My father thinks it's funny to get him drunk, and my mom was teaching him to make cocktails."

Jesus. His own father didn't seem so bad, suddenly. "You're an awfully good sister."

She gave him a wry smile. "So I'm brave, I'm honorable, I'm a good sister… Where's my Nobel Prize?"

"You're also incredibly beautiful."

She rolled her eyes. "Freak of genetics."

So mentioning her looks was off-limits. "And smart."

"I almost flunked out of high school, Connor."

"Good grades don't mean much. I was valedictorian, and I'm a cook."

"I thought Jeremy Lyon was valedictorian."

"No. Salutatorian."

"You sure? Jeremy's so perfect. I can't see you beating him out there."

Fucking Jeremy. Every female in town, from Connor's own mother to his three-year-old cousin, was hung up on him. Oh, hang on. Jess was smiling. She was teasing him. Got it.

She was finished with her meal, and had drunk half her wine. But she wasn't making any noises about leaving, either.

Connor had had a few girlfriends in the two years since they'd slept together. Two. He'd had two. One and a half, really. No one who'd really…impacted him, as much as he would've liked that.

Not like Jess.

He looked at her a long minute. "Remember when we, uh… hooked up? When you came to the Institute for that class?"

"No, Connor, you were just another notch on my bedpost." She straightened out her fork and knife to the three o'clock position on the plate. "Yes. Of course I remember."

"I didn't sleep with you because of what you said, you know."

"What did I say?"

"That I slept with you because I could. Because you were Jessica Does."

"But that *is* the name you used." She cocked an eyebrow at him, still keeping up with the cool-chick-with-an-edge attitude.

"It just…came out." A crap answer, and yet the truth. That stupid name had been given to her young, and it had been liberally used throughout high school. Jess herself had used it.

"So why *did* we sleep together?" she asked.

"Is 'because we're both red-blooded American heterosexuals' a good enough answer?"

The corner of her mouth hinted at a smile. “I mean, why did you bother? I’m guessing you have to beat the women off with a club.”

“Some days, sure. I try not to be too rough.”

“So why me, then?”

Was she serious? “I liked the way you ate dessert.” No game, he had absolutely no game. “And you smell nice.” Proof of his sorry, no-game state.

“Right now I smell like Irish Spring. You’re really living the cliché on that one, by the way.”

“A present from Colleen.”

“Ah. Well, most of the time, I smell like restaurant food and other people’s wine and whatever Davey’s wiped on me.”

“I like food. And wine. Not sure about what Davey’s wiping, so I’ll have to stay neutral on that. But you and I have a lot in common, Jess. We both work in restaurants—”

“Don’t. You’re a Culinary Institute–trained chef who has his own restaurant at the age of twenty-three. I’m a waitress.”

“So? It’s hard to be a good waitress.”

“It’s really not,” she said.

“Sorry. Didn’t mean to offend you. I bet you’re a horrible waitress.”

“Just stop saying nice things.”

“Okay. You’re a really shitty dancer.”

She laughed.

She didn’t laugh enough. Or maybe she did, but he didn’t get to hear it enough.

“And your outfit had no imagination,” he added. “Mrs. Adamson, at least she tried.”

Jessica Dunn laughed again.

Before he’d really planned on it, he leaned in, slid his hand around her neck and kissed her as gently as he knew how. Her lips were soft and full, and he was an addict, just like that, not just wanting to kiss her, but needing it like he needed breathing.

Then she kissed him back, and light seemed to spark through his veins, hot and electric, and God, she felt so good, her slender, vulnerable neck, the silky, damp hairs there. He teased her mouth open and tasted her, and she was suddenly gripping his shirt in both hands.

He probably shouldn't be doing this. Maybe this was…uh…what was the phrase? It was hard to think with his mouth against hers, their tongues sliding…

Oh. Right. Taking advantage.

He pulled back. Ran his fingertips along her jaw, the tender, smooth flesh just below.

Her pupils were dilated, making her eyes look darker, and her mouth was slightly open.

And then, just like that, she was back to the three-feet-away zone. Without so much of a flicker of an eyelash, the wall came down.

Someday, he was going to figure her out.

"Connor," she said calmly, "you don't want to sleep with a stripper."

"You're not a stripper. You got fired." He picked up her hand and kissed it. Twice. The Irish Spring smelled better on her.

She swallowed. "I should get back to Davey." But she didn't leave, either. And she was staring straight ahead, at his chest, not at his face. It was as though she was waiting for him to convince her otherwise.

In fact, it was almost like she was shy.

Jessica Dunn, who'd beaten up boys twice her size in middle school, then slept with most of them in high school, and yet who also seemed like an ice princess, totally untouchable…seemed shy. Even if her tongue had been in his mouth a few seconds ago, even if his shirt had been fisted in her hands.

She liked him. He was almost sure of it.

He wanted to say a hundred things, about taking care of her, and wanting her so much he ached, and how his chest felt punched when she came out onto that runway tonight, and how if he didn't kiss her again, fast, it might kill him, and if he couldn't sleep with her again, it would definitely kill him.

"Who stays with Davey when you're out?" he asked instead, his voice a little hoarse.

"Gerard Chartier. They're the same mental age."

"Can Gerard stay a little longer?"

There was a long pause, and Jessica was very still, and Connor's whole being clenched with wanting, with hope, with *please say yes.*

She nodded.

Connor didn't wait. He stood up, lifted her onto the bar and kissed her, a different kiss this time, hungry and full, his tongue against hers, his hand pulling out her ponytail and sliding his fingers through her long, damp hair.

She wrapped her legs around him and kissed him back, and that thrum of electricity became a lightning storm of white heat, and all that mattered was Jessica, her mouth, her neck, the shoulder blades that shifted under his hands, her long, beautiful spine and perfect ass.

He stopped kissing her for a second. "I live upstairs," he muttered against her neck.

She answered with a little smile, and that smile, it just killed him. "I guess I should walk you home, then."

Rather than let her walk him anywhere, he just lifted her up and carried her up the rickety stairs to his apartment, kissing her as he did. Kicked open his door, set her down and started on the buttons of her shirt, kissing her neck as he worked. His hand seemed to be cupping her breast. She wasn't wearing a bra, and her nipple hardened against his palm, and there it was, that blinding, stunning flash of want.

"Wait," she said. "Wait. Hang on." She pulled back a little, gripping his hands in hers. "This has to be a secret, okay? Because Davey will... He might... You know."

"Okay."

"Really?"

"Yeah." Right now she could've said *You have to cut off your right arm before we do this,* and he would've answered *Hey, not a problem!* "Don't worry. We can take it slow." *Slow. And fast. And hard. And—*

"I don't want your sister to be—"

"Nope. Me neither." Because Colleen would be insufferable if she knew.

Jess looked at him, and for the first time all night, she really looked at him, and Connor got the impression it wasn't easy.

Then she reached up and touched the scar on his cheek, and her fingertips slid down to the place under his jaw that dented in. The scars from Chico, all those years ago.

"Take me to bed," she whispered, and Connor couldn't help thinking that God *did* exist and was smiling on him for no good reason.

He'd take it. He'd take anything Jessica Dunn and the universe saw fit to give him.

CHAPTER SIX

Eight and a half years before the proposal…

For three weeks—well, twenty days—after her humiliating foray into the world of exotic dancing, Jessica, who wasn't the type to spin out happy fantasies of how wonderful everything would be, was starting to feel kinda happy and wonderful.

On day three of their…*thing*, she presented Connor her terms, written on a note card.

Rule number one: no telling anyone. God forbid she date one of Manningsport's favorite sons and have it not work out. She already had enough of a reputation to deal with. Plus, Davey. She had to figure a way to make him okay with this, and right now she had no clue.

Rule number two: no coming over when Davey was awake, and never without checking with her first.

Rule number three: no sappiness. Sappiness was just not her thing, and so no flowers, no cards, no *you make me want to be a better man* stuff.

Connor listened with a half smile and a raised eyebrow. "Anything else, majesty?" he asked when she was done.

"I'm sure there is. I just can't think of it right now." She put the index card back in her pocket.

They were walking on one of the paths on Ellis Farm, which was partially open to the public. It was cold, and she'd ridden her bike there, since her car was still acting finicky.

Hardly anyone came out to Ellis Farm on a cold, sleety November day, which was exactly why Jess had chosen it.

"So how long will we be a secret, Juliet?" he asked.

"As long as I say, Romeo. Is that a problem?"

"Anything for you." He gave her a crooked grin. "Can I kiss you? Do I need permission for that first? Are there guidelines for that on your index card?"

She pulled the card out and pretended to check. Playfulness. That was new for her, outside of goofing around with her brother. "Well…you can, but you have to make it good."

He did. He had the most beautiful mouth, his lips full, and he seemed to know just how to kiss her—gentle and soft, or urgent and hard, and no matter what, it made her insides curl and squeeze and light up in beautiful shades of purple and red. This kiss was long and slow and lovely, his mouth moving over hers, his hands sliding down to her hips to pull her against him, his razor stubble scraping gently. His tongue touched hers, and her knees buckled a little.

Then a dog barked, and they broke apart. Connor tapped the tip of her nose with his finger, smiled, and they continued walking. An Irish setter ran past, followed closely by its owner, not someone Jess knew.

"Horrible weather, isn't it?" the guy said.

"Sure is," Connor answered.

And when the man was gone, Connor took her hand.

That was all. They just walked, hand in hand.

Another first. Kind of embarrassing, the effect of Connor's big, warm hand holding hers so firmly, and acting like it wasn't a big deal. Boys hadn't wanted to hold her hand back in high school. They'd wanted to get into her pants.

And since high school, when she'd been working toward getting Davey and herself out of the trailer park and away from her parents, she hadn't dated anyone. There was no need to; Davey had a reputation as being liked by a lot of big, strong guys, and the bullying had mostly stopped. He was as safe as she could make him.

But now she was on a walk with a gorgeous man who was funny and thoughtful, who hadn't made her feel like trash when he'd seen her embarrassing attempt at rhythm and stripping, who scrambled eggs for her, who didn't ask prying questions about her family…who just seemed to *like* her, and who had been amazing in bed the five—and counting—times they'd done the deed.

She was pretty sure she didn't deserve this. Pretty sure the other shoe was about to drop.

Hence, the rules. Hopefully, they would soften the blow.

They met when she could get away, always at his tiny apartment, sometimes in the morning, when Davey was at school, sometimes late at night, just for an hour or so. She'd leave a note for Davey—*Going for a run!*—and a stick figure drawing of her doing just that, then ask Ricky, the guy who lived next door, to keep the baby monitor on his porch; the houses were so close together that if Davey woke up, which he rarely did since the kid slept like a rock, Ricky could hear.

Then she'd head to Connor's, her heart light and buzzing, a warm flush wrapping her like a hug.

On the night of the restaurant's grand opening, she arranged for Davey to stay overnight with their mom, who was enjoying a brief sober spell. Dad was at a casino, so he wouldn't be back for a day or so or longer. And Mom did love Davey, even if she was sloppy about looking after him. Jess had taken all the booze with her; she'd found Mom's stash and dumped the half inch of bourbon and the half bottle of cheap vodka into the sink. With

Mom's sobriety, it was always a question of when she'd fall off the wagon, not if. Then Jess asked Mrs. Cooper to check on Davey once or twice, to make sure Mom was "okay," which Mrs. Cooper knew meant awake and sober.

"You bet, honey," Mrs. Cooper said. "I owe you from all the times you watched Sarah."

The restaurant was jam-packed, and Jess knew everyone. Gerard Chartier talked her into joining the volunteer fire department, Colleen was making everyone laugh, Jeremy Lyon came back for the weekend from medical school, and this time, seeing him and Faith Holland together—still sticky-sweet in love—didn't give Jess a pang.

She had a guy now, even if it was on the sly. And Jeremy had always been too perfect, anyway. Leave him for Princess Super-Cute.

That night Connor occasionally came out of the kitchen to press the flesh, and every time, his eyes found hers and rested a beat too long, and that wonderful, hot tightening would start in the pit of her stomach, making her feel what she imagined drunk felt like—not like her parents' version of drunk, but happy and loose and hopeful.

The food was amazing. And free. Crab cakes, creamy lasagna, tiny cheeseburger sliders, quesadillas, salads, shrimp wrapped in prosciutto, slices of bread stuffed with garlic and spinach... every bite succulent and filled with layers of flavor. Colleen, ever gorgeous and lively, was putting on a good show, sliding beers down the bar, spinning martini shakers, but it was Connor's food that practically brought people to their knees.

O'Rourke's would be a smashing success; Jessica could see that. Because of Connor. Colleen was great, and Jess had always liked her, but Connor was the real star.

And he was hers.

The thought made her heart feel almost too big for her chest.

When the grand opening wound down, Jess waited in the

park by the lake until the lights went on in Connor's apartment, and then knocked at the back door.

A minute later Connor opened, hair wet from a shower, jeans on but not buttoned. No shirt, his muscular chest utterly perfect, the smooth skin on his ribs begging for her hands.

Her knees were already soft with want.

He leaned in the doorway, and a smile tugged one corner of his mouth.

"Jessica Dunn. What are you doing here?" he said, and his voice scraped against that soft, aching place inside her, and she wrapped her arms around his waist and kissed him.

Good God.

She spent the whole night.

A thought occurred to her in the dark, after Connor had made love to her for the second time and was sleeping, his heavy, beautiful arm around her, a dangerous thought, the kind she knew she shouldn't think, piercing into her brain like an ice pick.

She felt safe.

The thought itself made her almost jolt up in bed.

That was usually the forerunner of doom.

She'd thought she was safe when she was nine and her father actually won seven thousand dollars on a scratch-card, and that money was going to help them get a better place to live. It would be the start of a new life for them, where Dad could get a job he'd keep; he'd always thought he'd be a good mechanic, and they made lots of money, and Mom would sober up if they lived in a real house because it wouldn't be so depressing, and Davey could get into that nursery school with the nuns who'd help him more than the public school, where he was always pulled out for speech therapy or put in time-outs.

That weekend, her father went to Rolling Thunder Casino and lost the seven grand plus eight hundred more…everything they had. The electricity had been turned off for six weeks, and Mrs. Cooper brought them food.

She'd felt safe, too, when Mom had three months of sobriety when Davey was six and Jess was thirteen. She'd lain there in bed, Davey's soft little snores so sweet and lovable just a few feet away, and it dawned on Jess that at last, she wouldn't have to be the one in charge, that maybe she could stay after school for extra help in math, now that Mom was sober and life was normal.

The next day, Davey had an outburst in kindergarten. Mom was called in and after she collected Davey, stopped at the package store for a handful of little Popov vodka bottles. When Jess got home, Davey was asleep on the couch in front of *Terminator II,* his face covered with dried snot from crying, and Mom was passed out in bed.

When she was sixteen, she'd felt safe after her mother's mother came to stay, a woman Jess had only met once before. Mom was in the hospital with jaundice, and Dad was who knew where, and all of a sudden, Grandma had pulled into the trailer park with three bags of groceries. She cooked for Jess and Davey and did the dishes, too, and said she respected Jessica for having a job. She wasn't a warm and cuddly grandmother, but she was there, she was sober and she took charge. Davey was scared of her, but he'd get over it, and it was so, so *nice* to have a real adult in the house. On her second night with them, around 10:30, Grandma looked at her and said, "You have to get up early. Why don't you go to bed?"

No one sent Jessica to bed. No one cared if she got enough sleep. "Okay," she said, and she had the thought to kiss her grandmother. She didn't, but something filled her chest, something warm and wonderful.

Then, on the fourth day, Mom came home, still a little yellow around the eyes, and Grandma went back to Nevada. She died the next year.

So feeling safe…it was stupid. Nothing was safe. No one was safe.

But then Connor murmured in his sleep and pulled her a little closer, and she lay there, her hand over his heart, and tried not to feel safe.

★ ★ ★

Chico Three was a puppy, another pit bull, because their terrible reputation aside, they could be very sweet, gentle dogs. Chico the Original…well, he'd been fine with the four of them. But something had happened to him before they got him, and he was scary when strangers came around. Jessica had tried to take care of the problem by chaining him to the rusting aluminum railing that led up the two steps to their trailer. She should've known it would break. She should've checked. She'd been worried about Levi's little sister, who was only two, and even afraid for Levi and Mrs. Cooper. The fact that the railing broke…she should've seen that coming.

But their next dog, Chico Two (obviously named by Davey) had been a *great* dog, a genuine sweetheart. He lived to be a ripe old age, but last month when he could no longer stand or eat, Jess carried him to the car and drove out to the veterinarian, trying not to cry, telling him what a good dog he was as the vet injected him with the mixture that would stop his heart. Davey had been devastated, of course. Broke the bathroom door with his head-banging, though she'd managed to get his helmet on him first.

Jess waited a month or so, then called the shelter, and of course they had pit bulls—they always did. Chico Three was fourteen weeks old, and Davey fell madly in love with him at first sight. So did Jess, for that matter.

And she decided that she'd ask her boyfriend—her boyfriend!—over to see the new puppy. After Davey was asleep. The other shoe hadn't dropped, and, well, this was what normal people did. She thought so, anyway.

She called him up. "Hey. You want to come over and watch a movie tonight?" she asked. It was Tuesday, his night off.

There was a pause, and Jess actually flinched. Maybe he didn't want to come. Maybe she was just a booty call. Maybe—

"Yeah. Absolutely. What can I bring?"

"Um…nothing. Just…just show up. After eight, okay?"

"Thank you, Jess." His voice made her stomach contract in that strange, scary happiness.

She hung up and bit her thumbnail. Ricky, her next-door neighbor, who was always outside, waxing his beloved red Camaro, would see Connor coming. And while Gerard Chartier came and went, it was pretty well known that he was Davey's babysitter. Connor was not a babysitter. It might be pretty obvious, in fact, that she had a boyfriend.

Terrifying. Kind of exhilarating, too. Maybe.

She went to the three houses where she worked as a home heath aide and zipped through her chores, then raced home to clean the house. She was a little anal about cleanliness, as the trailer had had mold and sticky, decades-old shag carpeting, but with Davey and a puppy, there was always some mess to clean up.

The rental house wasn't much—cheaply built back in the seventies, identical to Ricky's, but Jess had done her best to make it nice. She shopped tag sales religiously, always the first one there, and over the years, had scored some nice things: charmingly mismatched pieces of Fiestaware, a painted ceramic bowl from Italy, a decent powder-blue couch that wasn't attractive, but *was* clean and comfortable, a wobbly bookcase she painted black and shimmed till it didn't tip anymore, and a kitchen table with three chairs for when Mom would come over for supper.

The backyard was mostly dirt, but there was a tree that was good for climbing. Davey loved to climb trees, and because he did, Jess did, too. Otherwise, it was pretty drab. Ricky was a great neighbor, though he had some dark times when he'd just disappear inside the house for a week or so, not answering the door, leaving the TV on twenty-four hours a day; he was a vet and had some pretty severe PTSD. Jess would bring him food and leave it on the porch during those times. The neighbors on the other side fought a lot, and Jess had had to call the police a few times, which didn't make them love her.

Someday she'd own her own place. A house with a backyard that was more than a cracked cement patio and crabgrass. She'd have a flower garden, the ultimate luxury, and grow tomatoes and basil, too. There'd be a porch with a glider and hanging baskets. That always seemed like the crown jewel to her...big, full baskets of flowers brightening the entire street, attracting hummingbirds, which always fascinated Davey, and butterflies, which her mom adored.

That was what normal people did.

But for now, this house was fine. It was shabby, but it was a real house, with a cellar and everything, and the landlord wasn't horrid; the rent was manageable.

Davey was extra tired that day, so somewhat miraculously, he fell asleep early, Chico Three snuggled under his arm. Jess took another pass through the house, flipped the seat down on the toilet since Davey never did. Straightened a towel. Cleaned off the counters.

She was nervous. She'd never had a boy over like this. Levi Cooper was the only one who'd ever come to their trailer to hang out, and that was only because he lived in the trailer across the way.

A half hour later, Connor pulled up in his truck. Her chest prickled with a flush, and her heart rate doubled. He held a pot of yellow chrysanthemums.

"Hey," he said, standing there on her stoop. "Thank you for having me."

"Yeah, sure," she said. "Thanks for the flowers. Um...you can put them on the step there."

He obeyed, then came in, filling the small kitchen. How tall was he? Six-two? Tall.

"This is nice," he said. "You have a...what does Colleen say? A good eye. For, you know. Color and stuff. It's very clean, too. It's great, I mean. Thanks for inviting me over."

So he was nervous, too. "We have to be quiet, okay? Davey's asleep. He doesn't usually wake up, but..."

"Okay."

He just looked at her with those eyes of his, those tangled lashes and the perfect, clear blue-gray color. Those eyes should be against the law. His hands, too. He smelled like soap; he'd showered before coming here, she could tell, and it was somehow very innocent and sweet that he'd taken a shower before coming here.

Clearing her throat, she said, "I guess I'll...make popcorn. Why don't you put the movie on?" They had an old TV and a VCR; probably the last VCR in existence, but it had been free, and Davey loved his movies.

Jess made the popcorn. It was so strange having Connor here, in the next room. In her house.

This was like a real date. This *was* a real date.

She dumped the popcorn into the Italian bowl and went into the living room. Was it supposed to be this awkward? It felt very awkward. "Want anything to drink?" she asked. Should've asked that before.

"I'm good. Thank you."

They sat on the couch.

"Thanks for doing this, Jess," Connor said, and she couldn't quite look at him.

"You're welcome," she whispered. Her pulse slipped and skidded, and she could feel her cheeks heating with a blush.

She was happy.

She was home, her brother was safe and she had a boyfriend. The first boyfriend ever. And God help her, this felt real. It wasn't just a quick escape; it wasn't so he'd be nice to Davey; it was because she *liked* Connor O'Rourke.

And he liked her.

He smelled so good. Her skin prickled and hummed, and she couldn't even remember what movie she'd picked up from the library, though the opening credits were rolling and some ominous music played. She could feel the heat of his arm, which was so close to touching hers.

Then he looked at her, and she was kissing him before she even knew it.

They kissed and shifted and kissed some more, and Jess turned up the volume a little to make sure Davey wouldn't hear anything. Nothing ever felt as good as his heavy, hard body against hers, practically on top of her now. How could a guy who cooked and ate all day feel so strong? The muscles in his shoulders slid and tensed under her hands, the long line of his back was smooth and lean. His hand was on her breast, teasing and gentle, his leg between hers, asserting all sorts of delicious pressure, and Jessica thought if they could just do this for the next fifty years or so, she wouldn't ask for anything else.

He pulled back, breathing hard, looked at her, eyes heavy, cheeks ruddy. Then he smiled. "This is fun," he whispered.

She nodded.

Then Connor looked over her shoulder. "We have company," he said.

It was Chico Three, wagging his tail, head cocked, like he was waiting for an introduction.

"Chico Three, this is Connor," Jessica said. "Connor, meet Davey's new puppy."

Connor disentangled himself, leaving Jessica feeling unfulfilled and a bit empty. But it was okay; the night was young. He sat up, scooping the puppy onto his lap. "Hey, boy," he said, and Chico wriggled with delight, wagging wildly, nipping Connor's chin, making little whining noises of delight. "Ow," Con said, smiling. "Those are some sharp teeth. No biting, Chico."

"What are *you* doing here?"

Jess jumped. Davey stood at the bottom of the stairs, hair rumpled, looking confused. Shit, shit, shit. *Play it calm, be matter-of-fact.* "Davey, you know Connor, right?"

"Hey, Davey," Connor said, still petting the puppy.

"What are you *doing* here? Why do you have my dog? Let go of him!"

"Honey, it's okay, he's not—"

"Let go of him! Don't kill him!" His face was getting mottled and red, and if she didn't stop this, it was going to be bad.

Jess stood up. "Davey, we were just watching, um, a spy movie. What's your favorite spy movie?" she asked. *Redirect.* That was what all the psychologists said, all the articles on the internet, but she was too late, and they were the wrong questions.

"Why did you let him in?" Davey yelled. He grabbed a photo frame from the bookcase and threw it at Connor, missing, then reached for a pinch pot he'd made her in pottery class, which he threw to the floor. It cracked in two.

"Take it easy, buddy," Connor said. "Everything's okay."

"Get out of our house! Get out!" Davey screamed, and he shoved past Jessica and launched himself onto Connor.

"Davey! Stop!" she said, trying to grab her brother's arm. Connor, God bless him, managed to put the puppy on the floor, and Chico fled into the kitchen, barking, but Davey was like a Tasmanian devil, screaming, flailing, hitting, and Jess could barely hold him; he was like a really big, really strong otter, writhing and twisting. Connor stood up, towering over Davey, and was promptly punched in the face. She grabbed Davey's arm. "No hitting! Just take a breath, Davey. Tell me who's better, Superman or Batman?"

Connor gave her an incredulous look.

"I hate you! I hate you!" Davey wailed. "You killed my dog! You killed my dog! Run, Chico Three! Run!" He twisted his arm free, sending another punch right to Connor's eye, hard enough that Connor rocked back.

"That's enough, Davey. Stop it," Connor said firmly. It didn't work.

"Davey, please. You're scaring Chico Three," Jessica said, recapturing his arm. The puppy was barking in the kitchen, and the last thing Jess needed was a pit bull learning about violence, and shit, shit, shit.

"*He's* scaring Chico Three! He kills dogs!"

"Buddy, calm down, okay?" Connor said. "I'm not killing anyone."

"I'm not your buddy! I hate you! Get out! Get out!" Spit flew from his lips, and despite her best efforts to hold him, he kicked Connor in the shin, broke free of her and shoved him in the chest.

"Davey, stop," she said firmly. The doctors told her to be firm, establish parameters and redirect his attention. Too bad they weren't here to help. "You need to go to your room right now."

He shoved her, too, and slapped her right across the face.

"Stop!" Connor barked, and he grabbed Davey, turned him so her brother's back was against his chest, and just held him tight.

Wrong move. Being restrained was the thing Davey hated the most. His screams grew louder, if possible, and he threw his head back, catching Connor square in the face. Connor let him go.

Davey grabbed the bowl of popcorn, smashed it on the floor, kicked the coffee table and then went to the wall and began banging his head against it. "Get out, get out, get out!"

"Davey, please, please stop," she begged, starting to cry. She forced herself between him and the wall, her shoulder taking the brunt of his blows, but it was too late, damn it; she should've had his helmet down here, should've prepared for this. His head was bleeding. She managed to get behind him and wrapped her arms around his chest, but he was too strong to take down, even with all her body weight in the effort. "Davey, this is not okay. Stop this right now."

"Out! Out! Out!"

Shit, hell and baby Jesus. "Connor, can you get him on the floor for me?"

"No! No! No! Don't touch me!" Davey bucked up against her.

Connor picked up his legs, and Jess sank back on the floor, almost holding Davey in her lap. She wrapped her legs around him and put one arm behind his head so he wouldn't break her collarbone, and another across his chest. He couldn't do himself any harm this way, but her ears rang with his screams, and he twisted and flailed.

And sobbed.

He needed his meds.

"Connor, take my place, okay? Just hold him so he doesn't hurt himself. Be careful not to choke him." She had to almost shout to be heard over Davey's wails and Chico Three's hysterical barking.

Connor obeyed. His eye was already starting to swell. "It's okay," he said to Davey, who was struggling wildly, his feet kicking out at nothing. "I'm not gonna hurt you." Davey screamed in response, and Connor looked a little freaked out. Who could blame him? This wasn't what most people dealt with.

Jess didn't have time to think about it. She ran upstairs to the bathroom and grabbed the Xanax, the only thing the doctor would prescribe for Davey's meltdowns, and liquid Benadryl, hating that it had come to this.

She was drugging her brother.

Davey was still wailing. Kicking, too, from the sound of it. Poor Connor.

Jesus, this was horrible. She ran back downstairs, filled a plastic cup with water. Chico Three was on his little dog bed, chewing a squeaky toy.

She hustled into the living room and knelt down. Her brother was now just breathing wildly, groaning, but still kicking. One time, when their father had missed his birthday, he'd put his fist through a window and needed five stitches.

This was much, much worse.

"I'm going to give you the sleepy medicine, okay, sweetie pie?" she said, feeling idiotic in the face of Davey's rage. "Then you and Chico Three can take a nice nap. And we'll watch *Batman*, okay? The one with the Joker? I love that one. I love the Batmobile."

She slid two pink pills into his mouth, then held up the cup. He bit it, but it was plastic for a reason. "Drink, honey."

"I hate you!" He tried to head-butt Connor again.

"Swallow the pills, honey. You'll feel better."

"Make him go away."

"I will, as soon as you swallow the pills, honey." He obeyed, and she gave him the Benadryl chaser.

She hated herself for medicating him. It was no better than getting him drunk. But it would work. Davey was very sensitive to drugs.

She didn't look at Connor. Couldn't bring herself to do that. He said nothing, just held her brother. There was a clear impression of teeth on his arm. Human teeth. Davey had bit him.

It was so fucking unfair that it worked, that she was reduced to this, to medicating her brother into submission. She felt like an evil doctor doing experiments on a kid.

Davey was wearing his Batman pajamas. That made everything worse. "Don't let him hurt me," he said, and Jess couldn't help the tears that slid down her cheeks.

"I won't. No one will ever hurt you, baby."

"Don't let him kill Chico Three."

"I won't. Chico Three is safe and sound, chewing on Squeaky Dinosaur."

He was getting sleepy. His body lost its stiffness, sinking back against Connor. There was popcorn everywhere, not to mention broken ceramic, a broken coffee table and a smear of blood on the wall from Davey's head.

"I hate you," Davey murmured, and Jess had to clamp down the tears that gathered in her throat, because she knew that one was meant for her.

Her brother's eyes closed, his lashes clumped together from

tears. She pressed her sleeve against the cut on Davey's head. It wasn't bleeding much. He'd had worse.

"Want me to carry him to bed?" Connor asked. He was going to have quite a shiner tomorrow.

"You're bleeding, too," she said, and her throat tightened more. She couldn't look him in the face.

"I own a bar. It's good practice for being a bouncer."

"Don't joke about this."

"I'm sorry. Let me bring him upstairs."

"I can do it," Jess said.

"I'm sure you can, but I've already got him, so why don't you let me do it this time?" He sounded irritable. Who could blame him?

She hesitated, then nodded. He picked Davey up easily and went upstairs. "First door on the left," she said, somewhat needlessly, because it would be obvious which room was his.

Worried the puppy would get cut, she picked up the pieces of broken pottery. The Italian bowl was way too shattered to be fixed with glue. As for the little pinch pot Davey had given her for her birthday, well, she couldn't think about that right now.

Chico Three sat under the table, the squeaky purple dinosaur in his mouth. "Come here, boy," she said, grateful when the puppy obeyed her. He didn't seem traumatized now, just waggly and sweet. She picked him up and kissed his head, and the little guy licked her chin.

"Don't be nice to me," she whispered, then went upstairs.

Davey was sleeping, the blue plaid comforter pulled up to his chin. Connor stood there, looking down at the boy. His eye was nearly swollen shut.

She set the dog on the bed, and he snuggled right up to Davey's back, turned in three circles and lay down with a sigh. Jess went into the bathroom, ran a clean facecloth under the cold water and got a Band-Aid, then went back to the bedroom. Wiped the blood away from Davey's head. Just a small cut, thankfully. No stitches would be needed, but his head would be sore in the morning, that was for sure. She put the Band-Aid on, her throat choked with glass.

"Will he be okay?" Connor asked.

"Yep." A tree branch ticked at the window. "Connor, you should probably go, okay?"

"Let me help clean up."

"I want you to go."

"Jessica, this is—"

"Please, Connor." Because if he didn't leave now, she'd start crying for real, and there was no way in hell she was going to let that happen. Bad enough that he'd seen what he had.

She went down to the kitchen, got some ice cubes from the freezer and stuck them in a plastic bag. "Hold that on your face."

He obeyed. "Jess, we can work this out."

"Sure. But I want you to go now."

He looked at her through his unswollen eye, then leaned in and kissed her cheek. "Okay. Call me later?"

"You bet."

She didn't call later.

Connor called her the next day; she let it go to voice mail.

The third day after Davey's outburst, when she couldn't put it off anymore, Jessica waited till O'Rourke's would be closed, checked on Davey to make sure he was asleep. She left him the running note on the floor outside his door and then went next door. Ricky answered right away. "Would you mind?" she asked. "I won't be long."

"No problem." He took the baby monitor. "You okay, Jess?"

"I'm fine. Thank you, Ricky."

Then she drove to Connor's and broke up with him.

"I'm sorry," she said. "I don't think this is going to work. He's my first priority, and until I can see if that new medication will work, I can't expose him to anything upsetting. You saw what happens." His eye was swollen. The rumor mill had it that he took a spill on his motorcycle. So he'd lied for her, apparently.

"Jess, I did some reading—"

"And now you're an expert?" Her voice was sharp. People had been giving her advice on how to handle her brother all her life.

"No, but I can help with some things. Maybe."

"Like what, Connor?"

"I can pay for the medication."

She could feel her face hardening into the Jessica Does expression—*Don't mess with my brother, and we won't have a problem.* Threaten first, give sex second.

It generally worked.

With Connor, though, the order was wrong, but it was the same thing, sort of.

"Let me help you," he said quietly.

"No, thank you." People meant well. Sure they did. But then they thought their money entitled them to something. If Connor funded Davey's medication, maybe he'd start saying things like, *I think I get a say, since I'm the one who's paying for this.* Or, if he didn't like how things went, what if he decided to stop paying?

No. It had to come from her. She was the only one she could rely on. She'd made this problem; she was the one who had to deal with it, and if it meant she didn't get a normal life, so be it.

"Maybe I can help in other ways," Connor said.

"What ways?"

"I don't know yet. This is new to me. But I know a little. I read a lot of articles, and—"

"Well, it's not new to me. Don't think you can figure this out because you've spent three hours on the internet, Connor. I've been living with this since I was seven. I love him. I know what's best for him. I've talked to doctors, read every article there is. I know what he can and can't handle, and he can't handle me having a…a thing right now."

"A thing? Is that what we are?"

She swallowed. "Yes. I'm sorry."

He just looked at her a long, long minute. "I'll miss you, then."

For a second, she could feel her face wobble, her tough-girl *don't mess with me* front slipping, and oh, God, what if he saw how lonely she was?

"I have to go. Davey's alone. I just ran over to tell you. Thanks for being so nice about everything."

With that, she turned and ran down the stairs. Pulled out of O'Rourke's parking lot so fast she slung gravel.

She didn't realize she was crying till the road went blurry.

CHAPTER SEVEN

Five years before the proposal

It wasn't that Connor gave up on women after Jessica cut him loose. No. He was a normal healthy American male. He dated. And he did try to *date*, rather than hook up, because he wouldn't want some asshole guy to sleep with Colleen and never call again. In fact, if it was up to him, Colleen would've joined the Sisters of Mercy long ago.

And then there was Savannah, who was as sweet as they came, a sturdy little kid who got dropped off at O'Rourke's every Friday night so Colleen and Connor could spend some quality time with her, and babysit while Pete and Gail went to some other, fancier restaurant.

So being a well-behaved guy was kind of paramount. Savannah already had a shitty male role model, though Pete was Mr. New and Improved Father 2.0 with her. Even so, she didn't need a brother who slept around.

So Connor dated. Just not very well.

Not many women made it past the two-week point. They were nice and all… They just weren't Jessica.

He kept waiting for her to come in and tell him things were under control, and could they pick up where they left off. It didn't happen. She came into O'Rourke's every Wednesday night with the rest of the volunteer EMTs and firefighters, and she always said hello, just as nice as pie— "Hey, Con, how's it going?"

And he'd say something like, "Just fine, Jess. How's your brother?"

And she'd say, "He's doing okay, thanks for asking."

Then the copper wire that connected them, ever since sixth grade, would light up with electricity and heat, a reminder that no matter what, they were locked in.

And then it'd go cold.

Or, more likely, Jess would flip the switch. She'd go back to the firefighters, who were more of a drinking club, at least on Wednesday nights, and get dealt into the poker game or make wisecracks with Gerard Chartier. She'd have one glass of white wine, which she never finished.

But every once in a while, if he was having a particularly rough day for whatever reason, Jess would pop into the kitchen, that mysterious half smile on her face, and say something nice. Something like, "That crab-cake special…it was proof of God, Con." Or she'd say, "Heard a joke the other day and thought of you." It would be inevitably filthy and hilarious, and he'd crack a begrudging smile and shake his head, the wire warm with current and tangled around his heart.

Almost like she was checking up on him.

Then she'd go back to the bar and not finish her drink.

If she waited on him at Hugo's, she'd drop a hand on his shoulder and give it a little squeeze. But she did that with Jeremy and Gerard, too, he'd observed, and did even more with Levi, like messing up his hair, which invariably made Connor stupidly jealous. Levi and Jess went way back, friends since they were toddlers, practically.

Being relegated to friend…it was discouraging to say the least.

So one day, when a gorgeous redhead came in, and Colleen was too busy flirting with Levi Cooper, who'd just been promoted to police chief, Connor came out and took her order. Started talking.

Kim Garvis was the town clerk in Bryer, the next town over. She was in Manningsport for a training session on new software and decided to get dinner before she headed for home; said she'd heard good things about O'Rourke's.

She was smart. She was nice. She was gorgeous. She was interested.

There was absolutely no reason not to ask her out, so he did.

Connor had kind of forgotten how it was to date someone without sneaking around. They didn't hang out at O'Rourke's. The restaurant was closed on Mondays, and Connor's day off was Tuesday, and he really didn't feel like staying in the building where he lived and worked in his free time. Plus, there was the Colleen element—his sister loved nothing more than to get into his business and offer color commentary. So he'd get on his motorcycle and drive over to Bryer and hang out with Kim, or take her out to dinner or a movie.

And everything was very nice. Couldn't ask for anything more. It was great.

So long as he didn't think about Jessica Dunn. Whenever she did come into his head, he'd remind himself that she'd made herself clear, had other priorities, and he had to get that through his thick Irish head.

Then one night Kim surprised him by showing up at the restaurant. There'd been the spring biplane show on the lake, and O'Rourke's was packed and loud and fun. Kim didn't mind; she sat at the bar, chatted with Colleen, who'd guessed, using her psychic twin powers, that he was seeing someone. Kim seemed completely at ease, laughing with some of the regulars, and Connor, glancing out, smiled, seeing his girlfriend there.

"Rafe, you have the conn," he said. Though Rafe was not a Navy man, he did love submarine movies, especially those starring Matthew McConnaughey or Denzel Washington.

"I have *you*, Con, and aye aye, skipper," Rafe said, taking over the grill.

Connor washed his hands and went out, weaving through the crowd till he got to Kim. "Hey, you," he said, and gave her a casual kiss on the lips.

"Hey, back," she said, grinning. "Thought I'd come see you in your element."

"His element is lead," Colleen shot back. "The densest element. Oh, snap!" She high-fived Gerard and pulled a Guinness.

"The densest element is osmium, idiot," Connor said. "Though a good case can be made for iridium, too."

"No one cares," she said. "It was a great joke. Kim, you know you can do better than this guy, don't you?"

"I see you've met my irritating twin," he said. "And clearly, I got her through chemistry. She's quite slow."

"And yet he works for me," Colleen said. "Kim, ignore him. I'm much more interesting."

"Unfortunately, I'm not a lesbian," Kim said. "But if I were, you'd totally be my type."

"I'll take that as a moral victory," Colleen said, sliding a beer down the bar.

"I have to get back in the kitchen," Connor told Kim. "You need anything?"

"What time will you be done?" she asked.

"Kitchen closes at ten."

"Then I'll need you at 10:02." She smiled. Colleen made a gagging noise.

Kim stood up, gave him a kiss—a real one, getting some cheers from the gang—and then sat back down.

Connor grinned and turned to go.

Jessica was looking right at him, looking as if he'd just shot her in the heart, and Con's own chest felt like the good old broomstick had just skewered him, hard and dull, splintering bone and tearing organs.

Then she blinked, and there was the *three feet away* face. She turned away and laughed at something Theresa DeFilio was saying.

Connor turned back to Kim. "I'll see you in an hour."

"Great," she said. "Colleen was telling me about the time you hit her in the eye with a potato."

"Happy times," he said, then went back into the kitchen.

But something was wrong.

Hannah and Monica, his cousins and waitstaff, kept passing in the orders, but Connor's rhythm was off. He put sweet potato fries on one instead of the truffle-oil potatoes, cooked a tuna steak instead of the swordfish. After the fourth mistake, Rafe gave him a look.

"Sorry. My girlfriend's out there. I'm distracted." Except it wasn't Kim he was thinking of.

"Well, then, get out there, big man," Rafe said. "Any cute gays for your lonely sous-chef?"

"Jeremy Lyon."

"Yeah, but he's fresh out of the closet, and celibate or something. Creepy. Be on the lookout. I'll finish up."

So Connor went out. Got a table with Kim. Had Monica freshen her drink, asked about work. Showed her a picture of Savannah. They talked about movies.

It was very nice.

Except Kim seemed to be mad. And getting madder.

"Everything okay?" Connor asked.

"Yep."

"You sure?"

"I'm fine." She raised an eyebrow.

Oh, shit. The *F* word. "What's wrong, Kim?"

"Nothing."

"I have a twin sister. I know what that means."

"What does it mean, then?" she asked.

"It means I've fucked up somehow."

"Then you're not as dumb as you look."

"Okay, if we're fighting, can I at least be told why?" he asked.

Kim stood up. "I'm leaving."

"What? Why? Uh… I'll walk you to your car. Kim, what—" She was really leaving. He had to hand it to her. Indecision was not one of her flaws.

He followed her into the back parking lot. "Kim, please tell me why you're mad."

"Who's the blonde?" she asked, whirling on him.

Holy Mary. Kim missed her calling. Should've been with the FBI. "What blonde?" he said, hoping to play the *men are thick* card.

"Don't play obtuse with me. The blonde you won't look at."

To bullshit, or not to bullshit? "We're pretty crowded here, Kim. Can you be more specific?"

"The gorgeous one," she said sharply.

Busted.

"Oh. That's Jessica. We went to school together."

"You slept together, too."

"Uh…yes. A while ago."

"And you're in love with her."

"Look, I don't—"

"Don't bother, Connor," she snapped, flicking back her beautiful hair. "You've *never* not looked at me the way you wouldn't look at her."

"Uh…how am I supposed to respond to that?"

"You saw her, and my God, the air just changed, Connor. So don't bullshit me."

He held up his hands in surrender. "She and I dated very briefly, and that was… I don't know. Two years ago." Twenty-seven months ago. "It didn't work out."

"Why?"

He wasn't about to spill Jessica's personal issues or family history. "She just didn't think it was working."

"Well, it's clear you want to be with *her*, so good luck." With that, Kim opened her car door and got in. "Nice knowing you."

"How am I the bad guy here?"

"You just are. Deal with it." She slammed the door, backed out of her spot, then rolled down her window. "You have no right dating someone when you're in love with someone else."

Then she gunned the motor, ran over his foot and was gone, tires screeching at the corner.

"Ouch," Connor said.

He tried his foot. Bruised, maybe, but not broken. With a sigh and a curse, he went back inside, limping a little.

"Another one bites the dust, huh?" Colleen called.

"I hate women. Especially you, Dog-Face."

"They hate you back, Troll Boy."

Rafe was finishing up the last order. "I'll clean up," Connor said.

"I thought you were with your woman."

"She dumped me. Get out, go home, have fun."

"If you were gay, I think we'd make a really nice couple. Just putting that out there."

"Don't make me fire you."

"That's what I get for trying to be nice. Ciao, boss."

Connor grunted. Got to work. Cleaned the mess from the entire night, shooed off the cousins, ignored Colleen.

When the place was empty, he started cooking. Lasagna. Vegetarian lasagna with sautéed red onions, portobello mushrooms and fresh baby spinach. Made a thick white sauce with whole milk, flour, ground pepper and lots of butter. He made the dough, cranked it through the press—pasta from a box tasted about as good as the box, whereas Connor's could make an Italian grandmother weep. Ladled out the sauce, gently layered in the noodles, vegetables, sauce and freshly grated Parmigiano-Reggiano, not the fake American stuff, that he special-ordered a few times a year from the Italian market in Philly.

Jessica had no right to look at him like that, like she'd just been mown down. Two frickin' years—twenty-seven months—and she hadn't once indicated the wish to get back together. And then, with one look, she blew a perfectly nice relationship with a very nice woman.

"So, brother mine, you want to talk?" Colleen asked, coming into the kitchen from where she'd been stacking chairs in the restaurant.

"Nope."

Colleen didn't say anything for a minute. Then, because it was physically impossible for her not to speak, she said. "I'm sorry about Kim. She seemed nice."

"Yep." But he looked up. "Thanks."

"See you tomorrow." She punched him on the shoulder, just hard enough to hurt a little, and he flicked some white sauce into her hair. Then she left, and the quiet of the empty restaurant settled around him.

Cooking always grounded him. To be a good chef, you had to understand food, let it speak to you, inhale its scents, watch it cook. You had to *feel* the pasta, assess its stick against the wooden spoon, taste it, to know when it was done. You couldn't just look at a clock. You just had to know when it was right.

Cooking was a way to stop time. To make a family take a half an hour and sit, relax, eat and taste. There was a Zen sense to it, a way of making a dozen separate ingredients into something transformative and new and special, something that would sustain and nourish and bring happiness to those who experienced it, at least for a little while.

Small wonder he'd started cooking when his parents' marriage began to crumble, years before his mother knew anything was wrong.

He put the lasagnas in the oven and got to work cleaning the kitchen until every surface gleamed.

He loved this place. It was his true home.

And he didn't like getting slammed in the chest at home.

By the time the six lasagnas were done, it was 1:00 a.m. He loaded them into his truck, drove to the soup kitchen—they'd given him a key when he opened O'Rourke's, and he dropped by about once a week with this kind of take—and left five of the lasagnas in the fridge with a note on heating. Then he got back in his truck and drove to Jessica's.

She answered faster than he would've expected. "Connor," she said. "Is everything okay?"

"I brought you a lasagna."

She frowned. "Uh…thanks. Why?"

"I'm mad at you."

"No, I get that. The lasagna tells the whole story."

Okay, sure, it was dumb. "My girlfriend didn't like the way I didn't look at you. So she broke up with me."

"And clearly a lasagna…does what, exactly?" There was a hint of a smile at the corner of her mouth, and Connor felt an answering tug in his chest.

"I don't know."

Her smile grew. "Would you like to come in?"

He followed her inside the house. The kitchen, though plain, was immaculate. On the table were an open textbook and a notebook. She closed both and put them on the chair. Message received: *whatever I'm studying is none of your business.*

He put the pan on the stovetop, turned and leaned against the counter.

Jessica Dunn looked beautiful in pajamas, even if the bottoms were green plaid and the top was a T-shirt that showed a cat wrapped in a tortilla. *Purritto,* it said. Funny.

"So why are you here, Connor?" she asked.

"My now ex-girlfriend pointed out that I'm still hung up on you."

"Did she now." Jess swallowed and looked at the table. Straightened the napkin holder.

And that, friends, made Connor very happy. She was nervous. For some reason, he knew that was a good thing.

"You ruined a perfectly good relationship." He bit down on a smile.

"By existing?"

"Yep." He let his gaze wander over her. Her hair was down, and he loved her hair, the cool, smooth texture of it, the graceful swing. Her cheeks were flushed, and she was now fiddling with the drawstring of her pajamas. Double-knotting it, in fact.

Connor had always been good with knots.

"Do you want me to stop coming to O'Rourke's?" she asked.

"No."

"Then what do you want?"

"You."

She went to put her hands in her pockets, then discovered she didn't have any. Folded her arms, instead. "So you're bribing me with lasagna?"

"Yes. Is it working?"

She shrugged. "A little. It smells fantastic."

"Jess," he said quietly, "you didn't like seeing me with someone else. So be with me."

She huffed. "I have no problem with you being with someone else, Connor. If you like her, that's great. I'm glad."

"You almost sound sincere."

"I am," she said.

"Liar."

The kitchen was quiet except for the hum of the refrigerator. He kept looking at her. The pulse in her neck was visible. And fast.

"She was right, you know," he murmured. "I *am* still hung up on you."

"Sorry to hear it."

"No, you're not." He went toward her and took each of her hands in his. She swallowed again, her cheeks pinkening. "Jessica," he whispered, leaning down to kiss her cheek. She shivered. Didn't pull away. "Be my girlfriend." Kissed her jaw, then just below her ear. "You have to. I made you lasagna." Her skin smelled like lemons and vanilla.

"I can't... You shouldn't..."

"Lasagna, Jess. All those layers. Homemade pasta."

She laughed a little. "Connor, I'm sorry. I wish I could... I wish you were still with her. Your girlfriend."

"I don't."

The comment seemed to hit her where she lived, because her beautiful green eyes softened, and her gaze fell to his mouth.

Connor didn't wait for more of an invitation. He kissed her, slid his arms around her to keep her close, and there it was again, that locked-in perfection, like they were made to kiss each other...and only each other. Her mouth was soft and giving, and a small sigh came from her and he couldn't wait any longer, because for crying out loud, they hadn't been together for twenty-seven months, and he missed her, he ached for her, and no one else would do.

They ended up making love right there, Jess on the counter, her legs wrapped around his waist, long, hot kisses and long, half-clothed foreplay, until she couldn't wait anymore, ordered him to do her in a breathy, urgent voice.

And Connor was not about to disobey a direct order. No, sir.

After they'd eaten a hearty serving of lasagna, they went into the living room and talked, whispering so they wouldn't wake Davey, and kissed and made love again. This time was slow and sweet, and afterward, they lay on the couch, wrapped around each other, a soft green blanket to keep off the cold.

He watched her as she slept, the long lashes brushing her cheek, her hand curled around his.

This was all he wanted. The circumstances didn't matter.

He could win Davey over. He'd buy a two-family house and Davey could live with them, and they'd have a couple of kids, and she could quit her job and get her degree in whatever it was she wanted, and every night could be like this one, them together, naked and warm under the quilt, the wind gusting at the windows, the two of them safe inside.

At an hour so early the birds weren't even singing, she woke him and told him he had to leave before Davey woke up.

He looked at her a long time, then smoothed her hair back. "This time, we're in a relationship, Jess. This is not just sleeping together. Okay?"

"I—I have to think about my brother."

"I know. We can go slow, but this is happening. Okay?"

She bit a fingernail, then put her hand in her lap. "Okay." A muscle in her jaw flexed.

"It'll be fine," he said, kneeling down in front of her. "You'll see."

"Sure," she whispered.

She was terrified. Could hardly look at him, and it made Connor all the more determined to make her see this could work.

And it did work. For months. Were they still sneaking around? Absolutely. But he'd take it. He'd do anything for her. He was completely, utterly smitten, and happier than he'd ever been in his life.

Getting close to her wasn't going to be easy, he recognized. A lot of people had let Jessica down over the years, and it would take time to make her see he wasn't one of them.

But she was giving him a chance.

What he saw—and what he was pretty sure she didn't know—

was that he was the lucky one here. Jessica was hands down the best person he knew. Taking such good care of her brother, working so hard at two or sometimes three jobs. She didn't mention her parents, but he'd heard things… She gave them money, paid off her father's gambling debt. Levi had to arrest Keith Dunn one night for drunk driving, and she had to leave Connor's to take care of things.

He didn't complain about their erratic time spent together. Just asked if he could do anything. Made chili for her to bring to Davey when she told him it was his favorite. Waited for her to call, accepted her cancellations. He tried to pay Gerard for watching Davey, but Jess would never let him.

For a good long stretch, they were getting somewhere. Colleen gave him an inscrutable look at work and left him alone, possibly sensing that this time was different.

And then one day, Jessica came to O'Rourke's in the middle of the day, her face white. "Can I see you for a second?" she asked.

She had never asked to speak to him alone in a public place before. He knew it would be bad.

"Clear the kitchen, guys," he said. Rafe and Omar, the dishwasher, went out obediently.

"My mother died," she said. "Last night."

"Oh, honey," he said, taking her in his arms. But she just stood there, stiff as a statue.

"I… It was sudden, but I guess it was a long time coming. Liver failure."

"I'm so sorry."

She stepped back, and he knew what was coming. "Davey's wrecked."

"And how are you, Jess?" he asked.

"I'm…okay," she murmured. She wasn't. She was far from okay. "But I… I have to put things on hold with us."

"You don't, Jess. Let me help."

"Help with what? With Davey? I don't think that would work."

"With you. Let me help you."

"I don't need your help," she said, and holy crap, there it was again, the broomstick through the sternum.

"You don't need anyone? Even when your mom just died?"

"I'm fine. But thank you."

She was already gone. This talk was just a formality. He wanted to be mad, to tell her for God's sake, just let him in and let him take care of her.

Except he knew that she'd hate that.

And he also knew she had loved her mother.

"I'm very sorry for your loss," he said.

"Thank you," she whispered.

"I'll wait."

"You don't have to."

"I will."

"Well, I don't want you to, Connor," she said, her voice ragged. "I don't need that guilt trip. Just…go find some nice, normal person and marry her, okay?" The broom handle twisted, just in case there was still any living tissue that needed killing.

"Guess I can't win for losing here," he said.

"I need to focus on Davey and get through this. My father—You know what? I have to go."

"Okay." *Her mother just died*, he reminded himself. *Be a prince.* He hated that his conscience sounded like Colleen. "If there's anything you need, call me, okay?"

Her eyes filled.

That was the thing. Jessica Dunn did a tough-girl act like no one else. And *act* was the key word.

He hugged her again, and this time, she let him. He stroked her hair, and then she stepped back. "Take care," she said.

"You, too."

He went to Mrs. Dunn's funeral with Colleen. Actually, most

of the town went, which was a tribute to Jess more than Jolene Dunn, the sloppy drunk who never could break free from the bottle.

After the service, Connor kissed Jess on the cheek, tried not to take it personally when Davey shrank from him and wailed a little louder and buried his face in Jess's chest. He shook Mr. Dunn's hand. The man smelled like cheap beer and body odor, and Connor had to fight the urge to punch him. *Take care of your daughter, goddammit.*

Through Gerard, Connor heard that Davey had to sleep with Jess every night, that he'd had some outbursts of the heart-wrenching kind, some of the fist-through-the-wall kind, and sometimes he even forgot that their mother had died.

The poor kid.

Jessica never did call or green-light their relationship or do anything toward him at all. Connor gave her all the space she needed, watched her for signs that the time was right.

None came.

After seven months, he went again to her house after hours, and once again, she seemed almost to be waiting for him. Chico Three, who was now full grown, pushed his head against Connor's leg, his tail wagging, and crooned in delight. It was a sharp contrast to Jessica's reaction.

She didn't open the door all the way. "Davey's having a bad night," she whispered.

Connor said nothing.

"I'm sorry." She started to say something else, stopped, then sighed. "I'm very sorry."

"Okay," he said. Then he handed her the large Tupperware bowl he was holding. "Chili," he said.

She took the container, and when she looked back up at him, her eyes were suspiciously shiny. "See you around," she said.

"Okay." He walked back to his truck, because there was nothing else to be done.

CHAPTER EIGHT

Four days after the proposal

It hadn't been fair, Connor proposing like that. Since the other night, all Jessica had done was stew over it. For once, she'd resented the long weekend—Manningsport Day, when all the local businesses closed for some historic, unknown reason. Her job at Blue Heron Winery was the perfect antidote for personal problems, and she really didn't want the free time.

Marriage? Seriously?

Granted, Jess realized that most people would think the whole proposal was really romantic and all, but it wasn't fair. Connor knew the rules.

When they'd gotten together for the last time, she'd made it clear.

She liked Connor. Very, very much. But her life was not typical. She had Davey, and he would always be her first priority until the day she died, and she wouldn't have it any other way. Who else loved Davey the way she did? Who else could take care of him? He had fetal alcohol syndrome, and, the doctors had surmised, post-traumatic stress disorder, courtesy of that asshole Pete O'Rourke, who'd made sure a little boy had seen his beloved dog dragged away to be put down.

And to someone like Davey, time didn't heal all wounds. He still cried for Chico the Original. Still cried for their mother. Still asked if Dad would be home for dinner, though Keith Dunn had disappeared the day of their mother's funeral and hadn't sent a single note, or dollar, since.

Chico One… Yes, he should've been put down. But it could've been handled so much better. In Davey's mind, it was Connor who'd caused the dog's death. No amount of Jess explaining could undo what he thought was true, and her parents hadn't helped with mutterings of *Those fucking O'Rourkes* or *Why was that kid bothering the dog in the first place, huh?* And so, according to Davey's logic, Connor killed dogs. Her brother's limited IQ prevented him from viewing the story another way.

The result was that for the past twenty years, Davey had been terrified every time he'd seen Connor. That time when Connor had come over to watch the movie…that had been the worst, and Jess understood. Davey had been betrayed. There was his dog-killing enemy, in his own house, with his *sister.* It had taken months to gain his trust back.

Over the years, Jessica had read enough to get a doctorate in the subject of fetal alcohol syndrome. She'd talked to dozens of school counselors, therapists, psychologists, pediatricians, neurologists. She once talked her way into a conference on the subject—her looks came in handy once in a while—and let an expert buy her a drink and stare at her cleavage while she peppered him with questions.

In the end, they all said the same unhelpful things. But Jessica was the world's foremost expert on her brother. She understood things like executive function, processing deficiencies, impulse control. She understood that if she said something like "Don't hit the car with that stick," Davey might think it was perfectly okay to hit the car with a rake.

He could read a little bit, and unless you studied his face and knew what to look for, you'd never know he had any problems. People would hear him quoting endlessly from *The Hobbit*, but they wouldn't understand that to Davey, it was just a cool adventure story with swords and a dragon. Themes of betrayal, friendship, the corruption of wealth, loss of innocence…those higher concepts were invisible to her brother. And because he could quote movies and he spoke fluently, people often got frustrated with him for not understanding what seemed so obvious to them.

Like Connor. He just didn't want to accept that to Davey, he'd always be a dog killer. The day Chico had been dragged away by Animal Control had been the worst day of his life. Worse even than when their mother died.

Connor thought he could win her brother over. He was wrong.

Davey wasn't going to change. He wasn't *able* to change.

But even putting Davey aside—which she really couldn't, but just for the sake of argument—Jessica…well, she didn't *believe* Connor. He didn't know what he wanted. Like a lot of guys, he saw her as a challenge. Once, she'd been slutty; after that, she'd become essentially celibate.

Except for him.

She was careful to keep things with Connor controlled. They'd always had a casual relationship…well, no. That wasn't the right word. But a *fluid* relationship, because that's just how it had to be. She'd always told him he was free to find someone else. He had, in fact. During their in-between times, he'd dated a little bit, and why not? She'd had to break up with him three—four?—times for various reasons. She understood if he needed to move on. She would've been happy to see him with someone else.

She was almost glad when he'd had a girlfriend, that redhead from Bryer. Let him move on and leave her alone and stop bringing up all those dangerous feelings. After all the times she had to break things off, she'd have understood if he one day introduced her to a fiancée.

But he didn't. He kept coming back instead, and Jess had to wonder why. To make up for Chico One, all those years ago? To rescue her? She didn't *want* to be rescued, thank you very much. A lot of people saw her as poor Jessica, white trash from the trailer park with the drunk parents and slow brother; Jess who had worked as a waitress for half her life, and yes, for about two minutes as a stripper. She could see how people had always seen her, Julia Roberts in *Pretty Woman—Come here, honey, all you need is some money and a nice hot shower and some good clothes, and you'll be exactly what I want.*

No, thanks. There would be no Cinderella story here. She could save her own damn self, and Davey, too.

And she had. It took her nine years, but she got her master's in marketing. She had a fantastic job with Blue Heron now, something she couldn't have called five years ago, working for the family that had once brought her hand-me-downs.

She had a decent place to live. Her brother was stable and doing well with his job, packing boxes at Keuka Candles. She was practically respectable now. The last hurdle would be owning her own house, and that was only a year, maybe fifteen months, away. She was planning to buy a place in the Village, a place that seemed as magical to her as Narnia, the sweet Victorians spreading out from the town's tiny green, views of Keuka Lake from every street. It would happen on her own terms, because Jessica had learned a hundred times that she was the only one she could count on.

Three years ago, after her mom had been gone awhile, and Davey had finally seemed to adjust, Connor and Jess had a week together, their shortest stint yet. Her appendix ruptured on the eighth day, and it was ugly. Full-blown peritonitis and everything, because that was the way things seemed to go for the Dunn family.

When the nurse had told her that Connor was there to see her, she said no. What if Davey came in? He was upset enough, terrified that she would die, and the fact that Connor was probably a little terrified, too…well, she just couldn't take it. They didn't have an ICU kind of relationship. It would make things seem more solidified than they were.

Her emergency drove home the fact that she had to find a conservator for Davey, and as soon as she was out of the hospital, she started talking to lawyers and trying to find someone who could be his guardian just in case. All those years, and it had never occurred to her that she could die and Davey would be alone.

Connor didn't even bother coming over after that one. He didn't have to. Being turned away in the ICU… *Sorry, your name is not on the list…* She'd been pretty clear.

And still he was nice to her. Still she came home to a fridge full of food, a packed freezer and clean sheets on her bed and Davey's, too.

This last time she and Connor had started seeing each other, it was because of a sneak attack at his sister's wedding. For months before, she'd suspected he'd been dating someone, and she'd been so, so careful not to let it bother her. He deserved a great relationship. A full, normal relationship with a woman who didn't have conditions and rules and a stunted ability to trust. She hadn't gone back to him in all that time, because she hadn't wanted to leave him again.

Colleen and Lucas's wedding day last fall had been perfect—a sunny and beautiful day, a huge tent in a meadow, and good old Colleen, who'd always been nice to Jess (and had a bit of a reputation herself, though not quite as nasty as Jessica's) had been so happy.

And there was Connor, doing his shtick as single brother of

the bride, dancing with everyone from Carol Robinson to Paulie Petrosinsky to his mother.

He hadn't brought a date.

And then he asked Jessica to dance, too, and she said yes, because it was the Chicken Dance and nothing romantic, and it had been fun.

She pretended her heart wasn't stuttering and that he was just an old friend from high school, the guy who made the best burgers in the state of New York, the charming brother of the bride who made everyone cry with his speech.

When they were done flapping wings and twisting and clucking, he'd smiled, thanked her and then said, "I miss you."

How was a woman supposed to handle that? Huh? For the rest of the wedding, it felt like bees were humming under her skin, and it was hard to remember how to breathe.

She ended up at his house that night. The second Davey was asleep, she asked Gerard if he could watch Davey overnight. The second he got there, she took off for Connor's. He opened the door, and she pretty much devoured him right there in the front hall. Not that he minded.

And afterward, with her dress lying in a puddle and her panties MIA, she spelled out exactly how it could and couldn't be. Again.

Three people knew about her on-again, off-again thing with Connor, three rather unlikely people. Gerard, her old buddy from the fire department. They'd slept together once in high school; Gerard had been on the football team, a big, strong guy, and a nice guy, too. Just one hookup, in his car at the edge of the soccer field, and he'd been her friend ever since. Looked out for Davey, too.

Gerard had always been her go-to guy for babysitting, physically big enough to handle her brother if he went into one of his rages, nice enough that Davey really liked him. The fire trucks didn't hurt. So he knew, because he had to know, since he was the one who kept Davey company on pizza nights. Ricky was the other person. He didn't mind doing a few hours of baby-monitor listening at night, either.

It worked. In the almost seven months since Colleen's wedding, it worked.

And then *wham*, Connor got down on one knee. Held up a *ring*, for the love of God.

Why did he have to do that? It ruined everything. And it hadn't been easy, sitting there, pretending to be casual and... and...calm, not when he was rocking her world, and most definitely not in the good way. More like he was taking a baseball bat to her world.

Once or twice a week had been safe.

Marriage... God, no! The thrill of their illicit relationship would wear off, and he'd think *Why did I want to marry her again?* and then, just assuming they somehow pulled off a miracle and Davey wasn't an issue...then Connor would leave her. And she'd be worse than Jessica Does. She'd be Jessica Was, as in *Jessica was married to Connor O'Rourke, but obviously, he moved on.*

There were times when what she felt for Connor was so... big...it was a terrifying. Times when they were in bed and his hands were on her. When he smiled, and she felt it in her bloodstream, in her lungs and stomach and bone marrow. When he said her name in that soft growl, when he just appeared at her door at one in the morning, when he looked at her on Wednesday nights at O'Rourke's, and there was that hard, almost painful pulse between them that no one else could see or feel.

It was almost too much. Anything else, anything more, was just not possible.

Jess liked to get to Blue Heron about an hour before anyone else. Davey got on the bus to the candle factory where he worked every morning at 7:45, so she was generally at the vineyard just before eight.

And this morning, after the weekend she'd had, she could use the quiet time to get her head straight.

The beautiful April day did little to brighten Jessica's mood as she drove to work. The apple trees were starting to bloom, the air infused with a hint of grapes, and Keuka, called Crooked Lake because of its odd shape, winked blue in the distance. The Holland land stretched from the lake all the way up to the ridge, hundreds of acres of farm, field and forest, and right in the center, the compound—the barns where the grapes were turned into wine, and the big, graceful post-and-beam tasting room, which also housed the gift shop and the corporate offices.

A few hundred yards away was the Holland residence, where Honor, Jess's boss, lived. Mr. Holland, Honor's dad, and his wife lived over the garage, and way up on the ridge was Jack and Emmaline Holland's house, only visible if the sun hit the windows just right, almost camouflaged up there. Across the field and through the woods was another Blue Heron structure—the old stone barn that had been renovated two years ago and turned into an extraordinarily popular wedding venue.

Growing up in the shadow of the Hill, in the grubbiest trailer in the trailer park, Jess never lost the slight rush of nervousness when she went to work.

She unlocked the big oak doors and went in, through the gorgeous tasting room, named one of the prettiest tasting rooms in America by *Wine Spectator*, past the racks of Blue Heron wine, hundreds of gold-foil logos winking in the light. The gift shop sold everything wine-related you could imagine—T-shirts and corkscrews, glassware and cheeseboards, dishcloths printed with grape leaves, mugs and wine charms.

Just past the tasting room was the corridor to the office wing. Jess's desk was in front of Honor's office. She liked being almost a watchdog for her boss. Honor was kind of perfect—calm, smart, able to delegate, complimentary when someone did a good job, helpful and informative if someone was stuck.

If Jess ever got fired, it'd kill her. She had it made here. She'd been working here since last winter, her first job in marketing, her first nine-to-five job ever. Honor was the vice president of operations for the vineyard, which meant she did everything outside of farming the grapes and making the wine. She ran sales, distribution, special events, marketing, PR and supervised all their employees. As her assistant, Jess did whatever Honor said. Sometimes it was give a tour of the wine-making operation, sometimes it was organize an event, write a press release, handle an event at the Barn, which took up more and more of her time these days. Whatever Honor asked, Jess made damn sure she did it right, fast and well.

It was still thrilling, being able to work behind a desk. To write things and come up with ideas for the vineyard, sit in on meetings and make suggestions that her boss took nine times out of ten. A far cry from waiting tables, though she still did that a few nights a week at Hugo's.

All of the Hollands worked for the vineyard in one capacity or another—Honor's older sister, Prudence, was the farmer. Her brother, Jack Holland, was the head winemaker, along with Mr. Holland and old Mr. Holland. Ned Vanderbeek, Prudence's son, was now the fourth generation of the family to be working at the winery. He handled about a third of the vineyard's sales and was one of the few who actually used his office. The other Hollands were always off in the fields or barns.

Honor's sister Faith, who was married to Levi Cooper, didn't officially work for the vineyard, but she was the one who'd renovated the crumbling stone barn, and she was here quite often, checking the plantings up there and visiting her family.

The Hollands were a tight-knit clan, always coming in and out, bickering amiably, having family dinners and weddings and baptisms, holiday meals and vineyard events. You never saw one without at least one other.

It was the type of family Jessica would've sold her left lung for.

She only had Davey. No cousins, no grandparents, no aunts and uncles. Her mother had had a brother who died in high school, the start of Mom's drinking problems. Somewhere, maybe, her father was still alive. Otherwise, no one.

Well. She *did* have Davey. Last night, he'd brought her outside to hear a crow call. The bird had been sitting on a telephone wire, yacking away, and Davey thought it was the funniest thing ever, and they'd sat on the back steps, just listening to the crow, Davey giggling till tears ran down his face, until it got too dark for the bird.

People often thought—wrongly—that she was a saint for taking Davey in, for not putting him in a home. They didn't know about how much he gave her back. A smile from him, a drawing, his joy over a really good cookie…those things lifted her heart like nothing else.

Jess was working on some press for Blue Heron's upcoming events when Honor walked in, her tiny dog poking its head from Honor's purse.

"Morning, Honor," she said. "And good morning, Spike." She petted the dog's tiny head. "Can I get you some coffee?"

"No, thanks, I'm good," Honor said, setting Spike on the floor. "How was your weekend?"

Kind of crappy, Jess thought. *My boyfriend proposed. Don't you hate when that happens?* "It was great. How about yours?"

"Very nice. Can you come in my office for a minute?"

Jessica did as she was told. Shit. Adrenaline needled through her knees. She was about to be fired. Her throat locked, and her face felt hot, but she took a seat in front of Honor's sleek, tidy desk, her mind racing. She had health insurance here, for both her and Davey. She had vacation time, not that she used any. The pay was really solid. Where else would hire her? Would—

"I'll get right to it," Honor said with a smile. "You've been promoted."

Jess's mouth fell open. "What? Really?"

"You deserve it. Congratulations. Hiring you was the best move my father ever made."

"Honor! I— Thank you!" Jess's cheeks were on fire, her legs limp with relief. "Um…promoted to what?"

"In a nutshell, you'll be taking over most of the PR and marketing. You're good at it. Better than I am, really."

"I highly doubt that."

"And the Barn is just too busy for you to handle, on top of everything else you do." She didn't say anything for a minute. "Can you keep a secret? What am I saying? Of course you can." She smiled. "I'll be needing some time off in about seven months."

"Oh, Honor! Congratulations!" Jess jumped up and hugged her boss, then, a little embarrassed, sat back down. Honor and Tom had been married almost a year. Jess was very fond of him, and Charlie, his not-quite stepson who'd come to live with them a little while back.

A *baby*. For a second, longing surged hard and strong. Then she cut it off. No point in going there.

Honor smiled. "Don't tell anyone, okay? So much can happen in the first couple months, and you know my family. And with Charlie still being a little new here, I want to keep it quiet for as long as I can."

"Gotcha. I'll keep good thoughts."

"Thanks. Anyway, remember we were talking about hiring an event planner at our staff meeting last month?" Honor asked. Jess nodded. "Well, I put out a feeler, and then a couple weeks ago, I met someone in the city when I was doing sales calls. Everything fell into place, and she starts today. I forgot to tell you. Pregnancy brain, I guess."

"Wow. Okay, great!"

"Her name's Marcy Hannigan. She's got great references, and with the season picking up, I figured we'd get her started as soon as possible. And now you'll get to do more real marketing and less dealing with hysterical brides."

"I don't know how to say thank you," Jess said. "But thank you."

"Thank *you*," Honor said. "You know how...particular I am about things, and you're the only one I don't feel the urge to micromanage."

"I resent that," said a voice from the doorway. Ned, late as usual, adorable as usual, too. "And the word is *anal-retentive*, not *particular*."

Honor smiled. "Hush, child, the grown-ups are talking. And you don't want Jess's job. You're doing great in sales."

"My good looks and charm?" he suggested, winking at Jess.

"Exactly," Honor said. "Now go." Ned obeyed. "So the new position," Honor continued. "You're our first ever director of marketing." She handed a paper across the desk. Jess glanced at it; in typical Honor fashion, it was numbered and bulleted, outlining her new duties.

"Wow. I have a title." She couldn't help grinning.

"And an office. We've finally accepted the fact that my father will never set foot in one, so you get his."

"Really?"

"You also get a raise, Jess. You've been fantastic, and we don't want to lose you." She handed over another piece of paper.

Tears stung Jessica's eyes.

Eight thousand more a year. Eight *thousand*.

"Thank you," she whispered.

"We'd like to take you and Marcy out tonight, okay? Bring your brother. O'Rourke's, seven o'clock. The whole family, plus spouses and kids."

Jess was afraid to look up. She didn't want her boss to see her crying.

Honor sensed it, anyway. "Why don't you pack up your desk

and get settled in your new office?" she said kindly. "Marcy will be here around noon to meet everyone."

An hour later, Jess closed the door to her first-ever office.

Honor had already hung a name plaque on the door. *Jessica Dunn, Director of Marketing.*

Was it wrong to want to take a picture of that? Maybe later, when no one was around.

On her desk was a picture of Davey when they got Chico Three. She had a coffee cup—*This mug may contain wine* with the Blue Heron logo, one of her ideas from a couple of months ago. She'd pitched the notion of a little more humor in some of the merchandise, and Honor liked it, so they now had a line of items in the gift shop that were more lighthearted and selling like crazy.

Almost hesitantly, Jess sat behind her desk. Her window overlooked the western vineyards—the 1780 Rieslings and Maisy Chardonnays.

A view. She had a view. Her throat tightened again.

Jess took a breath and considered the office. She might need a few more things to personalize the space. One photo and a company mug didn't say much.

Honor's office had beautiful photos of the vineyard in the different seasons, taken by Jack, who was a pretty good amateur photographer, at least a dozen framed photos of her siblings and their kids. There were also a slew of Tom and Charlie, including an absolutely gorgeous shot of Honor and Tom on their wedding day, dancing together, their foreheads touching, Honor's eyes closed, a small smile on her lips.

It occurred to Jessica that there was not a single photo of her and Connor together. Not one in the entire world, unless someone had snapped one of them doing the Chicken Dance at Colleen's wedding.

All those times together, and not one photo.

The thought gave her an unexpected pang.

But you know what? No negative thoughts were going to take place here. She had a raise, a title and an office! Maybe she'd get some plants. African violets or orchids. Davey tended to overwater houseplants, so they all died swiftly. But her office (her office!) had a wide windowsill perfect for just such a thing. In some ways, it would be more her space than anywhere but her bedroom, a room only Davey had seen. And once, Connor.

It dawned on her that she'd be going to O'Rourke's tonight. This wasn't exactly a new experience, but going to the place owned by the guy whose marriage proposal she'd just rejected… that *was* new.

Nervousness jangled through her limbs.

Had he told anyone about the proposal? Would Colleen spit in her drink? Would the O'Rourke cousins refuse to wait on her? Would Connor do anything, like storm out of the kitchen and dump a plate of nachos in her lap or…nah. Of course he wouldn't. There was some pride at stake, after all.

And Connor wasn't violent.

An image of his bruised, stitched twelve-year-old face flashed in front of her. *You can hit me. It's okay.*

Her heart folded in on itself like a wounded animal.

Well. The sooner she started acting normal around him again, the sooner things would actually *be* normal.

Time to get to work. She had a story to pitch on Ned becoming the fourth generation to currently work at Blue Heron. She clicked on the document and read what she'd written so far, then revised a little, wrote a few more paragraphs. She was pitching it to *Wine Spectator,* so it had to be brilliant.

A knock came on her door.

"Jessica Dunn, meet Marcy Hannigan, our new events planner," Honor said, stepping aside for the new hire. "Marcy, if you have any questions, just ask Jess. She handled your job until this morning."

"Hi, Marcy. It's very nice to meet you," Jessica said, standing to shake Marcy's hand. Her hair was black and choppy like an anime character—really cute—and she wore black-framed glasses. Her cheeks were ruddy with good health. "And absolutely, let me know if I can help."

"Don't worry about me!" Marcy said, her voice strong and robust, matching her sturdy frame. "I doubt I'll need a thing! I've been doing event planning for ten years, and you wouldn't even *believe* some of the venues I've handled, or some of the personalities I've worked with. Donald Trump, hello? Talk about high maintenance on *that* wedding! But in the end he told me I was the best planner he'd ever worked with! He even offered me a permanent job, but I'm the type of person who thrives on diversity. Who cares if I had a million-dollar budget? That gets old so fast, you wouldn't believe it, I kid you not. And even if he did send me an entire case of Cristal to try to woo me, I said, 'Donald, I'm sorry, you're going to have to settle for my runner-up! I'm just not interested!' So this place will be a piece of wedding cake for little old me! I told Honor when I interviewed, I foresee absolutely no problems!"

Wow. That was quite a soliloquy. A lot of exclamation points. Jess glanced at Honor, who didn't seem affected. Then again, Honor was very chill.

"Well, uh, welcome to Blue Heron."

"I'd love to stay and chat, but as I told you, Honor, I want to hit the ground running. No time like the present! We all have twenty-four hours in the day, but I'm the type of person who doesn't like to sit around on my butt, staring at a computer screen. Nice to meet you! I guess I'll see you later!"

"You bet," Jess said. Had she just been insulted?

Marcy's office was right across from hers—no mere desk for her—and for the next two hours, the woman hauled stuff in—boxes, photos, a huge ficus tree, curtains—curtains? Why would anyone want to block the view of the fields?—an upholstered chair, a coffee table. She clattered. She hammered. Jess heard Honor get up and close her door, and after a while, she did the same.

Marcy had energy, she'd give her that. And if Honor had hired her, she must be a helluva wedding planner.

At that moment, Ned stuck his head in the door. "Hey. Got a minute?"

"Sure. Come on in, and close the door."

"Yeah. Noisy out there." He sat down. "Congrats on the promo."

"Thanks, buddy. What's up?"

He tilted his head back against his chair and sighed. "You know I've been living in the Opera House, right?" he asked.

Jess nodded. The Opera House was a beautiful old building converted into apartments a few years ago, right there on the green in the heart of Manningsport.

"Well, I can't really afford it anymore. I'm a spendthrift youth."

"Uh-oh."

"Yeah. I bought a new truck, couldn't resist a big-screen TV, bought a necklace for a certain girl who will remain nameless, and now find myself in debt."

Jess smiled. Everyone knew Ned had a crush on Levi's little sister, who was still in college. "You irresponsible pup. What can I do for you?"

"You have an extra bedroom, right? Ever think about renting it?"

Jess blinked. "Um…no, I never did." With Davey's issues, it had never crossed her mind.

"Well, I could pay you I don't know…a couple hundred a month? And I could hang out with Davey, too, if you needed coverage or something. I have no life, except when I'm driving to Geneva to date She Who Cannot Be Named."

A couple hundred a month, plus the raise, would mean home ownership a lot faster.

And Ned and Davey got along great; they were pretty close in age, and Ned, like Davey, was a dork about comic books and action movies. It might be really nice to have another adult in the house.

"Let me ask my brother," she said. "If he says yes, it's a go."

"Great. Because if I have to move back home, I'll kill myself." He stood up. "Gotta make some calls. See you at O'Rourke's." He rose and opened the door, almost bumping into Prudence. "Oh, shit, hey, Mom. Gotta go."

"Is that how you greet your mother?" Pru said. "Give me a kiss, you thankless slob."

Ned rolled his eyes and kissed his mother's cheek. "You look young and beautiful today, Mother," he said.

"That's more like it. Now get out of here. The grown-ups are gonna talk." She came into Jess's office and nodded approvingly. "Heard about the promotion. Well done, Jess."

"I can't thank Honor enough."

"You know what would look great in here?" Pru said. "A cutout of Captain James Tiberius Kirk, USS Enterprise. Or Khan. Even better." She threw herself into the chair. "So how was your weekend? Got anything good to tell me? Carl and I stayed in and did the usual. Watched HBO, fooled around, got caught by Abby *again*, it's like the kid *wants* to see us naked."

"I'm positive that's not the case."

Pru smiled. "How about you? You and Connor do anything fun?"

Yes. Prudence was the third person who knew, strangely enough. Ever since Jess had started working here, Pru, who was about fifteen years older than she was, had just sort of decided that Jessica and she were friends. It was as easy as that. Almost every day since Jess started, Pru would come in from the fields, smelling like grapes and fresh air, plunk herself down in the chair and talk.

Then one day about six months ago, Jess and Pru had been

at O'Rourke's, and Connor made a rare appearance from the kitchen. He went over to a couple who practically fell over themselves with compliments, then glanced over at Jess and Pru. Gave a nod, then turned his attention back to the couple.

"You two doing it?" Pru had asked.

Jess had been so surprised, she jolted, spilling her root beer.

"Don't worry," Pru went on. "I won't tell anyone. I totally get the allure of a secret fling. That's the problem with being married for twenty-five years. Not a lot of secrets. So how is he? Is he fantastic? I bet he's fantastic."

Jess's face had hurt from blushing. Couldn't exactly deny it when it was put so bluntly.

But she found that it was pretty nice to have a girlfriend.

Oh, Jess had plenty of pals. Colleen, Emmaline Neal, who worked with Levi and had just married Jack Holland, some of the women on the ambulance corps. Faith was nice, too, and Jess liked seeing Levi so happily married. Honor was close to being a friend, but Jess always felt like that was a line she shouldn't cross, given the whole boss/assistant thing.

But Pru... Pru was different. Funny, way too open about sharing her sex life, but really, really kind. And to the best of Jess's knowledge, she never did tell anyone.

"Hello? Jess? You're not saying anything," Pru said now. "Did you guys have a fight?"

Jess glanced at the closed door. "Well, he proposed," she said in a low voice.

"Fantastic!" Pru held her hand up for a high five. "Bring it here, girl!"

Jess didn't.

"Oh, shit." Pru sank back into her chair and crossed her legs. "Did you say no?"

"Of course I said no."

"Why?"

"Because...you know. Davey wouldn't go for it." She looked

out the window, to the sweet green fields, the grape leaves fluttering in the wind. "Besides, even putting Davey aside, it'd be a no. Connor and I are just friends."

"Who get it on like starving ferrets."

"I'm quite sure I never used the word *ferret* for anything, Pru."

"Still. You sure you don't want to marry him? He's so hot. And he cooks. I mean, come on, sister. Don't be greedy."

"No, no. He's great. He is. But…marriage is just not for me."

"Ouch. Poor Connor." She winked, taking the sting from her words.

"I better get back to work, Pru."

"Sure. Me, too. Hey, have you met the wedding planner?"

"I did."

"Talks a lot."

That was almost funny, coming from Prudence, who was rather free with conversation, as well. "Part of her job, I guess."

"I guess. See you at O'Rourke's later on. Oh, will that be weird for you? Since you broke his heart and all?"

"His heart is not broken. Seriously. He was just going through the motions."

"If you say so. See you later. It'll be fun." Pru smiled and stood, hitched up her Carhartts and thudded down the hall, and Jess tried to get back to work.

She hadn't broken Connor's heart. She was almost sure of it.

CHAPTER NINE

The second Connor walked into the restaurant on Tuesday morning, Colleen swiveled around from her place at the bar, frowning.

Times like this, the magical twinsy bond really sucked.

"What are you doing here? It's your day off. You look like your dog just died, and you don't even have one."

"Don't want to talk about it," he said.

"Con—"

"No." He strode into the kitchen and set his bags down. Time to get to work.

Yesterday, Manningsport Day—such a dopey holiday, though one he usually liked— he'd gone to five Mennonite farms. Bought cilantro and baby romaine, goat cheese and lamb. This morning, he'd driven to the fish market in Corning and bought some gorgeous haddock that had been swimming in the Atlantic the day before. Fish tacos would be the special, then, with a side of creamy coleslaw. Burger of the day would be lamb with cheddar, sautéed baby Portobello mushrooms and artichoke hearts. Soup du jour, Potage St. Germaine, perfect for spring with the new peas and fennel. Rafe could do something with rhubarb for dessert. Maybe a nice Chantilly cream on the side.

"Connor." Colleen stood there, a frown on her face, idly rubbing her enormous belly. Hard to believe she still had two months to go.

"Yes?" he said with great patience, slicing a leek, then chopping it at lightning speed.

"What happened?" Her voice was quiet.

So it was that bad, then. She was actually concerned.

"Dog-Face," he said after a minute, "you know how you love fixing people up?"

"I do, indeed."

He began with the carrots, four of them across, the rhythm of the knife underscoring his words, the slices wafer-thin. "So. Do your thing with me."

"What? Seriously? You want me to find you a woman?"

"Inside voice, please."

"So you *are* straight, then." She grinned.

"Just do it. Find someone nice."

"Marriage nice?"

He glanced at her. "Yeah. What? Don't look at me that way. I want to get married. As long as it's not a disgusting sappy mess like you and Lucas."

"Soon-to-be-born child of mine, ignore your Uncle Idiot. He's jealous of Mommy and Daddy's wedded bliss. Sure, I'll find you someone. Jessica Dunn."

"Not her."

"Why?"

Connor was careful not to make eye contact. "We're just friends. She's not my type."

"Because she was a slut in high school? Who cares?"

"It's not that. She's just not my type."

"How can that be? I'd sleep with her, and I'm straight. We're talking about Jessica Dunn here, Con."

He didn't answer. Didn't look at her. Just kept slicing those sweet little carrots.

Colleen covered her mouth with one hand. "Hail Mary, full of grace, you've already dated her, you lying liar of lie-land! Why don't you marry her, then?"

He grabbed another four carrots, cut off the ends and began dicing again, the knife making a satisfying rhythm against the cutting board.

"Oh, Connor," his sister whispered. "She turned you down?"

"Moving on," he said.

"Are you heartbroken?"

"Colleen, let's not do this, okay?"

"But you—"

"No." *Thunkthunkthunkthunk.*

"I could—"

"Absolutely not." Another leek, slit, turn, dice.

Colleen scootched herself up on the counter. "Would it kill you to sit on a stool?" he asked. "I'm cooking here."

"Are you okay?"

He stopped chopping. Looked at his twin. "Yes. Thanks. I'd just like to meet a nice woman and get married."

"Do you love her?"

"Shut up."

"Connor..."

"You know what? I can register on Match.com."

Her mouth dropped open. "How dare you! Fine. Be your normal constipated self. You want someone, the ground rules are, you have to do what I say."

"You know what? Forget it."

"No! I'll never forget it! And I'll do a good job, I promise. But you have to listen to me, all right?"

"You'll be serious, right? No freak shows."

"Of course!" she said so emphatically that he immediately distrusted her. "But love can be deceptive at first glance, dear boy, so if I tell you to ask someone out, you have to do it and trust your big sister."

"You're my little sister."

She sighed. "By three minutes, and yet so much wiser in the ways of the world. So that's my deal. Take it or leave it. Just remember that I have something like twenty couples to my credit. If you're tired of being pathetic and alone, you have to listen to me. Deal?"

"Deal."

It wasn't what he wanted. He wanted to be telling Colleen that Jess would be her sister-in-law, because Colleen really liked Jessica, always had. He wanted to tell his sister she'd be his best person, just as she'd predicted last fall at her own wedding.

But he wasn't going to spend his thirties the same way he'd spent most of his twenties, waiting for Jessica to let him off the sidelines and into her life.

He had a little pride, after all.

Colleen was still staring at him, her eyebrows puckered. Luckily for Connor, the kitchen door swung open.

"Hola, mia." Colleen's husband came into the kitchen and kissed her. Connor winced.

"Not in my kitchen," he said. "I'm holding a big knife, Lucas, and you did knock my sister up."

"True, true." He kissed Colleen again then put his hand on her stomach.

"Connor wants to get married," Colleen told him.

"Marriage is great." Lucas smiled and kissed Colleen again.

"Stop it! Jesus. Get out of my kitchen, both of you."

Colleen paused at the swinging doors. "I'll find you someone great, Con," she said in a rare moment of sincerity.

He nodded. This would be good. Almost like an arranged marriage. No work required on his part, just show up and smile.

Jess didn't want him, and that was fine.

His knife slipped, slicing into the tip of his thumb, and a thin red line of blood appeared.

CHAPTER TEN

By the time Jess got home after work, her head was pounding. And she had to go right back out, because the nice Hollands were wining and dining her.

Her and Marcy, that was.

Her first impression of her new coworker wasn't great. The voice, for one—it could cut glass. The self-praise, for two... To be honest, Jess envied people with that much self-confidence. She had no idea what it would be like to walk into a very cool job and have no worries that she could handle it, that her employers would like and appreciate her, that she wouldn't get fired. It had taken her months to relax at Blue Heron. Today she'd seen Marcy with her feet up on her desk, bellowing laughter into the phone.

All that being said, she had faith that Honor had hired someone competent.

"Davey, do you want to go to O'Rourke's for dinner tonight?" she asked.

"Can I have nachos *and* chili?" he asked. Somehow, he'd never really put two and two together and didn't realize that his archenemy owned the restaurant. He *loved* Colleen. All men did.

Either he didn't realize Connor worked in the kitchen, or it was an out of sight, out of mind thing. Jessica wasn't about to ask.

"Sure," she said. "There'll be a bunch of us. The Hollands are taking me out. I got a promotion today." And a raise. A significant raise. The thought still made her flush.

"What's a promotion?"

"It means I have my own office," she said, swallowing some ibuprofen. "You can come see it this weekend, okay?"

"Okay. So a promotion is good?"

"Very good. It's your boss saying you're doing a great job, so now you can do other stuff, too."

"Will I get a promotion? I do a great job."

"You probably will, then." Jess would have to ask Petra, the manager at Keuka Candle, to give Davey—and all the special-needs workers—a certificate or a sleeve of stickers. The company was great that way.

"I need another picture of you," she said, smoothing back his blond hair. "I have to decorate my office a little bit." Not with a ficus tree and a couch, but with something.

"I can decorate your office!" he said. "Wait right here!" He ran up the stairs.

"Put on a clean shirt!" she called. Thumping noises came from his room, then he pummeled down the stairs—honestly, it always sounded like he was falling.

"Ta-da!" he said, beaming, and he was so stinkin' cute with that smile and those lashes. He held up his offerings: one of his Beanie Baby stuffed animals. Prickles the Hedgehog, and a candle. "This is for your new office," he said. "A decoration. And a candle, so it will smell nice." He got defective candles free.

"Oh, Davey, thank you! Is this Vanilla Sugar Cookie? My favorite!" She hugged her brother and kissed his forehead, then smiled at his sweet face. "Hey, guess what? You know Ned Vanderbeek, right?"

"He's my best friend," Davey said. He had a lot of best friends.

"Well, he was wondering if he could stay with us for a while. In the spare bedroom."

"Where the boxes are?"

"Yes. What do you think? Would that be okay with you?"

"Does he have a bed?" Davey asked.

"I bet he does."

"Then sure! I love Ned! We can watch movies together!"

"Great. We can tell him at dinner. Come on, honey-boy. I'm starving."

The Hollands commanded not just a table, but an entire section of the restaurant. Davey and Jess got there last. Davey had wanted to take his Flip the Cat Beanie Baby, which, after an extensive search, turned out to be buried under his beloved Wonder Woman comic books.

Marcy had gone in a few steps ahead of them. She hadn't held the door, either. She was just now being assisted out of a very gorgeous and expensive-looking brown leather coat by Jeremy Lyon, who had the manners of a prince.

"Hi, Jeremy!" Davey said, waving Flip at him. Jeremy was Davey's doctor. Jess's, too, not that she went too often.

"How are you, Davey?" Jeremy asked. "Hi, Jess."

"*He's* incredibly hot," Marcy murmured to Jess.

"Gay."

"Of course."

She caught a glimpse of Connor through the pass-through window in the kitchen. He didn't see her.

Good. She guessed that was good, even if it felt like she'd swallowed a stick.

"Our guests of honor are here," Honor said, standing up. "Let me make the introductions, Marcy. I know you've met some of us, but I'll just go through the list. My grandparents, Goggy and Pops, rarely known as John and Elizabeth Holland. My dad, another John, and my stepmother, Mrs. Johnson, sometimes called

Mrs. Holland, but mostly Mrs. Johnson. You've met my brother Jack, and that's his wife, Emmaline, who works with Levi there, the chief of police, and Levi is married to my sister Faith, and that little butterball on her lap is my beautiful nephew, Noah. And you met Tom already, and this is our son, Charlie."

Jess winked at Charlie. She had a soft spot for the kid, who'd recently gone from miserable teenager, something Jess well understood, to pretty nice person.

"Next to Charlie is my niece, Abby," Honor continued, "who's home from college and seeking gainful employment for the summer. And where's Pru? Oh, there she is. You met her this morning, right? And that's Carl, Pru's husband. Guys, meet Marcy Hannigan."

"Excellent to meet everyone!" Marcy said. Her voice carried easily over the crowd.

"Sorry to overload you, Marcy," Honor said. "A necessary evil, introductions. And guys, I think you all know our new director of marketing and her charming brother." This brought a round of applause from everyone, and Jess felt her cheeks heat up with pride and embarrassment.

"Over here, Davey, my boy," Ned said, though he was younger than Davey. "I saved you a seat."

"'I am fire! I am death!'" Davey said gleefully. Davey had something of a savant-like memory when it came to movies, and *The Hobbit* trilogy was getting a lot of play these days.

"'There you are, Thief in the Shadows,'" Ned returned, also a *Hobbit* geek. "How's it going, bud?"

"You're living with us!"

"I am? That's great! Thanks, guys."

Jess moved down the table, saying hi to everyone in turn, to where two empty seats sat at the end, for her and Marcy. Marcy was still working the crowd, shaking hands and laughing. Though Jess loved the Hollands, these events always made her a little sweaty. Luckily, there was an ally who might understand.

"Hey, Levi," she said. "Hi there, tiny Levi." Noah Cooper, who was two months old and change, was already the image of his father, sleepy eyes and crinkly forehead. "How's it going, Faith?"

"Hi, Jess! Congratulations on your promotion," Faith said, smiling. Jess always felt a small flash of shame where Faith was concerned; she'd been pretty hard on her back in school days. Water under the bridge, largely thanks to Faith being incredibly nice.

"So this Marcy person," Faith said in a low voice. "Lots of energy."

And speaking of the energetic devil, she tapped a glass with a knife. "I just want to say hellooo, Team Holland! Thank you for taking me out! Fantastic to join all of you! I'm thrilled to be working with all of you and look forward to an amazing year!"

"Hear, hear," came the chorus.

Marcy maneuvered into the seat next to Jess. "Oh, a baby!" she said. "I love babies. Well, I should say, they love me! Some people have a way with kids, and it's not like I try, they just gravitate to me. Look at how he's smiling at me!" She glanced at Levi. "You must be the father, since he looks just like you."

"Levi Cooper," he said, shaking her hand. "Chief of Police."

"So if I get a speeding ticket, I should talk to you," Marcy said, laughing merrily.

"If you get a speeding ticket, I probably gave it to you," he said, not smiling. Good old Levi.

Hannah O'Rourke took their orders, no small feat with the elder Mrs. Holland unable to decide between the filet mignon and the sole almandine, asking for rice instead of potatoes and green beans instead of Brussels sprouts. Davey got chili and nachos; he ate like Homer Simpson, no matter that he was skinny as a pretzel stick.

Several bottles of Blue Heron wine were brought over, and Jack poured her a glass. As always, she'd drink some of it—and appreciate it; she had nothing against wine. But one glass and one glass only was her protection against the family history of alcoholism. Sometimes, Colleen would pour her a refill on the house, but Jess never drank it.

Speaking of Colleen, she came over, her stomach ripe with baby.

Strange, to think that if Jessica had said yes to Connor two nights ago, Colleen would be her future sister-in-law. The baby percolating in there would be her niece or nephew. Connor was thinking it was a girl. A little girl who'd call her Auntie Jess, who'd—

She cut that thought off at the pass.

Colleen was looking at her.

She knew. Oh, shit, she knew.

Then she smiled, right at Jess.

So maybe she didn't know.

"Hey, everyone!" Colleen said. "I hear congratulations are in order. Well done, Jess. Hi, there," she said to Marcy. "Colleen O'Rourke Campbell, half owner of this fine establishment."

"I love it! So homey! So cute! Very charming! I'm Marcy, the new event planner for the Barn! Totally thrilled to meet you!"

"Same here," Coll said, and Jess didn't miss the assessing look she gave Marcy. "Jess, do you know any experienced bartenders looking for a summer stint? I don't see myself yanking beers with a newborn in my arms."

"I'll ask around."

"Maybe Hugo knows someone?"

"I'm working tomorrow night. I'll ask." It dawned on her that with Ned moving in and her raise that she might not have to wait tables this summer. It would be the first time in seventeen years. She could come home, every night, and stay there. That one job would be enough.

The thought was staggering.

"You bartend?" Marcy asked.

Jess looked at her. "I can. I waited tables for a long time. Still do a few shifts a week."

Marcy's eyebrows raised.

Judgment had been passed.

There was no shame in working hard. Jessica knew this. She also knew some people were snobs and looked down their cute little noses at people who worked in the service industry.

"Do you cater?" Marcy asked, turning back to Colleen. "I'm putting together a list of area restaurants and caterers that I'll approve to make sure every event at the Barn at Blue Heron has a certain *élan*."

"I'll send our chef out to talk to you," Colleen said. "My brother, Connor. He runs the food end of the business."

Shit.

She'd have to get Davey to wash his hands or something. Maybe they could go throw stones in the lake for ten minutes or so. It would also give Jess a perfect reason to avoid him.

"Now, Levi, pass me my godchild!" Colleen said. "I've been standing here for a solid minute and I'm dying to smooch those cheeks! Right, Noah?" She gathered the baby into her arms and rested her cheek on his head. "Who loves you? Auntie Colleen does, that's who! Faith, if I have a girl, let's just do an arranged marriage, okay?"

"I thought that was a given," Faith said.

"You guys enjoy your dinner," Colleen said. "Nice to meet you, Marcy. I'm taking this baby with me. Come on, Noah, let's schmooze, honey." The baby burped.

Jess watched her go off to show Noah off to Gerard and Lorelei, who were dating, asking them if the baby wasn't the cutest thing in the wide world.

"Wow, she's stunning!" Marcy announced. "I always feel like a total hag around a beautiful woman, don't you?" she asked Jessica. "Faith, you're gorgeous, you can totally hold your own, but Jessie and I, we're like *trolls* where she's concerned, aren't we?"

Okay.

First of all, no one called her Jessie. It was Jessica or Jess.

And secondly, what did you say to that? *You're right, Marcy, I'm a troll!* or *Are you kidding? You? You're so cute!* She was fairly sure Marcy was waiting for the latter.

She said nothing.

"I don't think anyone would call either of you a troll," Faith said, saving the moment. "I always thought you could be a model, Jess."

Jessica could feel Marcy practically quivering as she waited for Faith to compliment *her.*

Faith took a bite of her nachos. Levi, always a man of few words, cocked an eyebrow at Jess, then gave his wife a sleepy smile and stroked the back of her neck.

"Where's my sword?" Davey asked. "Jess! I don't have a sword." His face was getting that pre-cry look.

"I'll get it, sweetie," she said.

Davey's drink—a Shirley Temple—had been served without the little plastic skewer. He collected them, and…well. Jess stood up, went to the bar and snagged one, went back to the table and popped the sword into her brother's drink. "There you go, hon."

"Thanks, Jess!" he said, grabbing her hand and giving it a loud kiss. Crisis averted. She ruffled his chick-down hair and went back to her seat.

Glanced at her watch surreptitiously.

She wished she liked these events more. It was just that she always felt a little…on guard. As if at any moment, one of the Holland clan was going to reminisce about the time when Keith Dunn ran into their mailbox, or when Jess's mother puked at the eighth-grade chorus concert.

The Hollands love you, she reminded herself. She took a sip of wine and forced a smile at Jack Holland, who gave her a wink and turned his attention back to Emmaline.

Couples, couples everywhere.

"What's wrong with your brother?" Marcy asked, and Jess's head whipped around.

"Excuse me?"

"Oh, is that politically incorrect? I'm sorry, I just wondered. Was I not supposed to notice?"

Jess felt her heart turn to a fist of ice. Marcy smiled brightly and raised her eyebrows, waiting for an answer. The smile was as fake as they came.

"He's intellectually disabled." That was the newest—and kindest—label the medical community had given it. Sure beat a lot of ugly words kids had used growing up.

"What happened to him?"

Silence settled on their end of the table. Pru gave Jess a look and rolled her eyes. Levi and Faith were both listening, and both knew exactly what *happened* to Davey…everyone in Manningsport knew. But who the hell would ask so baldly? And why did Marcy think it was any of her business?

Jessica could feel her heartbeat in her stomach, a sure sign of rage. She raised an eyebrow, keeping her expression cool, and stared Marcy down.

A beat passed. Two. Three.

Marcy's smile slipped, and she gave a bark of laughter. "Oh, okay, I guess *that* subject's off-limits. So sorry. I just have one of those personalities. I'm naturally curious, that's all. People interest me. They fascinate me." She broke eye contact with Jess and beamed across at Levi and Faith. Neither smiled back, God bless them.

"Tell me about your promotion, Jess," Faith said. "Honor said you'd be doing more marketing."

Grateful for the change of subject, she turned to Faith and answered. The Barn was Faith's creation; Jess wondered how she liked Marcy, or if she'd had any say in hiring her. But those things weren't her business, and unlike Marcy, Jess was good at knowing when to keep her mouth shut.

After dinner had been served—and devoured—Ned and Davey went to the back to play pinball. The Hollands had rearranged themselves, changing seats so they could talk to everyone. Marcy had shaken off the gaffe from earlier (though Jess would bet she saw nothing wrong with what she said) and was talking—loudly, *God*, her voice was loud—about a celebrity wedding she'd handled. Unfortunately, Abby was fascinated, peppering her with questions.

Then Connor came over to the table.

Three days without seeing him, and she felt his presence like a rogue wave, unexpected and devastating.

Why was that? They'd broken up before. They'd fought before, sort of. He'd come around.

She missed him. Three days, and she *missed* him, and what was that all about?

"How's everyone doing?" he asked.

A chorus of compliments and assurances rose from the group. "You sure can cook, Connor," Pru said. "That rib eye was the best I ever had. I'm seriously thinking about gnawing on the bone."

"Thank you," he said, always a little uncomfortable when he had to field praise. She'd noticed it over the years, how he was always reluctant to come out of the kitchen and accept the coos and compliments from his patrons.

That being said, he had always loved watching her eat. Once, he even fed her dessert when they were naked in bed. Crème brûlée with caramelized orange zest and the tiniest hint of nutmeg, and the second she was done, he'd shagged her so—

Ah. He was speaking.

"Congratulations, Jess. You got a promotion, I hear."

"I did. Thank you."

"How's your dinner?"

"It was excellent, as always." She couldn't remember what she'd ordered.

"Glad you liked it."

So pleasant. You'd never know her heart was shuddering in her chest.

This will be the last time you break up with me.

He couldn't really mean that.

It suddenly occurred to her that he could.

Then he looked at Marcy. "Hey. I'm Connor O'Rourke, the chef and half owner. I hear you're the new event planner."

"I am!" Marcy boomed. "We should get together and talk! I'd love to have you on my list of approved caterers! The Barn at Blue Heron can't be serving just any kind of food. I mean, I heard the last event served Kentucky Fried Chicken! That's *so* not the image we want to portray, right? It's much more upscale than that."

The event to which Marcy was referring was one Jess had arranged. And yes, they'd served fried chicken in buckets, but no, not from KFC. From The Chicken King, a small franchise owned by one of Manningsport's wealthiest residents (and Connor's mother's boyfriend). The event raised money for the animal shelter in town, and no one, including the Hollands, had worried about their image.

"You haven't had the Chicken King's Bacon Buttermilk Batter Bombs," Faith said to Marcy. "But Connor, we'd obviously love to have O'Rourke's on the list, if you guys are interested in doing catering."

"Probably not," he said. "We have our hands full here."

It flashed through Jessica's mind that he was saying no because of her, because she worked for Blue Heron, but that was stupid, because Colleen and Faith were best friends, and—

"Let's get together for a drink just the same," Marcy said. "I'd love to talk. You could recommend some local outfits, pastry chefs, whatever." Her eyes dropped to Connor's left hand. No ring, of course.

Well, shit.

Colleen walked behind her brother and smacked his head. He didn't look at her. "Sure," he said belatedly. "That'd be nice."

"It's a date, then. Here. Put your number in my phone." She handed over her enormous smartphone, the latest model, encased in a Burberry plaid case.

The rest of the table was talking about something else, and little Noah was being passed around. Smelling his head seemed to be a thing. Mrs. Holland was advising Faith on how to get him to sleep through the night, and Mrs. Johnson was asking for another piña colada, the only one of the group not to drink wine.

Yes. Look anywhere but at Connor, who was giving an age-appropriate, attractive and very confident woman his number. She twisted the ring she wore on her thumb—her mother's wedding ring. Look how much happiness marriage had brought her mother. None. Fights and drunkenness and poverty, though chances were, Jolene probably would've found those without marriage, too.

"You okay?" Levi asked, and Jess jumped a little.

"Yeah, I'm great. Thanks. Just a little headache."

"In this crowd? I can't imagine." He smiled, and she was grateful. Like her, Levi understood being a little…separate. But now he was securely in the Holland clan, having found his place with Faith.

Jess would never have that, and that was just fine. It was better to be on her own. She couldn't rely on someone else when Davey was at stake.

Besides, if she didn't count on anyone, no one could let her down.

She suddenly found herself with the baby in her arms. "Hey, Noah."

His head *did* smell so good. She gave Levi a smile. Her old friend deserved every happiness, but suddenly, that feeling of being left out gripped her throat in a fist.

And then the shit hit the fan.

"What are you doing here?" Davey was back, glaring at Connor, who didn't hear him, as Marcy was talking about the *amazing* apartment she'd left in Manhattan.

"Want to head home, Davey?" she said, passing the baby back to Levi.

"I hate you!" Davey barked, and Connor turned around. "You're not invited! You should go home! This is Jessica's party!"

Connor knew better than to answer. He'd been coached on it, in fact.

"Whoa," Marcy said. "Okay, this is a *little* awkward, isn't it? Is he all right?"

"Let's go, Davey," Jess said. "We can watch *The Avengers* if you want."

"I'm going, too," Ned said, standing up. "Got to get my beauty sleep, right, Davey?"

Davey's eyes flickered to Ned. "Right. I—I have to get my beauty sleep, too."

Ned tossed her a wink. She forced a smile back.

Gratitude could be wearying sometimes. Jess appreciated the people who understood her brother, but it was tiring, always hoping people would understand, always going into the most ordinary situations having to wonder if her brother's temper would flare, if he'd be scared, if something would trigger a rage.

Ned walked Davey up front, and Jessica got out of her chair, then stood there, looking around the table. "Thank you all so much for tonight." She paused. "For everything." *Thank you for giving me my first real job. Thank you for your faith in me. Thank you for accepting my brother. Thank you for making me feel normal.*

For a second, she almost thought she might cry.

"We're lucky to have you, Jessica," the younger Mr. Holland said.

"I can't believe I ever managed without you," Honor added, and Jack agreed, and before Clan Holland could stand up and start hugging, which they did a lot, Jessica gave a quick wave and made her way to the front of the bar.

Marcy didn't acknowledge her, just leaned back in her chair and laughed at something she said, then laid a hand on Faith's shoulder and laughed again.

The Hollands liked Jess, she knew that. But she couldn't help feeling a little uncomfortable that Marcy would be staying when she would not.

Near the front door, Ned was checking his phone. Davey was talking to someone. Jess pulled on her jacket—it was still chilly at night, April or not—then froze.

Davey was hugging the person he was talking to. And Davey didn't hug many people.

Someone short. Someone skinny. Someone with reddish-blond hair.

"Jess, look!" Davey said, turning. "He's here!"

The floor dropped out beneath her, and she took an involuntary step back.

There he was, his nose crooked from so many fights, hair shaggy as ever, half his face taken up by his big blue eyes, same as Davey.

Keith Dunn. Their father.

He smiled hugely. "Jessica," he said, and those eyes filled up with tears. "How's my baby girl?"

CHAPTER ELEVEN

"Absolutely not."

"Connor! You said you'd do whatever I ordered." Colleen huffed mightily and folded her arms on her watermelon of a belly. "You said you'd go out with her!"

"I was being polite. Now move, because I have to cook."

"Give me five minutes, for God's sake." She turned to the sous-chef. "Rafe, tell him to listen to me."

"What's the harm?" Rafe asked, leaning against the stainless-steel counter. "Expand your horizons. Get laid. Smile a little."

"She's really not my type."

"We talked about this," Colleen said. "You have to be willing to try or you'll just be at home, brooding and sulking. Like always."

Connor sighed.

"Don't you Catholic sigh at me," Colleen added.

They were talking about what's-her-name. The new person at Blue Heron who'd been in the other night. Marie or Marsha or whatever.

"You said you'd listen to me," Colleen reminded him. "I'm

pregnant, and if you upset me, Lucas will stab you." She folded her arms on her stomach. "Besides, you'll never get—"

"Fine. I'll do it."

Because she was just about to say *You'll never get over Jess if you don't start trying.*

Jessica had made herself crystal clear. And maybe Colleen was right. There was a first time for everything.

"Good," Colleen said. "I texted Marcy from your phone and told her you'd meet her for a drink. Of course, I pretended to be you and was very charming, so don't be surprised if she expects a little fun."

He closed his eyes. "You're such a hemorrhoid."

"You want to be godfather to this baby or what? I can always ask Rafe here."

"I think it's clear who'd buy the best presents, especially if it's a girl," Rafe said. "A gay faux uncle versus your hetero brother. No contest."

"It's a girl," Connor said. Colleen and Lucas had decided not to find out, but Connor knew already.

Colleen raised an eyebrow, one of her better tricks. "That's a good point, Rafe. Connor, can't you just stop whining and man up and go on this date, damn it?" She burped. "Do you have any Tums? God, this heartburn is murder."

"When will this baby be born? Seems like you've been pregnant for two years."

"Oh, is it hard on you? Do you think you should say stuff like that when we're in a room full of sharp objects? Huh?" Rafe handed her a roll of antacids, and she scarfed down two.

Okay, so she was really uncomfortable. Her back hurt; he knew that without her saying anything. Irritatingly, he had a sympathy backache. And she was scared. Lots of things could go wrong. He felt a flash of fear himself, and before he could stop himself, he found that he had his arm around her shoulders. "You'll be fine, Dog-Face. And hopefully the baby will look like me."

"Will you please go out with Marcy? Have I ever been wrong in my entire life?"

"Yes, and yes. I'll go, but only because you threatened me with a knife."

"Now see? Was that so hard? I can already see the write-up in the *Vows* section. 'They went on a date after Connor's beloved twin threatened to stab him.' Oh, and I'm interviewing a temporary bartender, so don't growl and scare her away."

"Get out of my kitchen, both of you," Rafe said, flapping his hands. Connor gave him a look but obeyed. It was Rafe's kitchen on Tuesdays and on Friday nights, when Connor and Colleen had dinner with Savannah.

While Colleen fussed around behind the bar, Connor got his laptop from the office, sat down at a booth and focused on his project of the last fifteen months.

O'Rourke's Brewing.

In the land of small vineyards, there was also a fair number of microbreweries popping up here and there. Some were quite good; some were mediocre. But who better to be an owner of one than Connor himself? He knew flavors. O'Rourke's had the best beer list in the Finger Lakes, or so said the *New York Times,* thank you very much. Why not branch out into something a little different?

He didn't want to be a brewer himself per se; his true love was food. But he'd always done some home brewing, though he really didn't drink too much; one beer on an empty stomach was enough to give him a buzz. But Connor knew a guy, Tim Parsons, who'd jump at the chance to be a brewer and do the actual work, almost like a sous-chef. He was just waiting for Connor to get things in place, content with his day job as a schoolteacher.

The restaurant was his first priority, but Connor wanted

something a little more to his name. He and Colleen had owned O'Rourke's for almost ten years now, and they were both incredibly proud of it.

Problem was, it ticked along like clockwork. They had a great staff; Rafe was almost as good a chef as Connor, and a little better with desserts. Colleen ran the bar perfectly, Hannah and Monica were excellent servers. In tourist season, they hired a couple more kids to bus tables and wash dishes. They got stellar reviews and were featured in virtually every article that mentioned Manningsport.

So that goal had been met. The other goal—marry Jess—had gone down in flames.

It hadn't been easy to see her the other night with the Hollands. But she played it cool, that much-hated *three feet away* face on in full force. It was her specialty, after all. So he played it cool, too, even if he did burn the next order he'd cooked.

Time to focus on the microbrewery. He and Tim had already developed seven varieties of beer in Tim's garage, and they were utterly fantastic, in his humble opinion. But the first step to creating an actual brewery would be to find funding. He had a chunk saved, as well as a bank loan, but he'd still need investors, people who wouldn't mind being silent partners and ponying up the cash. Connor had a successful business to his name; he already had an in with distributors as the co-owner of the bar; and he was a professional chef. He was keeping an eye out for some real estate that would house the business.

All he needed was about half a million dollars more, and he'd be all set.

"Daydreaming about your brewery?" Colleen asked.

"Yeah." He turned the folder so she could see his notes.

"Dogface Ale? Aw! Thanks, brother mine." She smiled, rubbing her belly. "You know, Dad would be—"

"I'm not going to ask Dad to be an investor."

She sighed. "He's not Satan, you know."

"I know. But this is going to be mine. Not ours, and certainly not his."

"Well, our high school reunion is coming up. You could tap some of our old classmates. You should start with Jeremy. He's richer than God."

He hadn't thought of that. It might be uncomfortable, casually asking Jer if he had a few hundred thousand dollars lying around. Then again, why not? Jeremy might get a real kick out of it.

"Do you have any plans at all?" Colleen said.

"I have this spreadsheet," he said.

"That's just money. What's your vision?"

"Um…what?"

"You need to pedal vision. Why would I buy O'Rourke's beer instead of anyone else's?"

"Because you're my sister?"

She rolled her eyes. "What sets O'Rourke's beers apart? You have an attractive twin. How will you leverage her charm and good looks to help your business grow?"

"I won't. She's not as cute as she thinks."

She smiled and gave him the finger. "I'm even cuter. Oh! The baby kicked. Want to feel?"

"That's okay. I have sympathy back pain as it is."

"You do? That's kind of sweet, Connor." She toyed with her hair, as she always did when she was thinking, then sat up a little straighter. "You know who could totally help you? Jessica."

Connor's stomach dropped. "Uh…have you forgotten a little something?"

"No. But come on. You two have known each other for decades. You gonna nurse a broken heart forever?"

"I was thinking a day or two."

"Drama queen."

"You're the one who spent ten years—"

"Hush! I'm pregnant. Be nice to me. No, seriously, Con. Jessica knows a lot about marketing. She has contacts through the vineyard. And she's always on the prowl for extra money. Did you know she even stripped for a while?"

"How do you know that?"

"I know everything. Plus, it would help you start to get over her. You can't not speak to her. We've known her since forever."

It was an irritatingly logical suggestion.

Connor was saved from further comment as the door to the bar opened, and in came a very pretty (and very young) woman Connor didn't know.

"That's Jordan. My bartender candidate." Colleen struggled to stand up, and Connor pulled the table back to give her more room then offered his hand and hauled her up. It wasn't easy. "You sure you're not percolating a calf in there?" he said.

"Shut up. I'm glowing, and you can't even tell I'm pregnant from behind. Check out my ass."

"I will not."

Colleen waved to the girl. "Hi! We're over here."

The young woman came over, looked at Connor and blushed a deep red. "Hi. I'm Jordan Reynolds."

"I'm Colleen, and this is my brother, Connor. He's the chef, so he's not important and you can just ignore him. Let's get you behind the bar and see what you can do."

"Nice to meet you," Connor said.

Her eyelids fluttered, and her mouth opened slightly.

"Don't you dare crush on him," Colleen said, ushering Jordan over to the bar. "He's disgusting. That hair is a wig, and he's wearing contacts to cover his reptilian eyes."

Connor was only half listening. Colleen's idea about tapping some of their classmates might be a good one.

The one about asking their father…that would never happen.

Connor had suspected his father was cheating long before he had confirmation. It was in all the movies…the late-night meetings, the phone calls he would only make from his den, door firmly shut. The weekend business trips, the number of which increased sharply when the twins were in high school.

But he didn't look too hard. His father had never been that interested in him, and Connor tried to return the favor. Mom and Colleen worshipped the ground he walked on; Pete O'Rourke didn't need or want Connor's adoration.

It was when he was doing a winter internship in Corning that he learned for sure that his father was a cheat.

He was working at a tapas restaurant owned by a Culinary Institute graduate, a nice gig so he could be home for the holidays and still working. The place had a window between the kitchen and the restaurant, so patrons could watch the busy kitchen as their food was prepared.

One night, a woman caught Connor's eye. Caught every male's eye, in fact. She was a redhead, for one, and built like Scarlett Johanssen for two. Hard to miss. Add to this, she was staring right at him, and when he met her eyes, she gave a sly smile.

He came out after her dinner was served; she was with two other women. "How was everything, ladies?" he asked, and the other two giggled and complimented him. The redhead just looked at him. "I'm Gail," she said, offering her hand. "Gail Chianese."

"Rhymes with easy," one of her friends murmured, and the three of them all laughed. They talked for a few minutes until Connor had to get back to the kitchen. When they left, a server came back with a note. "Someone left a phone number for you, Con."

Gail.

Telling himself it would be good to date someone after the Jessica debacle last fall, Connor called Gail. He took her skating; old-fashioned, he thought, and fun for a winter afternoon, which was the only time she'd said she had available. She was *incredibly* hot, four years older than Connor, a flight attendant who'd traveled all over the world.

She didn't know how to skate, pressed into him at every opportunity, and he appreciated it. It was pretty fun, he thought. She seemed to be having a nice time, though she kept glancing at her watch. Also, she hadn't really dressed for the outdoors, though he'd told her to, and she was getting cold. Conversation didn't exactly flow, though she was an excellent flirt.

He drove her home at the end of the afternoon and kissed her on the cheek.

"You're adorable," she said. "You sure you don't want to come in?"

"I'd love to, but I have to be at work in half an hour." He also had a hard and fast rule about not sleeping with someone on the first date.

"Mmm. Not *nearly* enough time." She stretched her arms over her head, revealing a strip of toned stomach. "I guess you'll have to ask me out again."

"I guess so." The truth was, he was a little put off by the constant innuendo, the cute looks, the obvious body language. So different from Jessica. The thought of her made his chest hurt. Since their hookup, and their conversation over Christmas, he hadn't seen her.

"I'll call you," Gail said, narrowing her eyes. Then she turned and went inside, waving coyly over her shoulder.

She did call a few days later and asked him to meet her for an early drink just down the street from where he worked. They got a seat in the window. "How've you been?" she said, looking him up and down.

"Great. And you?"

"I've been *wonderful*."

Okay, she wasn't his type. But he was here, so he'd make conversation (he could mentally hear Colleen laughing at that one), and then they'd be done.

The Market Street section of the little city was packed with holiday shoppers, snow was falling, and it looked like a Norman Rockwell painting, a few glass-blowing demonstrations going on, a brass band playing in front of a bakery.

Gail was beautiful, that was true. She was also pretty boring. At least skating had given them something to do. He asked her about her travels, assuming she'd have some good stories, but got a vague answer. Asked her if she'd gone to college. She had not. Racked his brain for another question and came up empty.

"So how much does a chef earn, anyway?" she asked.

Subtle. "Depends on the restaurant."

"Those celebrity chefs make a lot, I bet."

"Probably."

"You have the looks for that kind of thing. A TV show and stuff."

"Not really my thing." He suppressed a sigh. Great ass or not, she seemed fairly vacuous.

Then his father pulled up on the street right in front of the bar.

Pete O'Rourke owned commercial property all around Manningsport as well as a few places in Corning and Dundee; half of his life was spent in his swanky little Mercedes coupe, driving to and from places to talk to building managers and tenants and lawyers.

Pete got out and fed the meter. Connor sat still, hoping his father wouldn't look his way.

"That's a cute car," Gail said.

"And that's my father in it," Connor said.

"Really?"

"Yeah." Pete went across the street to another building—probably one of his properties—and went inside.

"What does he do for work?" Gail asked.

"He owns buildings," Connor answered.

"Is that right." Gail sucked on her straw again, smiled at Connor for no reason, then dropped her eyes. You had to wonder if she practiced that in the bathroom mirror. She checked her phone, then said, "Whoopsy! I have to meet some friends. Thanks for the drink!" She air-kissed him, and he said it had been nice to see her, and expected never to see her again.

The truth was, it was fine. She was gorgeous, yes.

But she was no Jessica Dunn.

A few weeks later, when Connor's shift was over, he walked down the block to his car. Christmas was over, and Corning was quiet under the dark winter sky. A dog barked somewhere. The frigid cold felt good after seven hours in the steamy, hot kitchen, and Connor stopped for a second in the alleyway to the parking lot, taking a deep breath of the clean air.

Then he heard a familiar voice.

He turned, and there was his father in the doorway of the building he owned.

Kissing Gail, his hands on her spectacular ass.

It was one thing to have suspected his father was a cheater. It was another to see it.

All Connor could think about was his mother, his sweet, loving mother who adored her husband. Who'd made her traditional bacon and eggs on Christmas morning and beamed when Pete gave her a puffy red bathrobe as a present.

Gail was twenty-six; Pete was in his fifties. Hardly a new story, but slimy just the same.

Connor left.

At home, he tried to be extra nice to his mother and gave Colleen a wide berth so she wouldn't pick up on anything on the twin radar.

He didn't know what to do. Tell? If he told his mother, it would break her heart. If he told Colleen, ditto, and she'd tell Mom. Granted, this probably—definitely—wasn't the first time Pete had cheated.

But this time, Connor knew for sure.

The fact that he'd inadvertently introduced Gail to his father made him feel sick.

He owns buildings, he'd said. Might as well have said *He's a sugar daddy.*

He avoided his father, and doubted Pete even noticed.

And Connor decided not to tell. He thought about it a thousand times. Once, he even started to tell his mom, opening by asking if she was happy, and when she said, "Oh, my heavens, *yes,* honey! Why would you even ask such a thing?" And she smiled so sweetly that he just couldn't do it.

That was a mistake.

In April, Pete dropped the bombshell. He was divorcing Mom.

Gail Chianese-Rhymes-with-Easy was pregnant.

Colleen was devastated. Mom was shattered.

Connor was not surprised. Not very, anyway.

He did his best to try to avoid his father and Gail. Told his father not to come to graduation, moved to Manhattan to work. But then one autumn day when he was home visiting his sister and mother, he ran into the happy couple, almost literally, right in front of the Black Cat.

"Son!" Pete said. "Uh…hey. How are you? You look good."

Connor didn't say anything.

"This is Gail."

Connor looked at her, and saw the nervousness in her eyes. Saw her pregnant belly.

"Nice to meet you!" she said, giving a fake laugh. "Pete talks about you all the time!"

So she hadn't mentioned him. Dad had no idea that his son had gone on two dates with Gail the Tail, as Colleen called her.

"You're going to be a brother pretty soon," Pete said. "Isn't that great?"

Jesus. "I already am a brother." He waited a beat, then added, "I hope it's healthy." That was the best he could do.

And that's pretty much how it had been for the past ten years.

Savannah was a great kid, and Connor saw her often. He and Colleen babysat once a week almost from the very beginning. When she was two, she started having dinner with them every Friday night at O'Rourke's. When she was five, she started playing T-ball, and Connor went to every game he could. He gave her piggyback rides and took her swimming in the lake. Once a year, Connor took Savannah to Yankee Stadium, just the two of them. He bought her cool presents and sometimes stopped by her school to say hi at lunchtime, just because she loved when he did.

When she was nine, she was good enough to play on the town softball league, the youngest player in the history of the league to qualify, and Colleen made sure she was on O'Rourke's team.

And he avoided her parents as best he could. Was polite if he had to see them, like at Savannah's birthday parties or games. Gail made his skin crawl, and his father was worse.

Colleen had made her peace with their father. Connor had not. After what Pete put Mom through, Connor saw absolutely no reason to invite the slick bastard back into his life.

He certainly wasn't going to give him the chance to invest in a business.

Well, he could sit here all day, or he could get out and do something. Go for a run, hit the boxing gym, see if Tom Barlow was around and up for a few rounds.

Running won.

He went home to change. He owned a two-family Victorian a couple blocks off the green. Until recently, Colleen had lived upstairs, and though he wouldn't admit it, he missed having her there. Missed Rufus, her giant Irish Wolfhound mutt.

The downstairs apartment had always seemed too big. Three bedrooms, a living room, den and kitchen. Colleen called his style "Generic American Male," but he didn't see anything wrong with that. He'd bought his furniture in one fell swoop, basically ordering page 21 of the Pottery Barn catalog. He had three framed photos: one of him and Colleen the day they opened the bar; one of him, Mom and Colleen at Collie's wedding last year; and a photo of Savannah at bat.

Not one of him and Jess.

Yeah. The place was too quiet. Too big, too quiet, too empty.

Then again, it was supposed to have been for a family.

"You're an idiot," he said aloud.

Maybe he'd get a dog. A new girlfriend seemed like too much work. Bryce Campbell, a former classmate, ran the local shelter; maybe he could hook Connor up with a new best friend.

He changed into running shorts and an O'Rourke's baseball team T-shirt. Their slogan for this year was *O'Rourke's: Manningsport's Reigning Champions. As Usual.*

It was a perfect spring day in the Finger Lakes. Trees were in full flower, the sun was shining, the town bustling with tourists and townies alike. He waved to Julianne, the librarian, and Emmaline flashed her patrol car lights at him as she passed. He headed out of the Village—someone was cooking pork, and it smelled fantastic—then headed up to the Hill, where the vineyards sat like crown jewels of the area, the fields green against the bright blue sky, clouds slipping past.

Three miles of hard, uphill running cleared his mind. He'd get some investors and start the brewery, a place that would almost be a spin-off of the bar. Five or eight varieties to start with, a tasting counter, a few little tables. Maybe he could hire Faith Holland to design a little outdoor terrace. He had to finalize the loan from Sherry at the bank. Needed to investigate the real estate market and see about an old barn that could house the brewery, which would be the perfect building for such a place.

He was coming up to the top of the hill, where the air smelled like grapes; the farmers used the crushed skins as fertilizer. There was Prudence Vanderbeek on a big John Deere tractor. He raised a hand, and on impulse, turned into the drive of Blue Heron Vineyard. The Hollands' place, where Jess worked.

He'd never visited her at work before; having a secret relationship meant he couldn't drop by with flowers or just to kiss her.

But his mother worked at the vineyard, too, as a pourer in the tasting room. The perfect excuse.

Inside, several couples were taking down notes, chatting with Mom, smiling. And why not? The Blue Heron tasting room was one of the prettiest around, and chances were high that one of the Holland family had come out to schmooze, which customers loved, according to his mom. Mom herself was good at her job, none of the Debbie Downer stuff she saved for her children.

One couple wore matching sweatshirts with pictures of mustangs running across a desert. You had to wonder where those were sold. Connor sat next to them. "Hi, Mom."

"My son is here!" Mom announced. "Hello, sweetheart! How nice to see you! I called you yesterday, but you didn't call me back." It wouldn't be a visit with his mother without a guilt trip, but she looked pleased nonetheless, and Connor knew he scored points by stopping by.

"My son and daughter own O'Rourke's," Mom told the drinkers. "It's the best restaurant in town."

"Thanks, Mom. You'll get your cut later." He winked at the patrons, who smiled back.

"What are you doing here?" Mom asked. "Is something wrong?"

"Nope. I was out for a run. Thought I'd stop by and say hi."

His mom beamed. "The best son in the world."

"Why stop at son? How about best child?"

"You know I don't have favorites." She smiled at him. He was her favorite, of course.

"So how are you, Mom?"

"Excellent." She poured a taste of pinot gris for the mustang couple, then answered a question for someone else. She came back and ran a hand through her hair. Repeated the gesture.

"Notice anything different about me?" she asked.

Oh, crap. "Your hair looks great," he said. She'd let it go gray recently, and it did look nice.

"My hair is the same."

"Um...well. You look nice."

"Don't I?" She clasped her hands in front of her chin. "Anything different?"

Connor stifled a sigh. What was it? A facelift? New lipstick? He had no idea. "Uh...are you wearing makeup?"

"No."

The door behind the tasting room opened, and in came Jess. She halted at the sight of him, and his stupid heart slammed against his sternum. "Hey, Connor," she said, her voice perfectly normal.

"Jess." He managed a nod, he was pretty sure.

"Here to see your mom?"

"Yep." His mother was frowning at him now and kept shoving at her hair.

"You *still* don't notice anything different about me?" Mom asked.

"Can I have a taste of the Gewürztraminer?" one of the men asked.

"Let me pour that for you," Jess said. She pulled out a bottle and stepped a little bit behind his mother, then pointed at her own hand.

Her left ring finger, to be precise.

Connor's eyes widened. He looked at his mother's hand. Sure enough, there was a diamond there, as big as a cherry tomato.

"Hail Mary," he said.

"I know!" Mom crowed. "Ronnie and I are getting married!"

"Holy shit."

"Stop cussing and hug your mother," Jessica said calmly.

"Mazel tov," said the lady in the horse shirt, clinking her glass with her husband's.

There were a lot *more* cusses that wanted to come out, that was for sure. His mother? Getting *married*? She was…sixty, maybe? Did she really need to be married? Because marriage implied… Okay, gross. And to Ronnie Petrosinsky, the Chicken King? Didn't he have ties to the Russian Mob?

Was his mother actually having sex with the Chicken King? Connor's stomach rolled.

"He's choked up," Jess said. "Aw. Look at him, Jeanette."

"You'll still be my best boy," Mom said, coming around to hug him.

"Uh… I'm so happy for you, Mom," Connor murmured. The wine tasters cooed.

Jessica gave him a wry smile. He smiled begrudgingly back, then hugged his mother a little harder.

This would be good. Ronnie was a decent guy, loved his only child, made fistfuls of money with his fried-chicken empire, and Mom would have someone to look after, and someone to look after her.

Connor wouldn't have to plow his mother's driveway every time it snowed. He wouldn't have to worry about her if the power went out during a thunderstorm.

He wouldn't have to worry if she was lonely.

"Okay, let me go. I'm having a hot flash," Mom said, and Connor realized he was hugging her very close, indeed.

Maybe he *was* a little choked up.

"Have you set a date? I don't want you shacking up with this guy. Would've been nice if he'd asked my permission first," Connor grumbled.

His mother laughed. She did look happy. And younger. And pretty. "Sometime this summer. I also might be quitting Blue Heron."

"Don't even joke about that," Jessica said. "Folks, no one knows our wine better than Jeanette except the Hollands themselves," she added, filling glasses. "You have the privilege of talking with a real connoisseur today."

"Oh, Jessica, you're too nice!" Mom said. "But she's right, I do love wine. Have you tried our Chardonnay? It's lovely, and we have both oaked and unoaked." She glanced at him. "Connor, sweetheart, I'll see you later, okay? You and Colleen are coming to dinner this week. Is it me, or is she huge?"

"I think she looks beautiful," Jess said.

"She's huge," Connor said. "Congratulations, Mom."

His mother beamed.

Good. She deserved happiness. She'd been something of a ghoul these past ten years, moaning and mooning after Pete. High time she got over him.

"Jess, can I talk to you for a minute?" he asked.

The faintest blush worked its way into her cheeks. "You bet. Come on back."

She led him down the hall, past Honor's office and into hers, a smaller version of the same. On the door was a nameplate: *Jessica Dunn, Director of Marketing.*

He could guess what that meant to her. The office overlooked the vineyard. She'd decorated with a couple of photos of her and Davey, or Davey alone. A stuffed animal sat on one shelf, as well as some books on marketing and wine. Otherwise, it still looked very new.

"Have a seat," she said, going behind the desk. She picked up a pen, then put it down.

"Congratulations to you, too," he said. "On your job promotion. I'm really—" *proud,* he wanted to say "—happy for you."

"Thanks." The flush deepened. "What can I do for you, Connor?"

He could think of roughly eighty-seven things immediately, all of which involved sex. "Uh…well, I just… I wanted to say…" Shit. Talking was hard. He took a deep breath. "No hard feelings, Jess. I understand."

Her face didn't change, didn't move, but her eyes flickered.

There were a hundred stories there, and none that he'd get to hear. She'd told him all she was going to.

She nodded. "Thank you." Her voice was low.

"I just don't want to… I mean, it'd be nice if we could…"

He *hated* talking.

"I know. Me, too." She gave him a little smile. Words had never really been their thing, anyway.

"Is everything okay with you?" he asked, because there were shadows under her eyes, and he wasn't dumb enough to think he'd caused them.

She picked up the pen again. "My father's back in town."

A hot, slow wave of anger flooded Connor's chest. Keith Dunn had screwed his family over more times than anyone could count. Left Jessica completely in charge of Davey after her mother died.

"Want me to get rid of him for you?" he asked before he remembered that wasn't his job anymore.

She shook her head. "Thanks for the thought. I'll take care of it."

Or Levi would. After all, he was a cop and could actually do something other than threaten. As ever, the old pang of jealousy sounded.

It wouldn't be smart to ask her to help him with the brewery. She didn't want to marry him; he should give her, and himself, some space.

"I was wondering if you might be available for some freelance work," he said, because why not? It's not like he was emotionally intelligent. He'd proven that more than once.

And being around Jessica, in any way, was preferable to the alternative.

"Bartending? Colleen already asked me."

"No. Marketing."

She raised her eyebrows. "O'Rourke's needs help?"

"No. The brewery. You know."

"Um...no, I don't."

Right. It was quite possible that Connor had never told her, since they'd never had a normal relationship with talking and meals and all that. "Well, I've been working with Tim Parsons about opening a brewery, and it seems like a good time." *Because now that you left me, I have quite a bit of time on my hands.* "I figured it could be...you know. Good." Captain Eloquence, that was him.

"Connor, that's great," she said. "I think that's a fantastic idea."

"Really?"

"Yes! Who better than you, right? You know food, so you'd know what to drink with it."

"Yeah. That's what I had in mind. You know how restaurants always recommend a wine pairing. No one recommends beer, and why not? So I'd consult, basically, and Tim would do the real work, but I'd tell him what flavors I wanted to go with different kinds of food, and serve them at O'Rourke's, and kind of...go from there."

She was smiling. Just a little, but he felt it in his blood cells, all of which were marching south, whistling happily.

Get up, doofus. Her answer to his proposal echoed in his mind.

The whistling stopped.

"Let me check with the Hollands and see if they'd mind," Jessica said. "If they say it's okay, I'd love to help."

Connor stood up. "Great. Work me up an estimate if they say yes."

"You don't have to pay me."

"Yes. I do."

Those words shut down the warm light in her eyes. But he did have to. They could be friendly, and maybe they could work together, but he couldn't go back to begging for scraps from her table.

A door opened, and the hallway was suddenly filled with chatter. "You're going to love it, it'll be so fab! And I love your idea of having people arrive by horse and carriage! Oh, my God! Connor! Hi! Are you looking for me?"

It was what's-her-name. His date. "Hey," he said, standing up. "How are you?" Molly? Mary? Maybe? No, not Maybe. Marcy, that was it.

"Elizabeth, this gorgeous guy is Connor O'Rourke," Marcy continued, stepping aside so another woman could peek in. "He owns the cutest little tavern in the Village here. You should book him for your rehearsal dinner! Seriously. The food is ah-mazing!"

"Hi," said a smiling woman. "If Marcy recommends you, it must be great."

"Thanks." Maybe he should say something else. "You're getting married at the Barn?"

"I am," she said. "Totally fell in love with it when I saw it online. And Marcy is so helpful."

Connor glanced at Jessica, who hadn't yet been acknowledged, then back at the bride. "Good."

"By the way, Connor, I got your text," Marcy said, leaning in Jessica's doorway. "I totally can't wait. Where should we meet?"

"Uh, your choice," he said.

"Okey-dokey," she said. "I'll text you later. Come on, Elizabeth, we have tons to go over! This will be the most special day of your entire *life*! I promise you! That's what every one of my brides says to me. Without fail. I kid you not."

They went into her office and closed the door.

That had been fairly exhausting. Marcy was very cute, if you somehow silence that voice and cut her energy level by, oh, ninety-eight percent.

And now Jessica knew he had a date with her. She sure didn't seem to care. He looked at her another minute. She returned his look, calm as Buddha. *Three feet away, pal.*

"Send me that estimate," he said. "And thank you, Jessica."

With that, he went back out, waved to his mom again and turned his five-mile run into ten.

Maybe exhaustion would get Jess out of his head.

CHAPTER TWELVE

Jessica's hands were shaking as she got out of her car in front of Hugo's. She took a calming breath, looked out over Keuka Lake, and took another.

When her father had just appeared like that, Jessica thought that maybe, for the first time in her life, she might pass out. Her skin crawled in a massive, wriggling wave, and her heart started thudding so hard she could feel it in her eyes.

Davey, the traitor, hugging him.

And then Keith called her his baby girl.

She'd grabbed Davey by the arm and dragged him to the car. "I want to see Dad!" he said, and she could feel his anger building up and knew she'd be faced with a huge rage storm back home, and she didn't care.

"Get in the car. Now," she ordered.

"But it's Dad! He came back for us!"

"Get in the car, Davey! Right now!" *Right now* was their code for emergency, and Davey's eyes widened. He did as he was told, shoulders bent, and Jess felt two inches tall.

Their father was running down the street to catch up. "Jessica, honey, I know I have a lot to make up to you—"

"Shut up." She turned to her father, her fingernails digging into her palms, her fists were clenched so hard. "You don't get to do this," she hissed. "You don't just pop in and start hugging. You stay away from my brother or I will kill you."

She hadn't meant to say that. It felt true, nonetheless. And it felt evil and powerful and *good.*

"You have every right to be mad," he said. "I accept that, and I take full responsibility."

"So what?" She got into the car, shoved the key in the ignition and peeled away from the curb.

"Jess?" Davey's voice was small. "Aren't you happy to see Dad?"

"No, sweetheart. I'm not." Her voice was odd, and she ran the stop sign. Shit. She took her foot off the gas and slowed down.

"I love Daddy."

Jess glanced in the rearview. His eyes were wider than usual. He was scared.

She had scared him.

The lump in her throat was strangling her. "Let's talk about this later, okay?"

"Will Dad come live with us?"

"Later, Davey."

"I want Dad to come live with us."

She tried to relax her choke hold on the steering wheel. "He's not."

"Well, I *want* him to!"

"That's too bad, Davey. He's probably only in town for a day or two. To go to the casino, not see us."

"He *said* he missed me! He *said* he loves me!"

He doesn't.

The words practically tore her chest apart trying to get out.

The next day, she'd found a note taped to the front door. Keith—he didn't deserve the title of *Dad*—wanted to talk. He'd been sober for a thousand days. He wanted to make amends and try to rebuild his relationship with his children.

The only thing missing from the note were kitten stickers, a drawing of a rainbow and the winning Powerball ticket.

But he was in Manningsport, and Jess couldn't see a way around talking to him, because if she knew her father, he'd take the path of least resistance. And that was through Davey.

So she called the number he'd left and tersely agreed to meet him at Hugo's, because O'Rourke's would be too busy and full of people she knew. Hugo's catered more to the out-of-towners.

And Connor didn't work there.

When he offered to get rid of her father for her, she almost cried. Wanted so, so much to find herself in his arms and let him take care of her, and yes, let him beat the shit out of her father, and scare him so bad he'd never come back.

But if she started to let stuff like that come out, who the hell knew when it would stop?

She could deal with Keith Dunn on her own. She *had* to deal with him on her own. And she would. No one else could do it.

"Hello, Miss Beautiful," Hugo said as she came in. "I have the corner reserved for you."

Good old Hugo. He knew about her history with her father.

Keith Dunn had been a pretty high-functioning alcoholic. Better than Mom, who truly was addicted, who once drank hand sanitizer at the hospital when she was desperate, who tried over and over and over to quit, failing each time.

No, Keith was a beer man—Pabst Blue Ribbon, a twelve-pack a day even when they were on food stamps. Though he was skinny, he looked bloated, as if beer would leak out of his pores if you brushed against him.

But he never seemed drunk the way Mom did. It made it worse somehow; like he made the conscious decision to let everything fall to Jessica, and he'd just pop another beer and watch TV.

The corner table was as private as Hugo's had, often reserved for marriage proposals. Today, the interaction that took place here wouldn't be so pretty. Jess sat down and straightened the butter knife.

She hadn't gone home to change first, wanting to look as professional as possible. Gray pencil skirt, white blouse, black pumps with a strap across the ankle, hair in a plain French twist.

"You look hot," said Felicia, who, like Jess, had been here for years. She handed over a menu. "The whole corporate thing… you look like a porno about to start. Just let down your hair and start flipping it around."

"Not really the look I was going for."

"I'd take it in a heartbeat. Don't tell me you have a date."

"My father."

Felicia winced. "Shit."

"Don't take our order, okay? We won't be long."

Felicia put her hand on Jess's shoulder. "Gotcha."

"Wait, Felicia. Um…bring me a glass of wine, okay? No, a beer. It doesn't matter what kind."

Because a beer was *his* drink. It would be a challenge, would weaken her father, distract him and remind him.

She twisted her thumb ring. Man, she didn't want to be here! The urge to bolt back home and lock the door shimmered like a mirage. Davey playing with his Avengers figures, a big bowl of pasta with garlic and olive oil for dinner, HGTV or Robert Downey, Jr. on the TV.

Instead, she was here, waiting for her worst nightmare to arrive.

Felicia returned with her beer, gave her a smile, then went to wait on a large party that had just come in.

Shit on a shoelace. Jess felt suddenly, horribly alone.

And then, like a miracle, there was Pru and Carl, Honor and Tom. Felicia led them to a table a little ways away; out of earshot, but close enough. Honor gave her a reassuring nod, Tom a little salute. Carl waved, but Pru came over.

"I happened to run into your father today," she said. "Asked him why he was back in town, and he said he wanted to make amends. He mentioned you were coming here. Thought you could use a little backup."

Sometimes a knight in shining armor was actually a woman dressed in flannel. "Thank you," Jess whispered.

"We're here. But you got this, Jess. You do."

It was very, very hard not to cry. Prudence smiled at her. "Besides, Carl and I have exhausted every superhero sex game we can think of. We're going old-school tonight. Just two middle-aged married people having dinner with family."

Jess gave a shaky laugh.

"Good luck, hon." With that, Pru went over to her husband.

For most of her life, Jess had hated the Holland family, hated them for being everything her family wasn't. And here they were, backing her up. Being her friends.

This was going to be an emotional night.

Jess took a sip of the beer just to remind herself that she could. She was better than her parents. She'd never been drunk in her life.

Then in he came. Looked around the restaurant, saw her and smiled.

It was the first time Jess could recall seeing him at Hugo's sober, since he used to visit her here when he needed her tip money for an "emergency." Happy times, Keith talking too loudly, Jess trying not to have their business broadcast to everyone, inevitably giving him money to make him go away.

Now, Keith walked over to her table, and Jess's hands curled into fists. She was sweating. Hopefully, she looked like fury encased in ice.

"Hi, Jess. I really appreciate you meeting me," he said. "Is it all right if I sit down?"

"Sure."

He looked healthier, Jess had to give him that. His bright blue eyes weren't bloodshot; his shirt wasn't stained. And aside from a few lines around his eyes, he was the same.

"You look incredible," he said, smiling. "You look like you could be the President, you're so classy."

"Why are you here?" she asked. No point in bullshitting.

"I want to make amends."

"The program works if you work the program?" Hey. She knew AA. Or at least, she knew Al-Anon. Some kids in high school played soccer, some were in drama club, some worked twenty hours a week and went to meetings for kids whose parents were drunks.

"Exactly," Keith said.

"Don't get your hopes up." She took a slow, deliberate sip of beer.

"My hopes are pretty low," he said, his eyes on the drink. He tapped his forefinger against the tablecloth. "Jessie, I've been sober for one thousand and fifteen days." He fished something out of his pocket. A coin from AA. Big deal. You could buy those on Amazon, probably.

"Congratulations. Don't come around here anymore."

"I'd like to have you and Davey back in my life."

"Permission denied."

He nodded, not quite looking at her. "You're angry, I understand that. And I can't undo what I did. But I love you and Davey—"

"No, you don't."

"I have a disease, Jessie."

"I don't want to hear it. *Mom* had a disease, remember? She died, if you recall, and right after that, you blew out of town, took out three credit cards in my name and put me fourteen grand in the hole while I waitressed to support your disabled son."

There was a clatter from the Holland table. Jess had the impression that Pru had just grabbed a sharp object, God bless her.

"Yes," Keith said. "I did all those things. And I regret them, and I'll never do them again, and I am very, very sorry."

"I don't care. I really don't. You're as dead to me as Mom."

He looked out the window, blinking. "I'd like to earn a place in your life, Jessie. And Davey's. I've been sober for almost three years."

"So what? Davey's all grown up, and I've finally managed to get out of that trailer park. I have a decent job with health benefits. We don't need anything from you."

"I'd like a chance to do better."

"I'm thirty-two years old. I don't need a daddy. Not anymore."

"Davey might."

Her hands went ice cold. "Well, I've been mother *and* father to him all these years, so if you think you're going to waltz in here and take him to a ball game or a movie and make everything right, think again. Best thing you can do for us is leave and never come back."

"I have a job at the salt plant over in Dundee. I rented a little place there. I'm here to stay, honey. And I don't care how long it takes. I'll make this up to you."

"How do you make up someone's childhood? How do I get a do-over on that, huh?"

"Okay, you're angry. I accept that."

"How generous of you."

He sighed. "But I have to say, I think you're exaggerating how bad things were," he said, and that's when Jessica completely surprised herself and threw her beer in his face.

Connor was in a particular circle of hell known as *the date who never stopped to draw breath.*

Marcy.

"So there we were, and not to toot my own horn—" as if

she'd been doing anything else since they sat down "—no one wants to be the one responsible for an Oscar winner's wedding disaster, am I right? So I say, in Italian, did I mention I'm fluent? I say, 'You there! Put on this striped shirt and row! I don't *care* if you can't swim! Ah ha! Ah ha! Ah ha ha ha!"

That was her laugh. The first time she'd let it rip, Connor thought she was coughing up a hairball. Also, she yelled all her sentences. People were looking at them, but Marcy seemed unaware.

They were in the little bar at Hugo's, because he hadn't wanted to go to O'Rourke's, since Colleen would be there. Also, it was Wednesday, when the volunteer EMTs and firefighters had their meeting there, which consisted of pool-playing and dirty jokes.

And Jess was on the fire department. He didn't want her to see him with another woman. It just felt wrong.

Marcy sounded like a flock of geese, honking incessantly. No, geese sounded too nice. That comparison wasn't fair to geese. Chickens. She sounded like a thousand chickens. A stadium of chickens.

Fortunately, his participation in the conversation wasn't required. Marcy told stories. Namedropped a lot, not that Connor knew who any of these people were, but he'd already learned to simply nod and pretend he did, because otherwise, she'd tell him in excruciating detail.

His phone buzzed, and though he hated when people checked their phones while out with real live humans, he suddenly understood the urge.

Whenever he'd been with Jess, he'd turned off his phone completely.

The phone buzzed again, urging him to sneak a peek. It was Colleen.

Stop being so negative. There must be something you like about her. Try being positive for once in your life.

He glanced around Hugo's tiny bar area to see if his sister was there. Nope. The magical twinsy bond struck again.

He looked at Marcy, who was laughing at her own joke. *Positive, positive.* Well, she was cute, he'd give her that. Her hair was black and shiny, and though her eyes were small behind her glasses, they were a nice blue color. Average rack. A little thick around the middle, which he only noticed because she kept sucking in her stomach like she was about to blow out the candles on a centenarian's birthday cake.

In the twenty minutes Connor had been on this date, Marcy had probably said more than Jessica had said in ten years.

But Jess could say one word, and it would mean everything. *Yes*, for example. Yes would've meant everything.

"So I'm standing there, and this guy says 'I love your outfit,' and I'm like, 'Hello? This shirt is ten years old! You have pretty lousy taste, pal.' And then I realize it's Michael Kors! I kid you not! Ah ha! Ah ha! Ah ha ha ha!"

This date would never end.

Then all of a sudden, Tom Barlow came through the bar, half dragging Keith Dunn by his collar, and escorted him none too gently out the door.

There was only one reason Jess's father would be here.

"Excuse me a second," Connor said. Without waiting for Marcy to answer, he went into the main section of the restaurant and saw Jessica at the corner table, surrounded by her friends—Honor and Pru and Hugo. The tablecloth in front of her was sopping wet.

"Jess?" He knelt down in front of her and took her hand. If anyone didn't realize he was in love with her, they were blind or stupid. Her hand was icy, and he rubbed it between his. "You okay?"

Her eyes were dry. No. Jessica Dunn never cried, but that copper wire connection between them flared with heat.

"I'm fine," she lied. She squeezed his hand and pulled it free. "Just lost my temper a little bit."

"As you should have," Pru said. "I would've broken the damn glass over his head."

"Me, too," Honor said.

"Let me take you home," he said, standing up and offering his hand.

"Good idea," Pru said. "Jess, let him drive you home. It's been an upsetting night."

"I'm really fine. But thank you." Her eyes met his, and the wire lit up. She wasn't fine. She *needed* him, damn it. But she didn't take his hand. He let it drop.

"What have we here?" Shit, it was Marcy, and she cozied right up to him. "Wow, it's my boss! Hey, Honor! Hi, Prudence! Food must be great here! Connor and I were just having dinner, and then I was like, whoa, they're actually kicking someone out! Kind of exciting! Does that sort of thing happen a lot around here? But everything seems to be under control now. Can Connor and I do anything, Jessie?"

Jessica looked up at her. "I go by Jessica or Jess," she said, and her voice shook the tiniest bit. "Please don't call me Jessie."

"I'd be more than happy to take you home," Connor said. The urge to take her home, to *his* home, to take care of her, made him want to just toss her over his shoulder and carry her out.

Tom Barlow came back in. "All right, then, Jess?" he asked.

"Yes. Thank you so much, Tom." She smiled at him, and though Connor liked Tom Barlow quite a bit, he had the sudden urge to punch him.

There were too many people here.

But Jessica needed people. Especially with her father back in town.

"We can definitely give you a ride, Jessica." Marcy reached out and gave her a pat on the shoulder. "Listen, we all have crappy dates. You wouldn't believe some of the idiots I've been out with."

"Why don't you have dinner with us, Jess?" Honor suggested. "We'd love that."

"You guys are the best," she said. "But I think I'll go home. Ned's missing the fire department meeting, watching Davey, so I'll get back and he can go."

"I'll drive you," Connor said.

She put her hand on his arm for the briefest second, and he caught the faint smell of lemons. "I'm good, Con. But thank you. Thanks, everybody. Sorry for the drama."

"I totally wish I'd seen it!" Marcy said. "You go home, pour yourself a nice big drink and relax, okay? Poor kid."

"Have a good night, gang. Thank you again. I… I really appreciate it." She walked gracefully through the dining room. Hugo stopped her and gave her a hug, and Felicia touched her hair.

"Well, let's get back to our date!" Marcy said brightly. "Too bad about poor Jessie—whoops, *Jessica*—because we were having a super time! Ah ha! Ah ha! Ah ha ha ha!"

Prudence rolled her eyes.

Because he couldn't figure out a way around it, he went back to the bar with Marcy.

"So am I wrong in thinking there's some history there?" she said, beaming brightly. "Between you and Jess?"

Connor looked at her a few beats. "We're old friends."

"Is that what the kids are calling it these days?" Another hairball laugh.

"Listen, thanks for meeting me," he said. "I'm afraid I have to get back to O'Rourke's. It was very nice talking to you."

"Oh, definitely! And we didn't even get to talk about you being a caterer for the Barn events! We'll have to get together again, won't we?"

He hated catering. “That’s not a service O’Rourke’s offers,” Connor said. “But I appreciate your asking.”

“You bet! Well, maybe we’ll see each other around, of course we will, tiny town and all that, so until next time! Whoops, I have to race off, so busy these days, not that I’m complaining, I thrive on this schedule. Maybe I’ll go check in with Honor.”

Poor Honor. Well, she hired the woman, after all. “Good night,” he said, and left a twenty for their drinks.

By ten o’clock that night, Jessica’s heart had stopped thudding erratically, and her hands had stopped shaking. A pint of Ben & Jerry’s Red Velvet Cake had taken the place of dinner, and rather than the big drink Marcy had suggested, she was self-soothing with a *Love It or List It* marathon on HGTV. Ned and Davey had been at the gym when she’d met her father, and Davey had crashed at about 8:30, thanks to maniacally running on the treadmill, which was one of his great joys in life. Ned was in his room, talking on the phone to Sarah Cooper, which seemed to be his ritual before bed.

She shouldn’t have been surprised that her father had minimized the way things had been. That was nothing new.

But good God, the words had been like a kick in the stomach.

She wasn’t sorry she’d thrown the beer. A horrible, hard part of her hoped the taste and smell of it had knocked him right off the wagon, because it would be a lot easier if he’d just crawl back into his hole and stay there. She didn’t want the New & Improved Sober Keith, doling out apologies like breath mints.

There was a soft knock at the door. Chico Three lifted his head and wagged his tail, but the dopey thing was the type of dog who’d offer a serial killer a chew toy, rather than protect her and Davey. She got up and went to the door.

If it was her father, she’d call the police.

It wasn’t.

It was Connor, holding a foil pan. "Lasagna," he said with a half smile.

God. It would be so easy to love him.

Chico Three raced to the door and went straight for Connor's crotch. "Would you keep your dog from molesting me?" Connor asked, his voice quiet, the smile still on his face.

"Sorry." Jess grabbed Chico's collar. "Be polite, Chico."

"Can I set this down?" Connor asked.

"Of course."

He went into the kitchen, and he looked so natural there, so familiar. Maybe he'd ask her to come over to his place. She could ask Ned if he'd mind her leaving for a little while.

And she could use that. She could use Connor's arms around her, his mouth, his callused, strong hands. She could use some naked time with this beautiful man.

Instead, he put the pan down on the stove. "Is there anything I can do?" he asked.

She didn't answer for a second, her throat tight. "No, I'm fine," she answered.

He looked at her for a few heartbeats. "Okay." Then he leaned in and kissed her cheek. "See you around."

With that, he left, closing the door quietly behind him, leaving Jessica alone in the dark and orderly kitchen.

CHAPTER THIRTEEN

"Come on, Connor! Work that arm! What are you, a six-year-old girl?"

"Easy, Yogi. I'm just warming up." Connor stared down from the pitching mound at his little sister, who was giving him the sign for a fastball. Savannah was a catcher—a good one, and she didn't like him throwing what she called "kitten pitches."

However, his fastball was somewhere around 80 miles per hour, and he didn't want to hurt her.

"Come on, wuss!" she taunted.

"You've been hanging around Colleen too much," he answered, and let the pitch fly. She caught it without visible movement, her glove just closing around the ball.

"Is that the best you can do? Because my mother can throw that hard." She threw the ball back to him. Hard.

"Okay, smart-ass," he said. "Don't go crying if you can't handle the heat."

He let loose. Another perfect catch.

She was good, all right.

She gave him a three and pointed to her left thigh. Curveball. Not a problem.

They threw for about a half hour, swapping mild insults, Con occasionally giving her a little advice, Savannah occasionally returning the favor. When they were done, Savannah took off her catcher's gear and they started running, part of her fitness regime. Her goal was to play on the Little League team with the boys, rather than on the girls' softball team, and speed wasn't her thing. Since Connor had always been a pretty decent athlete, he'd appointed himself her coach. Better that than having their father give it a try, and dropping dead of a heart attack in front of her.

"So how are things at home?" he asked, jogging backward to see her face.

"Fine, I guess. Mom's been sick."

"Is she okay?"

"I guess so."

Connor turned back around and didn't ask any more. If there was something to be worried about, Colleen would ferret out the news and tell him. The most he'd said to Gail these past ten years were essentially, "Hi, how are you?" and "I'll bring her back by nine."

But Savannah was a good kid. His father and Gail were doing something right. Certainly, Pete was better at the second round of family life than the first, which saved Connor the trouble of beating him up.

"Connor, do you have a girlfriend?" his sister asked as they rounded the last corner of the block.

He glanced down at her strawberry-blond head. "No."

"Why not?"

"Oh, God. I thought you were the nice sister."

She giggled at that, her face flushed but not too red. "Is there someone you like?"

"No. I don't like anyone. Especially little sisters who interrogate me." Another giggle. "Is there someone *you* like?"

She stopped running as they came back onto the field. "Yes."

Well, shit. "You're ten. I forbid you to like anyone."

"Don't tell anyone," she said. "It's an older man."

Connor was suddenly drenched in a cold sweat that had nothing to do with running. *And I will kill that older man.* "Who, honey?"

"He's in seventh grade. Sawyer Bickman."

So that made him fourteen to Savvie's ten. Predator material. Clearly, this Sawyer person needed to have a six-foot-two adult scare the living shit out of him.

"He told me I made a fantastic play last week," Savannah said, looking down. Connor didn't miss her smile. "The big kids came to our game."

"Is that it?"

"I thought it was pretty great, Connor." She cut him a mildly hurt look.

"I mean, that was all he said? Did he…do anything?"

"Ew, Connor. Yes, that was all he said."

"And have you talked since?"

"No." She flopped down on the grass and stared at the sky, which was a perfect, clear blue today. "He probably has a girlfriend."

"Honey, you're—"

"Don't tell me I'm only ten years old. I know how old I am. And my mom has already told me, in case I forgot."

Connor lay down next to her.

He'd been twelve the first time he'd fallen for Jess. The only time, really, since it never went away. "So you like him."

"I think it's more than that."

Savannah had an old soul that didn't match her slight (and adorable) lisp. "Young love can really pack a punch," he said.

"You're telling me." She was quiet for a minute. "He's really nice to people. Not just me, but everyone."

Connor nodded. "That's a good sign."

She turned to face him, her little round face earnest. "Should I do anything? Write him a note or something?"

"Maybe you should ask Colleen. She's pretty good at this stuff."

"But you're a boy. What would you think if you got a note from a girl who liked you?"

Crap. "Uh…well, what would this note say?"

She sat up straight. "'Dear Sawyer, when you told me I did a good job tagging out Aidan Priestley, it was the greatest moment of my life. My chest was burning and I was so, so happy, it felt like birds were flying inside me. I think about you all the time. I know I am only ten, but if you wait for me, I will love you forever. Respectfully, Savannah Joy O'Rourke.'"

Quite the recitation. And *respectfully*? Connor ran a hand over his jaw, hiding his smile.

"That's…uh, very poetic. I liked the part about the birds flying. But here's the thing, Savvie. If he's fourteen, it's a pretty big age gap. But when he's… I don't know—forty, it won't be." Yes. Forty. He could see his little sister dating when she was thirty-six. That felt about right.

"Forty?"

He gave a conciliatory shrug. "Or maybe even sooner than that. But right now, I think the best-case scenario is that he'd be really flattered that you liked him, and he'd admire the guts it took to send the note."

"Great!"

"On the other hand, though, if he did have a girlfriend, or if, say, the girl who was writing was a little young, he might feel…uncomfortable. He might worry if it was appropriate, if she was only ten. He might think, 'Doesn't that girl have a big brother who's really scary?'"

"You're not scary, Connor." She smiled at him. She'd lost another tooth, he noted.

"Everyone knows I'm *extremely* scary. But do you know what

I mean? You might put this nice guy in a tough spot. He might want to be friends with you, but if it's romantic, he can't be."

Savannah pondered, then sighed. "This is probably good advice."

"Well, sure. I'm your big brother. I'd just keep playing good baseball, maybe focus on that. Keep it at a level where you guys could talk about sports without anything being misinterpreted."

She nodded. "Got it. Keep him in the friend zone."

"How do you know that phrase?"

"Everyone knows that phrase. Wanna throw some more? Or are you too weak and exhausted?"

He stood up and grabbed her as a response, tossed her over his shoulder like she was a sack of rice and ran around the bases, her happy shrieks filling the air.

When he took Savannah back home that day, he waited as he usually did until she was inside the house. Usually, she'd just open the door, turn and wave, then run inside.

Today, however, the door was locked. She rang the bell, then stood there a minute. When no one came to answer the door, he joined her on the porch.

His father's house was, unsurprisingly, huge, showy and soulless. It was the last house in the cul-de-sac, the biggest house in the development, which was cloyingly called Whisper Winds Way. He'd been inside for Savannah's birthday parties, and it was the same on the inside as it was on the outside.

"My mom said she'd be home," Savannah said.

Connor knocked. Loudly.

No one answered.

Savvie had said Gail had been sick.

"Well, come back to the restaurant with me," Connor said. "I'll put you to work, how's that?" He'd have to call his father.

Just then the door opened, and there was Gail. "Hi, baby girl!" she said. "Did you have fun?"

She looked awful. White-faced, her hair dull and disheveled.

"You okay, Gail?" he asked.

"Yeah. Just a little under the weather."

"I'm starving," Savannah said. "Bye, Con! See you later!" She darted inside the house.

Gail shaded her eyes and looked at him. "How was she?"

"Great."

She really looked like hell. Usually, she wore tight, tight clothes, low cut on top, high cut on the bottom, not a fan of the *less is more* philosophy. Today, she was wearing yoga pants and a sweatshirt. Connor was actually surprised she owned a sweatshirt.

"I was napping." She lowered her hand. "Your father would love to speak to you," she said. "He's out right now, but maybe you could call him."

"Maybe. Feel better."

"Maybe *we* could talk sometime, too."

"Why would we do that, Gail? Are you really sick? Is there something I should know?"

"No, no, it's just..." She sighed. "I've always felt a little bad about...you know."

"About what?"

"Dating your father right after our...thing."

"We didn't have a thing. We met twice." He didn't really mean to sound like such an asshole. Honestly, he had no problem with Gail, except that she made him want to take a shower.

"Well, I just hate thinking that it's partly because of me that you and your father are...distant."

"You weren't his first mistress, Gail. You were just the woman who stuck. My father and I were distant long before you graduated from high school, not to worry."

"I do worry."

"Don't. Get some rest. Feel better."

He went back to his truck.

Well, shit. If Gail was sick—really sick—what would happen then? If she had cancer or something? He'd bet his father would hire a nurse and spend as little time as possible with her, then get married before the dirt had settled over her grave.

Savannah could always come live with Connor.

Shit. He'd have to report to Colleen so she could figure out what was wrong.

CHAPTER FOURTEEN

It had been a quiet week since the debacle at Hugo's. Even Davey had been subdued, though they'd had a nice half hour the day before, watching the tulips grow. Well, staring at the tulips she'd planted in the tiny scrap of front yard they had. But Davey was convinced that the sunshine was warm enough that they'd open, so they'd sat there together, Chico Three lying motionless on his back as Davey scratched his belly, all three of them looking at the flowers.

It was moments like these that she loved most of all with Davey—the way he could appreciate the smallest thing, that, when you stopped to look with him, turned out to be pretty remarkable.

Their mother had been like that, a little. Every time a butterfly drifted into their grubby little yard at the trailer park, Jolene would call everyone over to see, each time as delighted as if she'd never seen a butterfly before.

But Davey wasn't talking much, and this bothered her. She'd have to watch *Iron Man* with him tonight. That always perked him up, though she could recite the movie by now. Still. Robert Downey, Jr. It could be worse.

Davey hadn't mentioned their father again. Keith had sent her two emails at work, finding her through the Blue Heron website. Both were full of the expected AA lingo. *Make amends. Powerless over addiction. Take full responsibility.* He understood that dealing with him was her choice, and he would respect that.

And then the killer—*But Davey will always be a child, and I'm praying you'll give me the chance to be a better father to him than I was to you.*

Three years sober. If he was telling the truth, that was. There was no reason to trust him. He'd lied, cheated and stolen all her life.

Give me the chance to be a better father to him than I was to you.

A father figure was one thing she really couldn't be to her brother.

Well. She had work to do—show Connor the marketing plan for his microbrewery.

As always, O'Rourke's was cheerful, immaculate and happy. "Jessica!" Colleen said from behind the bar, where she stood with a pretty girl. "My idiot brother is expecting you." She turned toward the kitchen. "Connor!"

"Colleen, inside voice," he muttered, coming through the swinging doors in his chef's whites, two days of stubble, his thick hair slightly mussed.

Damn. Had she ever seen him clean-shaven? Did she ever want to?

"Hey, Jess," he said, and her uterus trembled.

There was that feeling again, that dangerous feeling, that they were meant to be together. Scratch the surface of that, and you'd end up unhappy and worse than when you were alone...but *still.*

"Your brother is so handsome," breathed the young woman behind the bar.

"You need to get over that, Jordan," Colleen said. "First of all, he's really ugly. Secondly, he's your boss."

Connor ignored them both. "Let's go sit down." He put his hand on her back and guided her to the last, most private booth.

Jess found that her mouth was dry. Other parts were not.

Had she actually broken up with him? Or was it the other way around? And what was the reason again? Because not only could the man cook—that lasagna had been un*freaking*believable—he looked like a sullen angel, that dark, dark brown hair, the blue eyes, those big, manly hands, the smear of something across his chest.

"How are you?"

"Oh, good. Good, good. I'm good."

"Good." There was a smile in his eyes. "Things okay with your father?"

Right. She shrugged. "Things are stable."

He nodded. He had the most beautiful mouth; lips that were full and soft and brooding—could lips brood?—and when he smiled, she could actually feel it, a warm force that practically knocked her on her back, and hey, if she was on her back, they might as well—

"Let me get you a drink," he said. "Sorry, I should've offered first thing. Seltzer and cranberry, lemon twist, right?"

"Yes. Thanks."

He went off to the bar. There was a crash as the new girl dropped something, then the low rumble of Connor, reassuring her, no doubt. He went behind the bar and the girl—Jordan, was it?—swayed on her feet, her face fire-engine red as Connor bent to pick up the pieces of whatever she'd broken. Her heart, maybe.

First a date with Marcy. Now the pretty bartender with a huge crush.

She was going to have to find a way to make that okay in her head.

Connor deserved to be with someone great. Rumor had it

that Colleen was on the case, so it'd be a matter of months before he was in love with someone.

She remembered the time she'd seen him kiss that redhead, and how it felt like a razor slice with an acid chaser.

But she'd turned him down for all good reasons, and he'd been generous enough to offer his friendship, anyway.

She wondered if everyone knew how incredibly decent Connor O'Rourke was underneath his grumblings. How many men would do that?

She could only think of one.

"First-day jitters for Jordan there," he said, setting her glass in front of her.

"And a massive crush."

He rolled his eyes and sat down across from her. "So what have you got?"

"Behold," she said. She dragged her laptop out of her bag and opened it, clicked a few buttons, then turned the computer so Connor could see it.

The first slide was the brewery logo, using the same font the pub used. But it was even better; Jess had enhanced the colors, giving the brown letters a shadow of gold, adding some Victorian-style corners.

Connor nodded. "Nice."

But this was dumb. She slid around to his side of the booth and sat next to him.

He was warm. He smelled like garlic. Her uterus trembled again.

The next few slides were mock-ups of labels for the types of beer he planned to produce: India Pale Ale, Amber Lager, Pilsner, Porter, Stout. Each had its own label—the Dog Face IPA was her favorite, featuring an antiqued photo of a collie, after his sister. She glanced at his face; there was a slight smile there.

"You'll have to give me a description of what each beer will taste like," Jess said. "Same kind of idea as wine tastings—boldly hopped, caramel maltiness, whatever you have in mind. I made these up, obviously."

"Boldly hopped, huh?" His smile grew.

The next slides detailed some data—the fast rate at which microbreweries were expanding into the area, the increased revenue for five comparable breweries, the tourism statistics for the Finger Lakes.

And then a picture of Connor himself, at the stove in the restaurant kitchen, flipping a pan of something, flames leaping. His face was intent and serious, and he looked ridiculously handsome.

There was that tremble again. The thought that she was sitting right next to Smokin' Mc*Damn* made it almost painful.

"Where'd you get that picture?" he asked.

She cleared her throat. "Colleen. She gave me the numbers on the restaurant, too."

Connor's credentials were listed in bullet points—education, experience, awards, reviews. Next came O'Rourke's booming success and statistics—fourteen hundred percent profit growth in the first three years, sustained growth since. A little bit about Tim Parsons and his experience in brewing—not much, but enough.

Then came the point that would set O'Rourke's Brewing apart from the other microbreweries. Connor's knowledge of flavors, beer that was sophisticated and elegant enough to pair with the best meals, as well as to be enjoyed on its own. She'd lifted pictures of beer from the internet, as well as pictures of Connor's signature dishes, taken from their website.

"I was thinking you could include recipes to go along with each different beer," Jess murmured. "Buy a growler, get free recipes so the customer could really see how that particular beer enhanced the meal."

"Good idea." He glanced at her, and she felt it, the pull of him. Jordan wasn't the only one affected. Hopefully, Jess's face wasn't beet red, however. She had more practice, after all.

A few more slides showed four fermenting tanks, bags of hops and yeast, all attractively arranged. The dollar amounts Connor had emailed her and what they would go for. Targeted advertising and demographic research.

Then the last slide. The logo again, and the simple message. *Make every day special. Drink O'Rourke's.*

She looked at him. "What do you think?"

"This is...perfect, Jess." He looked at her, his eyes so damn beautiful, halfway between blue and gray. "Perfect."

She looked away. "I'll just need you to answer some questions about the flavors and correct any mistakes, and you'll be good to go."

"There aren't any mistakes."

"Hey... Hi." It was Jordan, staring with puppy-dog eyes at Connor. She seemed about to swoon, the poor thing, struck dumb with the wonder that was Connor Michael O'Rourke.

"Yes?" he said when Jordan failed to speak further.

"Right. Um, Colleen? She says your mother? She's here."

Colleen herself came over. "You guys almost done?" she asked. "Time for wedding talk, Con. Jess, our mother is marrying the Chicken King and will soon become the Chicken Queen."

"I know. Congratulations."

"Oh, of course you do! You work with her. Well, it's a little freaky, but thank you. We're happy to get another sister, right, Con?"

"I already have too many, but yes."

Jessica nodded. Paulie Petrosinsky was one of the nicest kids from their graduating class, an only child, Jess thought. She'd make a great sister to just about anyone.

"Jordan, sweetheart," Colleen said, "go make my mom a white zin and 7-UP, because I just can't bear to do it, okay?"

The girl gave Connor one more longing look and went off, bumping into a table on her way. "Call me crazy, Connor, but I think she has a crush on you. Don't go sleeping with the staff, now." Colleen winked at Jess.

"She's a little young for me," Connor said.

"Yeah, and don't you forget it."

"Why would I forget it? I'm not even—"

"Stop talking," Colleen said. "By the way, I do have a date for you. Tonight. Be here and be clean, okay? Is it so much to ask? And shave that scruff. You look like you're half grizzly bear. Come on, what are you waiting for?" She waddled off.

"You guys are still so cute," Jessica said, standing up.

Connor stood as well, towering over her. "If she wasn't my sister, I'm pretty sure I'd hate her."

"Liar." She paused. "Does she know?"

"Know what?"

Jess swallowed. "Know about us? Me?"

Connor's eyes dropped for a second. "I didn't tell her. But yes. She does. The twin thing."

Jess nodded. "She's being really nice. I thought she'd stab me if she knew."

"Her stabbing days are mostly past." He just kept looking at her, and she wondered what he wanted to say. It would wring her heart one way if he said he missed her, and it would wring it the other if he didn't.

He looked over at the other table. "Well. I have to go off to hell now and talk about weddings. Colleen's was bad enough. Now my mom."

If she'd said yes, they'd be planning their own wedding. Or maybe, they'd already be married.

"Hey, dude," came a voice. Paulie, who was about five-foot-three and solid muscle. "Jess. How's it hanging?"

"I… I never know how to answer that question. But I'm good. Congratulations about your dad getting married."

"Yeah, it's pretty cool!" Paulie said. "And Con, that means you and Coll and I are kinda related."

He grinned and punched Paulie lightly on the shoulder. It was hard not to feel jealous. "I should get back to Blue Heron," Jess said. "My break is almost over."

"I'll email you with those beer descriptions," Connor said. "Thanks again. This was great." He reached into his pocket and pulled out a check.

"Oh. Um…thanks," Jess said.

Transaction completed.

Maybe he was over her, she thought as he went over to the table where Jeanette was sitting with her fiancé and Colleen.

This will be the last time you break up with me.

He really did seem…fine.

Jess's throat was tight.

It would've been nice if she felt the same way. An unexpected wave of longing for the way things had been made her knees wobble. Those secret dates at his place, the way it felt when he opened the door and smiled at her, the way he hugged her so tight. The way he kissed her.

All told, she'd slept with twelve men, eleven of them when she was in high school. Only one since. The only one who'd ever made her feel…cherished.

"Jessica?"

She jumped.

It was her father. "What do you want?" she said, all her soft thoughts blown away.

"Do you have a minute?"

"For what?"

"Just a minute to talk, Jessie."

She glanced around. The bar was mostly empty; the O'Rourke-Petrosinsky group the only people sitting at a table in the back. Victor Iskin was sitting at the bar with his latest taxidermied pet there on display, and Jordan was eying Connor and wiping the same spot on the counter over and over.

"I have to be back at work in fifteen minutes," she said.

"I won't take that long."

With a deep breath, Jessica sat back down in the booth she'd just shared with Connor. Heard him laugh from across the room. Connor didn't know Keith was here; he'd be at her side in a heartbeat if he did.

"What is it?" she asked.

Keith sat down. "I was wondering if you'd given any thought to my request."

He smelled like soap. This was new. In her memory, her father always had that rank smell of cheap beer and stale cigarette smoke. His eyes were clear and blue, the long, straight lashes just like Davey's. He'd lost the gross little beer gut he'd sported and was now skinny as a shoelace.

She didn't say anything.

"I miss him, is all," her father said, his voice husky.

"I'm sure you do," she said. "Eight years is a long time to go without seeing someone."

Another chorus of laughter came from the O'Rourke table.

"I owe you an apology for what I said last week," Keith said. "You didn't exaggerate anything. Your mother and I let you be the adult while I did nothing. I acknowledge that, and I'm sorry, Jess. You deserve the Medal of Honor as far as I'm concerned."

"I love my brother more than anything or anyone. When I tell you I would kill anyone who'd hurt him, don't think I'm exaggerating."

"Oh, I believe you," her father said with a sad smile. "You always were so fierce. Listen, I just want to see him. You can breathalyze me. Call my sponsor at AA if you want. I've waited over a thousand days for this, to make sure it would stick this time, that I could do it. Please, Jess. It can be however you want it. Just give me a chance to see him."

She could feel the pulse in her stomach.

Davey had been so quiet this past week. A little somber, which was so unlike him, except for when Mom had died.

And he'd been so happy to see their father the other night.

Jessica glanced at her watch. Then she looked at her father. "We have drum circle tonight at seven over at the Art League. Next to the pizza place. You can come to that. Nothing afterward. You tell Davey you have to go when he asks if you can come over."

"Oh, Jessie, thank you," he breathed. "Thank you."

"It goes without saying that if I ever smell even the faintest hint of alcohol on you, I'll get a restraining order. I used to sleep with the police chief, don't forget." She stood up, suddenly desperate to get back to work, to her clean office, to her tidy computer files.

"Understood." Her father grabbed her hand. "I won't let you down."

She pulled her hand away. "That would be a first."

"Come *on*," Davey said. "I don't want to be late for drum circle! I love drum circle! Jess! We're gonna miss drum circle!"

"We're not late. See? It's ten of. Just calm down." But Davey was out of the car and running for the entrance the second she pulled into the parking lot.

Jess got out and sighed. This wasn't what she yearned to do in her free time, but boy, did Davey love it.

Drum circle was exactly what it sounded like—a circle of people sitting on hard metal chairs with a lot of different types of percussion instruments to choose from, from bongo to Toca to maracas to Davey's favorite, the cowbell. Jess generally went for the wooden block and stick, one of the less desired instruments each week.

Davey wasn't the only special needs person here; Brody Tatum, a Downs kid, was here with his parents; Jess had waited on them dozens of times. Miranda Cho, who worked with Davey at the candle factory, was also here with her mother, who waved to Jess.

"Hi, Miranda," Davey said, running up to her. "What's your favorite instrument? Mine's the cowbell. I love cowbell!" They had this conversation every week, verbatim. Well, Davey did. Miranda didn't answer; Jess had never heard her speak. But she glanced at Davey with a shy little smile and went to the center of the circle, grabbed a big African drum, then sat down. Davey sat next to her, and Jess next to him, block and stick ready.

Tanner Angst—his real name—sat down on Jess's other side, the better to bathe her in his tormented artist black cloud. Tanner felt he should've been the next Dave Matthews back in high school—and yes, she'd slept with him, once, and he hadn't even been that good at looking out for Davey. He'd been the king of cool back then, but one semester at Berklee College of Music had shown him he wasn't quite the special snowflake he thought. He now taught music at the middle school. Four years ago, he'd asked Jessica out and hadn't yet forgiven her for turning him down, yet also couldn't stay away from her. Some people could pull off brooding, Jess thought, picturing Connor. And some people just looked stupid.

She kept looking at the door. She didn't have to wait long; Keith Dunn came in at two minutes before seven.

"Dad!" Davey was out of his chair and racing across the circle to greet their father.

"Hey, son!" Keith gave him a long hug, then tousled his hair. "Is it okay if I stay?"

"Yes! Yes, it is, Dad! Come sit with us. Come on! Get your drum. Or you can have the triangle! Here! Here's the triangle! This is my best friend Miranda. Miranda, this is my father! Jess! Dad is here!"

"So I see."

"Isn't it great?"

"Yes." She managed to smile at her brother, but her heart was thudding. "Sit next to me, why don't you?" she said to her father. That way, she could smell if he'd been drinking. She turned to Tanner. "Do you mind moving over a seat?"

"Oh, Jessica. I didn't see you there," he said. "Fine. Whatever."

Her father smelled like Ivory soap. Not a hint of booze, and Jess was an expert.

She felt a tiny stir of hope, then cut it off. Her father was here; he was sober at the moment; Davey was happy. That was all. Reading into it, or expecting it to last, would be idiotic.

"Thank you for this," her father said quietly. She nodded once.

The circle was full now, and populated with some of the odder ducks in Manningsport, the creative souls who yearned to break free from the constrains of ordinary life. Jess stood out a little, as someone who had no rhythm—as shown by her aborted attempt at stripping—and as someone with no yearning to express herself artistically, someone who would quite love ordinary life.

"Gang, we're here to express ourselves artistically," said Debbie Meering, who ran the Art League. "This is a time for us to reach deep into our souls, envisioning our primordial roots in the swamps of time."

Every week she came up with something weirder. Jess tried, unsuccessfully, not to roll her eyes.

"Let's think back to the heartbeat of the brave little frog," Debbie went on, "who decided to be the first to venture out of the slime of the past and bravely leaped onto the shores of today."

Her father snorted.

Jess turned to look at him. He cut her a guilty smile, then looked at Davey. "I love cowbell," he said. "I got a fever, and the only prescription is more cowbell."

Well, well. Her father had a sense of humor. Same sense of humor she had, apparently, since she loved that old *Saturday Night Live* skit.

"Are you sick, Dad?" Davey asked. "Do you have a fever?"

"No, no, Davey. Just joking around."

"Tanner," Debbie said with a disapproving frown at Jess and her father, "will you lay down a rhythm for us, the rhythm of that brave little frog's heartbeat?"

There was another small snort, and Jess almost smiled herself. Weird, the idea of laughing with Keith Dunn.

Tanner started with a basic rhythm, which the drum circle picked up. Even Jess could follow it, so long as she didn't think too hard. *Tap. Tap. Tap. Tap.* It was when people started getting fancy that she screwed up. *Taptap. Tap… Tap.* Okay, time to fake it.

Her father wasn't much better, pinging away at a triangle at irregular moments. Davey was pretty good, though, and Miranda kept whacking out the, er, heartbeat, steady and loud. There were two actual drummers in the group who made them all sound pretty fantastic, adding beats and riffs and whatever else they were called.

After ten minutes or so, Jess put her block back in the center and grabbed finger cymbals. She took a seat across the circle so she could watch her father and Davey.

Davey smiled nonstop. He saw her watching and smiled even bigger. She waved, feeling a smile herself.

Her father looked happier than Jess could ever remember. Not secretive, not sly, not falsely innocent. He kept looking at Davey, pinging away on the triangle, happiness and sorrow mingling in his expression.

Years of crushed expectations had taught Jessica better than to get her hopes up. But being Davey's sister…well, he had some wisdom to impart, too, and Jessica knew it. Be in the moment. Try not to worry. Stop and watch the clouds drift past.

So maybe, just for this hour, she'd stop gnawing herself to pieces inside and take in the sight of her father and brother having fun.

A hand pressed on her shoulder. Ned, who'd played drums

in the high school band. "What's our theme this week?" he whispered.

"Primordial frog heartbeats," she said, and the two of them dissolved into wheezing laughter. Then Ned took her cymbals and actually made them sound cool, a swish-swish-swish that, Jess imagined, sounded just like brave little Froggy's ventricles, pushing the blood through his heart so he could make his great leap of faith.

At the end of drum circle, Davey towed their father over to Jess's side of the circle. "Can Dad sleep over?" he asked.

"I can't, son," Keith said.

"Dude, there's no room," Ned reminded Davey. "I live with you now, remember?"

"Oh," Keith said. "Are you, uh… Never mind."

"No," Jessica said. "We're not. He's practically a child."

"Still holding out for you to go cougar, Jess," Ned said, checking his phone. "Oh, missed a call from Sarah. See you guys at home."

"Well, I'll… I'll be on my way," Keith said. "Great to see you both."

Davey looked crestfallen. "Can't you stay?" he asked. "Please?"

"I actually have to work," Keith said. "But I'll see you soon, I hope."

"Why don't you come for dinner one day this week?" she said, and holy crap, *that* hadn't been planned.

"Yes!" Davey said. "Yes, that's a great idea, Jess! Okay! Bye, Dad! See you at dinner one day this week!" He charged over to Miranda, whose mother was chatting with Debbie Meering.

"Are you sure?" Keith asked her.

"No. But come on Thursday. Five-thirty. He likes to eat early." She turned and went to corral Davey before she said anything else she might regret.

CHAPTER FIFTEEN

So far, Colleen was batting .000 in the matchmaking department. She'd said, quite convincingly, that she really thought he and Marcy would hit it off. "I mean it, Con! You're the silent, grouchy type. She's all sunshine and marigolds, and very outgoing. Someone has to drag you out of your cave. Give her another try."

He'd refused.

Then came Gwen, who met him at O'Rourke's. She seemed nice enough. Worked as a fourth-grade teacher. She was pretty. They made it through the crab cake appetizer without incident, until Connor asked one of Colleen's required questions.

"So, tell me a fun fact about yourself, Gwen." He winced at the words *fun fact* and reminded himself that Colleen had fixed up dozens of couples.

"Hmm." Gwen leaned back in her seat. "Well, I like to target shoot."

"Oh, yeah? You any good?"

"Hell, yeah! Once, I shot a baby raccoon at about two hundred yards. I'm that good." She winked. "So. Would you rather burn to death, or be buried alive?"

And now, Bailey, who hadn't killed any baby animals. At least there was that. Otherwise, not so much to recommend her.

"This is my first choice for my dream bouquet. See these ribbons? A perfect color match to my maid of honor's dress. See? Beautiful, isn't it?" The woman looked up at Connor, a religious glow in her eyes. "And then, wait for it…my *dream shoes.* Aren't they *beautiful*?" She spun her iPad around for Connor to see.

He was going to kill Colleen the second her baby was born. Then he would take his little niece and raise her himself, though Lucas would probably have an issue with that. He glared at his twin from across the floor, where she was very ungracefully maneuvering behind the bar. She gave him an innocent look. *What? Wipe that look off your face.*

This cannot be a serious date.

Free your mind, idiot.

Free his mind, please. It was hard enough not to just bolt from the restaurant. Here he'd had a perfectly nice day off, going for a run with Jeremy Lyon, then heading up to Tim's garage, smelling hops and tasting their latest batch and scrubbing out the fermenting tanks. Then Colleen had to go and ruin it.

Bailey Something, his date for the night, was, according to his sister, everything he needed in a future wife. She was an attorney—brains—had been on her college swim team—health—and represented a women's shelter pro bono—heart. She was attractive, he guessed. Brown hair, brown eyes. Medium height. The rest of her was hard to see, as she was hunched in front of her iPad, which showed some kind of online collage entitled *Bailey's Dream Wedding.*

"Connor?" she asked. "You haven't even said if you like the shoes."

"They're nice," he said, glancing longingly toward the kitchen. The restaurant was packed, and, regrettably, it was his night off. Hannah and Monica were racing orders in and out; Jordan was doing okay behind the bar, though she wasn't as good as Colleen. Rafe had a nice thing going on with the salmon special, though Connor might've used a little more dill and the Black Sea salt rather than the truffle salt. The regulars were all lined up at the bar: Gerard and Ned, Victor and Lorena, Mel Stoakes and the nice lesbian couple whose names he couldn't remember.

"I'm torn between *this* lace, and *this* lace," Bailey said. Connor closed his eyes.

"Hi, Connor!"

"Hey, kid!" Reprieve, in the form of his ten-year-old sister. He opened his arms for a hug. "This is my sister, Savannah," he told the wedding chick.

"Oh! How darling!" She practically slid off the seat in rapture. *All this and he loves children, too!* Yes. Connor would kill Colleen.

"Hello, son."

"Dad. Gail."

"Hello there," Gail said.

"I'm *Bailey.*" Bailey held her hand out to Gail. "You must be Connor's parents! What a *wonderful* job you've done raising him." Gail grimaced. Well, at least there was that. Gail wasn't even forty, and she'd just been taken for Connor's mom. She looked a little better than the last time Connor saw her, and back to her slutty-style outfits: skin tight and low cut.

"My father and stepmother," he said, because he had to.

"*So* nice to meet you!" Bailey said. "We were just talking about weddings!"

"My brother loves weddings," Colleen said, appearing with all the subtlety of the obese manatee she resembled these days. "He gave me away at mine. We're twins, did he mention that?"

He had not, given that the entire date, all seventeen agonizing minutes, had been devoted to Bailey's Dream Wedding.

"I *totally* want to have twins," Bailey said, her eyes widening. Connor sensed he'd just risen even higher on her Husband Material scale. "Girls. Identical. Wouldn't that be so perfect?" Maybe she had a collage for that, too. *Bailey's Dream Identical Girl Twins.*

"Connor wants many children. At least four," Colleen said.

"You do, son?" Pete asked.

"Those words have never come out of my mouth," he said.

"Okay, his eye is twitching. Come on, guys, have a seat," Colleen said, ushering the other O'Rourkes away. Dad and Gail coming in to eat was new. Just last year, they never darkened the doorway. Those were the days, he thought wistfully.

"Want to see my dream centerpieces?" Bailey asked. "Orchids. I *adore* orchids!"

Connor's left eye was indeed twitching. Maybe he needed a vacation. Far, far away. He'd meet some cute little Tahitian woman who didn't speak English, bang out a few kids, maybe stay there.

Just then, the town siren went off, and thank you, baby Jesus, it gave Connor the excuse he'd been dying for. "Gotta go. Volunteer firefighter," he was pretty sure he said, bolting for the door into the sunshine like a racehorse at the bell.

Technically, he *was* on the volunteer fire department, though his work kept him from going on too many calls. He didn't have his pager tonight, though, and had no clue where the call was.

"Connor, want a ride?" asked Ned Vanderbeek.

"That'd be great," Connor said. "Where's the call?"

"Rushing Creek. Patient combative with staff."

"Hopefully not your great-grandparents," Connor said, getting into Ned's sweet new truck.

"Nah, they're generally only combative with each other," Ned said cheerfully, flicking on the blue flashing light.

Connor knew Ned was living with Jessica and Davey. He knew Ned was involved with Levi Cooper's little sister—everyone knew that except Levi. Connor knew Ned had gotten himself into a hole financially and was trying to dig out, and he knew that Jessica almost never said no to the chance to earn a little more money.

It didn't stop him from being irritatingly jealous. Ned got to see her every day. Here Connor was on a date with a woman who'd been planning her wedding since she was, according to her, a newborn, and Ned got to see Jessica in her pajamas. Maybe even in a towel.

"So was that your girlfriend?" Ned asked.

"Shut up."

Ned laughed. "Oh, you poor slob."

"Don't make me sic Levi on you, son."

The laughter stopped abruptly. "Sorry, dude."

They pulled up in front of Rushing Creek Retirement Home, the first vehicle on the scene. The truth was, Connor would rather be chasing down combative seniors than back on that date.

Nothing thrilled the residents more than a visit from Manningsport's first responders, so there was a crowd waiting.

"Oh, Ned's here! That's my great-grandson. Isn't he handsome! Hello, Neddy-Bear!" called Mrs. Holland. "And hello, Connor dear!"

"Hi, Goggy! What have you done this time?" Ned asked as they headed for the front door.

"Oh, it's not me, honey! It's Arlene Piller. She's naked and on the run. And armed."

"Armed?"

"With a cane."

The facility was set up on different floors and wings, depending on the level of care required. The Hollands were in the residential unit, which was basically a posh apartment complex. It went from there to people recovering from surgery, people with chronic medical conditions, a hospice unit, and the highest level of care, the dementia unit.

A grumpy staffer stood in the hall, holding an ice pack against his face. "She's in the conservatory. And she's stronger than she looks. Swinging like Derek Jeter. She hit three of us."

"What's her medical condition?" Connor asked.

"Well, she's older than the puppy God got as a child, and

she weighs about ninety pounds, but she's like a ninja with that cane. Dementia."

"Fun," Ned said. "Okay, we got this, right, Connor?"

"Hey, guys."

It was Jess.

"Got your lasso ready?" Ned asked. "She's already taken out three orderlies."

There was a crash from the conservatory, a great glass-domed structure. The smell of soil and humidity was rich in the air. A tiled walk led through the enormous room; it was one of the bigger selling points of Rushing Creek, and Connor could see why. Orchids—Bailey's favorite!—roses, even lilac trees were in bloom. There were orange and lemon trees, and Connor caught the scent of basil, chives and coriander. Good. Fresh herbs improved virtually every dish. Maybe he should teach a cooking class for seniors here.

"It's awfully quiet," Ned said. "Hold me, Jess, I'm scared."

"Be professional," Connor muttered. "Mrs. Piller?" he called. "It's Connor O'Rourke. I'm an EMT with the fire department. You doing okay?"

"Bite me!" came a creaky voice.

"What a sweet little old lady," Ned said.

"Con, you have such a way with the elderly," Jessica added.

"You're both so helpful," Connor muttered. "Mrs. Piller, you need to come back to your room, okay?"

"No! Not okay! Take a bite of this, mister!" With that, she shook her withered shanks from behind a potted palm.

"Oh, my Jesus. I'm too young for this," Ned said. "I'll get backup. Where's Levi, anyway?"

Actually, the rest of the emergency services department was standing in the conservatory entrance, shooting the shit and laughing, from the look of it. Levi, Emmaline, Gerard, Bryce Campbell, a few others Connor couldn't see. "Hey, Connor,"

Emmaline called. "You were first on the scene. You've got this, buddy."

"We're here if you need us," Levi seconded, grinning.

"Thanks," Connor said.

"I'm never going back!" Mrs. Piller yelled. "And you can't make me! I have a cane! I will hit you! I will hit you hard!"

Connor looked at Jess, who seemed to be enjoying herself. She was wearing a cute little white shirt and cropped jeans, canvas shoes on her feet.

As ever, the most beautiful thing he'd ever seen.

He was done with dating, he decided then and there. He'd rather be alone than with someone who wasn't Jess. He didn't want kids if she wasn't going to be their mother. He'd be Uncle Con, and a great brother to Savannah and Colleen, and Paulie Petrosinsky, for that matter.

The decision made him feel strangely lighter.

"Let's go get her," Jessica said.

"Don't you dare!" Mrs. Piller said. There was a rustle of leaves and a flash of bluish-white skin as she scurried from one tree to another.

"Mrs. Piller, we just want to make sure you're okay," Jessica said. "Can I come closer?"

"Only if you want a cane in your eye."

Connor grinned. Had to admire the old lady's spirit. "How about if we just hang out for a while?" he suggested. "Just the three of us."

"I don't trust women," came the answer.

"Me neither," he said, looking at Jess and feeling his mouth tug. "How about just us two, Mrs. Piller? You and me?"

There was a pause. "All right."

"Out you go, Jessica," he said.

"You sure? I don't want her to hurt you."

"I have a thing for women who hurt me, as you well know." She smiled in response, always a good sport.

"Good luck, you big hero," she said, and she left, closing the French doors behind her. "This is not a show, people," he heard her say to the rest of the squad. "Give me that phone, Ned."

Maybe Connor and Jess really could be friends. They'd known each other too long not to like each other anymore. If it felt like his heart was being ripped out of his chest every time he saw her, then so be it. Being friends with her was better than dating Not Jessica.

He walked slowly toward where he thought Mrs. Piller was. She was stroking the petals of an orchid, naked as the day she was born. Her knees were swollen with arthritis, and, well, gravity had taken its toll on just about everything. A wave of sympathy rolled over him. If this had been his grandmother, he'd want her to be treated with dignity.

"How was your day, Mrs. Piller?" he asked, walking slowly toward her.

"Call me Arlene. It wasn't my best," she said.

"Any reason?"

"I just… I get sick of needing people. I hate people."

"Me, too." She held her cane, but it seemed like her batting impulse was over. "Hi," he said, extending his hand. "Connor O'Rourke."

She didn't shake it. "That's a nice name. I'll still hit you if you try to catch me, but that's a fine Irish name."

"On behalf of my mother, thank you." She smiled at that. Didn't seem demented to him. He started unbuttoning his shirt. "How about if you put this on?" He shrugged out of it and offered it to her.

She looked him up and down. "Very nice."

"Thanks."

"Do you lift weights?" she asked, struggling to her feet.

"Sometimes. Let me help you with that." He pulled his shirt around her. Her hands were shaky with age or exertion; he buttoned it up, relieved not to have to see her naked anymore. Not because she was old…just because it was so personal. The shirt hung down to her knees, she was so tiny and frail.

"I suppose you're going to put me in a straitjacket and tie me into a wheelchair now."

"Not really my thing," he said. "But we could talk if you want."

"I'm too exhausted to run anymore. Go ahead, lock me up in this hellhole if you want."

"I'm good. Can you tell me where we are and what day it is?"

"We're in death's waiting room," she said, and Connor couldn't help a laugh.

"How about the town?" he asked.

"We're in Manningsport at Rushing Creek—there's no creek that I can see, by the way. And it's May something. In hell, all the days run together."

"Fair point. Any pain anywhere? Did you fall down or hurt yourself?"

"No."

"And as for being naked and running around the place, got an answer for that?"

"Because I hate being called *honey* by some know-it-all seventy years younger than I am. Thought I'd shake things up a little and rebel."

Connor laughed again.

"It's not funny, young man."

"It's pretty funny." She gave him a begrudging smile. He looked around. "I didn't expect to see so many flowers in hell. Even more than in my yard."

"Do you live in a nice place?"

She was lonely. And he could see it, having to come live here, maybe not by choice. Having staffers treat you with kindness, but maybe not respect. "My house is a two-family Victorian," he said. "It's got a nice front porch, and an apartment upstairs. I bought it because I wanted to marry a nice girl and have her brother live with us."

"She turned you down, did she?"

"She did. So now it's just me."

"You should get a dog."

"I'm thinking about it."

"I like dachshunds myself."

"They're okay."

"I suppose you like the big, manly breeds." She gave his torso another appreciative look. He smiled at her.

She sighed. "I'm ready to go back, Connor O'Rourke. Thank you for treating me like a person."

He stood up and offered his hand. "It was very nice meeting you. Maybe I can come back and visit you."

"Are you hitting on me, as you young people call it?"

"Would you have me?"

She laughed merrily. "No! You're young enough to be my great-grandson."

"Why don't you give me your cane and take my arm and appreciate how young and strong I am?" he said.

"You're quite the flirt."

"Only with women of a certain age."

"It's my lucky day, then," she said, and she handed over the cane and held on to his arm. He led her through the sunroom to where the onlookers were waiting.

"Mrs. Piller," began a nurse in a sharp tone.

"Arlene has had a hard day," Connor said.

"It got better when you stripped for her," Ned quipped, and everyone laughed, even Mrs. Piller. Connor winked at her and helped her into the wheelchair.

"I suppose you want your shirt back," she said.

"You keep it," he answered. "I'll get it when I come visit you."

Her eyes, surrounded by wrinkles and sagging skin, lit up like a little girl's at a birthday party.

Mrs. Piller was wheeled away, and Connor had the impression

she'd be something of a hero today, whacking the staff, streaking, flirting with a young stud such as himself.

"I can't wait to tell this story at our reunion next week," Gerard said. "Our valedictorian, slayer of hearts. Age not an issue."

Jessica handed him the top of a pair of scrubs. As usual, while everyone else was just taking up space, she'd been useful.

"That was very sweet," she said.

"Thanks." He pulled the shirt over his head.

Levi smacked him on the back. "Good job, Con. I'll fill out the paperwork on this, since you must be feeling dirty." More laughter. Connor smiled begrudgingly.

"You want a ride home, Connor?" Jessica asked.

Friends. He could do friends. "That'd be great."

It was no surprise to Jessica that Connor had been the hero of that little drama. He was good at things like...well...calming down drama. She drove toward his house, his wonderful cooking-and-soap smell filling her car, his arm just a few inches from hers.

Didn't manage to say a word. Then again, the drive was only two minutes.

She pulled up in front of his house.

"Thanks for the ride," he said, opening the door.

"I miss you," she said suddenly, and her heart banged in her chest. "Nothing has changed, but I want you to know that."

He looked at her for a long minute, his lashes so thick and curly that they were tangled in the corners. "Every time I think you can't break my heart again," he said, "you find a way."

The words were like a hot knife into her heart. "I don't mean to," she whispered.

"Which makes it even worse." He got out and leaned down to look at her again. "I still love you. That hasn't changed, either."

She looked at the steering wheel. *Don't you dare cry,* she told herself. *You'll only make it worse.*

"You were really great with that old lady," she said.

She could feel his eyes on her still. "Good night, Jess."

Then the door thudded closed, and she pulled away as carefully as she could, not looking in the rearview mirror, looking only ahead.

CHAPTER SIXTEEN

On Friday afternoon, Honor asked Jessica to come into her office. As always, Jess felt her stomach clench. "Close the door," Honor said, not smiling as she looked up. Spike, her little teacup Yorkie, snored from her little bed.

Jess swallowed. "What's up?" she asked, taking a seat.

"Take a look at this," Honor said, handing over a piece of paper.

It was a press release about Blue Heron and the planned expansion to clear four acres and put in a new grape varietal—Aromelia, the first new grape to come from Cornell in a few years. There were high hopes for the grape to do well; it was a hybrid, and Jack Holland, a Cornell alum, had consulted on its development. Pru had started clearing the land two weeks ago.

Jessica had the file on Aromelia. She'd interviewed Jack in March about the grape and had all her notes in a folder, as well as a draft of an article. It was on her calendar for next week—*finish Aromelia article and pitch to science editor at NPR.*

This article was solid and factual, if a little dry. And the contact name listed was Honor Barlow...not Jessica Dunn.

"Marcy wrote this," Honor said.

Jess looked up. "Why?"

"I was going to ask you that. She sent it out already."

"*What*?"

"She came in here earlier and said you were a little overwhelmed, so she'd taken the initiative. Are you, Jess?"

"No! This is on my calendar for next week. I have all my notes and everything." She didn't like the slightly terrified note in her voice.

"Marcy said she ran into an acquaintance from the *Times*. Pitched him the story, said it had to be done right then and there or we'd miss the window."

"So she sent this out without asking you?" *Or me?*

"Mm-hmm."

Jess would never have done that. Even with her new title, she would *never* have let something go out without Honor's approval. NPR and the *Times*? They were too big without a green light from the boss.

Marcy hadn't felt constrained in the least.

Jessica's face was hot.

"The thing is, the *Times* is going to run it." Honor folded her hands.

"Oh. I— That's great." Because yes, coverage in the *New York Times* was pretty damn impressive.

"I just wanted to check in," Honor said. "If you need help, or if you're swamped, I'd hope you'd tell me, Jessica. No one would think less of you."

Except of course they would. "I don't know why Marcy said that. I don't feel overwhelmed, and I never said anything to her. I barely see her. She seems very busy with her own duties, you know?"

That was certainly true. Marcy was constantly on her phone, the little earpiece like an appendage, parading down the hall with a bride or a vendor, constantly talking, talking, talking. Jess had begun playing classical music in her office to drown her out.

Jess took a breath. "What do you think about her, Honor?"

It was a risk, asking the boss about another employee. As soon as she said the words, she wished she hadn't.

Honor tipped her head. "Well…she's doing a really good job. Every event has gone like clockwork, and we've had great reviews and happy brides. There are a thousand details to keep track of, as you know, and I'm glad it's not my job anymore."

Jess nodded. Honor was way too classy to say anything negative.

"She's a little…much," she added, and Jess almost sagged with relief. "But she has a way with customers, especially brides. And I can't say I'm sorry we're being featured in the *Times*. But I did tell her all press goes through you. You might want to talk to her."

"Okay. Thanks."

She got up and went back down the hall, still feeling in the wrong, somehow. And shaken.

Marcy was out, probably interviewing vendors or trotting around with brides, since she was the type to micromanage… Jess had seen her at Lorelei's Sunrise Bakery the other day for a cake-tasting, and even the perpetually happy Lorelei looked a little frazzled.

But press was Jess's job.

An hour later, she heard Marcy coming down the hall. "I don't care what she says!" she was all but yelling into her Bluetooth. "If you want chrysanthemums, you've got them! Don't worry about it another microsecond, hon! I'm on it! Ciao!"

Jess opened her door. "Marcy, can I talk to you for a second?" she asked.

"Of course! I'm super-busy, but sure!" She came in and sat down, looking around her office. "You could really warm this place up, you know. I could help you if you're not good with interior decorating. It doesn't have to look like you're a temp here."

"I'm not a temp. I've been here more than a year. I just don't like clutter."

"Well, everyone has their own taste, I guess. What's up?"

Jessica sat behind her desk. "The *Times* piece."

"I know, right? Fabulous placement. I was so psyched, I kid you not. I mean, sure, Neil—the reporter?—he and I go way back, and the timing was perfect. Yay, Blue Heron!"

Jess nodded. "The thing is, I'm the media director here, and all press should go through me."

"Did Honor have a problem with the piece?"

"I don't think so. It was more how you handled—"

"So? What's the big deal? It's all good! We're all on the same team, aren't we?"

"Yes, but you don't need to do my job for me."

"Were you pitching the same story to the *Times*? I guess I missed that." She smirked. "Look, don't get your panties in a twist. I seized the moment, that's all. You have your hands full with that poor brother of yours."

Jessica felt her face freeze. "My brother is not poor. Nor is he any of your business."

"I'm just saying, you must be exhausted, taking care of him all the time, waitressing, all those extra jobs of yours."

Jess clenched her molars. "We're not having this conversation, Marcy."

"Fine. Sorry. Just concerned, that's all."

There was no further denying it. Marcy was a bitch.

Something occurred to her. "How did you even know about the new grape, Marcy?"

"Huh? I don't know. Ned, maybe? Pru? She and I had lunch the other day. What a hoot she is! Listen, I've got to go. I have a meeting in, like, thirty seconds." She stood up. "You're welcome, by the way. Getting a piece in the *New York Times* is pretty fucking amazing, in case you didn't know that."

With that, she left. Didn't close the door, either, which meant

Jessica had to get up and do it, or be subjected to that voice and those exclamation marks for the rest of the day.

Jess had dealt with mean girls her whole life. Somehow, they always surprised her, anyway.

She wished it didn't make her feel so nervous. And that Marcy hadn't scored so big with her first shot across the bow.

John Holland dropped in later that day, his baby grandson in his arms, Faith's golden retriever on his heels. "Say hello to Jessica, Noah," he said, making the baby wave at her.

Jess stood up. "Hi, handsome boy." The dog, thinking *he* was the handsome boy, came over and nudged her hand. Blue was something of a fixture here, and the dog had a point. He was as pretty as they came.

"Doesn't this baby look just like Faith?" Mr. Holland said. Jess smiled; this baby was a clone of Levi, and Faith was the first one to say it. "Your mommy was the most beautiful baby in the world," he told the infant. He looked at Jessica, his perpetual smile as much a trademark as the Blue Heron logo. "How are you, dear? I hear your father's back in town."

"He is, Mr. Holland."

"You can call me John, you know."

"I don't think I can, but thank you." She smiled. She wasn't sure if she was glad or not that he knew. Small town, though. No secrets.

"Is everything going all right on that front?"

"Seems to be." Keith had come over for dinner just last night. Ned had stayed home as backup, but everything had been fine, Keith engaging Davey about what movies he liked, if he liked working at the candle factory, what his favorite desserts were. He'd offered to stay and help clean up, but Jess had turned him down, and he'd left without a problem.

"If you need anything, let me know," Mr. Holland said. "Give him my regards."

The words were innocuous, but it was a threat. Gentle John Holland, making sure Keith Dunn knew he was being watched.

What would life have been like if Jess had had a father like this man, who was now blowing raspberries at his grandson? It was impossible to imagine. "Thanks, Mr. Holland."

"Are you going to the high school reunion tonight, Jess?" he asked.

Ugh. "I'm not sure," she said.

"Oh, you should! Everyone will be so happy to see you. Mrs. Johnson and I are babysitting so Levi and Faith can go." Noah started to fuss, and Mr. Holland turned him so he could pat his back. "All right, little boy. Let's take a walk so you can see the grapes, how's that? Come on, Blue. Have fun tonight, Jessica dear."

On the short drive home, Jessica thought about the reunion. She'd bought a ticket; Theresa DeFilio was in charge of it, and no one could say no to her. She was just too nice.

But if she went, there'd be the Jessica Does references. The mean girls giving her looks and whispering, same as high school. The guys, checking her out, irritating their wives.

More than half her class had moved away after graduation. Some had gone off to college and jobs, and then come back—Faith, Levi, Colleen, Connor, Jeremy, Gerard, Tanner Angst. That type had seen her a lot these years, waiting tables at Hugo's, doing the home health aide work in the winters, and most recently, at Blue Heron. They'd seen her taking care of her brother, seen her move from the trailer park to the rented house.

But the others would still see her as Jessica Does, class slut. Trailer park trash.

"Ah, screw it," she said aloud. "I'm going."

Ned was happy to stay home, since she deducted his babysitting fees from his rent; besides, Sarah had finals and had warned him not to come anywhere near her, so he had no problem watching *Thor 2* and making popcorn with Davey.

Jess opened her little closet and pulled out the best dress she had—a simple sleeveless white knit. She'd worn it to the Black & White Ball last year, and Honor said she looked like a supermodel. Black high heels. Little gold hoops. She put her hair up in a French twist, brushed on some blush and took a look at herself in the mirror.

In another year, she'd own a house. She'd have a front porch with hanging baskets bursting with petunias and sweet potato vine and lobelia. There would be pretty ceramic tiles featuring the house number. She'd have a porch swing, damn it. She'd already come a long way from West's Trailer Park.

"You smell nice," Davey said as she kissed him good-night.

"I would also like a kiss," Ned said. She smacked his head instead and drove across town.

The gym looked and smelled the same as all gyms in all high schools across America, more or less. Low lights, a few tables with candles, a DJ in the corner.

"Jessica!" Jeremy Lyon said, kissing her on both cheeks, as if she hadn't just seen him at Hugo's yesterday. "What have you been up to since graduation?"

"I invented Facebook," she said, grinning. "And you?"

"I'm a gay." He pulled a face, then put an arm around his boyfriend. "See?"

"Hi, Patrick. Yes, I seem to remember you coming out, since I was at your unwedding."

"So you were. You probably remember it better than I do. It was a blur of terror for me."

Shockingly, there were actually people who hadn't heard about Jeremy "turning gay," so that was one story making the rounds. Faith, who'd been engaged to the guy, was also squealed over by those who didn't know she'd married Levi.

Other stories were Tiffy Ames, who'd left the military and invented a computer program that did something so complicated that Jess would need another master's degree to understand it.

But she and Tiffy hugged tight; they came from the same place, and Jess was truly happy for her old friend.

"What's your house like?" Jess asked. Once upon a time, when they were kids playing in the creek behind the trailer park, they'd talked about where they'd live someday.

"It's on the water in Santa Barbara. Jess, you have to visit me. Please, please visit me."

"I would love that," she said. It was hard to imagine going to California, but what a nice visual!

"What about your place?" Tiffy asked.

Jess shrugged. "It's on Academy Street. We're getting there. Renting now, plans to buy next year."

"You'll invite me over when you're in, won't you?" Tiffy asked. She looked fantastic; no longer too thin, better dressed, her hair no longer bleached white-blond.

"Of course I will," Jess said. She held out her phone and took a selfie of the two of them. "Look at us. We're awesome."

"We are!" Tiffy said. "We should be the trailer-park poster children. Speaking of that, there's Levi. I gotta go squeeze those biceps." She laughed, then went to say hi to their old friend.

Jess sipped a glass of wine from a plastic cup and hung back a little, just watching. Funny, how things never changed that much. Colleen, the most popular girl in high school, was the most popular girl at the reunion. Her stomach was getting a lot of pats, and Lucas, who'd graduated with them but had only moved to Manningsport in their senior year, was having his back slapped a lot. Levi and Jeremy were still best friends. Bryce Campbell, the class pretty boy, was dating Paulie Petrosinsky, who'd worshipped him back then. Theresa DeFilio was still taking care of everyone, making sure people had wine, talking to the caterers.

People whipped out their phones to show pictures of their kids, bragging about their jobs or glossing over things they didn't want to discuss.

And yes, some people—women all—shot looks her way. She returned the looks steadily. Not everyone had aged that well; Tanya Cross had gained at least a hundred pounds, and Carleen Krasinsky had dyed her hair black and gone the "too big for nature" breast implant route.

But she couldn't see Connor anywhere. She hoped he hadn't stayed away because of her.

The DJ was playing "Rock Your Body" by Justin Timberlake, and a fair number of people were dancing, Faith and Jeremy taking up lots of room, since Jer was a terrible dancer and flailed like he was being electrocuted. Colleen and Lucas were looking far better, Colleen's pregnancy only making her look more beautiful. Bryce and Paulie were laughing. So cute, those two. Theresa DeFilio and her nice husband, slow dancing despite the up-tempo song.

"Jessica *Does*!" boomed a voice, and Big Frankie Pepitone put his arm around her.

That fucking name. "Hey, Frankie," she said.

"You still are *incredibly* hot," Frankie said.

"Since last week when I saw you last?"

He gave her a one-armed hug. "Remember the time we did it in my rec room?"

"Barely. Is your wife here?"

"Nah. She'd be bored. So what's up, Jess?"

"Hey, Jess," said someone else. Jake Green, one of the ones who'd left and never come back. He hadn't been nice back in high school, and he still looked like the entitled brat he'd been back then.

Yes, she'd slept with him, too.

"We havin' a party over here?" Chris Eckbert, who'd been like a puppy dog to Jake. "Jess! Good to see you. Happy, happy memories."

And she'd slept with him, too.

Mark Renner came over, too, looking much the same as he

had in high school. Another football player, and yep, him, too. "How you doin', Jess?"

"Mark. Nice to see you again."

Her charms, for lack of a better word, had worked on Frankie and Mark. They'd befriended Davey, and with two giant football players calling him *buddy*, Davey hadn't been picked on as much. Most guys had been good investments. Tanner Angst and Chris had been mediocre. And Jake…not at all. He'd been a waste, and one of her few miscalculations.

"You still a slut, Jess?" Jake asked now.

Great. He was already drunk. "No, I joined a convent after learning I had syphilis. And you are…?" Let him think she forgot him. He'd been forgettable, that was for sure.

"Jake Green. Bet I could convince you to go back to your slutty ways."

"You'd lose that bet." *Ass.*

"Jess, I for one want to say thank-you," Frankie said. "You sure made high school a lot more fun."

"And I'd like to thank you, Frankie. For looking out for Davey. You, too, Mark."

"Oh, man, yeah!" Mark said. "How is he?"

"He's great." See? It had been a fair trade. And now with the advantage of maturity, Jess could see that if she'd just asked Mark and Big Frankie to look out for her brother back then, they probably would've said yes just because they were nice.

"Tell the little dude I said hi, okay?" Mark said.

"I will. Thanks."

"Let's go somewhere," Jake slurred. "I'll make sure you remember me."

"Shut up, ass-hat," Frankie sighed. "You never could handle your booze."

"I'm fine here," Jessica said.

"Well, maybe I'll follow you home. We can party."

Did people still say that? "No, thanks."

"You think you're too good for me now? Trailer-park trash turned ice queen? We'll see about that."

And then Jake was on the floor, holding his hand over his mouth, which had just been soundly punched by Connor.

Oh, boy.

"Get up," Connor growled.

Immediately, there was a crowd around them. Jake stayed where he was.

"Get up so I can beat the shit out of you," Connor said.

"This is really unnecessary, Connor," she said, putting a hand on his arm. He glanced at her. Oh. He was *furious.* Was it wrong to be a little turned on? Probably. Still, though. He looked… Damn. "It's fine. Jake's just an ass, same as ever."

"He threatened you." Connor looked back at Jake. "Get up, Green."

Jake stood up. Great. "Fight," someone said rather cheerfully. Where was Levi? Why was there never a cop around when you needed one?

"You're gonna fight me over this whore?" Jake asked, and then Connor hit him again, and Jake staggered back, then swung at Connor.

Jess threw up her hands. "Stop it, please. Frankie, can you do something?"

"Are you kidding? Jake earned this."

"I always hated Jake Green," Colleen said. "Lucas, remember him?"

"I do. If Connor needs any help, I'm here. Also available for body disposal later on."

"Oh, stop! You know I love when you get all gangster on me."

"Does *anyone* care that they're fighting?" Jessica asked. Connor landed a nice hit to the ribs, and Jake grunted. "Jeremy? Nothing?"

"Doctor's hands," Jeremy said, holding them out. "It's a liability thing. Plus, I never could stand Jake."

"Where's Levi?" Jess asked.

"He stepped out to call my dad and check on the baby," Faith said. Connor took a hit to the face, then gave a rather beautiful right cross, knocking Jake right on his ass.

"Okay, that's enough," Jessica said. "Gerard! Get over here and drive Jake to his parents' place. I assume that's where you're staying, dumb-ass?"

Jake nodded sullenly, and Gerard hauled him to his feet and led him to the door. "Save me a dance, Jess," he said, grinning.

Right. There was dancing. The DJ put on a slow song—"Angel" by Dave Matthews—and couples began drifting out to the dance floor.

Connor was still bristling with anger.

"Come on, Connor, let's dance." She took his hand and pulled him to the middle of the gym. Put her hand on his shoulder, feeling the heat and hard muscle there. "That was really unnecessary," she said.

"I just defended your honor. Thanks would be nice." He wasn't looking at her, but his hand was on her waist, making her breath catch a little.

"My honor is beyond defending." His lip was bleeding. Just a little. She wiped it away with her fingertip. "I can handle the idiots, you know."

His blue eyes dropped to meet hers. Then he kissed her.

Aside from Dave Matthews, it sure was quiet all of a sudden.

Well, there went the whole secret thing. She almost cared.

Connor was *kissing* her. She tasted a little wine, and maybe a little blood, and his mouth was firm and hot and he was a little mad, and the kiss wasn't gentle. It was a statement of possession, and her insides pulled in a strong, hot squeeze.

He broke the kiss, then rested his forehead against hers.

Her heart was shuddering. Legs shaking.

"I'm going to make your brother love me," he said, and she laughed, because it was just *not* what she expected him to say. "I mean it, Jess. And you're gonna let me. I love you. I don't want to be apart anymore. I—"

"Okay, fine, you win," she said shakily. "Don't make yourself look any more ridiculous than you already have."

He kissed her again, more gently this time, and her fingers found their way into his thick, wavy hair. "You're not easy, Jessica Dunn," he murmured against her mouth. "You are not easy."

"Actually, I am. That's the problem."

He looked so sure, but her worries were already off to the races. What would happen when they were really together, and there was no chase anymore, and their everyday lives consisted of Davey and work and things like furnaces breaking and needing a new car? What would happen when he actually had her?

"Stop worrying so much," he whispered. He pulled her closer, going for the eighth-grade shuffle, and the feeling of his warm, hard body pressed against hers, slightly sweaty from the fight, made her insides light up in flashes.

Connor let his hand drop to just above her ass. "If I'd known a punch in the mouth would get me to this moment," he murmured, "I would've had Colleen hit me a long time ago."

Connor leaned against the brick wall of his old high school, waiting for Jess to make the call. The reunion was over; Connor was thanked and congratulated by quite a few classmates for beating the snot out of Jake, who'd always been a complete turd of a human.

"You kids have a fun night," Colleen said, lifting an eyebrow. *I told you she was the one.*

It's not like it's news, Dog-Face.

"Nice job beating on the little shit," Lucas said.

Connor nodded. His knuckles stung. He didn't mind a bit.

But now he was going to take his woman home and make love to her.

Finally.

Jessica was talking on her phone. “So you sure you don’t mind? I’ll be back by… Yes. Uh, yeah. How did you… Oh. Gotcha. All right. Thanks, Ned.”

She clicked off her phone and slid it into her purse. “We’re not quite the secret I thought we were,” she said.

“Sneaking around had its moments,” he said. *Had*. He was done with that.

She nodded. Didn’t say anything else.

Shy again. After all these years, even though it was only him.

“You want to walk home, Jess?”

“Okay.”

He offered his hand, and after a second’s hesitation, she took it. “Connor—”

“No more rules, Jess. No more lists. Okay? Let’s just be together.” He kissed her hand and started walking.

The town was quiet, and they didn’t talk. He couldn’t remember being happier, but she was nervous, holding his hand a little too tightly, not looking at him.

They came to the Village, and rather than cut across the green, he steered her toward the little park at the foot of the lake. Since the town rolled up the sidewalks by eleven, it was quiet now, just a few customers still in O’Rourke’s. The leaves of the maples sighed in the breeze, and a night bird called, then was silent.

Jess reached down and slipped off her shoes and took a few steps out onto the dock. Her white dress glowed in the moonlight, and she didn’t say anything as she looked out at the lake.

She was still nervous. It was oddly flattering.

He followed her out onto the dock, put his arms around her and pulled her back against his chest. Didn’t say anything, just breathed in the clean smell of her hair.

More than anything, he wanted to reassure her that everything would be all right. Wanted to tell her how beautiful she was, that he’d take care of her and never let her down, that she could trust him.

He kissed her neck instead, and rested his forehead on her shoulder.

"I forgot to ask," she said. "Did you talk to anyone about your brewery tonight?"

"No."

"Why? Tiffy Ames is—"

"Because I could only think about you."

She turned to face him, her expression unreadable in the moonlight. An owl called from not too far away.

Her mouth was soft and sweet under his, and he cupped her head with both hands and kissed her until she was melted against him, her arms around his neck, her fingers in his hair, and when a little moan came from her throat, it almost felled him.

"Let's go home," he said, and she nodded.

His house didn't feel so generic with her in it. The second the door was closed, he kissed her again, pushing her against the wall, lust tearing through him. *Go slow, go slow,* the last thinking part of his brain said, and he tried. Sort of. He failed.

He was starving for her, and she wasn't pulling any punches, either. Mouth, tongue, teeth, all in a greedy feast of flesh. She wasn't being sweet now, no, sir, and thank God for that. She shoved his jacket off, yanked his shirt out of his waistband and slid her cool hands up his hot sides, then went to the button of his pants.

He stopped her, pinning her hands by the sides of her face, and lowered his mouth to her neck. God, she tasted good, so many layers of flavor, the lemony soap, a hint of perfume, the taste of her skin itself. He released her hands and slid them down her sides, then up her front to cup her breasts. No bra, God, thank you. His thumbs teased over her nipples, and she bit down on his lip, reminding him of the hit he'd taken there earlier. Then her mouth opened and their tongues slid together, and his thigh was between hers, pressing hard, her dress riding up, and he was practically blind with lust now, just flares of light and the feeling of Jessica.

"Take your hair down," he rasped, and she stepped away from him and reached to the back of her head. Her hair slid down around her shoulders, swinging, catching the faint light from the street.

Then she reached down, grabbed the hem of her dress and pulled it over her head in one glorious move.

No bra. White lace panties.

Black high heels.

He'd die if he waited any longer. With one quick move, he scooped her up, all that silken skin, her hair as cool as water, and carried her to the living room and dumped her unceremoniously on the couch, falling on top of her.

She was laughing now, and the sound…the sound just told him what he already knew.

He loved Jessica Dunn.

He always had.

CHAPTER SEVENTEEN

"Look at that smile. You're gross."

Connor looked up at his sister. "Now you know how I feel about you and Lucas."

"So she finally took pity on you, huh?"

"Yep." Quite a few times over the past five days, as a matter of fact. He grinned.

"Stop smiling! You're disgusting. Congratulations."

"Thank you."

It was nine o'clock on Wednesday morning, and they were in O'Rourke's kitchen. Connor was working on the paella, a spicy New Orleans–inspired dish with shrimp, scallops, crawfish tails, mussels, chorizo, roasted red peppers, red onion and garlic, and the smell was making him nearly drunk. He also had to start the soup, which would be French onion, because it was cold and rainy today, and he'd guess they'd sell out of both.

Colleen was taking up space. More and more these days. "You feeling okay?" he asked.

"I guess so. Kind of uncomfortable."

"Got her name picked out yet?"

"You're so sure it's a girl, aren't you?" She smiled. "We want the name to be a surprise."

"And yet you'll tell your big brother."

"So Lucas thinks she'll be Amelia, but I was thinking it'd be nice to name her after his mom. Isabelle. She died when he was little."

"That's beautiful, Dog-Face."

She scowled at him. "I barely recognize you. You're all cheerful and nice. It's freaky. But listen, as long as you're on a roll, and don't be mad at me, because I'm pregnant and have horrible heartburn and you have to pity me. Dad's coming in this morning to see you."

"Why?"

"He has something to tell you."

"What?"

"Let him tell you. I have to pee. This baby must have both knees right on my bladder. Besides, Dad just walked in. Bye. Be nice."

She left, and Connor growled. Felt a pang of sympathy heartburn, which irritated him. He finished cutting the shrimp, then the sausage, then tossed them into the pot. Washed his hands carefully, twice. Wiped down the counter. He didn't mind making his father wait in the least.

Then, with a sigh, he went into the restaurant. Pete was sitting at a table. "Hey, son," he said, standing up. "How are you?"

"Fine. How are you?" Completely polite.

"Sit down, sit down." His father gave him that laser-white smile. Connor waited.

"So. Uh, things are good? Colleen says you're starting a brewery? That's wonderful. Can I do anything to help?"

"No, thanks."

"Well, if you change your mind, or need financing, or... I'm here."

Connor waited some more. Being the quiet twin had its advantages.

Pete O'Rourke took a deep breath. "I have some news. Good news, I think. Well, no, it's definitely good news. Um... Gail is pregnant. It's a boy this time."

So that was why Gail looked like hell lately.

Connor waited to feel something. Nothing came.

He'd be thirty-three years older than this kid. Old enough to be the father. His father, odds were, would be dead by the time the kid graduated from college. Gail the Tail was pushing forty herself.

Oddly, the only thing he felt was pity.

"Best wishes," he said.

"Son, I just want you to know that you'll always be—"

"I'm not ten. There's no need for a pep talk. I'll be a good brother."

"I already know that." Pete looked at him, with difficulty, it seemed. "Connor, it's just that ever since Savannah was born, there's been this distance between us."

"The distance was there long before Savannah. You just didn't notice."

"It seems to have gotten worse."

"Well, yeah. Come on, Dad. You made a laughingstock out of my mother. The middle-aged man with a hot babe on the side, proving his virility by getting her pregnant."

"But Gail and I have been married for almost eleven years now. Even your mother has found someone else. She's even getting married again. And I'm a good father to Savannah, aren't I?" The question wasn't boasting. He wanted an answer.

"You are," Connor conceded. "Listen, I have work to do. Congratulations on the baby. I hope everything goes well."

"That's it?"

"Did you think there'd be more?"

Pete looked at the table. "I guess not."

"I'm not trying to punish you, Dad," Connor said. "I just don't want anything from you."

His father flinched. "Got it."

Connor stood up and went back into the kitchen. Through the window, he could see his father, sitting at the table for another minute before getting up to leave.

Did Pete think they were going to toss a ball around? Go camping together? They hadn't done that when Connor was ten.

It was strange, therefore, that he felt an unsettling sense of guilt all the same.

Jessica left Blue Heron for lunch, something she didn't often do. "I hear you're sleeping with my son," Jeanette said as Jess went through the tasting bar.

"Oh...hi, Jeanette." Jess felt the blush creep up from her chest.

"I approve, don't worry," the other woman said. "Hey, I just had a thought. Would you like to be one of my bridesmaids? Colleen's my matron of honor, and Paulie's a bridesmaid, and Carol Robinson was saying that older women never get to be in wedding parties, so she's in, too. What do you say? It'd be nice to have my son's girlfriend here. Maybe you two will be next." She beamed at Jessica and raised her eyebrows.

Oh, God. What had Connor been telling people? Jess took a steadying breath. "What a nice offer, Jeanette." She'd never been a bridesmaid before, but serving at Jeanette's...it was an odd thought. A sweet thought, too.

"Guess what!" Marcy burst in the front door, shaking the rain from her hair like a puppy. "I just got John Holland approved as justice of the peace! Is that freaking genius or what? People can have the *owner* of the *vineyard* perform their ceremony! What a fantastic idea! I can't believe I didn't think of it before! High five, Jeanette! Hey, you want him to do you and the Chicken King?"

"Oh, what a great idea! Our daughters are best friends, after all."

It *was* a good idea. "Nice job," Jessica said. She'd give credit where it was due. Who wouldn't want John Holland performing the ceremony? Marcy was right.

Since the press release, Marcy had been doing more and more PR. Well, she'd been trying to. She suggested events for the vineyard, though none of them had been green-lighted; at this point in the year, the calendar was full with everything from a full-moon ride in a horse-drawn wagon to Wags and Wine, a pet show/wine tasting. Again, all Jess's domain, all firmly under control, all proven successes.

But at this week's staff meeting, Marcy had spoken up again. "I don't know if you do this kind of thing, but it might be really motivational if we hosted a sales retreat this fall," Marcy had said, going on to suggest contests and prizes for those who sold the most wine at the tasting bar, opened new accounts in stores and restaurants, came up with new promotions for the vineyard. "If it's in the budget, we could have a weekend retreat at a nice resort, or down in the city, complimentary massages or tickets to a show."

It was a great idea, and one that Jessica actually considered, as well. Almost to the letter. She'd outlined the idea about six months ago, but held off; a lot of companies did this kind of thing, but it was expensive, too, and the vineyard had taken a bit of a hit with all the snow last winter.

But Honor had considered it, asked a few questions and made a note on her iPad, all while Jessica mentally chastised herself for not going ahead with it. The worst they could say was no; she shouldn't have been so hesitant.

Well. That was water under the bridge, and Jess had a big lunch meeting today. Her, Davey...and Connor.

She got to Keuka Candle Factory where Davey and about ten other people worked, packing cardboard boxes with the different variety of candles.

"Hi, Jess!" called Petra, the manager.

"Hi, Jess!" Davey echoed. He ran over and hugged her.

"Oh, you smell good," she said, kissing his cheek. "What flavor is that?"

"Woolly Sweater," he said proudly.

"Yummy. You ready for lunch?"

They drove to the nearest Chicken King franchise, since A) the food was amazing, if loaded with cholesterol, and B) Connor's mother was marrying the owner, and it made Jeanette happy to hear Jess was going there, and also, C) Davey did better controlling his outbursts if he was in public.

Because an outburst would surely be coming.

Today was the day she was telling Davey about Connor. And yes, she was afraid. That time when Chico Three was a puppy, Davey had put the fear of God into her. It had been his worst outburst ever. Last fall, he'd had another one when he'd seen Connor at the grocery store one night and Connor helped Jess by reaching for something on the top shelf. That rage storm hadn't been as bad, but still pretty dreadful; she'd had to drag him out of the store, then go back the next day to pay for all the bananas and apples Davey had thrown, only to find that Connor had already taken care of it.

And now Davey had to be brought into the picture, because… well, because there was no way around it.

Shit. Just the thought made her knees wobble. He'd been so betrayed the last time, unable to believe that his sister had been sitting with the enemy in his own house. Thank God he hadn't seen them making out. It had taken him weeks to forgive her.

The rain was really coming down when they pulled into the Chicken King. She and Davey ran inside. As planned, they were here first, and Connor would come when she texted him that she'd broached the subject.

There was only one other person at the counter, since it was early yet.

"Dad!" Davey said, bounding over. Well, that was a coincidence. Hard to avoid in a town of fewer than a thousand people, but still.

"Hey! My two favorite kids!" he said, hugging Davey. "Hi, Jessie."

"Here's your Born on the Bayou Louisiana Rub," said the girl behind the counter, handing over a bag that was already staining with grease.

"Are you here to eat with us?" Davey asked. "You should eat with us! Please, Dad! Please!"

Keith looked at her. Eyes still clear, no alcohol odor, no tremor in the hand. Davey had grabbed Keith's free hand and was swinging it, chanting "Stay, stay, stay."

"Okay," Jessica said, surprising herself. "Um, Davey, look at the menu and decide what you want." She stepped away a few paces, her father following her.

"Are you sure?" he asked.

"Actually, yes. I have to tell Davey something that will upset him, and maybe it's good that you're here."

Her father's eyes lit up at the chance of being helpful. "Okay. Sure. What is it?"

She twisted the silver ring on her thumb. "I have a boyfriend."

His face softened. "Oh, Jessie, that's great."

"Davey's not going to think so."

"Why?"

"It's Connor O'Rourke."

Her father shook his head. "From the restaurant… Oh. Right! Chico bit him, didn't he?"

Mauled was a better word. Nearly killed. "Yes. And Davey thinks Connor killed Chico, more or less."

"Really?"

Jess bit down on a surge of impatience. "Yes. Things are very black-and-white for him. He was five when it happened, and it's practically carved in stone in his memory. All he remembers is that Mr. O'Rourke and Connor came over, and then Chico was taken away and died."

"Shit. I barely remember that myself."

"No, you were drunk at the time."

He flinched a little. "You're right. Well, maybe I can help now."

"The thing is, when he gets upset, he gets violent. And he's not a little boy anymore."

"Can I have Triple Batter Crunch, Jess?" Davey called. "And extra onion rings?"

"Get whatever you want, hon."

Keith's face was solemn. "Thanks for this, Jessie. For letting me help."

She sighed. "I hope it works." She got a plain chicken sandwich. She actually loved Chicken King food, but her stomach was jumpy. She then sat down at a table across from Davey and her father. Keith asked Davey questions, keeping things light, and Davey tore into his meal like a starved Viking.

"So Davey," Jess began. "I wanted to talk to you about something."

"I love chicken," he said. "They make it thirty-eight delicious different ways." He could quote all the commercials. "Joo-Joo Haitian Spice, Sweet Home Alabama Fire, Better than Grandma's Bacon Lard with Biscuits—"

"So, the thing is, sweetie, I…uh… There's a guy I like. And I want him to be my boyfriend."

He took another bite. "That's nice."

Keith raised his eyebrows at her. So far, so good, he seemed to be saying. He obviously had no idea what was about to happen.

"He's really nice," Jess said. "He likes animals, especially dogs. His sister has a big, funny dog, and he likes kids, too. He has a little sister and he plays baseball with her."

"Can I have your corn?"

She passed him the ear, dripping with butter. The Chicken

King's mission seemed to be to shorten lives. "So he'd like to meet you. Actually, he already knows you a little bit."

"Who knows me?"

"The guy I'm dating."

"Oh. Okay."

And now for the hard part. "The thing is, you might think at first that he's not nice, but he really is."

"Who is it?"

She took a deep breath. "It's Connor. Connor O'Rourke."

Davey blinked. A second later, he stopped chewing. "But he killed Chico One."

"No, he didn't, actually," Keith said, looking at Jessica for permission. She gave a little nod. "Chico was a bad dog that day. He bit Connor. Hard."

"So Connor *killed* him." Davey's voice rose.

"No, no, he didn't, honey," Jess said.

"He came to our house and they took Chico One away and Chico died! He killed Chico One!"

"It was my fault that Chico got off his chain," Jessica said. "So it was my fault that Connor got bitten. And when a dog bites a kid, they can't—"

Unfortunately, that was when Connor came in. Early. He was supposed to wait, damn it. "Hey, guys," he said.

"Get out!" Davey screeched. He grabbed his cardboard container of lunch and flung it at Connor, who ducked, chicken wings raining down behind him. "Go away!"

Keith put his arm around Davey's shoulders. "Settle down, Davey. Come on, now."

"Get out! You can't be here!" Davey said, furious tears spurting out of his eyes. Jess felt her own throat tighten.

"Davey, listen to me," she said, gripping his hand across the table. "I wouldn't be friends with someone who was mean to dogs, would I? I love dogs. I loved Chico One, and I loved Chico

Two, and I'm crazy about Chico Three. Right? You know that. I wouldn't let anyone hurt a dog."

"You let him take Chico One. *You* brought Chico One to the mean men." He started sobbing.

Oh, God. It was true, of course. Her throat locked with tears.

"Listen, Davey," Keith said, turning his son's face toward him. He took a napkin and blotted his tears. "Chico One did a bad thing. Mommy and I, we should've kept a better eye on him. You might not remember, but Chico One only liked us. He chased Connor and bit him, and when dogs bite someone like that, they have to…go to heaven."

Davey put his head on the table and wailed, and Jess felt her heart crack.

Keith stood to greet Connor. He gestured him over and shook his hand. "Hi, I'm Keith. Jessica's father. You must be the nice guy she's dating." He spoke clearly; the *nice guy* was obviously meant for Davey, who didn't look up.

Connor glanced at Jess, then looked at her father. "We've met before."

"Right, right. Of course. It's good to see you again."

"He's *not* nice," Davey said without looking up. His skinny shoulders shook. Jess swallowed, hard.

"He seems nice to me," Keith said. "Want to sit down, Connor?"

Davey looked up, his eyes darting between their father and Connor, his long lashes clumped together with tears. He looked utterly, wretchedly confused. Jess's stomach twisted. This wasn't fair. Things that were true for Davey stayed true. It spared him a lot of heartache in life, because when he thought of Dad, for example, he remembered the father who loved him. That Dad had left for eight years didn't matter; Dad loved him, the end.

And Connor was bad, the end.

She hated that he looked so lost.

Connor sat down and took her hand under the table and squeezed it. "Hey, Davey."

Davey's mouth tightened. "I want to go home."

"I'd really like to get to know you," Connor went on. "Jess loves you so much. She talks about you all the time."

"Shut up!"

"And I want you to know I never meant for Chico One to… go away."

"I hate you!" He banged both fists on the table. "Leave me alone! Jess! Make him go away!"

"This isn't working," Jess whispered. "Maybe you should go."

Connor looked at her. Scrubbed a hand across his jaw. "Okay. I'll call you later." He got up, touched her hair, then walked out.

He didn't even get to eat.

"Connor," her father called. "We'll see you again soon."

Connor waved and went out into the rain.

CHAPTER EIGHTEEN

One thing was clear to Connor—Davey Dunn was excellent at manipulation.

If the decision was left to Jessica, Connor would never darken their door again. She was used to caving to her brother. Con understood.

This would be just the two of them. Time to cut out the middle man, or in this case, the middle woman.

After lunch, he went back to O'Rourke's, cooked up five shepherd's pies with mashed potatoes so creamy they would make angels weep, did a few quick meatloaves from veal, pork and beef and made a vegan dish that could be served with regular or gluten-free pasta. Then he handed the control over to Rafe and said, "I'll be back in an hour."

"Hey," Jordan breathed from behind the bar.

"Hey, Jordan. Be back soon." The girl blushed and overfilled a mug of lager.

He drove up to Keuka Candle, which was a low industrial building just over the hill toward Dundee. Sat in his car for a few minutes, then went inside.

There was Davey, amiably chattering to a dark-haired girl

next to him, the trauma of lunch past, now that he'd gotten what he wanted. Yep. Manipulative. Oh, he might not know it, but he was just the same.

"Hey, Connor," said Petra, who managed the place and was a regular at O'Rourke's. "What's cookin', good-lookin'? Get it? Since you're a chef?"

"Yeah. Never heard that one before." She smiled. "Can I talk to Davey Dunn for a few minutes?"

"What it'll get me?"

"Nachos on the house?"

"Deal. Davey, over here, hon!" Davey looked up and, seeing Connor, his expression darkened. "He doesn't like you, does he?" Petra murmured.

"I'm dating Jessica."

"Ah. Davey, you be chill, you hear me?" Petra said. She took a few steps away to help one of the workers.

"What do you *want*?" Davey demanded, his fists clenched at his sides.

"I want to date your sister, and I need your permission."

"No, no, nope, never. I *hate* you."

"I understand that. But you're the man of the house, aren't you?"

Davey hesitated.

"You look after your sister. Right?"

"Yes," he said, though he sounded unsure.

"So I need your permission."

"Why don't you just go die?" Davey folded his arms, seeming rather pleased at his comeback.

"That was very rude." Connor glanced over Davey's shoulder. "Would that girl like hearing you say something like that?"

"What girl?"

"The one who's watching you. The pretty one."

Davey glanced back at the girl he'd been talking to. "Miranda?"

Bingo.

"Yeah. Miranda. I bet she likes nice guys, not rude boys." Davey scowled. "Look, Dave," Connor continued. "Your sister loves you. She loves you way more than she loves me, I know that. And that will never change. But I want to take her to the movies and come over sometimes. And I want her to come to my house sometimes."

"No."

"Just the way I bet you'd like to have Miranda come over and watch movies. And be your girlfriend."

Davey's face flushed. "She's not my girlfriend."

"Dude, we're all the same, us guys. She's cute. You like her. Don't you?"

Another scowl.

"Have you cooked for her yet? Girls like when a guy cooks for them." As Connor well knew.

"No! I can't cook!"

"Why?"

"Because!" Davey yelped. "I might hurt myself. Jessica doesn't let me even use the toaster."

That seemed extreme. The kid had a job, after all, and toasters weren't rocket science. "Guess what? I know how to cook. I'm a chef."

"I bet you're a *horrible* chef."

"You like the nachos at O'Rourke's? And the chili?"

"Duh," he answered. "They're great."

"I make those." Davey blinked in surprise, and Connor almost smiled. "You want a girl to like you, you have to cook for her."

"I didn't know that."

"And yet it's true."

Davey mulled that over. "Jessica won't let me cook, because I might get hurt."

Well, shit. It wasn't as if Connor had too many aces in his pocket. If Jess put the smackdown on this idea, he'd have to fold.

"I'll teach you to be safe," he said. "And you know what? It can be our secret, and then you can surprise Miranda *and* your sister by making her a cake or nachos sometime. How would that be? When you get really good, you could cook dinner a couple times a week and not have Jess always make it for you. Be the man of the house, you know?"

He didn't answer. Glanced back at Miranda.

"What do you say, Dave? Is it a deal?"

Still no answer. Davey might have a low IQ, but he wasn't dumb.

"Also, I need to pick out a dog," Connor said, throwing the Hail Mary pass. "And I was thinking you could help me find the right one."

"Will you kill it?"

Connor rolled his eyes. "No. Now, do you want to help me or not?"

When Jessica got home from work that day, she really just wanted to go to bed.

Or have a glass of wine. A normal person could have a glass of wine; she couldn't. Pity.

Chico Three would have to do as stress relief. He was up for the job, whining and wagging his whiplike tail, pushing his big head against her legs. "Hello, Chico," she said, kneeling down to pet him. "Who's a good dog? You? You are? I've heard that about you." She kissed the dog's head and scratched behind his ears.

He looked a lot like Chico the Original. No wonder it was hard for her brother.

At least Davey hadn't been worse at the restaurant today. She had to give her father credit. And that, too, was a dangerous thought.

She changed out of her work clothes and went to her computer. Did a quick bank-balance check; everything was still there.

She and her father had never talked about the credit card thing, but she'd been changing her banking password and PIN number every week since he'd been back.

While she was at the computer, she typed in *houses for sale, Manningsport, NY.* Another relaxation device in lieu of wine—real estate fantasy.

She didn't want a fixer-upper, though that was what she could afford at this moment. But she didn't have the skills needed to overhaul a place, even though she loved the shows on HGTV that featured people sledgehammering through walls. And she already had two jobs, though she was only taking two shifts a week at Hugo's. She could do some painting, some cosmetic work, but thinking about tearing down walls just made her feel tired.

Emmaline Neal had a great house that Jess had hoped would go on the market when Em married Jack Holland, but her sister had moved in—Angela, who taught at Cornell and spent weekends at the house. And it was a family house, so Jess really didn't see it going up for sale.

Anything on the lake or with a good water view was prohibitively expensive. There were a lot of trailers for sale, but Jess wasn't going back to one of those, even though some could be really cute. No. She wanted a real house. With a porch.

A house like Connor's would be perfect.

She snapped her laptop shut. Wishful thinking, she believed that was called. Today had been a big step backward in their relationship.

Maybe it was better if this ended quickly.

Or if they could go back to the sneaking around. Dancing together at the reunion…that had been both terrifying and the most wonderful thing ever, being there out in the open, everyone knowing…and judging. The other night, when Ned stayed home with Davey, Connor took her out to dinner in Geneva, the first time they'd been in the same restaurant at the same time and neither had been working. It had been strange. And wonderful, if nerve-racking. The whole time, she'd been thinking, *So this is what normal people do.*

She'd also been worrying about what happened when Connor got tired of this.

It wasn't that Jess felt as though she was a bad person. It was just that she felt a little…well…*dismissible* in the grand scheme of things. She'd failed every single time she'd tried to get her parents to sober up, and while she'd read all the literature, she couldn't help feeling that if she'd just been better, or smarter, or nicer, she would have found a way.

Yes, she was glad her father was sober, though how long he'd stay that way was anyone's guess. But it hurt that he'd only gotten that way when he'd been long away from her. All those talks, the pleading and begging from his own daughter, hadn't done the trick. She hadn't been enough.

No one except Connor had ever wanted more than sex, not even Levi. Levi sure hadn't fallen in love with her (nor she with him, but still). And back in high school, once sex was over, guys didn't exactly bring her home to their mothers. Despite her popularity in parked cars, not one boy asked her to the prom. She had to wonder if Connor was just fixated on her, and if, sooner or later, he'd learn what all those other guys had figured out long ago—she really wasn't relationship material.

A boyfriend… She didn't know how to have a boyfriend. When she and Connor had been out the other night, she'd racked her brain for fun and interesting things to talk about… and came up empty. That was why women like Marcy tended to drain the blood from her veins. The never-ending stream of confidence, whereas sometimes Jess felt as tired and gray as an old dishcloth.

She was hardworking. She was loyal. She believed she had a good heart. But it was hard to imagine she deserved the best guy in the world. He liked her. He said he loved her. And he still didn't know everything about her, about what she'd done to Davey.

But he'd kissed her at the reunion. He put that idiot Jake on his ass for her, and while it was all very medieval, she owed him at least an attempt.

"Hi, Jess!" Her brother banged into the kitchen and threw down his backpack.

"Hey. I didn't hear the bus."

"Guess what? I'm picking out a dog for Connor O'Rourke."

CHAPTER NINETEEN

The Manningsport Animal Shelter was like the Four Seasons for the Four-Legged, with hardwood floors, ambient lighting and a large, fenced-in dog park. The Cat Community Room, whatever that was, had dozens of carpeted perches and strange little bridges and structures to prevent boredom, according to the brochure in the foyer. And the Dog Lounge looked hauntingly similar to Connor's living room.

"Hey, dude!" Bryce Campbell called as Connor walked in. Last summer, Bryce had sunk a hefty sum into what was then a very modest, typical animal shelter and now ran the place. "What can I do for you?"

"I'm looking for a dog."

"Awesome. I'll give you the family discount."

"Oh. Thanks." Technically, Bryce was Colleen's cousin-in-law, and now, since Bryce dated Paulie, and once Mom and Ronnie got married in a few weeks, Paulie would be his stepsister, so Bryce would besomething. It was complicated. But Bryce was a good guy. Always smiling, extremely bright blue eyes.

He wondered abruptly if Jessica had slept with Bryce.

It was possible. He'd never asked for names. He knew some,

since the guys had been pretty proud of it back in the day, but… well, shit. It didn't matter.

"What kind of dog are you looking for?" Bryce asked.

"I don't know. Something kind of easygoing and low maintenance."

"Purse dog?"

"What's that?"

"You know. Like Honor Holland's dog. Fits into a purse."

Hell, no. "Something a little bigger. But not huge, either, not like Rufus."

Bryce nodded. "Here's your paperwork, bro. Fill it out and we can get looking."

"I'm waiting for Davey Dunn to help me pick one out."

"Cool. Yeah, he's great. Comes here a lot to play with the dogs, keeps me company."

"Hey there, Connor." Keith Dunn came in, Davey in tow.

That was something, Jess letting her father be in charge of Davey. Oh, but wait, Gerard Chartier was here, as well. That made more sense.

"Hi, Bryce!" Davey bounced over and high-fived their host. "Can I show my dad the cats?"

"Sure, dude. You know the way."

"Bryce, got any reading material for me?" Gerard asked. "I'll just hang here while you guys help Connor pick his puppy." He grinned at Connor and accepted the *Sports Illustrated* Swimsuit Edition from Bryce.

"You read it for the articles?" Connor asked drily.

"There are articles?" Gerard said, flipping through.

Connor looked at the application. Reason for wanting a dog. *To make my girlfriend's brother like me.* "Always wanted one," he wrote instead.

It seemed akin to adopting a child, all the questions about his income, his hours, who'd supervise the dog when he wasn't home. Was it wrong to put Colleen, when she'd have a kid? He put Lucas instead. Davey came back into the room with Keith.

"All set," Connor said, handing the application to Bryce. "Ready to rock and roll."

"Ready to rock and roll," echoed Davey. He hadn't yet made eye contact with Connor, but he wasn't smashing his head against the wall, either.

They followed Bryce back to the dog kennels, which were nicer than his first apartment, really—each one had ceramic tile floors, a plush dog bed, chew toys, animal-themed artwork on the walls and a little door to a fenced-in area outside.

There were four or five of the usual suspects—the Chico types, pit bulls or pit mixes. One growled at Connor, and he felt the flash of remembered fear, Chico One's jaws clamped on him, Colleen's eyes wide, the sound fading as he almost lost consciousness.

"These are all nice," Davey said. "These are like Chico."

"Yeah," Connor said. "Very nice." Chico Three *was* nice. A real sweetheart. Not a biter, not at all.

"Got anything else?" Keith asked, and Connor hated to admit it, but he was grateful.

"Well, we have this beautiful lady here," Bryce said, crooning over a speck of white fluff, about the size of the dust bunnies that roamed under Connor's bed. There was no way in hell Connor was going to get a fluffy white dog.

"So cute!" Davey said. "Hi, what's your name?"

"I've been calling her Lady Fluffy," Bryce said.

There was also no way in hell he was getting a dog named Lady Fluffy who was, according to the sign on the cage, a Maltipoo.

"That's a perfect name!" Davey said. "Hi, Lady Fluffy! Dad, isn't Lady Fluffy so cute?"

"She's gorgeous. Hey, sweetie!" The dog yapped in response.

"Dad, she's licking you! She likes you! Maybe *you* should adopt her!"

"I can't have dogs," Keith said. "The landlord won't let me."

Damn. "Got any golden retrievers?" Connor murmured.

"Dude, no," said Bryce. "When we do get one in, it goes so fast, you wouldn't believe it."

"Irish setter?"

"Nope."

"Weimeraner?"

"Dude, we're a shelter. We hardly ever get a purebreed." Bryce gave him a disapproving look.

"Get Lady Fluffy, Connor!" Davey said.

"She's definitely a contender," he lied. "But let's see all the others, too."

The next dog was a bullmastiff mutt who lay like a dead lion, gas escaping in long, poisonous hisses. "We're trying to figure out his diet," Bryce said, his eyes watering. "Hey, boy! How you doing?" The dog didn't move.

The last dog was a spaniel of some type. It seemed very, very old with a white face, milky eyes. "I didn't know they had diapers for dogs," Connor said.

"No, they do," Bryce said. "Really convenient."

Connor lowered his voice and tipped his head toward Davey. "I don't want to get a dog who'll, uh..."

"Go to the Rainbow Bridge anytime soon?"

"Exactly. Do you have any puppies?"

Bryce shook his head. "This is it."

Davey was cuddling Lady Fluffy under his chin. If Connor brought that dog home, he'd probably step on it and kill it and not even know. He was not going to put the poor Malti-whatever at risk.

So it was the dead lion, the octogenarian or a pit bull.

"Meet Lady Fluffy," Connor said two hours later, taking the dog out of his jacket pocket. "My new best friend."

"Oh, Hail Mary," Colleen wheezed, then bolted for the bathroom. Her gales of laughter could be heard loud and clear.

"That is one great-looking dog," Lucas said, fighting a smile. "Really manly. A poodle, is she?"

"Maltipoo. And shut up."

"You gonna put a bow in her hair?" Lucas broke and started laughing.

"I repeat—shut up. Jessica's brother picked her out for me."

"God, you are whipped," Lucas said.

"And you're not?"

"Point taken." He went over to the ladies' room and knocked. "*Mia*, you okay in there?"

Colleen emerged from the bathroom, wiping her eyes. "She's really cute, Con. When you said you were getting a dog, I just pictured you…with…with a…" The laughter started again.

"Get her out of here," Connor told Lucas. "Leave, Dog-Face. Go push out that baby rhino."

She stuck out her tongue, then said, "Rafe! You're godfather."

"I've already bought seventeen bisexual outfits in size newborn," Rafe called back, peering out the kitchen window. "Is that the term? *Bisexual?*"

"Unisex," Connor said.

"Got it. Why are you here? Get out. It's your day off."

"I wanted to show Colleen my new dog."

Rafe gasped. "Oh! She's beautiful! If I didn't have my hands in ten pounds of chicken breasts, I'd be all over her."

"Lady Fluffy is really cute, Connor," Jordan said, blushing.

"Thank you, Jordan," Connor said. She dropped a glass. Right. He wasn't supposed to look directly at her. "All right. Lady Fluffy and I are leaving. It's my day off."

"Oh, you have a life all of a sudden?" Colleen asked. "Lucas, I'm walking my brother home. I need exercise and fresh air if I'm gonna push this kid out."

"I'll be here, *mia*. Waiting for you." Another glass crashed to the floor. Apparently, Connor wasn't the only one to affect poor Jordan.

"I hate to be the one to bring it up, but strolling two blocks isn't really exercise," Connor said, putting the dog down on the sidewalk and clipping on her leash. She came up to his ankle. Lucas had a point; Fluffy might need a bow. They headed off, Fluff's tiny little paws blurring as she trotted along, happily snuffling the air.

"So what are you doing today?" his sister asked, waddling beside him.

"I'm teaching Davey Dunn to cook. But don't say anything to Jess. He wants to surprise her."

"God, you're so cute. You're adorable. I mean that. Connor O'Rourke, you are a sweet little cookie, that's what you are." She put her hands on her back and sighed.

"You doing okay?"

"Oh, sure. I'm thirty-seven weeks pregnant, I burp like a frat boy and hit my recommended weight gain about four months ago, and yesterday, I broke out in pimples. For the first time in my life, Connor! Faith looked like a goddess when she was pregnant. I look like a bloated hippo corpse."

"I can't disagree, sadly."

She smacked him on the head. "Sorry," he said. "You glow, Dog-Face."

"That's better. How you doing with Dad and Gail and baby makes four?" she asked.

He sighed. "I don't really care a lot. I mean, I'm sure I'll love the baby. I love Savannah. It's just… I don't know."

"You don't feel connected to them."

"Why would I?"

She shrugged, her expression a little sad. "I don't know. He's our father, yada yada. How's the brewery coming? You getting investors?"

"Actually, yeah. Jeremy somehow heard about it—" he cut

his sister a look "—and asked if he could buy in. But I have a meeting in a few weeks with some serious money people."

"That's great, buddy! This might really happen, then! Imagine, you doing something without me and not having it be an abysmal failure."

"Really appreciate the confidence." They waved in unison at Lorelei, who was walking out of the bakery with a cake box in her arms.

"Can I give you some advice?" Colleen asked.

"Why ask? You know you're going to."

"Let Jessica do the presentation with the investors. She's gorgeous, you're ugly, she's friendly, you're grumpy and can barely string two sentences together. And, brother mine, she can say great things about you, whereas you'll look grouchy, ugly *and* pompous if you say them yourself."

"Your faith in me…it's humbling."

"I know what I'm talking about. And you know I know." They were at his house now, where she'd lived until last fall. "Pick that dog up so I can kiss her. If I have to squat, I'll have the baby right here."

He obeyed. "You scared?"

"What? Me? Nah!"

"I'll come to the hospital if you want," he said, and suddenly, his sister's eyes filled with tears.

"I'm terrified," she whispered, and he hugged her, his tiny dog licking Colleen's face.

"You'll be incredible, Collie," he murmured, kissing the top of her head. "I know what I'm talking about, too. And you know I know."

"Everything will be so different. What if I'm not a good mother?"

"Then give the baby to me."

She sputtered with laughter, then smacked him on the shoulder. "You're a jerk."

"Coll. You don't need to worry about being a good mother. You already are."

Her eyes filled again. "I hate you." It was what they always said when emotions were a little too high.

"I hate you, too. Now, I have to go. You need someone to help you waddle back to the restaurant?"

"No. I think I'll go see Faith so I can sniff Noah's head. I'll just cut across the yard."

"Tell your husband where you are so he doesn't freak out."

"Admit it. You're starting to like him."

"I admit nothing. See you later."

He watched until she was in Faith and Levi's house; their backyard was diagonal to his own. When she was safely inside, he put Lady Fluffy down. "Welcome home," he said. "Try not to get stepped on."

An hour later, Davey sat in the kitchen with the dog on his lap. If Lady Fluffy could help Connor marry Jess, he'd commission a statue of her to be put in the park, like Balto, the dog who'd brought drugs to the sick kids in Alaska. Gerard had dropped Davey off and then went to the bakery to see Lorelei and said he'd be back around four.

"So you never cook at all," Connor clarified.

"I can use the microwave to soften my ice cream."

"You ever make popcorn or anything like that?"

"No." He scowled.

"Right. I thought we'd start with scrambled eggs. So first rule of the kitchen, wash your hands."

When Davey was clean, which took three tries, because he kept picking up Fluffy, Connor started him on cracking eggs. He had two dozen, since he thought it might be a little challenging.

It was. Davey crushed the first egg, getting it all over his hands. And table. And some on the chair. That was fine; Connor would do a bleach-down of the kitchen later on. "This is gross," Davey said, reaching down to touch Fluffy.

"No touching the dog, remember? You'll get it. Watch this." Connor cracked an egg with one hand.

"So what?"

"So it's one of my few tricks."

"I don't like your tricks." The kid—man—was suddenly angry. The good old internet had said his mood might change on a dime, and for reasons that were unclear to someone unfamiliar with Davey's issues. Little frustrations could build up, then explode.

"Listen, Dave," he said. "I know you don't like me a lot. And you don't have to. But I would really like us to try to be friends, even if it doesn't work."

"*I* wouldn't like us to be friends. You're a show-off."

Ah. Shouldn't have cracked the egg one-handed.

"I have a question for you about dogs." Redirect. That was one of the bits of wisdom that had been offered again and again. He remembered Jessica asking him about Superman or something when Davey had freaked out that time. Then, it had seemed she should've just told him to knock it off. Now it made more sense. "Do you think Fluffy would like it if I played music?"

"Yes." Davey's tone was sullen.

"Any particular kind?"

"No."

"Like… I don't know. I like the song from the *Avengers*. You know?"

"That's too scary."

"Right. Um, maybe…"

"'Spirit in the Sky.' That's a good one."

Connor nodded, then got up and wrote it down. "Thanks, Dave."

"Everyone calls me Davey." His tone was back to normal.

"I just thought Dave sounded a little older. Like someone who was old enough to have a girlfriend."

Davey looked down at the table and smiled.

"Here," Connor said, handing him an egg. "Let's try it again."

By the time Gerard came back from the bakery with cupcakes, Davey had successfully cracked three eggs out of fifteen attempts. The kitchen table was slimy, but Connor didn't care.

"What've you been up to, big guy?" Gerard asked, slinging his arm around Davey.

"It's a secret," Davey answered. "So I can surprise Jess. And Miranda!"

Lady Fluffy—that name, God—barked to be let out. At least she was trained.

"Can I go outside with her?" Davey asked, cupping his hands around his eyes to peer out the back door. "It's so pretty out there!"

"Sure." The backyard was fenced in. And, yeah, it was pretty. Landscaped with hostas and ferns, a big linden tree in the back, huge vegetable garden that he tended like it was a child. Hey. Connor was Irish. Gardening was a thing.

Davey let the dog out and ran outside with her, the two of them chasing each other.

So this is what it would be like to have a little brother. Or brother-in-law.

"Does Jessica know you're doing this?" Gerard asked.

"No," Connor said. "I'm trying to teach him to cook some basic things. And I'd appreciate it if Jess didn't know. We're gonna surprise her."

"Gotcha. Totally whipped, are you?"

"Yep. Here's your money, pal. Thanks for your time." He took two twenties out of his wallet and handed them to Gerard.

"You could just feed me for free this month," Gerard suggested.

"This will cost less. Thanks again, man." They shook hands,

and Gerard left, calling for Davey. Connor got to work scraping up the egg mess, Lady Fluffy amiably licking whatever had fallen to the floor.

"Think this is gonna work, Fluff?" he asked the tiny dog. "Yeah? Me, too."

CHAPTER TWENTY

On Saturday, Jess watched from the window as Connor pulled up in his truck. She jumped back, but he saw her, and a smile spread across his handsome face as he came up the walk.

"Spying on me?" he asked, giving her a quick kiss.

He was way too good-looking. She smiled, then turned and called over her shoulder. "Come on, people! The cows await!"

Connor was taking her and Davey to a 4-H fair up in Penn Yan, part of his attempt to win the heart and mind of her brother. Another guest—her father.

Keith had been solid and steady, coming to drum circle every week, not asking for more, accepting every invitation to dinner. He never had other plans. If she had to cancel, he didn't protest. He practically let her sniff him down like a bloodhound. He never balked at her rules and regulations and left the minute she hinted that he should.

On these visits, Keith spent more time with Davey than with her; Davey had no baggage, so she understood. But sometimes, her father would look at her and she'd see the sadness and regret there, and she'd have to turn away.

Too many times, her father had gotten her hopes up, and

she'd believed. That he'd stop drinking. Keep his job. Save money. Stay.

He'd never managed any of those things.

Until now. These past two months were the longest she'd known him to be sober. He did seem different. She wanted to believe. But believing had been bred out of her long ago.

Still, when Connor suggested the 4-H fair, and Davey asked if their father could come, she said yes.

A family outing…that was new.

"Guess what movie I saw last night, Dave?" Connor asked. *"Iron Man."*

"I love Iron Man!" Davey said. "'Iron Man. That's kind of catchy. It's got a nice ring to it. I mean, it's not technically accurate. The suit's a gold…' Jess, what's the rest?"

"'A gold titanium alloy, but it's kind of provocative, the imagery, anyway.'" Jess finished the quote for him, and Connor glanced over, a smile in his blue eyes. For a second, Jess thought about holding his hand, but didn't. It might be too much for Davey.

And her.

"A carriage! Look, Dad! A horse!" Though Mennonite horse and carriages were nothing new for the area, Davey always went a little nuts when he saw one, and there were plenty out today. The sky was heart-wrenching blue, fat white clouds sliding by like thoughts, and a breeze ruffled her brother's downy hair.

There were the expected pens of calves and alpacas, as well as sheep, goats, chickens and even a herding demonstration from one of the Mennonite farmers, whose border collies were legendary. "We should've brought Chico!" Davey said, running off to see the dogs.

"Wait, Davey," Jess called.

"I'll go with him," Keith said. "You kids wander around. It's not big enough to get lost." He met her eyes, and she knew what he meant—*if I'm screwing up, you'll be able to see it.*

"Okay," she said. "Um...thanks."

"Alone with my woman and all this livestock," Connor said. "Think of the possibilities. Which first? Beef cattle or dairy?"

"How about some food?" she suggested, and they followed the enticing scent of meat being cooked over an open fire.

"Seems kind of insensitive," Connor murmured as he paid for their meals. "The barns, the barbecue pit. The cows must be doing head counts every fifteen minutes."

Jess laughed. And this time, when they started walking again, she took his hand. It made her heart beat a little erratically, but she didn't let go, either.

Vendors had set up booths, selling everything from sweaters made from different types of wool, to wooden bowls and spoons, to silver jewelry made from old cutlery. Jess stopped in front of a table that sold pictures from long ago. Solemn-faced people with stiff postures, unsmiling. "Who'd give up pictures of their family?" Jess wondered aloud. People who died alone, that was who. People with no kids to want the photos, no cousins, no grandchildren.

People who ended up like she might. If she outlived Davey...

That was a thought she never could follow to the end.

"Come on, sweetheart," Connor said, and the endearment tugged at her insides. "Let me win you something and prove my manhood."

"I can't wait," she said.

"I'd prefer to prove it later, if Ned would be so kind as to watch Davey tonight," he murmured, pulling her in for a kiss.

This was what normal people did. They kissed at fairs and held hands. He pulled back and kissed her forehead and grinned down at her.

It was hard to look at him. There was so much in her heart, it was almost impossible to let him see all that happiness. Almost.

He tilted his head in question. Then she stood on tiptoe and kissed him. And kissed him some more, and more after that, until the only thought in her head was Connor O'Rourke of the perfect mouth and the curly eyelashes, generous heart and strong arms.

"So where's my prize?" she asked finally.

"Right," he said, his eyes smoky. "Coming up, my queen."

It was one of those little crane games that were nearly impossible to win. "Davey got stuck in one of these once," Jess mused as Connor frowned in concentration. She leaned against the glass box. "He climbed right in, and it took an hour and a half to get him out, but boy, did he have fun. They gave him eight stuffed animals."

"Hush, woman, you're breaking my concentration," he said. "What's your preference?"

She studied the prizes in the case. "The bunny with the bow in her hair."

"You got it." Connor maneuvered the crane toward the stuffed animal. The crane claw opened and dropped, and it did grab something, though not the bunny. It was a plastic bubble holding something green.

"Just what I wanted," Jess said.

"This thing is rigged," Connor grumbled.

"Really? Go figure."

The bubble dropped into the dispenser. Inside the container was a tiny little plastic creature with fangs and a tuft of green hair. It was quite cheerful. "I love it," she said.

"What did you win? What is it, Jess?" Davey said, careening over, his face sticky with cotton candy.

"It's a little green monster," she said.

"Can I have it?"

"Not this time," she said, looking at Connor. "This one's for me. What should we name it?"

"Yoshi," Davey said instantly.

"Let me see if I can win you something, Davey," Keith said,

and so it was that Davey ended up with the bunny, and Jess with Yoshi, the little alien monster.

"You want to trade?" Davey asked sweetly, knowing she liked rabbits.

"Not on your life," Jessica said. "Connor won this for me."

"It was difficult, yes, but the spoils of war were worth it," Connor murmured.

"And Dad won that for you," she said.

Her father stopped abruptly, then continued walking. His eyes were on the ground, but he looked up for a second, and she saw that those eyes were full of tears.

Oh.

She'd called him *Dad.*

First time in about twenty years. And she didn't want to take it back, either. She smiled at him a little, and something shifted inside her, like a shade lifting from a window, flooding the room with light.

Connor invited the Dunn family to eat at O'Rourke's that night, despite the sickening amount of food Davey had eaten at the fair. The kid could use some vegetables; Connor was hoping to get a salad in him after the cotton candy, three hot dogs and caramel corn he'd managed to consume.

He was on in the kitchen, at his best, a fast, smooth rhythm with Rafe and the servers, one of those nights when everything was going perfectly. The menu was gorgeous—seared scallops in a cilantro remolata and ginger-lime beurre blanc; filet mignon with a mustard cognac sauce; the Kobe truffle burger with shallots and Roma tomatoes, in addition to the O'Rourke's classics. Connor chopped, sliced, seared, roasted, plated and stirred, barely hearing his cousins call out the orders, but registering them nonetheless. In the Zen, Colleen called it.

Rafe's strawberry shortcake with Devonshire cream was a huge hit, as was the homemade ice cream with caramelized ginger and seared apples. Colleen wasn't working tonight, but

Jordan seemed to be holding her own, Monica helping her out from time to time.

And every time Connor looked out the kitchen window, he saw his woman.

Jeremy Lyon had joined the Dunns, which was nice, because without him, Jess might've felt a little uncomfortable—outed as his girlfriend, dining with her father, the former town drunk. But Jeremy was a master at putting people at ease. Even Prudence and Carl stopped by the table to talk.

It was pretty damn nice to be able to look at Jess and not have her pretend he was just her old buddy from high school. Nice that Davey didn't freak out at the sight of him. Nice that Keith was only drinking water.

"You should go out there and take a bow," Rafe said around nine-thirty, when the orders had slowed. "You were incredible tonight."

Connor usually hated doing that, but tonight was different.

He washed his hands, took off his apron and went into the restaurant. "Bravo, Chef!" Pru called, and sure enough, the restaurant patrons burst into applause.

Connor rolled his eyes and smiled, gave a little nod, then went over to Jessica's booth. "How was everything tonight?" he asked.

"Excellent, Connor, absolutely fantastic," Jeremy said, and Keith nodded in agreement.

"It was good," Davey said. "I had nachos and chili."

But Connor was really just asking Jessica. She didn't answer, just looked up at him with those beautiful green cat's eyes, and smiled.

His woman. In his restaurant. And everyone knew it.

He leaned over and kissed her, getting a little more applause from the bar regulars. She didn't pull away.

"I always thought you two were a great couple," Jeremy said smugly, reaching for his wallet. "Let me get this."

"Dinner's on the house tonight," Connor said. "And I better get back in the kitchen. See you later." Again, his eyes met Jessica's.

A perfect day. That's what today had been.

He'd drop by her place later, see if she was still up. If not, he'd stare at her window, because why not, right? He was stupid with love. No shame in that.

It was past midnight (late by Manningsport standards) when Connor turned off the kitchen lights. He'd sent everyone else home.

But something didn't feel right. Someone was still here.

A noise came from the back. From the ladies' room, specifically.

Connor walked back and knocked on the door. "Hello? We're closing," he said.

A squeaky sound came from inside. Then someone cleared her throat. "Just a second."

Water ran and was turned off, and then the door opened.

"Jordan. I thought you went home."

"On my way."

Her eyes were red. Ah, shit. She'd been crying.

"Is everything okay?" he asked, and immediately wished he hadn't, because her face crumpled, and tears practically popped out of her eyes, and that squeaky sound came out of her like hiccups. "Oh, hey," he said. "Come on, sit down."

He guided her to the nearest table. Got her some napkins to dab her face. She failed to dab. Got her a glass of water, which she didn't drink. She just sat there and cried.

Where was Colleen when he needed her?

"Jordan," he asked, "what happened, kid? Was someone mean to you?"

"Yes!"

"Who?"

"You!"

"What?"

"I love you and you have no idea," she wept. "It's so hard working here. I should quit."

Connor tried not to wince. "Uh…hey. There, there." He handed her a napkin. Her eyes produced quite a few tears. Quite a few.

"I'm completely invisible to you. You're dating that *goddess*, and of course you don't notice someone like me. That would never happen, and I'm so stupid. I'm so, so stupid, but from the second I saw you—"

"No, no," Connor said, just hoping to keep her from saying anything else. "Listen, you're not… It's not… You're…"

Young. Innocent. Sweet. Really, *really* young, though. She was what…twelve years younger than he was? Barely legal for her to bartend.

He thought of Savannah, with her crush on the kid with the dopey name.

"You're not invisible," he said gently, handing her another napkin. She took this one. "Not at all. I definitely see you."

"No, you don't."

"Sure, I do. You're a really good kid."

"I'm twenty-one."

Okay. An infant. "No, I know that. But you're very…nice, Jordan."

"You don't even know me."

"You're hardworking, you're always cheerful, you're a little shy, but hell, all the guys love you. Gerard, Ned, Jeremy, Mr. Iskin, all our regulars. They think you're great."

Her eyebrows raised.

"And you're very pretty, Jordan. You are. I mean, come on. You must have a mirror." He smiled.

"You would never go for someone like me."

Danger, brother mine, said Colleen's voice in his head. "You're probably right," he said, and her face fell again. "But not because of you. It's because I've been in love with Jess since I was in sixth grade. That's twenty-one years. That's your entire lifetime. Kind of pathetic, isn't it?"

"Totally," she said, taking a sip of water.

"Most of that time...like, ninety-nine percent of that time, we haven't been together. We're a little..."

"Star-crossed?" she suggested.

"Inept, I was going to say."

"But you're together now," she said.

"Yeah. Finally."

Jordan's eyes filled again. "I can't imagine someone waiting that long for me."

"Well, you're young. And I think you're one of those girls who, uh...who doesn't know how great she is just yet. Who doesn't see what everyone else sees."

"And what's that?" she whispered, wiping her nose.

"That you're very kind. And loyal, and dedicated." Sounded like he was describing a dog. "And you know, you listen to people. You do. I've seen it. People can talk to you. I can guarantee you're going to meet someone who sees how special you are."

She looked at him through her red-rimmed eyes. "Really?"

"Yeah. Absolutely. He's probably already met you and is just waiting for you to get over your crush on some old cook."

She smiled wetly. "Yeah, right."

"Trust me. I've been a boy mooning over a girl. I can sense these things."

She blotted her eyes and sighed. "I'm sorry."

"It's okay."

"Don't fire me."

"I won't."

She blinked at him a few times, then smiled. "You're really nice, Connor."

"Let's keep that between us." He stood up and offered his hand, which she took. "Can I walk you home? You live in the Opera House, right?"

"It's, like, thirty feet away. I'm good, Connor."

"Yes. You are. See you tomorrow."

She let go of him and smiled. "Yes, Chef."

Ten minutes later, Connor was knocking gently on Jessica's door. She answered almost right away.

"Hi," she whispered.

"Hi."

"Hi," said her neighbor, who never seemed to sleep. He was smoking on the front porch, the tip of his cigarette glowing in the dark.

"Good night, Ricky," Jess said, pulling Connor into the kitchen. "No lasagna tonight?"

"I already fed you."

"So you did. Listen, Davey's not asleep yet, and he's a little overstimulated from today, so you can't stay. I'm sorry."

"It's okay. I just wanted to look at you."

She smiled. "Is that all?"

"No. Other things, too." He leaned in and kissed her, felt her palm against his heart.

"Jess?" came Davey's voice from upstairs. "Jess?"

She broke off the kiss and held her finger to her lips. "Yes?" she called, not looking away from Connor.

"Where's my Wonder Woman comic book?"

She winced.

"Wonder Woman, huh?" Connor whispered. "He has great taste in women."

She rolled her eyes and turned to the stairs. "It's probably in your night-table drawer or under your disgusting pile of clothes."

"Found it!" Davey called. "Don't come upstairs for a while."

It was Connor's turn to wince.

"He's twenty-six," Jess said with a shrug. "Healthy American male in love with Wonder Woman."

So was Connor. A different type of wonder woman, but essentially the same. “Want to sit in the backyard and look at the stars?” he asked.

She looked at him for a long minute. “You’re quite a romantic, aren’t you?”

“That’s just a rumor. I’m really big and scary. You want to or not?”

And so it was that the perfect day ended on a blanket in Jessica’s small backyard, Jess on one side of him, Chico Three on the other, the stars so clear and bright overhead it seemed like everything Connor had ever wanted had been granted by a smiling, benevolent god.

CHAPTER TWENTY-ONE

Things are going well.

The second the thought came into her head, Jess tried to dismiss it. It was the kiss of death, thinking that.

But things were actually going well.

Davey was sometimes still a little grumpy about Connor if he thought about it. He'd sulk if Jess told him she was going out to see Connor, but having Ned around was a godsend.

When Connor came by, he always brought Lady Fluffy. The name made Jessica laugh every time Connor said it. Chico Three loved the tiny dog, who looked rather like a stuffed animal with its bright eyes and cottony fur, and it made Davey howl with laughter to watch the two dogs chasing each other.

Her father was still sober. Since the fair, he'd been coming around more and more, mostly to see Davey, always supervised by herself, Ned or Gerard. One of these days, she might let him take Davey somewhere, but she'd been in the car too many times herself as a child, arm braced across Davey as her father took a turn too fast and too wide. So while it was a future possibility, she wasn't rushing into anything there.

And between her boarder and her raise, and her two nights a

week at Hugo's, she'd finally saved up enough to really look for a house. Being terrified of poverty, she actually had more than she needed for a healthy down payment, because she wanted to have a solid rainy-day fund, in case the day came when she no longer worked at Blue Heron.

That day might come. She couldn't escape the sinking sensation she felt every time she saw Marcy with one of the Hollands, ass-kissing and complimenting, not to mention that barking, omnipresent laugh. But brides especially adored her, and the Barn schedule was packed full, every event going off without a hitch.

But Marcy was also still encroaching on Jessica's territory. She'd made a short video of the vineyard, even though Jess had scheduled a film crew to do just that. "I just thought it'd be good to have something *now*, while the season is really busy," Marcy said during a staff meeting.

"Well, I'm not sure we need an amateur video when a professional crew is coming in July," Jess countered. She'd chosen July for good reason; Blue Heron was hosting a hot air balloon festival, and the first haying was scheduled for that same week. The footage would be gorgeous.

"It'll just be a placeholder," Marcy said, dismissing Jess with a wave of her hand. "And listen, it's pretty good for an amateur video! I kid you not! You might even want to save the moolah, Honor, and just stick with mine. Ah ha! Ah ha! Ah ha ha ha!"

It was hard to argue with Marcy without making herself seem petty. So Jess let it go, or tried to. Kept her head down and kept working, hoping it would be enough. She didn't know how to work a crowd or promote herself. She didn't really want to, either.

On Tuesday evening, she met Connor at Scoop, the ice-cream shop that had just opened on the green. It was his night off, and their fourth official date. Ice cream for dinner—a good start. They ate their cones—strawberry for her, chocolate fudge for him—and walked through the little downtown, past Lorelei's, the antiques store, the new custom furniture place. Nice stuff in the window, Jess thought. The kind of stuff she'd buy for her house someday, graceful, sleek furniture made from beautiful grained wood. Probably cost a fortune.

Connor took her hand, and again, the strange, light thought came—*This is what normal people do.* He gave her a wry look, then licked his cone, and *hello*, did all men look this good eating ice cream?

"There's an alley here if you want to do me," he said. "But there are children around, so..."

"I have no idea what you're talking about," she lied, smiling.

Happy. That's what the feeling was. She was happy.

"I want to show you something," he said. They went down Lake Street toward the park. Little kids were running around, covered in sand, shrieking as they splashed in the cool water of Keuka. Someone was cooking hot dogs, and sailboats skimmed past. A barking dog caught her eye. It looked like Blue, Faith and Levi's dog, and sure enough, she saw the Coopers, Levi holding the baby, handsome in his uniform, Faith's red hair catching the light. Faith waved, and Jess returned it.

Connor turned onto Liberty Street. Just a short distance from the park and lake was a little stone-and-wood building, a hundred yards or so from the last house on the street. For as long as Jess was aware, it had been abandoned. A few years ago, there'd been a fire there—she'd been on the call, in fact—and whoever owned the place had just let it sit empty. A few scrubby cedar and wild raspberry bushes grew in front of it, and the grass all around it was long, making it easy to miss.

"Right this way," Connor said, leading her up to the wide doorway. That face of the building was wooden, and black from the fire. He opened the door, and the inside was similarly damaged. The floors were scorched, but the stone walls seemed sound, and the windows were arched. There was a fireplace on the western wall.

"Welcome to the home of O'Rourke Brewing," he said.

"Get outta here! Really? Oh, Connor, I love it." Her chest filled with a strange, sweet pressure, and she squeezed his hand, then hugged him. "Congratulations!"

He laughed. "I'll have to do a good bit of renovating, but my brother-in-law's a contractor, so he'll help me. It used to be a storage building for Jacob Manning's boat company back at the turn of the century. It hasn't been used since the thirties. Then that fire a few years ago... Anyway, we just have to put in electric and plumbing. And stairs. And replace the door. And the floor. Great location, though."

"Definitely. Where will the tanks go?"

"Upstairs. Down here will be eight or ten tables. We'll serve a little food, just enough to get people to see how great a beer would be with dinner."

She finished her cone and brushed her hands off on her skirt. "And where will you put the tasting bar?"

"Watch your step. The bar will face the lake, of course. I'll have a little patio outside, sort of like an arbor. I'll probably hire Faith for that. Once I get the investors on board, we'll get started."

She looked around. The building seemed sturdy; Connor wouldn't have bought it if it wasn't. "Zoning approval and all that came through?"

"Yep."

Of course it did. He was an O'Rourke, half owner of the most successful restaurant on Crooked Lake, son of the man who owned most of downtown. And though Connor wasn't showy, she knew he had money.

The familiar, small flash of envy flared briefly. Jessica couldn't imagine what it would be like to have enough money to own a house, a booming business and still be able to invest in more.

He was watching her, and her chest ached again in the nicest way. "This is just great, Con."

"Thank you. I have a question for you, by the way."

Please don't propose again. Her heart started thudding at the idea. She grabbed her thumb and twisted the ring. "Okay."

He grimaced slightly. "I have four people coming in from Ithaca. Empire State Food and Beverage, this company that funds businesses like mine. I can basically show them your PowerPoint, but just the thought of talking to them makes me…sweaty. I was hoping you might do the presentation."

"Sure! Sure, of course! I can take the afternoon off from work, more than likely. I have a ton of vacation time." She was so relieved it wasn't marriage, she almost laughed. "You have to be there, of course."

"I'll just sit quietly and look pretty."

She grinned. "No, you'll have to answer questions. But, yes, you can look pretty, too. Maybe get a haircut. Wear a suit."

He came a little closer. "Thank you, Jessica Dunn." A little closer. His eyes were on her mouth.

She took a step back, only to find the cool stone wall there. That was fine. She wasn't going anywhere.

He cradled her face in his hands. "There's this old Irish saying," he murmured, pressing a light kiss on her lips, "that if you make love in a building that needs renovation…"

She started laughing. "A building that will become a brewery?"

Another kiss, and even better, because he was smiling now, too. "Yes, a building that needs renovation so it can be a brewery…if you can get a girl to take off her panties and she lets you do dirty things to her, then the business will be very, very blessed."

"Who came up with this saying?" she laughed.

"Some Irish guy."

"I want to see it in writing," she said, and he was laughing now, too, low and rumbly, his clever hands already under her dress, skimming up to her thighs.

"I'll show it to you later," he whispered, and his fingers went higher, sliding inside her panties, and she was very glad for the wall behind her.

He knelt down. Oh, God.

"Far be it from me to stand in the way of your profitability," she said, her breath shaking, and let him do what he wanted.

When they emerged from the building a while later, looking like guilty teenagers, no doubt, Connor took her hand again. This time, it didn't make Jess feel so strange.

It made her feel…wonderful.

"You look rather flushed, Jess. I should get you home to bed. My bed, I mean."

"I can't," she said. "Ned has a date."

They turned onto Putney Street, walking slowly. This was one of her favorite streets, just a few down from the green, on the opposite side of the Village from Connor's house. Connor's street had grander houses, bigger yards. Here, though, it was more quaint. The houses were small but graceful, and trees lined the street. Birds swooped and sang, getting ready for the night, and the sky over the lake was lavender and pink.

Then she lurched to a stop.

There was a for-sale sign in front of #34. "Oh, my God," she breathed, then ran up the street.

It was a brick Victorian with a porch. A porch! She knew the house, of course; she knew every house in the Village, but she hadn't known this had gone on the market. It was small, and the front yard was tiny, but hydrangeas bloomed along the porch, their flowers so blue it made her heart ache. "It's for sale!" she said to Connor. "Come on! It's empty. Let's peek inside."

When had this happened? She peered in the window and almost swooned. Dark-stained hardwood floors, original. Big iron radiator. A fireplace edged with green ceramic tile, and wooden cabinets and built-in bookcases with lead-paned doors. And speaking of doors, the front door was gorgeous, oak with a big long oval and brass doorknob.

"Great porch," Connor commented.

The front door was locked, but Jess peered through one of the glass panels into the entryway, the mark of a gentler time. You could put a little table along the little wall, and have a beautiful glass bowl for your keys and phone. A carved staircase turned ninety degrees. There was a stained-glass window on the landing. "You see that stained glass? Isn't it gorgeous? And that woodwork is amazing."

"Very pretty," he agreed, looking in, as well.

She couldn't see any more from the door, so she went in the side yard, which was lined with hostas and some kind of low-growing blue flower. A little statue of St. Francis with his hand outstretched. It looked like a fairy lived here, it was so beautiful. In the back, the yard was small and neat and bursting with potential… She could put in flower beds along one side, maybe a shade garden on the other.

There was even a sturdy maple tree Davey and she could climb. Jess would bet that tree turned the most beautiful colors come fall. She could replace the chain-link fence with bamboo, maybe; they used it all the time on HGTV, and it could be a little treasure of a garden back here, and Chico Three would be fenced in and safe. She could ask Faith for help, maybe. Or just do it herself, even better.

There was a garage in the back, too. Imagine that. Imagine parking inside and not having to scrape off the car every time it snowed or iced.

The windows on the side of the house were too high for her to peek in.

"You want to look inside?" Connor asked. Without waiting for an answer, he crouched down and put his head between her thighs. "Hello again," he murmured, kissing one, then lifted her onto his shoulders.

"Oh, my God, Connor, it's so pretty," she said, cupping her hands around her eyes to see better. It was the dining room, with a built-in china cabinet and sideboard. A chandelier that, if it wasn't original Victorian, sure looked that way.

This was her house. This was exactly what she wanted. It needed work, sure, but it was mostly cosmetic, she'd guess. Maybe a new furnace, given the age of the house.

"Put me down, okay?" she asked.

"Yes, my queen," he said.

She barely heard him. Pulling out her phone, she entered the address into Google.

There it was, listed on Realtor.com, 34 Putney Street. Three bedrooms, one bath—she could fix that, maybe, someday. Living room, dining room, kitchen, walk-in pantry—pantry! Full cellar.

She almost couldn't look at the price.

Then she did.

Her heart stopped.

In a bit of a daze, she wandered back to the front porch. Sat down.

"You okay, babe?" Connor asked.

"I can afford this," she said.

"You—you want to *buy* this place?" he asked.

"Yes! It's perfect! I should call the real estate agent right now." She did just that. "Damn, they're closed." The beep of the answering machine sounded. "Hi, my name is Jessica Dunn. I'm very, very interested in 34 Putney Street. If you could call me as soon as you can, I'd really love to see the inside of the house." She recited her phone number, aware that her hands were shaking. "Talk to you soon. Thank you so much."

Her heart was racing. She looked at Connor and smiled.

He didn't smile back.

Oh. Oh, shit. Right.

He sat next to her. A goldfinch fluttered past, a flash of yellow and black. "At the risk of pointing out the obvious," he said quietly, "I have a pretty nice house already. It also has stained-glass windows and amazing woodwork."

She was twisting her ring again. "Yes. You do. It's just that I've always wanted to own my own place," she said.

"Right."

She looked at the hydrangeas, the little walk out to the sidewalk. "I don't think you understand," she said carefully. "My parents didn't even own the trailer where we grew up. We were evicted twice. The place I'm in now is a house, at least, but it's not mine, and it's pretty ugly, and the landlord won't replace the floor in the kitchen, and—"

"You don't have to explain," he said.

"It feels like I do."

He looked down for the longest minute of her life. "No," he said, looking at her. "You don't." Then he kissed her hand and smiled. "Let me get you home."

And even though he didn't say another word, she had that horrible feeling that she'd just chipped off a piece of his heart.

Again.

CHAPTER TWENTY-TWO

"Grumpy again," Rafe sighed.

"And holding a very sharp knife," Connor said.

"I'm holding your heart in my hands, Connor darling. Tell Uncle Rafe what the problem is."

"Can't you just make the coconut cake, Rafe? Please? Just do your job?"

The sous-chef sighed a Catholic sigh—Colleen had taught him—and turned on the mixer.

Coconut cake with a dollop of homemade key-lime ice cream was the dessert special. The burger of the day was buffalo with a kale, mango, jalapeño and mint chutney served with a side of truffle fries. Soup du jour—a cold asparagus.

"What is this? These aren't the greens I asked for," he said, staring at the iceberg in the fridge. "Who the hell ordered iceberg? It's fake lettuce."

"Connor, for the love of God, stop yelling," Colleen said.

"I'm not yelling. And why are you sitting on the counter? Why, Colleen? Why? You're making more work for me. I have to clean that now."

"Stop looking at me as if you're planning to pick your teeth with my bones." Colleen shifted and winced a little. "What did Jessica do now?"

"Nothing. She's buying a house."

"That's great!"

"No, Colleen, it's not."

"Put the knife down, brother mine. Let's pretend you're a civilized person. Tell Rafe and me what's wrong. Talk. Move your mouth while making sounds. Express your emotions. You can do it."

He didn't *want* to talk. Everything was wrong. It had taken a Herculean effort not to argue with Jessica last night and tell her it was incredibly dumb to buy a fixer-upper when he had a mint-condition, perfectly restored house that would fit not just him, her and Davey but their future children, as well. Nope. He was Mr. Understanding, which had him clenching his jaw so hard his teeth throbbed.

Then, after he'd dropped Jess back home, his mother had decided to come in the bar and force him out of the kitchen to talk about her wedding. And not just her wedding. Her *honeymoon*. She wanted Connor to know that just because she was menopausal didn't mean that certain parts of her were dead. Why? Why? Why did she do this to him? Was he too old to file child-abuse charges?

Add to this, he ran into Gail the Tail when he stopped by the convenience store and had to make polite chitchat. *Hi, how are you, congratulations, how's Savannah, how are you feeling?*

Now, Colleen was still sitting on his counter, *and* still pregnant—eight days past her due date, and his back was killing him with sympathy pains.

And Jessica didn't want to live with him, which probably meant she had no plans to marry him and have his babies.

"Hail Mary," Colleen whispered.

"Full of grace," Rafe continued.

"Con?" His sister's voice was weird. "I think my water just broke."

He dropped his knife. "In my kitchen?"

"Oh, God," she said, and her face changed.

"Okay, okay, it's okay, Dog-Face, it's okay." Holy Mary, Mother of God, please don't let him have to deliver his niece. He helped her off the counter, and sure enough, her tent-size dress was wet. "In my kitchen, Colleen," he said, his voice cracking a little. "How dare you and all that. Can you stand? Are you okay? Don't push. Should I get a basket or something? Oven mitts? Call Lucas, Rafe."

"Shut up, or I'll have the baby right here. Rafe, call Lucas!"

"On it," Rafe said, his phone already to his ear. "Lucas, hi, handsome, it's Rafe, get your ass here, she's finally in labor."

Colleen was gripping Connor's arms hard. "You good? Still good?" he asked. "Want to sit? Should I move you? Wanna lie down? Should I call 911? Boil water? Collie?"

"I've always dreamed of delivering a baby," Rafe mused.

"Shut up!" the twins snapped in unison. Then Colleen squeezed his arms even harder. Her eyes widened, and Connor could actually see the contraction roll through her. "Holy St. Romeo, this hurts," she whispered. "That was enough. I don't want any more contractions. I'm good without them."

Connor's back spasmed. "You're okay. You're fine! You're really brave."

"No, I'm not! I'm a baby, remember? I'm terrible with pain!"

"No, no, no. That's a lie." His shirt was already stuck to him with sweat. "You're a champ. A hero. Uh…don't have the baby here. Please. Wait for Lucas." He glanced at Rafe. "Close the restaurant."

"We're not open yet."

"Close it, anyway!" he snapped.

"I don't want to have the baby here, Con." Her voice was high and scared. "Please don't let me have the baby here."

"No! No, you will not have this baby in my kitchen."

Her eyes met his, wide with shock. Another contraction clenched her in its fist, and her eyelids fluttered. A little whimper escaped from her mouth. Her knees buckled a little, and he held her up. "It's okay, Collie," he said. "You got this."

It was so good to be a man.

"I'm scared," she whispered.

"I know. But listen to me, Colleen," he said firmly. "This is a great day. Your daughter will be born today." His eyes stung abruptly. "And you're gonna do great, sister mine."

There was a screech of brakes outside the restaurant, and Lucas burst in, thank all the saints in heaven. Connor stepped aside, and Lucas took his wife in his arms. Said something low and reassuring, smiled at her and kissed her quickly. "Turn your backs, boys," he said. "I'm gonna take a look."

Connor obeyed, and fast. So did Rafe, who nonetheless held his phone over his shoulder for a picture. A dull, pounding ache rolled through Connor's back.

His poor sister.

"Call 911," Lucas said. "*Mia*, you don't mess around. I can see the head."

Connor's niece was born half a block from O'Rourke's. The ambulance had arrived in time to pack Colleen up, though she begged them not to touch her and practically bit Gerard when he got her onto the gurney. Ten yards down the street, the ambulance stopped.

Isabelle Grace Campbell was helped into the world by her father, as well as Jeremy Lyon, who would now drink for free for the rest of his life; Jer had heard the call over the scanner and raced in from his office; and Gerard Chartier, who admitted that he'd always wanted to see Colleen's girl parts.

"You can come in now, Uncle Connor," Lucas said, smiling

broadly from the doorway of Colleen's hospital room. "You okay?"

"Just much, much older than I was this morning," he said. "Has my hair turned white yet?" He shook Lucas's hand, then hugged him. "Congratulations, brother."

Then he went inside and saw his sister holding a little pink burrito, and his eyes filled up with tears.

"Connor, meet your niece and goddaughter," Colleen said, and her whole face was shining. "The most beautiful baby the world has ever seen."

She was, too. A thatch of black hair, fat little cheeks, a tiny rosebud mouth. Her eyes were closed.

"Can I touch her?" he asked.

"You can hold her." She handed the baby over to him, and before he could protest, his niece was in his arms. "Hey," he breathed. The baby pursed her lips and opened her eyes, then, apparently unimpressed, closed them again.

His sister's daughter. His niece. Another female to protect. And he would. She had tiny, perfect eyebrows and the cutest nose ever, and she was so tiny, it was just incredible.

Isabelle Grace. His little sweetheart.

"You did great, Colleen," he said, and his voice was husky.

"It was an exciting twenty minutes," she said, then laughed softly. "Oh, your face. I wish I'd had a camera. Lucas, we should've filmed Connor."

"We were a little busy. Connor, can I have my daughter?" Lucas took the baby, kissed her head and stared down at her, enraptured.

Connor's arms felt empty without her, his *niece*. Though he'd known it was a girl, the word filled his chest with a warm pressure. His twin sister's baby. "You feeling okay, Coll?"

"Kind of like a superhero, actually. You want to hear how many stitches I have?"

"I'll pay you not to tell me."

Just then, their parents came in. "Oh, Colleen!" Mom said, bursting into tears. "She's beautiful!"

Pete went to Colleen's side and kissed her forehead. "Thank you for the granddaughter, sweetheart. Oh, gosh, she's just perfect." His eyes were wet, and he glanced at Connor. "Heard you did great, son."

"He was moderately okay," Colleen murmured. "He didn't faint, I'll give him that."

"Our grandbaby, Pete," Jeanette said, and Lucas turned a little so Pete could see. "What's her name?"

"Isabelle Grace," Lucas said. "Your daughter picked it."

"Isabelle was Lucas's mother's name," Colleen said. "And Grace because but for the grace of God, she wasn't born in a restaurant kitchen. Connor, it was quite sloppy. What you saw was just the start. There was blood, there was—"

"Stop torturing your brother," Lucas said. "Tell them instead how incredible you are. She was incredible," he said to his in-laws. "Two pushes, and the baby was out."

Pete put his arm around Mom. "She looks just like Colleen, doesn't she?"

"She does. So much like her." She gave him a watery smile. "Savannah's going to go crazy, I bet. An aunt at age ten."

Pete smiled. "I'll pick her up from school and bring her right here, if that's okay, Colleen."

Strange, to have his parents getting along. And nice that Dad hadn't brought Gail along, or that Mom hadn't brought Ronnie. For the moment, it was just the biological grandparents. Maybe, though, it was a little nice, given that Lucas's parents were dead, that this baby would have step-grandparents.

Grandparents. Gail was a step-grandmother. The thought made Connor smile.

"All right," he said, "I have a kitchen to sterilize in bleach. I'll come back later, okay?" He went to his sister and bent down to kiss her head. "Nice work, Dog-Face. I'm proud of you." He shook Lucas's hand again. "Congratulations, grandparents," he said to his parents.

He smiled all the way home. Happy, with a shot of PTSD.

"So guess what?" Connor asked Davey Dunn. "I'm an uncle. Colleen had her baby today."

They were back at his house. Rafe had made a huge poster for the restaurant window: *It's a Girl! Isabelle Grace Campbell! Mother & Baby both gorgeous & healthy. Come back tomorrow—drinks are on the house!* That last line had been Connor's idea—it would make his sister very happy.

In the four weeks of their lessons, Davey had mastered scrambled eggs—well, not quite mastered, but they were edible. They were moving on to grilled cheese today.

"Now, this is pretty basic stuff, but if you buy really good bread and cheese, it can be fantastic."

"I like string cheese. The kind with two colors and it's all swirly and you pull it apart? The one with the rabbit on the package?"

Connor suppressed a shudder. "Yeah, that's not really cheese, Dave. So, the trick is, you want the frying pan really, really low. See the blue flame? Just barely on. Now, you remember the rule about the stove?"

"Always check to make sure it's on when you want it on, and off when you're done," he said in a sing-song voice.

"Right. And what else?"

"Never use the stove alone."

"Good. Okay, so with grilled cheese, you want to keep the heat low, and butter the bread all the way to the crust, see? Then you put it in the pan—other way, butter side down—great. Now put the slices of cheese on, and cover all the bread. Good! And now the tomato slices."

"I hate tomato."

Connor raised an eyebrow. "No one hates tomatoes when I'm the chef."

Davey laughed. "No one hates tomatoes when *I'm* the chef," he echoed, lowering his voice. He was something of a mimic, Connor had learned. And it was awfully nice to make him laugh.

"And now a little more cheese. And now the last piece of bread—butter side up this time, see. The butter will make the bread nice and crisp and golden, so it has to touch the pan. And now we wait a few minutes."

"Fluffy! Come here, girl!" The little dog came skittering into the room and pounced on Davey's shoelace. He laughed and picked her up.

"Maybe I should drop by the candle place with Fluffy," Connor said. "You could show her to Miranda."

"I don't think she likes me anymore," Davey said, his face falling.

"Why?"

"She hardly talks to me."

Connor nodded. "Well, you're good at talking, right? You have to ask her questions that are easy to answer." How Colleen would laugh, him giving romantic advice.

"Like what?"

Good question. "Oh, like…who's your favorite Avenger?"

"I like Iron Man the best."

"Don't we all. But ask her, anyway. And then say something like, 'Hey, me, too! Maybe you could come over sometime and we could watch it.' And then you make her this killer grilled cheese, and she won't know what hit her."

"What hit her?"

"Oh, uh, it's an expression." Davey was a very literal person. "She'll be happy and surprised. A guy with great taste in movies *and* who can cook."

His student nodded solemnly.

Connor slid the spatula under the sandwich. "Perfect. See that gorgeous color? And now we just flip it. Voilà."

"Can I flip it next time?"

"You bet. Oh, and also, you say something nice about how Miranda looks." He thought of Jess. "Or smells. Tell her her hair looks pretty."

"Miranda has really great boobs."

"Okay, don't say that."

"She does, though."

"Do *not* say that. It's a little too…personal."

"But she *does*." Davey scowled.

"That's great. But don't tell her that, or she might get mad."

"I like them. They're pretty. Why would she get mad?" Was he about to have a meltdown? And what would Connor do if he did?

"I don't know, Dave," he said. "Women are mysterious."

Davey burst out laughing. Phew. "Women are mysterious! Yes, they are! They are indeed!"

Connor found he was laughing, too.

CHAPTER TWENTY-THREE

A few nights after Colleen had delighted the town by having her baby in the back of an ambulance, Jessica texted Connor from work and asked him to come for dinner that night. His presentation to the investors was next week, and she wanted to go over it.

And, she admitted, she felt a little guilty.

She knew Connor wanted more than she was giving. Honestly, she hadn't even thought about living with him since the day he proposed in April…and she still couldn't see it. She and Davey were a team. Bring in a third person, and it wouldn't work. Ned didn't really count; he was a tenant, and would be moving out at the end of the summer, too, once his Visa bill was paid off.

She'd made an offer on the house in the Village. And even though it was something she'd always, always wanted, it somehow made her feel guilty. She didn't want to tell Connor, but she'd have to, of course.

The truth was, she didn't really know how to do—or give—more.

"More what?" Pru asked over lunch. They were eating outside, sitting on a blanket in front of the Barn, enjoying the view and the enormous sandwiches from Lorelei's. "More sex?"

"Well...no, we're good on that front."

"High five, sister."

Jess laughed and obliged. "I just feel like he's...waiting. For something. And I know what it is, but I don't think I can pull it off."

"What is it?" Pru offered her some chips.

She took a few. Barbecue, the best kind. "It's this sort of... happy wife kind of thing."

"Do you want to be a miserable wife?"

"No, Pru." She shrugged. "Maybe not a wife at all."

"Why? I would crawl all over that man if Carl would kindly make me a widow."

"Uh-oh. You guys having trouble?"

"No. I just fantasize about being alone sometimes. It's part of being married a long time." Pru balled up her sandwich wrapper and started in on Lorelei's amazing white chocolate macadamia cookies. "You know. No more husband farting in the chair next to me, someone new, someone who looks like Thor. Anyway, back to you. You afraid he'll leave you? That if he's not chasing you down like he's been doing for the past decade, he'll get bored?"

It sounded stupid when Pru said it so baldly. "A little. Maybe."

Pru stared ahead, chewing contentedly. The wind blew, and the clouds slipped across the blue, blue sky. "You see that tree there?" Pru asked. "The big maple?" She pointed to a giant tree with a near-perfect canopy. Brides often got their photos taken in front of it, especially in the fall, when it turned a deep, glorious gold.

"It's a beauty."

"We call that the Liberty maple. The first Holland who settled this land planted it in 1780."

"Wow."

"Yeah. We don't advertise it, even though it's big enough to get on the state registry of champion trees. You know how it is. People can be ass-hats, and we didn't want some dopey couple carving their initials into it on their wedding day, you know? So it's a little family secret, but hey. You're my best friend."

Such a little sentence, said so effortlessly. Jessica's throat tightened. Pru was her friend because she just crashed through whatever reservations Jess had about friends. Pals were one thing; friends were…harder.

Except Prudence.

"Anyway, Great-Great-Grandpa What's-His-Name planted the Liberty maple when it was a seedling. It says so in his journal, which Honor has under glass somewhere. And he also said that this tree was to show his faith in the future. He'd never live long enough to see it come into its glory, but he liked thinking that his descendants would. And we have. We've all climbed in it and slept under it and all that. He did good, that guy."

"Is this somehow advice for my love life?" Jessica asked.

Prudence's trademark big, booming laugh echoed out over the hill. "Yes, dummy. Have faith in the future. Maybe you can't see it now, but if you don't water your little seedling with Connor, you're not gonna see it grow into something great."

"You're such a farmer. Want to come for dinner this week?"

"Sure." Pru stood up and stretched. "Ow. I pulled a muscle during sexy time with Carl last night. Thought I could lift him. I was wrong." She brushed off the seat of her jeans. "Gotta get back to the fields, kid. The grapes are calling my name."

Connor came over for dinner, right on time. She opened the door as he came up the walk, a six-pack of root beer for Davey in one hand, a bouquet of roses for her—she presumed. Lady Fluffy trotted at his side, no bigger than a squirrel.

"Yo, Jess, is he a regular thing?" called Ricky, who was in the yard, waxing his beloved Camaro.

"Seems that way," she said.

"I am," Connor said, raising an eyebrow at her. He kissed her, and her insides tugged.

"You could do worse," Ricky said.

"Thanks."

They went inside, Chico pouncing joyfully on Fluffy, then racing into the living room to get her a chew toy to share. "Hey, Dave," Connor said. "Brought you some root beer."

The two men in her life were getting along surprisingly well. Not at all what she'd expected. Maybe it was the dog.

"Can I have root beer now?"

"Say thank-you, Davey."

"Thank you. Can I?"

"Half a glass," she said. Connor stood there a second, looking at her.

"Your hair looks pretty," he said, and Davey cracked up. Connor shot him a look and a half smile, and she could swear they had an inside joke.

"What smells so good?" Connor asked.

"Chicken oregano, roasted potatoes and spinach salad."

"I hate spinach," Davey said.

"No, you hate cooked spinach," she answered. "This is salad."

"Oh."

"Thank you for inviting me," Connor said. "I hardly ever get a home-cooked meal unless I make it."

"Is Colleen a good cook?" Jess asked.

"Is that a joke?"

"How about your mom?"

"She's more of the *bake it till it's string* school of Irish cuisine," he said.

Jess smiled. "I'm gonna tell her you said that. Wash your hands, Davey."

"First rule of the kitchen," Davey said, going right to the sink.

She gave him a look. Usually, it was a struggle to get her brother to wash any body part.

Connor had been over a couple of times in the past few weeks, but this was the first time they were eating together, all three of them. She put dinner on the table—such a weird thing, doing this for a guy, though Connor had fed her more times than she could count. Davey lowered his head to his plate as if fearful that someone would steal it, and shoveled in the food in his typical way.

"You're gonna want to chew, Dave," Connor said, and she bristled the tiniest bit. Did he think she didn't know Davey ate like a starved Tasmanian devil?

But he had a point. And, shockingly, Davey listened immediately. "It's good," her brother said, smiling at her with a full mouth.

"Thanks, baby."

"It's excellent," Connor said, smiling.

This is what normal people do.

It didn't feel normal. It felt extraordinary and a little nerve-racking, as if at any minute, she was about to screw up.

But nothing bad happened.

After supper, she asked Davey to take the dogs in the backyard to play. "I have to help Connor with some computer stuff, okay?"

"Okay," he said, scooping up the dog and holding her over his head. "Come with me, Super Fluffy!"

"Hold her against your chest," Jess called, then got up to make sure he was.

"Okay," she said, getting her computer. "So I added a few things—"

"Come here," he said, pulling her down on his lap. He put the computer on the table and ran his hands up her arms. "Everything okay?"

"Yeah. Everything's fine."

"You sure?"

She took a deep breath. "Yes. It's just… I've never had anyone over for dinner before. Like this. Like…"

"A family?"

She hesitated, then gave a half shrug, half nod.

"How do you think it went?" he asked.

She looked at him for a minute, into those beautiful eyes. "It went well," she acknowledged.

His mouth tugged up on one side. Irresistible, that's what he was. "That's a good thing, right?"

"Yes." She smiled a little herself, and he kissed her, then, a long, deep kiss that homed in on her insides, making her feel soft and weak and burning with energy at the same time. Then he stopped, touching her bottom lip with one finger.

"And next week, my mom will be getting married, and you and Davey and I will be together again. With Colleen and the rest of my family. Will that be okay?"

She hesitated. The mental picture was a little like dinner with the Holland family…lovely, but a little on the terrifying side, too. "That will be okay."

"Maybe something you could get used to."

Her heart seemed to swell. "We should do the, um, the thing. On the computer."

He smiled. "Okay, boss, show me what you got."

She got off his lap and sat in the chair next to him, opened her laptop. "I wrote up some talking points for you."

"I thought we agreed I'd just sit there and look hot."

She laughed. "No. The thing is, the investors aren't investing in your company. They're investing in *you*."

"Great. A grumpy chef who doesn't really like people all that much."

"You're not really fooling anyone, Connor," she said. "You're not that grumpy. You think you're a big tough guy, but you're a big softie. Everyone knows it, too."

"No, they don't. I'm incredibly tough and very intimidating."

"Heard you cried when you saw your niece."

"I'm gonna muzzle that Colleen one of these days, new mother or not." He gave her a long look. "You ever think about having kids?"

The question was like an icicle through her chest. See, this was why she didn't want a relationship. These kind of heartbreaking talks. "No," she said.

"Why is that? Because of Dave?"

"Why do you call him that? Everyone calls him Davey."

"Davey's a boy's name. He's twenty-six."

"He's a boy. He always will be."

"Why don't you want kids?" he asked.

She folded her arms in front of her. "I don't think I'd be a very good mother."

"Are you kidding? You're incredible with your brother. And I've seen you with Noah Cooper. You get that dazed, happy look—"

"I like kids. I just don't want them."

"Why?"

Fine. He wanted to have this talk now, fine. "Because then I'd have to tell them what I did. How I am. Was. Whatever." *They won't want to have friends visit. They'll dread every time there's a parent thing at school. The other parents will talk about me, and their kids will make fun of mine, and my kids will get into fights to defend me, and then resent me for it.* "They'd...be embarrassed." Ashamed. "I don't want to do that to a kid."

He tilted his head. "What do you think you did, Jess?"

From the backyard came the yips from Lady Fluffy, the deeper barking of Chico, Davey's voice egging them on to catch the squeaky toy.

Connor hadn't looked away. She shrugged. "School slut, for one."

"Jess, you're too—"

"Well, I was. And that kind of reputation doesn't die. And

then there's the white trash stuff. Trailer park, drunk parents, all that."

"Everyone's got something in their closets, honey." The word made her heart hurt. "You know that."

She looked at the table. *Tell him.* Yeah. It was time. She cleared her throat. "I was also my mom's bartender." She looked him in the eye and squeezed the ring on her thumb hard. "I used to make her drinks. I could make a vodka tonic before I could read."

Connor took her hand. She took it back.

"Jess, you were a little kid."

"Not that little. Not for long." She paused. "I'd mix her a drink every day when I came home from school, and I'd keep them coming all afternoon and evening till she went to bed or passed out."

"That's not your fault."

"I did it when she was pregnant, too."

Connor closed his eyes for a second, then looked at her again.

So now he knew. She'd made Davey the way he was. Yeah, yeah, she'd been a kid. But she'd been an old soul even when she was seven. She knew it wasn't good that Mom was drinking so much.

"My mother was a sad person," she said briskly. "She was happier with a few drinks in her. I knew it wasn't healthy, and I probably even knew that it wasn't good for..." Her voice cracked a little, but she forced herself to keep going. "For the baby, but I did it. Until I was maybe thirteen, I made sure my mom had plenty of booze."

"I repeat. You were a little kid."

"I was little when I was four. I knew better by the time I was seven. So putting me in charge of kids... I don't see that happening, Connor, and I know you want them, and I think you should really reconsider being with me. I don't know what keeps bringing you back, but I honestly think you'd be better off with someone else."

There. She said it. The words hung between them like a wall.

The front door opened, and Ned came in with Sarah Cooper. "Hi, Jess," she said. "Hey, Connor! How are you? Heard you're an uncle!"

"Hey," Connor said.

"Is it okay if we hang out here?" Ned asked. "Watch a movie, make some popcorn? Levi keeps giving me these looks, and I'm scared, frankly. I mean, the guy married my aunt. You'd think he'd cut me some slack."

"He keeps talking about guns whenever Ned's around," Sarah said. "*Such* a pain in the ass."

"That'd be great," Connor said. "Can you watch Davey?"

"Sure," Ned said.

"Hang on a sec," Jessica said. No one had asked her anything.

"I would really like to go somewhere and finish this conversation," Connor said, rather forcefully.

"*That* doesn't sound good," Ned said. "You kids need to talk, you just run along. We got this."

And so it was that five minutes later, Jess was sitting in the passenger seat of Connor's truck, being driven across town like a kid being escorted to the principal's office.

He was mad. So what? So was she, for no good reason. He didn't say a word. Barely even looked at her. Also, she felt sick.

She'd never told anyone about giving her mom drinks. About how she'd been afraid that Jolene would go away forever, because she'd been so sad, how Jess had tried so hard to be good and fun and helpful...and how she knew that alcohol made her mother feel better. How sometimes, she'd make her mother a drink without even being asked.

They got to his house, his beautiful, perfect house with the backyard all landscaped with hydrangeas and roses and irises. A completely wasted porch without a single chair or plant. He unlocked the door, pulled her inside, through the living room, down the hall.

"Connor, I was just being honest," she said, and horribly, it suddenly seemed as if she was about to cry.

He towed her straight into his bedroom. It was so obviously a man's bedroom—big solid wooden bed frame, no decorative pillows. Dresser, night table, everything matching. No pictures on the wall except one of the gorge in Watkins Glen.

He looked at her for a long minute, eyes inscrutable.

"Are you mad at me?" she said in her best no-nonsense voice.

"No."

Another long beat passed.

"You were seven years old when your mother had Davey," he said. "You are in no way responsible for his condition. I'm going to tell you that until you believe me, Jessica Dunn. You're the best sister in the world, you had shitty parents and it wasn't your fault. It just wasn't. The only reason Davey is so great today is because of you."

It felt like a razor blade was stuck in her throat.

Then his hands went to her hair. Pulled out her ponytail and slid his fingers through her hair. Held her close for a long, long time, warm and solid, just holding her, and it felt as though her insides were shaking, and it was all she could do not to cry.

Then Connor lowered his mouth to her neck and kissed her, a soft kiss that scraped her skin and made her entire side electrified. Another kiss, thank God, because this she could handle, then another just under her ear, his fingers still threading through her hair.

"I don't want anyone but you," he said, lips moving against her skin. "Stop telling me to find someone else."

He worked his way down her neck, then up the other side, and Jess's breathing became ragged, her legs wobbly. When his mouth finally touched hers, it was gentle and tender, just the lightest pressure. He kissed each corner of her mouth, framed her face with his hands, then kissed her again.

He was seducing her.

The thought surprised her. They'd slept together so many times, and still he was seducing her. His fingers found the buttons of her shirt, and he kissed her as he undid each one, taking his time, touching the skin revealed. Another button, and another. She could feel him hard and solid against her, heat shimmering off his body. His hands slid under the shirt, pushing it off her shoulders, then trailed down her back.

"Connor," she said, and her voice was ragged, and this time there were tears in her eyes.

"Shh" was all he said, kissing her again. His tongue brushed hers, then his mouth was back on her neck. His clever fingers unhooked her bra, which joined her shirt on the floor, and his hands skimmed over her breasts.

She felt heavy and humming with lust, her skin alive, her heart thudding. He stepped back and pulled off his own shirt—oh, God, he was beautiful, lean and muscled, then unbuttoned her denim shorts and kissed her again, the hair on his chest scraping her skin so deliciously that her knees did buckle then.

He moved her to the bed and unbuttoned his own jeans, finally, and then he was naked and on top of her, and she could barely hold a thought except *yes* and *please* and *more.*

And when he was inside her, it was perfect. They were perfect.

"Open your eyes, Jess," he whispered.

She did.

"I love you," he said. "I love you, Jessica Dunn."

Her eyes were suddenly full of tears that slipped down her temples, into her hair. Connor brushed them away with his thumbs and smiled. "I love you," he said again.

And for the first time, she knew it was true.

CHAPTER TWENTY-FOUR

Connor was making progress with Jessica. He was sure of it.

In hindsight, he could see popping the question a few months ago had been a dumb-ass move, completely out of the blue in Jessica's mind. But winning the heart and mind of Davey Dunn—that was flippin' genius.

The fact that Jess wanted to buy her own house was a setback, but since he didn't have a better plan, he just ignored it for the time being. Maybe her offer would be accepted, maybe not. Things like inspections and bank loans had to take place. She wouldn't be moving in next week.

And even if she did, that might be okay. He wasn't going anywhere.

What she told him about her childhood just about killed him. He knew he couldn't just tell her Davey's condition wasn't her fault and erase everything. But he could stay. He could show her he loved her.

He could show her she didn't have to do this alone, and show her that being happy didn't mean the other shoe was about to drop. He'd done a lot of reading about adult children of alcoholics. He was trying to understand, trying to work his way into her heart, because he wanted that more than he'd ever wanted anything.

Trust, and happiness. Two things that Jess hadn't had a lot of. And fun.

One night, he asked Jess and Davey to come to a town softball game. O'Rourke's was enjoying their seventh straight year of championship, even without Colleen, who nonetheless came as a spectator with the baby and Lucas and Rufus the Doofus. The Irish Wolfhound was like Nana from *Peter Pan*, sitting next to the baby's stroller, towering over it, glancing inside every thirty seconds or so.

Rufus wasn't the only dog here; there was Blue, Faith's golden retriever; there was Chico Three; and there was Chico's best friend and goddess, Lady Fluffy.

Savannah came over to say hi and bent down to scratch Fluffy. "I love her name," she said sincerely, and Connor tried not to flinch. "It suits her."

"I hear you're going to be a big sister, Savannah," Jessica said to her.

"Yep. Another brother. I'd rather have a dog."

"You can share Fluffy here," Connor said. "And brothers are great, have you forgotten?"

"Big brothers are."

"Little brothers are, too," Jess said, putting her arm around Davey.

"Well, I am *not* changing any diapers." Savannah grimaced. Looked like she was coming into some adolescent sulkiness, and Connor felt a little glad. Keep her parents on their toes.

"I don't like babies," Davey said. "They cry a lot."

"I know," Savannah said. "Mom says the new baby will be her *little prince*. Gross."

Connor glanced over his shoulder. There were Pete and Gail, schmoozing it up with the town's mayor. Pete never missed one of Savannah's games. Part of the new and improved fatherhood package.

"Well, my sister and I have a game to win," he said to Jess and Davey. "Wish us luck."

Davey held up Lady Fluffy. "Good luck, Daddy," he said, making his voice squeaky.

"Dave, come on! I'm trying to impress the women."

"Keep working on that," Jess said with a smile, and Savannah laughed.

The game was the usual slaughter, as no one could touch O'Rourke's, thanks to Colleen's aggressive recruiting strategy—free food and drinks on every winning night. In the seventh inning, Connor belted a long home run so far out of the park that no one even bothered running to the fence. Driving in the Murphy girls and Bryce for a grand slam, he touched home, high-fived Savannah and ran right over to Jessica and kissed her firmly on the mouth.

"Nice job, big man," she said, blushing.

"Yet another man doing Jessica Does," a woman behind them murmured, just loud enough to be heard. Jess flinched, and Connor jerked upright, looking around.

It had to be someone from high school. So far as Connor knew, he was the only guy she'd been with in a decade. A *decade*, for Christ's sake.

Tanya Cross was studiously checking her phone. She glanced at Connor, then smiled sweetly. She always had been a jealous pill. Used to try to tear Colleen down all the time.

"Did you say something, Tanya?" he asked.

"Hmm? Me? No. How are you, Connor?"

"Great. A very happy man these days." He looked down at Jess, who cocked an eyebrow. She was tough, his Jess, but he knew that name still hurt. "Very happy." Then he kissed her again, a little longer this time, a little softer.

"Stop kissing," Davey said. "It's gross."

Connor felt her smile.

"I have to agree with Davey," Colleen said, appearing with the baby and a big smile. "Jess, you know you can do better, but I do appreciate you taking pity on my brother. Can we sit with you guys? Gerard's giant head is in my way." She handed Isabelle to Jessica. "Want to admire the most beautiful baby that ever was?"

"Her face is scrunchy," Davey observed.

"If by *scrunchy*, Davey, you mean perfect, you're absolutely right. Oh, hey, Tanya. You okay, hon? You look a little under the weather."

Ah, Colleen. There were times when he'd cheerfully drown her, and then there were times like this. She winked at him. Frickin' psychic, that's what she was.

Connor tousled Davey's hair, put one finger on his niece's little head—she was wearing a hat with bunny ears on it, and it was crazy cute. Then he went back to the dugout to receive his much-deserved congratulations and slip Ned a fifty so he'd watch Davey overnight.

Fun and sex. And food. That's what Jessica needed.

One of these days, she was going to marry him.

On the morning of the big pitch to the Empire State Food & Beverage, Jess called him. "You nervous?" she asked.

He was lonely, that was what he was. This bed seemed way too big without her in it. "No, since you'll be doing all the talking."

"You'll do some. Don't worry. You're a good bet, Connor O'Rourke. I'd totally back you." The unintended double entendre hung there for a minute. "By the way," she said quietly, "my offer on the house was accepted."

"Great! Congratulations." *Shit.* He'd been hoping someone would swoop in and steal the house from under her nose. "That's fantastic, Jess." He'd be happy for her. He didn't have much choice, and besides, he understood.

"Thanks for saying so." There was a weighty pause, then she took a quick breath. "Okay, I have to make sure Davey brushes his teeth. See you later. Two fifteen, don't be late."

"I'll be there."

At 2:15, however, *she* wasn't there. Connor was shown into the small conference room at the Radisson Hotel in Corning. Manningsport didn't have a real hotel…plenty of B&Bs and a motel by the lake. But for this, Jess had suggested something a little more official, a place with a conference room and a projector screen.

Their meeting was at 3:00; Jess said she'd set up the conference room so it would look fantastic, flowers and stuff, one of the things she did at Blue Heron during press pitches or special events. That was good, because, being a guy, prettying up the conference room had never occurred to him.

The last time Connor had had a business meeting was when Sherry Wu, his old prom date, had him come in to sign the papers for his loan. He hadn't worn a suit; he'd worn jeans and a T-shirt, probably. Who could remember? Today, though, he wore a suit. And shit, his mother's wedding was *tomorrow*, and he'd have to wear a suit again. And a tie.

He was sweating profusely. When was the last time he'd worn a tie? A funeral probably. Colleen's wedding. Whatever. He felt like he was being strangled. Jeremy Lyon wore a tie every day. Every single day.

His phone buzzed. It was Jessica.

Running a little late.

Thank God Colleen had suggested Jessica, who was nothing if not grace under pressure. First, the Empire Food people would be dazzled with her good looks; three men, one woman.

Jess always looked understated and elegant; she looked that way in pajamas. Something about her posture.

He caught a glimpse of himself in the reflection of a painting. He looked like a hit man, the suit, the clenched jaw, tight shoulders. "Relax," he told himself. This tie was choking him, had he mentioned that?

He had a hundred grand for the brewery, thanks to a decade of saving. Jeremy was in for another fifty. The bank had approved him for a decent loan, but he still needed about $600,000. Renovations on the building, insurance, equipment, furnishings, supplies, Tim's salary, counter staff salary, a liquor license, advertising, and enough to cover the loss they'd be sure to operate under for the first year, maybe two.

Six hundred grand.

It seemed like so much money. But with it, he could get started right away. And the brewery wasn't just a whimsical idea. He'd been working on it for fifteen months.

Jess had run through the presentation again last night. She was damn good at her job, that was for sure. She'd had a dozen booklets made online, bound and everything, the kind of thing he would never have thought to do. The covers said *O'Rourke's Brewing: Investment Opportunity & Business Plan*, with a close-up shot of a Pilsner, a Stout and an IPA, taken on the bar of the restaurant. It was like beer porn.

Each page of the book was beautifully laid out. The first few pages were the labels; she'd hired a graphic designer to finesse her basic ideas. His favorite was for the Dog-Face IPA, which showed a picture of a very happy collie who actually did look a bit like Colleen. There were photos of the proposed building, taken by Jack Holland, who was a really good photographer, and then the "after" vision of the brewery—Faith had made a mock-up on her architect's software, complete with people sitting at the tables, leaning on the tasting bar, on the patio. There was a nice shot of him and Colleen behind the bar of O'Rourke's, taken a couple of years ago.

The marketing breakdown focused on Connor's experience as a chef, same as in the PowerPoint presentation. Why he was specially positioned to craft beers that not only stood on their own, but also elevated the beverage to enhance both fine and everyday dining. That was the part that made Connor the most nervous. The stuff about him.

Then came the financial breakdown, which Connor had emailed her, and which she formatted to look clean and professional—where the money would be spent, and how. Then the timeline, projected one-, three-and five-year costs and profits.

And then, finally, the last page—the logo for the company, and that great tag line—*Make every day special. Drink O'Rourke's.*

He could never have done this without her. Though she didn't know it, once the funding came through, he'd be making her a partner.

Last night as she'd done her thing, he sat there, entranced—not by the brewery, but by her. She was smooth and confident with a wry edge to her words, and he would've bought a shoe box full of dirt from her, because she had a way of making everything sound fantastic.

He'd meant to bring his copy of the book, but he forgot it at home. Didn't matter; Jess would have a bunch of copies, as well as her PowerPoint presentation and his talking points. The only thing Connor had had to bring today was the beer itself. He and Tim had been working for weeks to get just the right flavors and fermentation.

He had them here, in a cooler, seven growlers full of the different varieties, as well as glasses and napkins from O'Rourke's. "That will be the most important part," Jess had said last night. "I'll warm them up, and you bring them home. Talk about the flavors in each one, what foods they'd go best with, and then, if they seem happy, we can take them to O'Rourke's for dinner so they can see what a successful business you've got going."

We. She may have been talking about the business *we*, but it sure felt like the couple.

Connor cracked his knuckles and looked at his watch. 2:30. The investors were coming at 3:00. A hotel staffer poked her head in. "Is there anything you need, Mr. O'Rourke?" she asked.

"No. Thank you."

He texted Jessica.

You close? I'm here.

Nothing. She was probably driving. She'd be here any second.

He had a text from Colleen: a picture of sleeping Isabelle, and the tender words Good luck, Uncle Idiot!

Still nothing from Jess. He checked his email. Checked the Blue Heron Facebook page and Twitter accounts to see if there might be a hint of why Jessica was running late. Not that she was *really* late just yet. Traffic, maybe. He called her phone. "Hey, you're probably in the car." Her Subaru didn't have Bluetooth. "Um, just checking in."

He went out of the conference room to the hotel bar. "Can I have a glass of ice water?" he asked.

"Sure. Lemon with that?"

"Sure." His eyes fell on the array of taps. "Can I also have a pitcher of, uh… Pabst?" Yeah. He'd bring in a mass-brewed beer as a compare and contrast. That'd be smart.

He carried his water and the pitcher back in the conference room and checked his phone again. Still no Jess. No call, no text, no email.

It was 2:48 now.

He texted her again.

Everything okay?

Waited for the little dots that would show her answering. Nothing.

Then he heard voices in the hallway. "Mr. O'Rourke is expecting you," said the hotel staffer, and there they were. Fresh sweat broke out under his arms.

Shit.

"You're early," he said. "Come on in, come in. I'm Connor O'Rourke. Uh...my, um, my business associate isn't here yet, but please come in."

They shook hands all around—there was Amy Porter, a woman of about fifty or so; Mark Something, a balding white guy whose name Connor knew he was destined to forget immediately; Trey Williams, who looked like a really well-dressed NFL player, gray suit, white shirt, shaved head, at least six-five, perfect teeth that gleaned against his dark skin; and Gary Gennaro, a ginger-haired guy who was packing a hundred or so extra pounds, the president of Empire State Food & Beverage. *Use their names*, Jess had advised.

He swallowed drily. Tried to smile. Wondered if he looked like he was snarling instead. Wondered why it was so hard for him to remember names when he'd studied them all week. Wondered if his sweat was showing.

They all said things about the weather and *nice to meet you* and all that crap.

"Why don't we get started?" said the woman—Porter, Amy Porter, Porter like beer, good, he hadn't forgotten her name.

"Sure, *Amy*," he said." Just give me one second to see where my business associate is." The second time he'd said *business associate* in thirty seconds. He already sounded like an ass.

The call went right to voice mail. "Jess, is everything okay? I know you're running late, but they're here." *They're here.* Sounded so ominous, probably because it was. "Call me, okay?"

He texted that as well, just to make sure. What the hell good was technology if you didn't use it, huh? Huh?

He took a deep breath, unstuck his sweaty shirt from his ribs and went back inside the conference room. *Names. Names. Use their names.*

"Jessica is on her way," he said. "So! Trey! Amy! And um… all of you! I guess we can just get to know each other. Uh, I'm Connor. I own O'Rourke's Tavern in Manningsport, and I have a new niece! My twin sister had a baby two weeks ago. I also have a ten-year-old half sister and a half brother on the way. Crazy, huh? Big age gap there."

Oh, Jesus. Kill him now.

Trey, the handsome devil, stared at him. The fat guy—Generic? No, Gennaro—was taking notes. Amy, also staring. The guy whose name Connor had forgotten was looking pained.

"So. I… I feel uniquely qualified to make beer, since I'm a chef," Connor said. "And I do have, uh, financial stuff. Papers. Projections. Just not *with* me. Jessica is bringing those, and she'll be here very soon, I'm sure. What would you like to know?"

Trey went first. "What kind of facility are you envisioning, and where would it be set?"

"Right. Okay, uh, there's this burned-out building right near the lake. Keuka Lake, that is. And it's great. I mean it's really… nice. Or it was, before the fire." He took a napkin and blotted his forehead. "Needs work, but a perfect locale. Location, I mean. Whatever."

Colleen babbled when she was scared. He used to make fun of her for it.

"You know what?" he said. "Obviously, Jess is the pitch man here, and I'm not sure what's keeping her. Why don't I do what I do best, and let you taste some beer? How would that be? Or is it too early for y'all?" He had never in his life said *y'all* before. Good God.

"It's three o'clock in the afternoon," Trey said.

It felt like four in the morning to Connor. Where the *hell* was

Jess? Had something happened? "Well, just a sampling, of course. I don't mean to encourage alcoholics. Right? Can't do that!"

"My father's an alcoholic," Amy said.

Of course he was.

"Pour away," Greg Generic said, thank God.

Connor lined up the growlers in a row. They were labeled—India Pale Ale, Amber Lager, Pilsner, Porter, Stout. He started with the Porter. "In honor of you, Ms. Porter," he said, pouring her three ounces. She didn't smile. He poured the same for the three men, and then one for himself.

"Nice, huh?" he said, gulping his down. "Dark and strong, really good head."

Oh, shit, that sounded like a porno line. He glanced at Trey, who was also dark and strong. Hopefully, he didn't notice the, uh, similarities. "We used rich dark malts, and you get this smoky, buttery flavor with the earthy hops." Did he sound stupid? It felt like he sounded stupid. "Medium-range body with an enticing firmness, but so creamy." More porn. Jesus. "What do you guys think?"

"I don't drink," said Trey. Fucking fantastic.

"It's very smooth," No-Name said. "I like the little hint of bitterness at the end."

"Yes," Connor said. Good, good, here was someone he could talk to. "Bitter. Exactly."

"Hit me again," No-Name said. Connor obliged. Filled his own glass, too. Took another healthy sip. *Just settle down*, he could hear Colleen saying. *You can do this.* He also remembered her saying that Jessica should do the talking. That he could barely string two sentences together.

Jess had told him to be friendly. Okay. He could do that.

"You look a lot like that guy on *House of Cards*," Connor heard himself say to Trey. "You know. The handsome one? Remy?" Now he sounded like he was hitting on the guy. "Not that I'm gay."

"I am."

"Really?" More sweat flooded out of every single pore. "One of my best friends is gay." *Please, Jess, please come in right now.*

"And I bet you have a best friend who's also black."

"Uh…well, no, not *best* friend. Friend, though. Marcus at the gym. But my *best* friend is really my twin sister, I guess."

Oh, fuck. There was really no other word for it.

He wiped his forehead again. "Let's get back to tasting. This is the IPA, which is a personal favorite." He poured more glasses for the Fab Four, minus the gay nondrinker. "This one has a very creamy head—" Sphincter! "—and good retention and lacing. Kind of a spicy pine hops in the nose and on the palate with just enough malt for balance."

Okay, so maybe that wasn't that bad.

"So it's very, uh, fresh, very bright with some citrus notes. Great for casual fare like burgers and nachos, but also with a delicate white fish, for example, or a pasta primavera. See, I'm a chef, I think I told you already. That's one of my goals. To bring beer to fine dining. Wine's been in charge long enough, don't you think?"

"I'm half owner of Wilson Vineyards," Ms. Porter said.

Connor drained his glass. "Well. I also love wine." Poured some more beer and drank that, too.

No-Name smiled and scribbled some notes. Pushed his empty glass back. Generic was not smiling, but was taking notes. Trey—cool name, was as well, and with that NFL physique, he could probably model. Bet he had a boyfriend. Too bad Jeremy was seeing Patrick. Trey and he would have beautiful babies.

This line of thinking reminded Connor about a certain pertinent fact regarding himself.

He was a lightweight. Colleen got all the drinking genes in the family.

And now he had *quite* the buzz on.

He checked his phone. Nothing from Jessica. Nothing.

He kept going. Through the Pilsner, the Amber Lager, the Stout. Everything he said seemed laden with sexual innuendo, and the *House of Cards* guy began to appear to be carved from stone. But Amy sipped every sample and took notes; Generic did the same; No-Name pounded back every pour and asked for more, and Connor wondered if the floor of the conference room should be on a forty-five degree angle, as it seemed to be.

"What's in the pitcher?" Amy asked.

"Oh, yeah, I forgot about that," Connor said. Shit. He sounded sloppy. "This is your typical American beer. I thought I'd use it for comparison purposes. So we've gone through all *my* beers, and now you can taste this *blecch* beer and really see—no, really *experience*, because that's what O'Rourke's Brewing wants to do. Create. A taste. Experience." He used his forefinger to punctuate the words. Maybe not a good idea. "Here. Let me pour you some. It's Pabst. Or Genesee. I forget."

And with that, he poured Amy some beer. Except he missed the glass and dumped it right down her front.

"Damn it!" she said, pushing back from the table.

"Oh, shit," Connor said. "Here, let me help." He grabbed some napkins and started blotting her front. Implants, given the way they jutted out at the same angle as a unicorn's horn, and like the unicorn's horn, felt like they were made of a very hard substance. "Are these new?" he asked, dabbing some more.

She smacked his hand away. "We're done here."

"Thank God," he said. Probably shouldn't have said that, but oops. "Great meeting you. I'm so sorry Jess couldn't get here. She, uh, she's fantastic. And she would've made me look really good."

"Take care," said No-Name.

"I'll call you?" Connor suggested.

No one answered. They left the conference room, and Connor sat back down. Put his head on the table and sighed.

That didn't go so well, it seemed. When he was sober, he'd find out for sure.

He checked his phone again. Still nothing.

It was a little past four.

This was not running late.

He bolted upright and hit his sister's name. "Where's Jess?" he barked.

"Oh, Con, she didn't call you? I just found out myself. She's at the hospital. There was a fire at her house. Everyone's okay, but—"

He was out of the conference room, running. He grabbed the nearest bellboy. "Get me a cab. It's an emergency."

CHAPTER TWENTY-FIVE

Jess had just gotten into her car at Blue Heron, about to head for Corning when she decided to swing by the house and bring Connor a good-luck charm—Yoshi, the little green plastic critter he'd won for her at the 4-H fair. Today would be tough for him, and wicked fun for her. The little monster would remind him to relax and smile a little.

And she'd remind him of that, too. It was really something, knowing that she'd helped him in this. Sure, he could've hired someone else to do it, but he'd hired *her*, and she'd done a great job, and she'd done it without guidance from anyone. He *wanted* her there. He wanted her to pitch his brewery to these people, with more than half a million dollars at stake, and he'd picked the girl from the trailer park, the class ho, to handle this for him. Not because she was sleeping with him—when he hired her, she hadn't been. Because he had faith in her, in her intelligence and professionalism.

That morning, she'd put on her best suit, black and simply cut, the kind that would never go out of style. A low-cut white silk V-neck underneath it; still classy, but with a sexy little edge. The black heels with the strap across the ankle. She pulled her hair up into a perfect French twist and put on her makeup carefully.

"Hello, Older Woman Fantasy," Ned murmured as she came into the conference room for a staff meeting.

"Shush, child," she said, grinning.

"Will you spank me if I'm naughty?"

"Behave, Ned," said Honor. "Jess, feel free to sue him. But you do look fantastic. Today's the day, huh? Good luck. Tell Connor not to sweat or growl at anyone."

Marcy burst in on her usual wave of energy and noise. "Sorry I'm late, so busy, have this superwealthy bride, and I want to— Uh." She broke off at the sight of Jessica. "A little overdressed, aren't we?"

"I have a presentation off-site today," Jessica said.

"For what?"

For none of your business, she thought. "For Connor O'Rourke."

"Why?"

"He's opening a brewery," Ned said. "And Jess is his woman."

"And a marketing genius," Honor added with a smile.

"Are you kidding me?" Marcy said. "You two are *dating*? I had no idea!"

"Jessica's private life aside, why don't we get to work?" Honor said, passing out some papers.

"No, of course, it's just that I'm *buried* in my work these days. Busy, busy! No time for extracurricular fun, I kid you not." She didn't look at Jess. Great. Another reason for Marcy to dislike her.

For the first time since Jess had started at Blue Heron, the morning dragged. All she could think about was the presentation, which she'd practiced until eleven last night. It would be a home run. She just knew it. And yes, Connor could sit there and look hot, and when she was done with the presentation, he'd field questions with ease, because Empire State Food & Beverage would be begging to give him the six hundred grand.

When the meeting ended and she went to her car, she thought of that little green plastic creature. He could keep it in his pocket, and maybe remember that beautiful, simple day at the 4-H fair, and that she'd kissed him. In public.

She drove down toward the Village, taking a right at the bottom of the hill. Soon, she'd be taking a left and going right into the Village, into her own little house.

And strangely, the thought didn't bring her as much happiness as she'd imagined it would.

But owning a house was something she was going to do. She'd come too far to move into someone else's place. She'd given Ned notice that she and Davey were moving, and it was fine with Ned. He'd paid off his credit card bill, and was moving back into the Opera House.

So it would be just her and Davey again, same as always.

There it was once more, that pang of...something.

She turned onto her street. Saw Ricky running up her steps.

The dread hit her before the facts.

There was smoke. There was smoke and a bad smell, and oh, God, a fire, a fire, but it was okay, it was okay, because Davey was at work—

And then Ricky came out the door and down the steps, his arm around Davey, and Davey's arm was in front of his face, and his hands were bright, bright red.

"Davey!" she screamed. She pulled over so hard she hit the curb. Threw open the car door, fell, and was up and running. "Davey!" She didn't recognize her own voice, it was so choked by fear.

"He's okay," Ricky said. "Just a little burn. Fire's out, but I called 911 already."

Tears streaked Davey's sooty face. Dear God, thank you, he seemed okay, but there was a livid red streak up his cheek, and his hair...his chick-like hair was uneven, because a good chunk of it was singed off.

And his hands, his poor hands were bright red. "Oh, honey," she said, and she was shaking so hard, and her chest was heaving. "Oh, God, oh, honey, what happened, are you okay?"

"My hands hurt," he said, sobbing. "It wasn't my fault! I'm sorry, Jess."

"No, no, it's okay. We'll get your hands taken care of. What happened? Why are you home?"

"I wanted to surprise you," he said, tears pouring down his face. "I wanted to cook you supper the way Connor taught me."

Levi was first on the scene, screeching up in his patrol car, Emmaline right behind him. The fire department was there in minutes, Gerard and a few other firefighters so reassuring in their gear, tramping through the house, checking the rooms, using the thermal imaging camera to see if there was fire in the walls, just to be sure. Pru sat with her, telling her it was okay, abject terror was just part of raising kids. Honor came, and Faith, baby in her arms, and Lucas Campbell. Tanner Angst and Debbie Meering from drum circle…just about everyone in town had come as soon as they heard it over the scanner—*structure fire, 159 Academy Street, disabled person in residence.*

Somehow her father found out. Keith arrived as they were trying to convince Davey to go to the hospital.

"Davey, you're hurt," Jess said. She was still shaking so hard she couldn't stand, and they were sitting on the front steps of Ricky's house, wet towels over Davey's arms. Jess was pressing a cool cloth against his face.

"I want to watch the firefighters," he said.

"If you get an infection, it's really going to hurt."

"It wasn't my *fault.*"

"I bet Gerard would use lights and sirens for you," Levi said. "You still love that, don't you, bud?"

"No. I want to stay." He was getting frustrated, Jess knew. His mouth had that stubborn, tight look to it.

"I've never ridden in an ambulance," Keith said. "I've always wanted to. Would you let me go with you, son? It'd be really fun for me."

Davey went to scratch his head, then stopped, wincing at the pain in his hands, and Jess bit down hard on the tears. "Okay, Dad," he said.

"Come on, Jess," Levi said, offering his hand. "You can ride with me."

At the hospital, they were shown into a room and told to wait. And of course, Jeremy Lyon wasn't on duty; he was away at a conference, so there was no friend present at just the right time, the way there had been for Colleen when she popped out her baby. No, for Davey, there was sit and wait.

Her poor little boy. If his hair didn't grow back…if he had a scar… Yeah, at least he was okay, but this was huge. What if he had night terrors again, the way he had after Chico the Original was put to sleep, after Mom died? Was the house okay for them to sleep in?

This was why she'd never wanted kids. This heart-stopping terror.

Prudence, Levi and her father were all in the waiting room. She wanted to be alone with Davey; he'd been getting more and more upset, concerned that he'd be in trouble for the fire. She'd assured him this wasn't his fault, then stroked his hair. Some of the burned strands broke under her hand like dust, and the smell was dreadful. After a few minutes, he dozed off, exhausted from the shock and fear.

He wasn't the one who should be worried about getting into trouble.

She stepped in the hall to make some phone calls and figure out how the *hell* this had happened.

Her screen showed three missed messages from Connor. Four texts. Oh, she'd be talking to him soon enough, that was for sure.

First on her shit list, however, was Petra, the manager of the candle factory. Jess told her what happened and chewed her out in a whisper. Petra was supposed to notify Jess if Davey left the candle shop early, and it didn't *matter* if Davey had lied and said she was home, she was supposed to *check*, and who *cared* if he'd never done anything like this before? This was policy for damn good reason!

"I'm so, so sorry," Petra said, and it sounded like she might be crying. "Davey said you and he were going to make dinner together."

"Well, he lied." First time, too. Connor had taught him more than cooking.

According to Davey, he and Connor had been meeting secretly for weeks. Weeks! Connor had been teaching him to cook so he could get a girlfriend. How to talk to girls, how not to mention their boobs, how to tell them they smelled good, but mostly, how to cook.

Davey had also said that Connor told him never to use the stove when he was alone.

Connor had never mentioned the oven.

And that was the problem. People didn't understand how Davey thought. The letter *A* was not necessarily followed by the letter *B*. She knew that. Connor did not. He had some nerve, going over her head. She, who'd taken care of Davey her entire life.

How dare he?

She had never been so angry in her life. Her entire body shook with fury from the bone marrow out. Connor had no business deciding that Davey—*her* Davey—was capable of being around flame and heat and sharp objects. He had no idea.

Davey had been trying to make an omelet for her and Keith. This from the kid who couldn't make his own toast. And since Connor hadn't mentioned *not* using the oven, he'd used the oven. Put it on broil, stuck the big frying pan right inside. When it started to smoke, he opened it up, flapped a dish towel inside the oven to clear it. The dish towel hit the heating coil, caught fire, and Davey tossed it in the sink, where the curtains caught.

He pulled down the curtains and turned on the water, effectively ending the fire, but burning his sweet face. And hair. And hands. He looked like a sooty chick, and those burns had to throb.

Where the *hell* was the doctor? The self-important nurse had come in briefly, told Davey in a saccharine voice that he was a brave boy and told him to make himself comfy.

He has second-degree burns on his hands and face, bitch, Jess wanted to say. *You get comfy with that.*

But Davey did doze right off. Probably the shock.

Her poor honey-boy.

Jess was an EMT. She knew the signs of a third-degree burn. Charred skin, no sensation because of nerve damage, difficulty breathing. Davey had none of that, thank God. But it was bad enough that there were two blisters on his right hand, one on his left, and both hands were a little swollen. The skin on his face was angry and tight.

She hoped it wouldn't scar.

She took off her suit jacket—oh, yeah, a century ago, she was going to give a presentation—and looked at herself in the little mirror in the exam room. She was as white as her shirt. Her knees stung; she'd fallen getting out of the car and skinned both of them.

She took her hair out of its twist and ran her fingers through it. Pinched her cheeks to bring some color.

Tugged down on her white blouse so the V showed enough cleavage, then tucked it in really tight. Got her bag, dug out her lipstick and put it on. Took a deep breath and went into the hall. Walked toward the nurses' station, making sure her hips swung.

There were three women and a man sitting behind the

counter. One of the women was the useless nurse; the man was sitting with his feet up, eating an apple.

She went to the man. *Tucker Simmons, MD.*

Perfect.

"Hey," she said, leaning onto the counter, her arms folded under her chest. "I wonder if you can help me." She wound a piece of hair around her finger and gave him a little smile.

"Sure!" He tried very hard not to look at her cleavage. He failed. One of the women snorted in disgust. Jess didn't bother looking at them.

"I know you're really busy today," she murmured, "but my little brother got hurt in a fire, and he's special needs, and we've been waiting forever. Do you think you can peek in at him? I bet all he needs is to be checked and maybe get a prescription for some painkillers."

He nearly fell out of his chair getting up. "Yeah, absolutely, I can do that. Sorry you had to wait so long."

Jessica Does struck again.

The lump in her throat didn't matter. What mattered was Davey. That was all.

CHAPTER TWENTY-SIX

Thanks to a car accident on Route 17, it was after six when Connor's cab pulled up in front of Jessica's house.

She hadn't answered a single text or voice mail.

He paid the driver, got out and went up the walk to her door. Ricky, her neighbor, was waxing the Camaro, and Connor lifted a hand in greeting.

"There you are, dude," Ricky said. "You hear?"

"A little. What happened?"

Ricky scratched a tattoo on his bulging biceps. "Kitchen fire. I hear the smoke detectors go off, I rush in there. Fire's already out. The kid has some burns on his hands, but he's okay. Jess, though…kinda hysterical. It's good that you're here, man."

Connor wasn't so sure. "I'm glad you were around, Ricky."

"Me, too." He grinned and went back to worshipping his car.

Connor knocked on Jess's door. She opened it right away. Stood there in yoga pants and a cardigan, feet bare, hair wet.

Her eyes were red.

Her face, however, was completely expressionless. "Are you okay?" he asked.

"You smell like beer."

"Yeah, uh… I spilled some during the presentation."

"Have you been drinking?"

"Yes. At the presentation. Jess, are you all right? How's Davey? And why the hell didn't you call me?"

She grabbed him by the shirtfront and yanked him inside.

"This was your fault," she whispered. "You're teaching him to *cook*? To *cook*, Connor? Jesus!"

"Okay, okay. Let's just talk. What happened?"

"Keep your voice down. He's sleeping. He's on Tylenol with codeine for his burns."

Connor flinched. "How bad?"

"Bad enough. Second degree, on his hands and face."

"Oh, Jess…"

"Shut up. How dare you go behind my back—"

"Hi, Connor." Keith Dunn walked into the kitchen.

"Hi, Mr. Dunn."

"Jessica, honey, I'll just…take a little walk, how's that?"

"Great. Thank you."

Her father gave him a possibly sympathetic or possibly murderous look. It was hard to tell. The effects of all that beer hadn't worn off.

The kitchen curtains were gone, and there was a black streak up the wall.

Connor suddenly felt sick, thinking of Davey alone in a fire. "Can we sit down?" he asked.

"Absolutely not."

"Jessica, look. I was trying to do something with him, to…"

"To get him to like you."

"Yes. Exactly. And to get to know him."

"And to hook him up with a girlfriend?"

"Oh, Miranda?"

"How do you know her?"

"I went to see him at the candle factory. She was there."

Jessica wrapped her sweater around her more tightly. Everything about her was clenched.

"You shouldn't have been sneaking around with my brother," she said. "You should've asked me about teaching him to cook. He's not capable of that."

"Look every cook has a fire at some—"

"Connor, his IQ is roughly 50. He could've died because of you."

Connor closed his eyes. "Please, can we sit down and talk about this?"

"No."

"Jess, he did good, right? He put out the fire. He didn't panic. This house is still standing."

"He put the frying pan in the oven because you told him not to use the stove when he was alone in the house. You don't get it. If you tell him, 'Davey, don't eat cookies in bed because you get crumbs on the sheets,' he thinks it's perfectly okay to eat cake in bed, because you didn't say *cake*. He can't make the same connections you and I can. You had no right to assume you know what's best for him!"

"Okay, you're right about that. But Jess—"

"And this stuff about a girlfriend! You don't even know Miranda!" Her whisper yelling was scary.

"She seems nice," he said.

"Based on what, Connor? Your many conversations with her? Have you ever talked to her?"

"No. Doesn't mean she—"

"You've been coaching him on how to have a girlfriend," she hissed. "Did you ever think about what happens if she doesn't like him, Connor? What if she breaks his heart? What if he actually loves her and it doesn't work out. What then, huh?"

"Who are we talking about here? Davey, or you? Or is it maybe me?"

Her eyes narrowed. Perhaps that hadn't been the right thing to say. She looked like she might be about to stab him.

Connor rubbed his eyes. "Jess, I'm so, so sorry there was a fire here today. I'm sorry I didn't check with you about the cooking lessons. I just wanted him to like me, so you'd see things could work out with us, and guess what? He does like me."

"He was burned today in a fire. You're missing the point! And you reek of beer."

"I spilled some."

"I cannot believe you came here drunk."

"I took a cab. While you were toughing it out alone at the hospital, I was still trying to give that stupid presentation, when I should've been with you. But you would never call me, would you? You'd never let me help."

"You're the *cause* of this problem."

"I said I was sorry. I am sorry. But Jess, I have to say I think *you're* the one missing the point."

She got very, very still. Connor was not so drunk that he didn't recognize this was not a good sign. "Oh, well, then please, illuminate me, because you must know I love when a drunk person gives me a lecture."

Well, he was in it now. Might as well go for broke. He took a deep breath. "I think you need to let him go a little bit. Let him do things without you watching all the time?"

"So you're an expert."

"I'm not. But he actually can cook. With supervision, yes. And today, all by himself, when confronted with a crisis, he took care of it."

She just glared at him.

What the hell. He was fucked now, might as well go for broke. "Have you ever considered that maybe instead of him needing you, you're the needy one here? That you get more out of this than he does? That if you're not Davey's savior, then you just have to be a person like the rest of us?"

She slapped his face. Hard. It stung. He closed his eyes and smiled. "You've been wanting to do that for twenty years, haven't you?"

"All I have to say is, it's a good thing I slept with half the fire department, because they were here in two minutes."

"Ah. So you're Jessica Does again, is that it? If you sleep around, then your brother will be safe."

"That plan sure worked better than having a boyfriend."

Ouch. The old broom handle through the chest, once again.

"And by the way, Dr. Phil, it's a little ironic to be lectured about emotional health from someone who's barely spoken to his father in twelve years. Just saying." She went to the kitchen sink, her back to him. "You can go now."

The next morning for some inexplicable reason, someone was banging on Connor's door, and the door felt hardwired to the surface of his brain, which seemed to have electrodes suction-cupped there, shooting pain into the deepest recesses of his cerebellum and down into his spinal cord.

The word, he believed, was *hangover.* He'd never had one before.

He had one now. Hail Mary, did he have one.

After Jess kicked him out, he'd walked home. Colleen had called and he'd told her he didn't want to talk, and then he'd turned off the phone to make sure she didn't call back, then decided a couple more beers seemed like the solution for everything.

"Connor!" his sister yelled now. "Get your ass out here!" She must be the cause of the horrifing banging. If he had the strength, he would strangle her.

He rolled over and fell right off his bed. Lady Fluffy barked, and Connor flinched. "Never do that again, puppy," he whispered.

God, he felt sick. Bad dreams about fire and being unable to find Jessica's house had haunted him all night long.

"Con! Come on!"

Pulling himself up made the headache worse. Fluffy danced around his feet, trying to kill him, and barked again, which *definitely* would kill him. He went to the front door, wincing in pain. His brain felt like a pulsing jellyfish of hate and poison.

"Shh," he whispered, opening the door for his sister. "You look nice."

Her eyes opened wider. "Our mother is getting married today," she said.

"Oh, shit."

"And you're hungover. Oh, man, I *knew* I should've come over last night." She turned to Lucas, who was sitting in his car on the street. "He's got a hangover!" she shouted, making Connor yelp in pain.

"Coll! Please."

Lucas got out of the car, then opened the back door and lifted out the car seat. "Work your magic, Colleen," he said. "Wedding starts in an hour."

"You are so pathetic," Colleen muttered, pushing her way in.

"Yes."

"All right. I have a cure, of course. I'm a bartender. I'm *the* bartender, and you are very lucky to have me." She stomped into the kitchen. Was she wearing tap shoes? Iron-soled work boots?

"Morning, Connor," Lucas said. "Sorry to hear about Jessica."

Yeah. His chest still felt crushed and broken and ruined. He looked down, half expecting to see a smear of ventricle on his shirt.

His baby niece blinked up at him. "Hi, Izzy. Who's my best girl?" She spit up in response. From the kitchen, the sound of the blender nearly sliced his head in half.

"You do not smell good, my friend," Lucas said. His brother-in-law wore a navy suit, white shirt and red tie.

"You're a very handsome man," Connor said. It was true.

"He's still drunk, *mia*," Lucas said.

"You don't say," she called.

"Why are you both yelling?"

"Drink this, loser," Colleen said, swishing into the foyer in her long dress. She handed him a foamy drink. "How's Davey?"

"You probably know more than I do."

"True. Well, he's doing fine. Levi stopped over this morning, and Davey's just great. Jess is calmer. So no worries, okay? She's dumped you fifteen times before. You'll get her back. Now drink this."

"What is it?"

"Gatorade, Motrin, kale, a banana and some Tabasco sauce."

"Hail Mary, full of grace."

"Oh, shush. Trust me. I'm your twin. Chug it and get in the shower. We'll wait."

An hour later, they were on the other side of Crooked Lake at the Chicken King's palace, a huge Victorian on a hill, decorated with a variety of bizarre chicken statues. His sister's remedy had made him feel minimally human again. Then again, Connor really hadn't had that much alcohol by normal-people standards. By his own…well, best not to think about it.

For the second time in a year, he was giving away a bride.

His mom came out of the bedroom where she'd been getting ready. "Ta-da!"

She looked…well. She looked like his mother. The face he loved, glowing with happiness today. "You're gorgeous, Mom," he said, his voice a little husky.

"So are you, honey," she said. "You should wear a tux every day. Oh, it's too bad Jess and Davey couldn't make it! They're doing okay, though?"

"Yes," he said, quashing the guilt. Best not to bring up any unpleasantness on his mom's wedding day. "Davey has a couple minor burns, but they're good."

"Glad to hear it. All right, let's get down with the others for pictures. Doesn't Colleen look fantastic? She lost that baby weight overnight, it seems! Which was good, because she gained so much, didn't she? And her cleavage is—"

"Ma. No."

His mother laughed. "Well. I'm a grandmother at last. Carol Robinson can't hold that over my head anymore. Can you, Carol?" she added as her bridesmaid came into the room.

"Oh, Jeanette, look at you! You look beautiful! And you're not so bad, either, Connor," Carol said.

Connor left his mom with Carol and the other bridesmaids—eight of them, including his sister—and looked around. Ah. There was the groom, leaning against a door and smiling at the women.

"So, Ronnie," Connor began.

"Call me Dad."

"I won't, but thanks. So, Ronnie, I know that you can buy and sell anyone in this town, and you're possibly connected to the Russian Mob, and the President is a personal friend and all that, but if you hurt my mother, you're a dead man."

"Got it, son!" Ronnie gave him a hard hug. "Good talk. Let's get going, shall we? Give that woman away, Connor. I'll take excellent care of her."

Ronnie went outside; Paulie followed as his person of honor. Then the bridesmaids began their march out onto the vast yard. "Oh, Mom," Colleen said, her eyes filling with tears. "This is a happy day, isn't it?"

"Knock it off and do your thing," Connor grumbled.

"Shut up."

"You shut up."

Jeanette laughed. "Oh, my kids. I love you both so much."

Seven minutes later, Connor had a stepfather.

With the exception of the food, the wedding reception was the same as all others, give or take. The chicken statues had a certain élan to them, Connor admitted. His headache had subsided to a dull throb.

He took Isabelle so Lucas and Colleen could dance together, and kissed his niece's little head. Sat on a bench under a tree so she wouldn't get the sun in her eyes. Her head smelled good, the silky black hair soft against his cheek. She made a little sound, and he patted her back.

He liked babies. Always had.

He missed Jessica.

He missed Davey, too.

His throat was suddenly tight at the image of Davey Dunn, hurt and scared. Everything Jess had said was right—he'd had no business going over Jessica's head. But it had seemed like a good idea at the time. Jess had seemed so close. He'd really thought that with Davey in his camp, maybe the knot on her heart would loosen enough for him to slip in there, but it didn't look that way. And he was out of tricks.

Jessica Dunn was not the forgiving type. Not where her brother was concerned.

"Hey there, son." Pete O'Rourke came down the stone steps to where Connor was sitting.

"Dad." Weird that both Dad and Gail were invited, but, hey, at least Mom was happy these days.

"A beautiful day, isn't it?" his father said.

"Yes, it is."

Pete was looking at Isabelle. "Want to hold her?" Connor asked.

"Oh, sure," his father said. The baby was passed, but Connor stayed seated, rather than find something else to do, his usual modus operandi for when his father was around.

Dad liked babies, too. Connor watched as his father leaned his cheek against Isabelle's head and patted her back.

"How's Gail feeling?" Connor asked.

"Oh, a little tired. The morning sickness is pretty bad. But she's good. The baby looks healthy."

"Good." The breeze came up off the lake, and the sound of laughter drifted in with it. The band was playing "SexyBack" by Justin Timberlake, and Connor winced at the thought of his mother dancing to it.

"Dad," he said unexpectedly.

"Yes?"

Huh. He didn't really have anything planned to say. "Uh… I just wanted to say something."

"Yeah, sure! Go ahead."

His father was a grandfather now. Despite the trophy wife, despite having a ten-year-old daughter and a new baby on the way, his father was getting old.

"You weren't that bad of a father," Connor said, then gave a little laugh at the lame compliment. "You were a good provider. You were hard on me to do well and in some ways, that was a really good thing."

Pete swallowed. Patted Izzy's back, same as Connor had done.

"And you're a really great father to Savannah. I'm sure you'll be the same with the new baby, too."

His dad's mouth wobbled a little. "Thank you," he whispered.

Connor stood up. "Now give me back my niece," he said. "I think I hear someone puking over by the green chicken statue, and I bet it's Gail."

CHAPTER TWENTY-SEVEN

A package arrived for Davey three days after the fire. Jess didn't recognize the handwriting, but the postmark was local. "Davey," she called. "You got something in the mail, hon."

He came galumphing down the stairs, sounding as ever like he was falling. It never failed to make her adrenaline spurt in familiar panic. "What is it?"

"I don't know. Want me to open it for you?"

"I can do it."

His hands were better. He said they felt tight, but they didn't hurt anymore. His face burn was a little more severe, so Jess had covered it with antibiotic cream and a four-by-four bandage.

He got the scissors out of the drawer. "Let me do that for you, sweetie," she said.

"I can do it, Jess." He sounded a little…patronizing, actually. She tensed as he ran the scissor blade across the tape. Didn't cut himself.

Inside the box was a blue knit scarf and a card. "It's from Miranda!" Davey said. His face lit up. "It's a get-well present!"

Now *that* was a shock. Jess had always thought the relationship was completely one-sided. "That's so sweet."

Davey grabbed the phone and, clutching the box, went into the living room. A second later, Jess heard him say, "Hi, Miranda! It's me, Davey!"

He had her number?

"Dave, I mean. Dave Dunn. Thanks for the scarf! Blue is my favorite color!"

Until a few seconds ago, red had been his favorite color. Jess smiled.

"It doesn't hurt much," Davey was saying. "I'll be back to work tomorrow. Hey, who's your favorite Avenger? Mine's Iron Man."

Looked like Miranda did talk after all. Or maybe she didn't need to, since Davey was going a mile a minute.

"Jess, can Miranda come over and watch a movie with us?" he yelled.

"Of course," she said. "Anytime. As long as it's okay with her mother."

Davey relayed the information, barely pausing for breath. "You can come now if you want. Or tomorrow. Or the next day. Oh, okay. Sure! Bye!" His face was so happy, bandage or not. Unable to contain his happiness, he ran out of the room and clattered into the backyard with Chico Three, the dog's happy barks echoing Davey's laughter.

So maybe Connor knew a little more on the subject of Miranda than Jessica did.

The door opened, and in came Ned. "Dry your tears, Jess, but I'm here for the last of my stuff."

"The new house has an extra bedroom, just in case you go back to your spendthrift ways."

"Good to know. When are you moving in?"

"Next weekend."

"Are you excited?"

"You bet." She really wasn't. She was tired, that was what she was.

Davey came galloping into the kitchen again. "I have a girlfriend! Ned! I have a girlfriend!" Davey yelled. Chico Three barked happily and jumped against his beloved. "I have a girlfriend, Ned!"

"Bring it here, my man," Ned said, fist-bumping him. "You'll come visit me in my new place, right? It's really nice. We can hang and chill."

"Hang and chill! Yeah!"

Davey seemed so happy, he was practically floating.

That night, as Jess was getting ready for bed, she saw Davey standing in front of the bathroom mirror, taking off his bandage. "Let me do that for you, pal," she said.

"I got it," he said, carefully peeling the tape away. He looked at the burn, which already seemed better. "Do you think I'll have a scar?"

"No, I don't."

"Connor says chicks love scars. Like his. From Chico One."

So they'd talked about Chico One during their mysterious cooking classes. And Davey had handled it. No meltdown.

He had a girlfriend. He had an age-appropriate male friend with an apartment. He had a good relationship with their father, and he had a steady job.

And he didn't need her help to take off a bandage anymore.

Jess knew that while those were all good things, her throat was unbearably tight nonetheless.

Keith's car was parked in front of the house when Jess got home from work the next day. Since the fire, she'd been letting him visit without supervision, just for small bits of time, a half hour here, fifteen minutes there, before she'd get home or if she had to run an errand.

"Hi, guys," she said as she came in, then nearly dropped the bag of groceries she was holding.

Davey was at the stove. Keith was sitting at the table.

"What— Davey, be careful," she said.

"Dinner is ready," he said grandly. "Scrambled eggs and toast. And ketchup."

Jess put the bag down. "You cooked?"

"I know how."

She glanced at her father. "Don't look at me," he said. "I've just been sitting here, listening and learning."

Okay, so Davey hadn't done anything alone. That was good.

But in a way, he kinda sorta had.

There was that vise on her throat again. She sat down at the table. Davey had drawn pictures on the paper napkins. Hers was a picture of a smiley-faced heart.

Davey put the plate of eggs on the table, then brought over the toast. Two pieces were just this side of charcoal, but the truth was, the toaster was finicky. "It smells fantastic," Jess said, her voice wobbling a little. She served herself some eggs, then passed the spoon to her father. Took a piece of the dark toast.

"This is the best supper I ever had," she said.

"You haven't even eaten it," Davey said, grinning that sweet smile.

"I already know."

"Perfect eggs," Keith said. "You did good, son."

After supper, they walked up to Ellis Farm Nature Preserve so Chico could get some exercise, and Davey could, too. He and the dog ran ahead, and Jess found herself a little jealous of Davey's endless energy.

It was a beautiful summer night, the sun beginning its slow descent over the hills, the clouds turning creamy, the sky behind them softening, pink and lavender edging the horizon. A rabbit ran across the path a few yards ahead, and a wood thrush was showing off from high in a treetop.

"Jessie," her father said, "I want to talk to you about something. I'd like Davey to spend some time with me. At my place. To stay with me part-time."

She jolted to a stop. "What?"

"I've been sober for almost three years now. I have a steady job and a decent apartment and a reliable car. I'd like to see my son more."

Jess closed her mouth. "Oh, really."

"Yes."

There was a bench nearby, overlooking the small pond. Davey was throwing a tennis ball in the water for Chico, who loved to swim. Jess sat down, keeping her eyes on her brother, making sure he didn't get too close to the edge of the pond. He could swim. But still.

"So you want…custody?" she asked. Her legs were shaking.

Her father sat, too. "I don't want to take him away from you, honey. I just… I'd like to see him more. Be more of a real father and less of a guest."

"A real father."

"That's right."

John Holland was a real father. Bet he never got drunk and threw up in one of his kids' beds. Levi Cooper was a real father. Lucas Campbell, too.

Keith Dunn was not a real father.

Chico Three barked joyfully from down the hill. Davey waved, and Jess and her father both waved back.

"That's a nice thought," she managed to say through the anger that was twisting through her like razor wire. "About thirty years too late—twenty-five for Davey, but still, a nice thought."

"I can't rewrite the past," he said.

"Save the euphemisms, Dad," she hissed. "You gambled away what little money you did make. I wore hand-me-downs from the rich kids in town. I never had a friend over in case you or Mom were drunk." Her chest started to jerk. "I've worked a full-time job since I was fifteen years old, and you stole my savings and put me in debt. I've never had a vacation. I slept with half the boys in my high school so they'd look out for Davey, because you were off in a bar somewhere, and I've never had fewer than two jobs. And you *let* me. Why didn't you want to be a real father back then?" Tears burned down her face like acid.

"Oh, baby," he said, his voice wobbling.

"You don't get to cry," she said, starting to sob. "Why didn't you want to be a real father when I needed one? Where were you when I tried to be a stripper so I could afford Davey's medicine? Where were you after Mom died and Davey fell apart? He needed a real father then. Not now." The sobs were out now, galloping through her entire body, kicking their way out of her throat. "Why weren't you a real father when Mommy was pregnant and I was bringing her drinks? Why didn't you stop me, Dad? Why didn't you stop me? Look at him! That's all my fault."

She pulled her legs up and wrapped her arms around herself and it *hurt*, this crying. It was horrible. It was like being trampled, and she had no idea how to stop.

Then there were arms around her, and her father was rocking her. "It's all right, baby," he murmured. "It's okay to cry. You're such a good girl. Such a good girl."

That just made her cry harder. She bent her head and just gave up, letting the hurt run through her, and sobbed, and sobbed, and sobbed.

But eventually, the sobs slowed. Her head throbbed, and she just didn't have anything left, not even enough energy to sit up straight.

Instead, she leaned against her skinny father. There was nowhere else to go. Couldn't remember the last time he hugged her. It had been decades.

Miraculously, Davey was still down at the pond with Chico. The best dog in the world, endlessly happy, always wanting to play and utterly, completely devoted.

She wiped her eyes with her sleeve.

"You know what I see when I look at Davey?" her father said, his reedy voice quiet. "I see the best kid in the world. He's kind, he's happy, he's healthy. He has a good job—better than a lot of the jobs I've had, honestly—and everyone likes him. He grew up feeling safe. That's all because of you, Jessie. You did that. No one but you." Her father held her a little tighter. "It wasn't fair, what your mother and I put on your shoulders. It wasn't right. But my God, what a good job you've done! I'm so sorry you had to do it, and at the same time, I'm so glad it was you. I would've ruined him."

More tears now, but these didn't hurt as much.

The past was so heavy. Too heavy to drag with her anymore. She was so tired of being Jessica Does. So tired of being afraid and alone and taking care of everything all the time. She just wanted to be. To be normal, to be happy, to be light.

A yellow swallowtail butterfly landed on Jess's knee and rested there, flexing its black-laced wings.

Her mother had loved butterflies.

"I'm so, so sorry, baby," her father said. "Davey being the way he is, that's all on me and Mom. Davey isn't your fault. He's proof of your goodness. Let me help, Jessie. Let me take care of Davey. Let me take care of you, even. Just a little bit."

Her eyes welled up again. "I'm not so good at that."

"You could be. You could try."

Davey came lumbering up the hill, panting, sweaty and filthy, happy as peach pie. His face fell at the sight of her tears, and his own eyes filled. "Why are we crying?"

She laughed a little. "I don't know."

"Is it happy crying?"

She sat up and wiped her eyes. Glanced at her father. "I think it is." She took a shaky breath. "Can I have another minute with Dad?"

He leaned down and hugged her. "I love you, Jess. Don't cry."

"Okay. I love you, too." She hugged him back and kissed his cheek. "My best boy."

He straightened up. "Come on, Chico Three! Come on! Let's go!"

She took another breath, less shaky this time. "Okay, Dad. We'll give it a shot. But I'm telling you, if you fall off the wagon, you never see either of us again. Ever. You have to stay in AA. I want someone to sign your time card or something. At least three meetings a week."

"I have no intention of stopping now."

"You get a breathalyzer for your car, so you can't start it up without a clean reading."

Her father smiled. "I already have one installed. Anything else?"

Her brain was soggy and tired. "Probably. I can't think of anything else right now, though."

He nodded and stood up, then offered his hand. "I love you, Jessica. I know I did a shitty job as a father, but I love you more than I can ever say."

CHAPTER TWENTY-EIGHT

Connor was the last person to leave O'Rourke's on Saturday night. He'd been working extra hours lately; Rafe had gone to Texas to visit his family, and the busboys were tired from a long run of packed nights at the pub. Monica and Hannah left after the kitchen closed, and Jordan had a date.

He scrubbed down the kitchen with more than his usual attention, then scrubbed down the bar, too, because while Jordan was a perfectly fine bartender, she lacked the OCD gene both he and Colleen had about cleanliness in the workplace.

He knew he was stalling. His house seemed to have grown in the past few weeks. He should probably rent out the apartment, too. "Ten more minutes, Fluff," he said out loud, even though the dog couldn't hear him; she was home, probably asleep on his pillow.

Thinking of his dog made him think of Davey.

He'd stopped by the candle factory the other day and practically sagged with relief at the sight of the kid, who ran over to see him. "How you doing, big man?" Connor had asked.

"I'm great! Did you hear I had a fire! And I put it out. And guess what? I have a girlfriend now. Miranda!" he called, "Want to meet my friend? This is Connor! Connor, this is my girlfriend, Miranda."

"Very nice to meet you," Connor said, though the girl opted not to come over. "Way to go," he said in a lower voice.

"I made her toast on Wednesday," Davey said. "With cinnamon and sugar. She liked it."

"Of course she did," Connor said, giving him a fist-bump. "So you doing okay, Dave?"

"I'm great!"

"I heard you got hurt in the fire."

Davey held up his hands. "I got burned. But it's better now."

Connor nodded. "Good. Glad to hear it. Well. I just wanted to say hi."

"Okay," Davey said. "I have to get back to work! See you later!"

Since his mother's wedding—it was easier than thinking *since Jess had dumped his ass,* or *since Davey had been in a fire*—Connor had made dinner for Colleen and Lucas when the pub was closed, and played with his niece, which basically consisted of holding her and seeing if he could get her to smile. He failed, but she did burp, which was pretty cute, too. He visited his mom and Ronnie in the Chicken Palace across the way. Went for a swim every day when he woke up. And even though the brewery was stalled, he spent his free time at the building, hauling out the burned floorboards and trash. May as well make it look nicer.

Anything to avoid thinking about Jessica.

The bar gleamed under the amber lights. There really wasn't anything else he could do here. He'd go home, wake up Lady Fluffernutter and take her for a walk, avoiding Putney Street, so he wouldn't have to see Jessica's new house.

He went out the back door, locked it and breathed in the smell of shale and water, a little garlic lingering in the air from the pasta carbonara special.

The night was as quiet as a closed casket. *Aren't we cheerful*, Colleen's voice said in his head.

"Hey, Connor."

He jumped. "Jess."

She was sitting on the split rail fence between O'Rourke's and the library courtyard, and got down. "How's it going?"

"Uh...good." As it had for the past twenty years, her beauty hit him right in the chest. Even now, when she wasn't smiling and was wearing that *three feet away* face he knew so well.

He guessed she was here to chew him out about going to see Davey at work the other day. "How's your new place?"

"Oh. Um, it's nice. We moved in this past weekend."

"I saw. You had quite a crew helping you." She hadn't asked him, needless to say. She *had* asked the rest of the fire department, more or less. "How is it, living in the Village?"

"It's...it's fine. It's good. Look, I'll get right to it. Would you like to get back together?"

He blinked. Twice.

One thing he could say about Jessica Dunn. There was no predicting her.

She grabbed her thumb and twisted the ring she always wore. "I'm sorry I freaked out about the cooking classes. I mean, I think I had some valid points, but... Anyway. I overreacted."

He didn't say anything. Felt his heart pumping too hard.

"So what do you think?" She cleared her throat. "We could go back to how things were."

Ah. Wasn't there an old movie called something like that? *The Way We Were*? His mother had watched it a lot after Dad first left. It didn't end well, Connor was pretty sure.

"What do you say?" she asked.

"I don't think so, Jess." Maybe he was a little unpredictable, too. "I can't. I still love you. But I... No."

She pushed her hair back with both hands, tucking it behind her ears, and he caught the faint aroma of her lemony shampoo.

"Why?" Her voice was small.

He rubbed his forehead. Good question. "I can't keep doing this. You've been leaving me for the better part of a decade, Jessica. You leave me. It's what you do. And here we are again, right? In a month or two, or three or five, you'll break up with me. Something will come up. Something big. I'm not saying you've ever done anything shallow. And I'll be right back here again. And I want...more."

The word hung between them in the dark summer night. For a heartbeat or two, Connor thought she might crack.

"Okay." Her voice was soft. "Sorry to bother you." With that, she turned and walked off, her footsteps quiet.

"You never bother me, Jess," he said to her back.

She didn't answer. Of course not. Far be it from Jessica Dunn to make a scene or a declaration.

Jessica saw that going differently. Much differently. She'd actually been pretty confident Connor was going to be really, really happy with her offer, probably because she was an idiot.

You never bother me, Jess.

After all she put him through, he could say something like that. He was right to want more. She couldn't blame him.

Life was a little weird these days. Her father had taken Davey off for the day, and Jess had spent the time unpacking and arranging. Her new house was adorable, bigger than the rental. She loved being in the Village with all its happy bustle. Davey had more freedom; he could walk to the green without her, and the shopkeepers all knew him and made him feel welcome. Lorelei had to stop giving him a free cupcake every day, though. Too much sugar.

But she hadn't realized how much the noise would carry from the lake with the summer people and their boats and parties. She hadn't realized how a room could echo if it was too empty.

Or, strangely enough, how much the smaller place on Academy Street had felt like home.

It was just new. She'd get there. After all, she owned her own home on a street she'd always loved. That was *her* name on the deed. The first person in her family ever to be a homeowner.

But it didn't pack the thrill she'd always thought it would.

And then there was work. For the first time ever, Jess didn't love going to Blue Heron.

It was Marcy. Funny, how one person could change the dynamic so much. Jess wanted to get past it, but good God in heaven, the woman annoyed her! Constantly bursting into Jessica's office uninvited to talk about what a great job she—Marcy—was doing. Constantly laughing that hacking laugh on the phone. If she said *I kid you not* one more time, Jess was fairly sure her head would explode.

On Wednesday morning, they sat around the big table in the conference room for a staff meeting. Prudence, Jack and Mr. Holland were out in one of the barns; they used to come to staff meetings, and Mrs. Johnson would make her famous lemon cake, and sometimes Faith would pop in, too.

That hadn't happened in a long time. Now it was just Honor, who looked a little green with morning sickness, Marcy, who was talking talking talking; Ned, who was staring out the window; and Jess herself.

She waited for Marcy to finish congratulating herself on last weekend's wedding. Jess had an idea to pitch—an exclusive foliage tour of the vineyard in October with a special dinner up at the Barn afterward. Very pricey, very exclusive, since the Hollands wouldn't want dozens of people tramping through their fields and forests.

Finally, Marcy finished. "Okay," Jess said. "I was—"

"Oh, and one more thing," Marcy said. "I was thinking that we could totally get a foliage piece into *New Jersey Lifestyle*," Marcy said. "Get people up from New Jersey, it's like, hey, New

Jersey, get off your ass and come on up, okay? We've got wine! We could put together this special tour of the vineyard for October, show off the trees, maybe do a dinner at the Barn. What does everyone think?"

How did she *do* that? How did she manage to scoop every idea Jess had had lately?

"And sure, foliage, who cares, everyone's got it, but we here at Blue Heron have something a little special, don't we? The Liberty maple."

Jess's skin prickled.

The Liberty maple. The tree Prudence had told her about, the one the first Holland had planted as a sign of his faith in the future.

The tree the Hollands didn't talk about except to their best friends. She looked at Honor, who was frowning.

"Right?" Marcy went on. "I mean, who else has a two-hundred-and-thirty-year-old tree planted by their ancestor, the war hero? So we could do this special wine called Liberty maple muscadet or something, Liberty maple merlot, it really wouldn't matter, and we could—"

"How do you know about that tree?" Honor asked.

Marcy stopped talking. "Excuse me?"

"How do you know about the Liberty maple?"

Holy *crap*. Jess's mouth fell open. "You hacked into Honor's computer," she said.

There was a beat of silence.

"What? I did not!" Marcy's eyes darted between Honor and Jessica. Her face flushed, a deep red.

Got you, Jessica thought. "And mine," she said.

"Um...okay, chill, Jessica. I can't remember who told me about the tree. Prudence, I guess. Maybe Faith. Anyway—"

"My sisters did not tell you about that tree," Honor said, her voice glacier cold. Ned wore a rare scowl on his face. "Nor did anyone in this family."

Marcy didn't answer. Her flush had spread down to her chest, leaving blotches of red on her neck.

"I never put it together," Jessica said. "But you've come up with quite a few ideas that were awfully familiar. The story on the new grape varietal, the sales retreat, now the foliage tour and dinner. You've been on my computer, reading my files. But the Liberty maple…there is *nothing* on my computer about that. That must've come from Honor's."

"I don't know what you're talking about, Jessica. I just… I had an idea. Sorry. I thought ideas were encouraged here."

"Holy shit, you did, didn't you?" Ned said. "You little weasel."

"You're fired," Honor said calmly.

"You can't fire me," Marcy sputtered.

"I just did. Ned, please escort Miss Hannigan from the premises."

"Hells, yeah. That sounds fun. Let's go, Marcy."

They left. Marcy, for once, speechless.

Honor and Jess looked at each other. "I couldn't stand her," Honor said, and she started to laugh. "She had a one-year contract with us, and I was counting the days. Good for you, Jess. Well done. I better call our lawyer, but thank you."

Jess spent the rest of the afternoon writing up the job description for a new event planner. Then, because Honor was the most efficient person on earth, a computer forensics expert came in. It wasn't hard to prove; Marcy had accessed the computers of Ned, Jess and Honor and in some cases, just copied files in their original state and rewritten them as separate documents, leaving the originals right there in the folder.

She'd also forged her own reference letters.

"This is on me," Honor said. "I hired her. Call it pregnancy brain. From now on, my dad gets to hire anyone new."

"What about me?" Ned asked. "Can't I hire people?"

"You didn't find Jessica." Honor smiled, then said, "Oh, hang on," and ran for the bathroom. A minute later, they heard her puking.

"I think I'm gonna have another cousin pretty soon," Ned said with wink.

Jess smiled. "I'd better get back to work."

"Fine. Shame me into working on this gorgeous summer day. Oh, hey, another beautiful woman. How's it going, Colleen?"

Jess looked up. Colleen had Isabelle in her arms and a rather frantic look in her eye. "Hi, Colleen. Here to see your mom? She's not working today."

"Nope. Ned, out you go." Colleen pushed past him into Jess's office and sat down. "I have to nurse."

"Please let me stay."

"I'm telling Lucas you said that."

Ned flinched. "I'll give you some privacy," he said, closing the door.

Colleen yanked down her shirt, did something to her bra and maneuvered the baby in place. She winced, then visibly relaxed. "Okay. Good. I can breathe again. So. My brother."

Jessica sat down. "Yes."

Colleen's eyes narrowed. "First of all, I know everything. The whole history."

"Really?"

"No. But I know enough. You and him, all this time. And then he proposes, and you turn him down, and I get that, I do, because he's a dolt and he rushes into things. And I did punish him by setting him up with those losers and buying you some time, so you owe me there."

"Um...thanks?" She wasn't completely sure what Colleen was talking about.

"But Jess..." Colleen's voice softened. "He loves you."

She nodded. There was that vise again, clamping down on her throat.

"So what's the problem? I know you love him. I mean, you

never once slept with him in high school. And you haven't been with anyone else except him since. Have you?"

Leave it to Colleen to know everything.

"And now Davey even likes him, and believe me, that wasn't easy. Do you know how patient Connor is? He isn't!" The baby squeaked at the sound of her mother's raised voice. "He isn't," Colleen whispered. "Not at all. Except with Davey. And you. So if you're just gonna sit there and let him find someone else, well, I seriously misjudged you." She popped the baby off her breast and switched sides. "Sorry about this, by the way. Now you've seen my boobs. Congratulations. So. Back to Connor. Go get him, Jess! I mean, what the hell?"

"He turned me down," Jess whispered.

"He what?"

"He turned me down. I asked him to get back together, and he said no."

Colleen frowned at that. "Oh. This surprises me."

They sat there in silence for a minute or two, the only sound of little Isabelle chugging away.

If Colleen had nothing to add, Jess was pretty screwed.

She swiveled her chair a little, her throat aching. The view of the vineyard stretched out before her. Honor and Tom were standing by one of the barns, talking to Jack, Honor's little dog biting at Tom's shoelaces. Up the hill were Prudence and her father in the 1780 Rieslings.

Beyond that was the Liberty maple, its branches wide and graceful, the leaves lush and green, rippling and bobbing in the breeze. Planted all those years ago, because one man had trusted that his family would thrive on this land.

Trust had never come easily to Jessica. But she had to hand it to the first Holland.

He'd been right.

She'd asked Connor to get back together, but nothing else. She'd had no faith in the future.

"Colleen," Jess said, not looking away from the tree, "is Connor working tonight?"

"Yep. He's been working every night."

"So he'd be there in, say, an hour?" She turned to face Colleen.

Colleen started to smile. "I can make sure of it."

"I'd appreciate that. Take as long as you need here. I have to run."

CHAPTER TWENTY-NINE

Jessica Dunn had not said the words *I love you* to anyone other than her brother in roughly twenty-five years.

She had never asked for vacation time.

She had never asked for a favor.

She had certainly never asked someone to marry her.

She was doing all of these things today.

The first person she talked to was Honor. Then Mr. Holland, the younger. Then Pru, then Keith. Then she called Levi and asked him to get a favor from the mayor's office.

Then she drove home to talk to Davey.

This was the most important favor of all.

Davey and their father were sitting in the backyard, laughing. "Jess!" Davey said. "Watch Chico Three! He can do a new trick. Chico, climb the tree. Climb the tree. Climb the tree, boy! You can do it!" Chico ran around the small yard, failing to climb the tree. "Well, he did it before," Davey said.

"He did. He made it to the crook," their father agreed.

"Dad, can I have a minute alone with Davey?" she asked. It still felt strange to call Keith *Dad*, but it also felt good. He nodded and went inside.

Davey bounced a tennis ball for Chico, who caught it neatly in his mouth, then dropped it at Davey's feet so Davey would do this a thousand or so more times. They were a match made in heaven, those two.

"Davey," Jess said, and suddenly her eyes were filled with tears.

"Are you sad?" he asked.

"No," she said. Then, after a beat, she added, "A little." The truth was, she had no idea how to ask him this. She'd never planned on it being anything but the two of them.

Her brother put his arm around her. "Are you lonely?"

Sometimes, she realized, she was as bad as anyone, assuming her brother couldn't understand certain things. Maybe Connor was right. No, he was *definitely* right. She needed Davey to need her. "A little bit. Yes."

"Maybe we should get another dog," he suggested, bouncing the ball for Chico.

She swallowed. "I was thinking, actually, that maybe we should get another person."

"Like Ned?"

"Well..." *Here goes nothing.* "I was thinking I might marry Connor." She bit her lip. "I would really love to marry him." Her heart shuddered. *Faith in the future. Faith in the future.*

"So he would live with us?" Davey asked, bouncing the ball again.

"Yes."

"Every day?"

"Yep."

"Where would he sleep?" Another bounce for Chico.

"With me. In my room."

"So gross," Davey said, and Jess laughed shakily. Her brother looked at her a minute, those long, heartbreaking lashes.

"Do you remember when I had my appendix taken out?" she asked.

"Yes. You were sick in the hospital, and Gerard stayed with me."

"That's right. And after that, I had to think about who would take care of you if I couldn't. You know, if I got sick again."

"Or if you died," he supplied.

"Right." Always blunt, her Davey. "I picked Connor."

Davey looked at her. "Why?"

"I knew he'd do a good job. Even though back then, you didn't like him, and you were scared of him, I knew he'd take good care of you."

"How'd you know that?"

She surreptitiously wiped her eyes. "Because he's always taken such good care of me." She swallowed. "So what do you think? Can I marry him?"

If he said no, that would be that. She'd have to deal with no, because Davey had to come first. She owed him that, and more important, she *wanted* that. So if he said—

"Okay," he said, then rubbed his nose with the back of his hand.

"Really?" Her heart leaped, and she sucked in a fast breath.

"Sure. I guess. Want a turn?" He handed her the tennis ball, and she threw it, Chico streaking after it.

She took Davey's hand, which was sticky with drying dog drool. "I'll still love you best," she whispered.

It was true. Since the day she'd first seen her brother's tiny, squalling face, her life had been defined. Everything had changed that day, when Jessica Dunn became a big sister. She grew up. She took care of someone. She was a hard worker and protective and focused because Davey needed her to be.

Everything good about her was born the day he was.

And even though she wanted to marry Connor so, so much, her heart was breaking a little. It had always been just the two of them. Her and Davey, all these years, from the trailer park to the rental house to finally making it here to their little house in the Village. The two of them together…that had always worked. Even when it was hard.

Three…three was a giant unknown.

Or maybe it was just faith in the future. Maybe she was just planting her roots.

"I love Chico best," Davey said. "*And* you. And Dad, and Miranda. And Ned, but I don't love Ned as much as I love Chico."

"So maybe we could go to O'Rourke's. What do you say?"

"Okay! Can I have nachos?"

"You sure can." She hugged him hard and kissed his cheek.

"Stop it," he said.

She kissed him again anyway, and again and again, until he wriggled away, laughing and wiping his face.

When she got to O'Rourke's an hour later, her father and brother right behind her, Jessica was shaking. Hard. Visibly. It seemed like her legs might give out with every step. Her heart was racing so fast it was quite possible she was going to faint.

Her father put his hand on her shoulder.

Colleen was there with Lucas and the baby, Levi and Faith and little Noah at the same table. Colleen gave her a smile and a thumbs-up.

Honor and Tom and Charlie were at another table, along with Mr. Holland and Mrs. Johnson, and Marian Field, the mayor of Manningsport. Pru and Carl were at the bar with Jack and Emmaline.

Pru came over, smiling. "Maid of honor, you hear? Don't you dare pick my prettier sisters. Come on, Davey, sit with us. You, too, Keith."

"Will you be okay, Dad?" Jess asked. "Being at the bar?"

"I'm fine, sweetie." He smiled and followed Pru.

Gerard, Ned, Lorelei, Connor's parents and their spouses and awesome little Savannah…the whole frigging town was here.

The shaking got worse. Hopefully, she wouldn't throw up.

She went into the kitchen. Connor was at the stove, Hannah was scraping a plate, one of the busboys was washing a big pot, and Rafe was whipping something with a whisk. "Hello, beautiful Jessica," he said.

Connor glanced up, then did a double take. "Hey."

"Hi," she said, her voice cracking. The kitchen was too small. Too crowded. Fainting was a definite possibility. Was there enough air in here? "Hey. Uh…can you come out here for a second?"

Rafe slid into his spot at the stove. "I got this, boss."

Connor wiped his hands and held the kitchen door for her. She went out and stopped in the little oasis between restaurant and kitchen, and stood just in front of the door, right where orders were passed from the kitchen. *Ask him in front of everyone*, Pru had advised. *Show him you mean business.*

She swallowed, her throat so dry it clicked.

Connor frowned. "What's the matter, Jess? Is Davey okay?"

"He's right over there," she whispered. "At the bar. He's fine."

"What can I do for you?" he asked. He glanced at the crowded restaurant, then back at her.

This was the moment. She twisted her ring. "Um, Connor… I was wondering if you'd…uh…marry me."

Though they were not very gracefully said, she saw the words hit him.

He didn't move. His expression didn't change. He didn't even blink.

It seemed to get very quiet.

"When?" he asked. "In another decade or so?"

"I was thinking tonight. Now. Now-ish."

His eyebrows raised. "Really."

"Yep."

"And why do you want to marry me, Jess?"

"Because…because…"

She looked into his eyes, and suddenly, the shaking was gone. "Because I've loved you since I was twelve years old," she said.

His mouth opened slightly, and those blue eyes softened.

"I love you more than I can say," she said, and tears flooded her eyes. God, she hadn't cried as much in her entire life combined as she had in the past three months. "I've wasted enough of my life *not* being married to you, so I'd like to fix that. Right now. Marian brought the marriage license from town hall, and Mr. Holland will do the ceremony, and…and we could be husband and wife in about ten minutes, if you want."

He was still just looking at her.

No doubt about it. The bar was silent.

Then he smiled. "Okay," he said, and he kissed her, and her whole being seemed to fill up with light and happiness, even if she was crying. A roar went up from the restaurant, but she barely noticed.

"Thank you," she whispered against his mouth. "Thank you for putting up with me."

He kissed her again, then rested his forehead against hers. "You know how it is, Jess," he said, smiling. "Anything for you."

EPILOGUE

Eleven months, one week and two days after the woman once known as Jessica Does became Jessica O'Rourke…

Connor O'Rourke really liked being married.

In the spring following their impromptu wedding, Jess, Davey and he had moved to Connor's bigger place on the other side of the green. Jess didn't want to add too much to Davey's list of life changes, so they lived on Putney Street through the fall and winter. And when Jess did sell the Victorian—at a tidy little profit, no less—she insisted on buying half of his house from him. It was the principle, she said.

He understood.

First thing she did was buy six huge hanging baskets for the front porch. A porch swing that dangled from the overhead beams. Wicker chairs and tables. Connor wondered how it was that he'd owned the house for five years and never thought to sit out here and watch the sky darken, wave to the neighbors, just sit with his arm around his wife and want for nothing.

Davey lived in the apartment, a little more independent than he had been. They had a security lock put on the oven and stove so he couldn't cook without one of them entering the code, and they'd done their best making the place safe. But he made his own toast now, and Connor was working on figuring out how to teach him to make his own nachos without starting a fire. Miranda came over to visit sometimes, always with her mom, and *The Avengers* had been played so many times that Connor could now recite it by heart.

And for three days a week, Davey stayed with Jessica's father. And that was very nice, too.

Connor had changed his hours so he could work more day shifts and let Rafe have a little more say over the kitchen. "A control freak changes for the love of his woman," Colleen had murmured. "Call the newspaper." Maybe it was true.

About six weeks after Jessica Dunn became Jessica O'Rourke, Connor got some surprising news. Greg Gennaro, also known as Generic, the president of Empire State Food & Beverage, ponied up the money. "Find someone else to be the face of the company," he advised when they signed the papers. "But you make great beer, son. Just go easy on it, you hear?"

In addition to the brewery, Connor also had a new brother—Ryan, a ten-pounder with a head of red hair. Connor visited them at the hospital, and even brought Gail flowers and thanked her, saying that since Colleen was clearly deficient as a sibling, he really appreciated Savannah and Ryan. This comment earned him a smack from his twin, as he'd known it would.

Life was good. He and Davey got along great for the most part, only one or two meltdowns, but not the head-banging kind. Connor was learning how to deal with his brother-in-law, how to be clear and specific, how to see his frustrations coming and hopefully help him deal.

And Jess…she was perfect.

Not really, of course. She still was learning to rely on him and not see it as weakness, but instead as what it was. Love. But every night when he came home, or sometimes in the middle of the night, he'd just look at her sleeping face, still a little stunned that she was his.

Then he'd wake her up. Slowly, kiss by kiss.

She loved him. She always had. Yep, *stunned* had it covered.

It was a beautiful evening, summer just a month away, the trees in bloom, the peepers calling. Connor was alone for the moment; dinner in the oven. He took a beer (a small one) out onto the porch to wait for his wife to come home.

Wife. The word still sounded so damn good. A hummingbird buzzed in for a drink at the hanging baskets, and across the backyard, he could hear Noah Cooper shrieking with glee, the Gomez kids shooting hoops down the block. Davey was at Keith's tonight, so it would be just him and Jess.

Con sat on the porch swing, then lifted Fluffy up to sit with him. Jess was a little late; she'd gone to visit Honor, who was still on maternity leave, and little Elizabeth, who was an extremely beautiful baby with wide gray eyes and a solemn way about her. A sharp contrast to Isabelle, a tiny tyrant, whose first word was *Con.* Connor planned on lording that over his sister's head for the rest of their lives. Colleen had another baby on the way. She hadn't told anyone, but he knew. Another girl, he thought.

Babies were all around, it seemed; just last night, Connor had rung the bell at the bar, offering a round of drinks on the house with the news that there was another John Holland in the world, courtesy of Emmaline—and Jack. Connor had always loved the Hollands, but now they were truly like his own family. They'd brought Jessica in and made her feel like one of them, so Connor was more than happy to part with $400 worth of alcohol.

And one of these days, maybe Jess would be ready to have a baby, too. They didn't talk about it too much, and honestly, if it never happened, Connor wouldn't mind. He had enough. His life was full. He had a niece and a baby brother and a little sister and an irritating twin. He had Lucas, and he had Davey.

He had his wife.

And speaking of… Jess pulled into the driveway and got out of the car.

"Hello, beautiful," he said, and she smiled. Looked even more beautiful than usual.

"Hey," she said, sitting down next to him. The smell of her shampoo, familiar as it was, still got to him. She kissed him, soft and sweet with a hint of sly and still that bit of shyness.

God, he loved her. She pulled back and smiled at him.

"How are Honor and Tom and their crew?" he asked.

"Everyone's great. But I actually had an errand to run, so I cut the visit short."

"What errand was that?"

She reached into her bag and pulled out a shiny piece of paper.

He looked at it. His beer glass slid out of his hand and thunked on the porch floor. Connor looked at the paper more closely.

Looked back at his wife.

Jessica was smiling. "Hope you meant it about having kids. Seems like we're having twins."

★★★★★

ACKNOWLEDGMENTS

As ever, deep thanks to Maria Carvainis, my wonderful agent, as well as Martha Guzman and Elizabeth Copps, who do so much for me. At Harlequin, I am blessed with an amazing team headed by my brilliant editor, Susan Swinwood, as well as Dianne Moggy and Michelle Renaud. A thousand thanks to them and all the others at Harlequin who work so hard to get my books out to the world. I have the pleasure of working with the energetic and brilliant Sarah Burningham at Little Bird Publicity, and the ever constant and lovely Kim Castillo at Author's Best Friend. Thanks also to Beth Robinson at MacBeth Designs for my beautiful website.

To Shelly Fisher and Douglass Schuckers, owners of the Brewery of Broken Dreams in beautiful Hammondsport, NY: thanks for a lovely afternoon of conversation, smelling hops and tasting beer. What a nice way to spend a day!

Many thanks to Stacia Bjarnason, PhD, for her sensitive and in-depth assistance in helping me develop the character of Davey Dunn. You're the best, Stacia!

I am forever indebted to the Fulkerson family, whose winery

is the basis of Blue Heron, and whose generosity with time and information have been key in writing this series.

For the use of their names in the Blue Heron series, thanks to Jordan Reynolds, Gerard Chartier (my friend!), Lorelei Buzzetta (my friend!), Norine Pletts, Shelayne Schanta, the fabulous Murphy girls, the Hedberg family, Allison Whitaker, Brandy Morrison, Laura Boothby, Dr. Buckthal (my friend's dad!), Grace Knapton, Ryan Hill, Dana Hoffman, Julianne Kammer, Nancy Knox, Luanne Macomb, Eleanor Raines, Kim Garvis (my friend!), Sharon Stiles and especially Carol Robinson, my darling and tolerant second mother. Special, heartfelt thanks to Anthony DeFilio, who asked me to put his late wife in a book three years ago—every time I typed Theresa's name, I remembered her and how much she loved her family.

To the world's best writing friends—Shaunee Cole, Jennifer Iszkiewicz, Huntley Fitzpatrick, Karen Pinco and the amazing Robyn Carr—how lucky I am to have you!

To the loves of my life—McIrish, Princess and Dearest—thank you for filling my life with such joy and happiness. You are my favorite people on earth.

And thank you, readers. From the bottom of my heart, thank you for reading my books.